Into
Suez

Stevie Davies has won numerous awards for her ten novels, and has been long-listed for the Booker and Orange Prizes. Several of her books have been adapted as radio and screen plays. Stevie lives in her home town of Swansea, where she is Professor of Creative Writing at Swansea University. She is a passionate sea-swimmer, cyclist and walker on the Gower.

Into Suez

Stevie Davies

PARTHIAN

Parthian
The Old Surgery
Napier Street
Cardigan
SA43 1ED

www.parthianbooks.co.uk

First published in 2010
© Stevie Davies 2010
All Rights Reserved
This edition published in 2011

ISBN 978-1-906998-37-0

Editor: Lucy Llewellyn

Cover design by Marc Jennings
Cover photo © Richard Heeps / Millennium Images, UK
Typeset by Lucy Llewellyn
Printed and bound by xxx

The publisher acknowledges the financial support of the
Welsh Books Council.

British Library Cataloguing in Publication Data

A cataloguing record for this book is available from the
British Library

To Emily, Grace & Robin
my beautiful three,
& remembering Frank

Gottes ist der Orient!   *God's is the East!*
Gottes ist der Occident!   *God's is the West!*
Nord- und südliches Gelände   *Northern and southern lands*
Ruht im Frieden seiner Hände.   *Rest in the peace of his hands.*

from *West-östlicher Divan,*
J. W. von Goethe, 1816

[Holding] Turkey and Egypt in the hollow of our hands, the Mediterranean is an English lake, and the Suez Canal is only another name for the Thames and the Mersey.
(from *Daily Bristol Times and Mirror*, 29/11/1875)

How many of [your correspondents] have had the 'privilege' of defending this filthy race from the onslaught of German forces at El Alamein only to be spat upon, hissed at, booed at, and in many cases even murdered?
(from *Tribune*, 14/8/1956)

I viewed the [Oslo] agreement as embodying a rare moment in history, the moment of recognition of the other. I exist, and you also exist. I have a right to live, and this is also your right. It's a hard and long road, ending in freedom and human rights of the individual, a road strewn not with roses but with struggle and patience ...
There is no end to the pain felt by most people when you suddenly raise their curtain of illusions and lies.
(from Ali Salem, *A Drive to Israel: An Egyptian Meets His Neighbors*, 2001)

Into Suez

Prelude

There they were again, larking in the alley. They'd all pour out and rock with laughter or stand in their petticoats with folded arms discussing some proposition in philosophy. *Wittgenstein!* they'd cry. *Sartre!* Which might lead to more laughing or crying or passionate wrangling, for such women could afford to be extravagant, in their emotions as much as in their clothes. Ailsa would look down on them, a timid spy, sash window suspended over her neck like a guillotine, peering through the geraniums she cultivated in a window box. She saw the tops of their fashionable heads: the ginger girl with her hair in a complex system of sausages; the luscious dark girl, caramel-skinned; others sleep-mussed, one sporting the grey-blue disc of an RAF officer's peaked cap. They had dash, they had flair, they had money and university education evidently.

Emotion next door was tumultuous, titanic at all times. The girls acknowledged no middle temperature. Uniformed men poured in and out. It was impossible to say who was

1

in love with whom, at any given moment. Meanwhile, through the membrane that separated them, Ailsa lived like a nun in the flat built above the stables of a Victorian brewery. You could still see the loose boxes in the wall and attachments for halters. Ailsa had been amazed to come upon such an ancient, secret recess within strolling distance of Buckingham Palace, down an alley at Brewers' Green. She lived up a steep staircase in the storey that had served as the brewer's granary. The bohemians next door racketed away just beyond a wooden partition painted a hideous flaking green. Ailsa heard it all: their water-fights, their singing, their lovemaking, their rows about Sophocles. Doing her washing-up in the bathroom (for the kitchen had no water, hot or cold) or hunched over her mean wartime gas fire, Ailsa wanted to tell them she knew exactly who Sophocles was: she'd read the *Antigone* for herself in Shrewsbury Library at the age of fourteen. She was a girl hungry for knowledge, endowed with what her family, who ran the village post office at Sutton Bridge, had regarded as 'the brain of a boy'. The late child of elderly parents, Ailsa had early set her heart on university and might have got there, for the Birches had been willing to stretch their limited resources to fulfil her aspirations. But her parents had died of pneumonia within three weeks of one another. Then the war had come along, with its altered horizons.

Ailsa bumped into one of the girls at the post box. It was the dark, charismatic one with liquid eyes who seemed more hysterical than the others. She wore a dark green coat with a black velvet collar and a scatter of dandruff on her shoulders: for all her messiness, she had a foreign, exotic air. Each made to post her letter and drew back in the other's favour, smiling. 'I say, aren't you the person next door?' asked the girl in peerless gentry English. Mona, she said. Mona Serafin. And then another arrived and said that her name was Billie and that Bobbie was on the way. Did they mostly have boys' names then, Ailsa wondered. Was that the thing nowadays? Ailsa, she said. *Gorgeous* name, Billie thought. Big Ben had sounded then and they'd agreed that the sound was reassuring rather than otherwise and that the mice at the Old Brewery didn't on the whole bother them. 'After all,' Mona or Billie had said, 'they've got lives of their own to live in their little world behind the wainscot.' Mona was *perishing*, she said. She had her own method of dealing with it, look. She opened her coat to reveal a hot water bottle slung from her shoulder and dangling across her belly.

Another time the redhead, hair as flaming as Ailsa's but more exuberant as to coiffure, knocked to ask if she'd like to come in for a party that evening. 'We'll make the most frightful racket and it'll be better for you if you're sloshed with us than having to hear it through the wall. Anyway, we all want to get to know you. We think you're so mysterious and glamorous.'

Of course Ailsa didn't go, although she was flattered at their view of her. Having invented some excuse, she was kept awake through the small hours. Anyway, she'd have been tongue-tied, out of her depth. Oxford and Cambridge types, silver spoon and all that. They all looked well-fed, to put it mildly, for they escaped the depressing rigours of the home front by eating on the hoof at cafés and grills.

One Sunday Ailsa watched the whole coven spill out into the cobbled courtyard wearing differently coloured berets, ginger, violet, red, cream and navy. Off they clattered in high heels that echoed down the alley. Berets at jaunty angles with tails like mushroom stalks. It was one of the few occasions when she'd seen them bother to dress up. They could wear hot water bottles slung across their chests and still be ravishing and superior. She gathered that they'd quit their undergraduate studies to work at the Ministry of Defence as clerks. Two of them spoke Serbo-Croat and Bulgarian; another was fluent in modern Greek, 'a doddle compared with ancient'.

Ailsa sat in her one armchair, her few possessions neatly arranged on an orange box covered in a cloth embroidered by her auntie in Church Stretton. Was she lonely? She examined a segment of her guarded face in the mirror of her powder compact: skin translucently pale, a scattering of ginger freckles, eyes blue-green. Ailsa ought to feel lonely but the freedom was too novel; solitude offered a roving eye on the boundless possibilities at the centre of the capital. If there were times when she was haunted by a kind of background hum – of the countless deaths in the ruins, void and emptiness – the thought of dull Shropshire reconciled her to London danger. Archie Copsey had gone down on one knee just before she left and she'd said no, Archie, oh no! He would wait, her cousin had promised. All his life if necessary. Don't do that for me, she'd thought, her forehead wrinkling in concern: I might not come back, ever. To be a farmer's wife and feed chickens held no appeal. So much history all around her. Ailsa loved to mingle with the Fleet Street hacks and watch the wigs pageanting up and down at the law courts. She attended concerts at the Albert Hall with her schoolfriend Betty, alike smitten with the capital. She'd go and hear the angelus at Westminster Cathedral. Once she saw Mona Serafin there, genuflecting to the altar. How did that sort with the socialism with which next door resonated? For they were all downright Commies, paid up too. Surely you had to make a choice between Lenin and Christ. Or was it not so simple?

But oh, the young men who came and went. Beautiful, willowy idealists, in officers' uniform or civvies, with great piles or flaps of hair, corn-coloured or conker-brown. Way beyond Ailsa's league. A pantheon of young gods – and older gods too, for owlish balding dons in hacking jackets hung about the girls, carrying a tribute of rare books instead of chocolates or flowers. But the young men, with the bloom still on their skin, instant Majors and Flight Lieutenants at the age of twenty-two, were all in transit, off to the ends of the earth to struggle, not for the Empire, but for the socialist new world, as one heard on breathless summer evenings when all the windows stood wide open. Once Ailsa saw a young man let himself out into the moonlight where, softly latching the door behind him, he sobbed aloud, face in his hands. One or all of them collectively had broken his heart.

Ailsa buttoned her tunic, tweaking at its basque; she pulled in her stomach and buckled her belt taut. She didn't have to worry about her stockings, all darned into a maze of lumps, for as a courier she wore slacks and boots. The motor bike was her version of their all-night party, yielding an exultant freedom, weaving in and out of traffic, enjoying a certain emancipation from ladylike rules and codes. Bike and rider made up a centaur, the machine an extension of

Ailsa's body and will, tuned to soar at the least touch of the throttle. She took a pride in maintaining its splendid engine.

Ailsa met Joe Roberts at a dance. They walked in St James's Park, bubbling with talk and chastely kissing; ate sticky buns in Lyons Corner House, washing them down with gallons of tea. Two weeks after meeting Joe, she was no longer Ailsa Birch but Mrs Ailsa Roberts, whose husband was an aircraft fitter from Glamorgan, stationed in the Western Desert. The blue air-letters on the door mat were her life line: she'd burst into the cold, dank flat and, if she were lucky, there would be her heart's desire. Her husband's uneven handwriting touched her, for Joe was not at ease with the pen, having left school at fourteen for the steel mill; he was a career airman who, having joined up at nineteen, felt his inferiority to his wife. She traced his journey from Libya and Egypt across the Mediterranean and up through Italy, the one precious life that drew her quivering compass needle.

She hardly registered her neighbours' absence until one evening, writing to Joe in Italy, and hearing the sickening silence that signalled that the doodlebug had reached its destination – hovering suspended above her own head, ticking with mindless purpose – Ailsa saw in a flash: she was a goner. There'd be no Joe, no babies, no great adventure. This was it. She tuned in at the same time to the silence of the lively girls next door. They'd vanished without her noticing.

6

Part One

Church Stretton, October 2003
The Empire Glory, June 1949

Part One

1

She had never liked her mother's bosom friend: a thoroughly bad influence on Ailsa, Nia reckoned. But she'd felt surprisingly moved when Irene died, in her mid-eighties: a full quarter of a century after Ailsa. An era ending. Now, a fortnight after the funeral, the boys phoned. Irene had held on to a box of Ailsa's, which Topher and Tim had found when they were sorting the lumber.

Nia, visiting her stepfather and half-brother on the farm at Lyth Clee, borrowed the Land Rover to go over to the Whites' house at Wenlock. Mam and Irene had been in one another's pockets. Whatever did they find to gas about? In her memory the two of them were forever winding wool by the log fire, Ailsa's big strong hands holding the skein, Irene's smaller hands a whirling blur as she wound it off into a ball. This memory went back and back to when things were clearer and more vivid, when she and Topher (also the bane of his mum's life, and this was the bond between them) would play rugby with the ball through the sitting room or roll it for the kitten.

Later on Nia had gone right off Topher. Their two kinds of hippiedom branched in different directions – his toward dropping out and dope and the affectation of calling himself a poet; hers into political activism. Which was the more angry, Topher in his sullenness, Nia in her bitterness? The two of them went back forever. To Egypt, scene of her first memories, as vivid as they were mysterious. Looking through a wire netting grid at the desert, suffused in pink, the sun at its horizon like blood in a yolk. She recalled khaki men with rifles rushing through a grove of palm trees, barking like dogs. The strange and beautiful daily sound of the muezzin calling believers to prayer, which years later she recognised when visiting Bradford, stopping dead in her tracks. The White boys featured as vague but stubborn presences in these memories. And if Nia grew to detest Topher's droning monologues, this was the everyday contempt of a sibling.

They had in common their mothers' shuddering dis-approval: Ailsa and Irene being Air Force widows who had been fighting, as Nia once put it, for Queen Victoria, the Raj and table manners. Not that Ailsa had been given to making reactionary speeches. It was the stiff quality of her silences that betrayed archaic allegiances. And actually Ailsa was too intelligent for the opinions Nia intuited: too bright, come to that, for airhead Irene. But something bound the two women tightly to one another, so that when Ailsa had remarried and moved back to Shropshire, Irene came to live nearby. Nia's Peace Movement activism had landed her in court on a couple of occasions. And Topher had been called a degenerate by his mother, he expressing

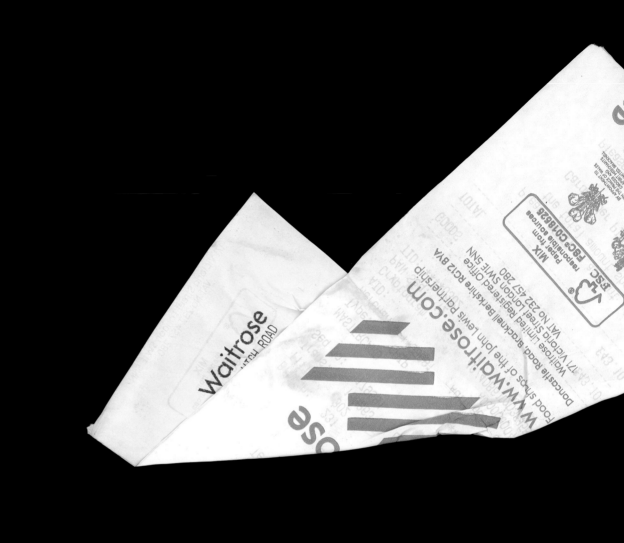

Please

Cardholder P

please DEBIT my account +

the total amount +

TOTAL

GOODS

AID:
Cryptogram:
PAN Seq: 12
TID: ****#0302

40/4DB6

£43

Waitro

171 Victoria Street London SW1E 5NN
VAT No 232 457 280

MIX
Paper from
responsible sources
FSC® C018626
FSC

surprise that she knew the word. An aura of disgrace had hung above these children of the crumbled Empire – even before (so Nia felt) they had done much to merit it.

She'd not seen Topher for several years when he rang about the box. His fair hair had hardly greyed but much of the centre had fallen out and his face had weathered into a thousand wrinkles. He affected a thin pony tail. *Male pattern baldness*, Nia thought as he stood in the stairwell calling up to Tim, who was busy upstairs emptying the loft where the box had been stored. 'She's here, Bruv!'

'Oh, right. Down in a sec. Make the lady a brew.'

Irene had laid great stress on the importance of an Aga in any well-regulated home. The kettle was kept forever simmering on the hob. Topher made them mugs of coffee, heart-stoppingly strong stuff he drank all day, the aftermath of various addictions he'd fought and (chiefly) not fought for twenty years. He was quiet. He's been weeping, Nia thought. Why that should have surprised her, she couldn't think. Hadn't she been crying inside for Ailsa for a quarter of a century? And yet, to put it mildly, mother and daughter had not got on. All the more reason to grieve, when you'd been at daggers drawn.

Topher sat at the other side of Irene's kitchen table. She put out her hand, covered his briefly. He bit his lip and looked away. Following his gaze, she saw, with a start, that the brothers had removed the picture of their father that had enjoyed pride of place over the hearth for as long as Nia could remember. This portrait of a young man in dress uniform had loomed over the White boys' childhood, their mother referring to it as likely to be disappointed in this or that behaviour of her sons, particularly the elder. It was

11

supposed to be a picture of heroism. Nia remembered catching sight of Irene through the door, raising her eyes to the portrait as if in worship. It was the first time Nia had ever thought, *Poor soul*. She'd got an inkling of the fact that Irene had lived most of her life in loss. Which explained and mitigated a multitude of sins.

The two women had returned from Suez widowed, their husbands war heroes. This had happened in the run-up to the so-called Suez Crisis, the first oil war, when the British Empire had been sent whimpering with its tail between its legs. Ailsa and Irene had been flown home in 1952, the year of the Egyptian Revolution. Four years later when President Nasser nationalised the Suez Canal, Britain had hatched a mad conspiracy with France and Israel: Israel would attack Egypt over the Sinai; Britain and France would go to 'save' the canal from both Israel and Egypt, thieves disguised as policemen. The tiny island made of coal and surrounded by fish and ruled by gentlemen-fascists had been cut down to size by American pressure and its own near-bankruptcy. Nia remembered sitting by the big brown Marconi hearing, rather against her own will, the news reports, for the wireless was insufferably dull to the child. Looking back, Nia could see that Suez politicised her childhood by making her elders look fools.

Sergeants Roberts and White must have been killed by terrorists in the build-up to the fiasco. You knew not to penetrate Ailsa's forbidding silence on this theme. But Ailsa, unlike Irene, had married again – her cousin, Archie Copsey. And she'd united herself to a man so lovable that, if Ailsa had not managed to be happy with Archie, well, that was her own stupid fault. She might have learned a thing or two from him too, for the mild Archie, a Quaker, had been a conscientious objector in the war. He worshipped the ground Ailsa walked on; in his eyes she could do no wrong. He had loved Nia as his own, taking her part even against the two boys born to Ailsa and himself. When Nia was bolshy and impossible, Archie had been a presence whose wry quietness had drawn the sting from countless quarrels and made the earth firm under her feet. She hardly remembered her own father, who was never talked of. No picture of Joe Roberts stood above the hearth or anywhere else in the house.

Irene on the other hand prattled interminably about her husband. Roy had been a saint. If only Topher could have taken after him even a little bit. She'd spoilt the younger brother, Tim, very much at Topher's expense: *Oh, darling, you're so like him.* But Tim had grown up a bit of a creep, not above stealing from his mother's handbag. He was all right these days, as far as she knew.

Now Roy White counted as a fallen warrior. Nia saw that his homely face had been turned to the wall among a stack of pictures the brothers had stripped from Irene's world.

'How are you doing, Topher?'

'Oh – you know. Hits you a bit, doesn't it? There was stuff I wanted to say to Ma and ask her – it was so sudden.'

When the blow came that took a life, it changed all the lights and shades, as Nia knew too well. Topher could have said those crucial things to Irene any day for the past four decades. But he hadn't. He'd begrudged the words that might have touched his mother's speechless heart. Topher had nourished a rankling grudge that had knitted itself into his very flesh and become part of him. Ignorant of where it came from.

13

'Better for her that way,' Nia said. 'Going in her sleep. A heart attack can be quite a merciful thing.'

'For *her*, maybe.' Tears seeped from his eyes. She saw again the boy in the man. A pale-haired child crouched with bucket and spade in the sand, his bare shoulders covered in calamine lotion, crying because – and surely she had made this up – enormous hail stones were being shot at them from the sapphire blue sky. But I was never a cry-baby, Nia thought: I picked one up, big as a ping pong ball, and sucked it. She saw all this in a flash, even as she said, 'Yes, it's a mercy for Irene. You will feel that later, Toph, when you're less raw. You really will.'

Tim stood in the doorway, carrying black bin bags. 'Hi, Nia darling, good to see you. You've not changed one bit,' he said insincerely. It seemed to be the only way he could speak. Yet she had a sense that sincerity was there under the surface, repressed. He was still, in middle age, a handsome-looking man, with his mother's delicate features. He'd done a bit of acting in his time which had delighted Irene. Nia remembered being carted along by Ailsa and Irene to an open-air production of *Hamlet* in the grounds of Ludlow Castle. It had rained. She could see Irene, sitting forward in her seat under the umbrella, cowled in her gabardine, ecstatic. She'd mouthed every word of Tim's hammed-up Guildenstern. He still trod the boards as an amateur.

Hamlet, thou hast thy father much offended rang through her mind. They were three over-age Hamlets picking over the funeral baked meats.

'I'm really sorry for your loss, Tim.'

'Thanks, Nia love. We're devastated. What are you doing with yourself these days?'

'Still teaching – and some advisory stuff.'

'You were in the news – last year, was it? Quite a celebrity. Didn't you help change the law on something or other?'

'Young offenders. Only through a committee report.'

'You were always the intellectual. Your mother was so proud of you.'

'You think so?' It was the kind of thing people said. Especially when it wasn't true. But she half-recognised the implicit truth of it. Ailsa had been proud of Nia behind her back. Behind her own back. Nia's heart gave a huge throb and then stopped dead. She wanted Ailsa back now, this minute, more than anything in the world. To embrace her, in every sense.

'And how's the lovely Poppy?'

'Lovely,' she said. 'Got it in one.' They'd been on another march against the invasion of Iraq last week, walking hand in hand. In her own time, your child circled back to you and linked arms as an equal. It was a miracle.

'How's the poetry going, Toph?' she asked.

'Yeah,' he said. 'Yeah.'

Was that an answer? He seemed to think so. Topher nodded his head; started constructing a roll-up, pinching up the tobacco, daintily licking along the paper. His teeth were stained brown. He offered her the joint, between thumb and forefinger. She shook her head. Topher's poetry, a wild and snarling animal in the sixties, had been tamed into a pussy cat of verbose affectation. But then, what did Nia know? She'd never seen the point of poetry.

Tim said he'd bring down the box.

He came crashing down the stairs two at a time and

15

placed a cardboard crate on the table. They all three looked at it. Nia's full name was printed in block capitals on each of the four sides. Once it had held Archie's new-laid free range eggs: 'Lyth Clee Farm, Best Salop Eggs'. They didn't sell eggs any more: the few chickens laid enough for the household and friends in Wenlock. Why had Ailsa stored the box with her friend rather than leaving it with Archie? There it had remained in Irene's attic gathering dust while Nia had aged to nearly her mother's final age, fifty-seven.

'Right then,' Nia said. 'Thanks for that, both of you. I'll be on my way – leave you guys to get on.'

'Don't go, Nia,' said Topher.

But she made her excuses and left, eyes smarting with Topher's smoke. She had the feeling she'd been smoked over in her crib, both parents pouring out their toxins.

Starting the engine, relieved to be on the road, Nia remembered her mother's intensely secret world. Ailsa lighting up, for instance: she could never kick the habit, though she pretended to have done so. Nia knew that Archie knew. Like a teenager, Ailsa would smoke out of the dormer window, looking over to the mountain, stubbing out the fags in an ashtray she kept in a shoe box. Did she really imagine it was a secret? Nia, prowling her mother's terrain, would count the lipstick-stained butts in the ashtray, poke at them with her finger. Always a little apart, Mami was a figure in green wellies digging in her market garden. Or crouching in the small barn with the vintage motor bikes she collected and never rode but tinkered with and polished up, humming all the while. Happy with her head in a book, she was always, as Nia put it to herself, *over there*. Her mother would take off with no notice when the spirit took her, letting herself slyly out of the far gate where the ground began to sweep up towards the Long Mynd. Sometimes she'd let Les tag along, the younger brother who was 'no trouble' and did not disturb her reverie. Nia would see Ailsa framed in the lattice window, striding off to where the turf was emerald in the low western light, becoming a stick figure, as she began to climb the purple Mynd. Always at heart alone.

Archie would know to let Ailsa be. When Mami went on one of her wanders, he'd lay a hand on Nia's arm to detain her, diverting her attention to some project of his own, helping with the calves, cleaning Mami's tools so they'd be shiny for her. Now, driving along the bridleway to Lyth Clee, Nia saw her mother as doubly recessive, walking away into the wilderness of death.

And Nia, from her earliest days at the farm, would cycle off alone through the mighty landscape, singing at the top of her voice, on her own adventure. But this was a different matter, apparently. Going AWOL, normal for Ailsa, counted as incorrigible naughtiness in Nia.

She set the box on the floor by the dead grate at Lyth Clee; cut through the tape and string and peered in. Coming from the yard, removing his boots at the door and going to wash his hands, her stepfather asked, 'What have you got there, lovely?'

'Don't be upset, Dad,' she said. 'It's some stuff of Mam's. For some reason it was stored at Irene's.'

Wiping his hands, he peered inside; saw the neatly packed notebooks, letters in their original envelopes, an album.

'That would be Mam's journals. Always busy with her writing, bless her.'

That was all he said, level and apparently incurious. Settling down in his usual armchair, he closed his eyes, stretching out socked feet as he had every evening for as long as she could remember. Archie at eighty was lean and spry, fit as a man two-thirds of his age. Only he had less stamina for the hours of arduous labour and lapsed into stillness at the end of the day. Of course Don took the bulk of the heavy work and all the farm business, which Archie had always found a chore. Nia looked over at him. Fairly obviously he did not want to examine the contents of the box. He preserves his inner balance, she thought; he is a spirit level.

Without opening his eyes, Archie made a loose fist of his hand and gently tapped his chest, in the region of his heart, as if knocking at a door.

*

The quiet sky buoyed Nia: she rode a thermal that came bouncing off the edge of the Mynd, circling so that she could look down on its spine at the sheer valleys deep in shadow dropping from Pole Bank. The homely irregularity of Archie's farm was spot-lit, its quilt of fields green and tawny yellow; the stand of oaks like broccoli. The red spot that winked would be Don in the tractor. Turning west, the glider sighed its way over Caer Caradoc; then towards Wenlock Edge.

That passion should be so peaceful, she could never have imagined before taking to the skies twenty years earlier. Ripped veils of cloud travelled beneath her, hiding and revealing the vast presences of the hills.

At peace, Nia thought: Ailsa too is at peace. They'd scattered her ashes on the Mynd all those years ago. Now looking down on the volcanic rock of Caer Caradoc, the sandstone Mynd, the rich soil of the flood plain, the coral reef of Wenlock Edge, Nia thought: those atoms of Ailsa might have drifted anywhere. Or everywhere. The whole of this is my mother.

Ailsa's moment; the six hundred million years of the massif. The mind fainted at the time scale of that. When the tectonic plates buckled and the volcanoes were born, Shropshire had been south of the equator. So Ailsa belonged to the body of the round earth. Nowhere was she a foreigner.

Nia made a sweet landing. Les came down ten minutes later. More and more, sister and brother lived for this, the necessity to earn their crust being intervals in their dream. In midwinter, when the mountain was white and icebound and nearly impassable, they'd struggle up in the Land Rover if they heard the club was open. Her brother met her in the clubhouse, where they clinked their customary glasses of brown ale.

'I thought of Mam up there,' she said.

'Oh, right? What in particular?'

'Not sure. A sense of her. Do you ever feel you're walking in her footsteps?'

Les shook his head and smiled. He was a literal, practical guy who managed a small chain of sports shops and called a spade a spade.

'Do you remember the raindrop fossil she brought down from the Mynd?' Nia asked him.

'I do. Where is it now?'

'She gave it to the museum at Carding Mill, didn't she?'

'That's right. We ought to go and see it again.'

One person couldn't claim ownership of such a treasure:

so Ailsa had declared, though anyone could see the avarice in her eyes. It was a fragment of telltale rock about the size of a brick, from a sandstone layer that had weathered out on the Mynd. The rock was imprinted with the marks of a passing shower that had fallen on to dried mud. The mud dried; a new layer of mud silted down, dried fast and locked the raindrops' traces in. And one day six hundred million years later, Mrs Ailsa Copsey of Lyth Clee Farm, climbing an exposed edge, had become aware of that passing shower.

'Yes,' said Les. 'We'll definitely visit. Not today. We're out to supper.'

'Have you phoned Nicki?'

'Yes, don't worry.'

Nicole did not much like her husband's fad for gliding and he was required to phone her whenever he was safely on *terra firma* again. Nia had shown him the photos and he'd begun to read Ailsa's journals. But he'd broken off abruptly, blushing to the roots of his hair: face, throat, everything, brick red. Would not say why. It was not his history. And this woman was not, in any way he comprehended, his mam. Perhaps that was it. Nia perfectly understood why he should be shocked, though she didn't share the reaction. Not at all. The Ailsa revealed in the journals was someone as nakedly close to Nia as a second skin.

Mother and daughter were alike, that was the thing, in ways Nia had rarely suspected. She'd had a couple of the tiny black and white pictures enlarged, so sharply had they affected her. They'd been taken on the voyage out to Egypt, obviously, since mother and child had been flown back in 1952. Enlarged, the prints looked strikingly modern. They might have been taken last week, except for the blanching

round the margins that turned them into a̶̶̶̶̶̶̶̶̶̶̶̶̶̶̶̶̶̶̶̶̶̶̶̶̶̶̶̶̶̶̶̶̶ ̶hᵉ
photos. One was a group portrait of Ailsa, th̶̶̶̶̶̶̶̶̶̶̶̶̶̶̶̶̶̶̶̶̶̶
and an unknown fair-haired woman. Toph̶̶̶̶̶̶̶̶̶̶̶̶
flaxen cherubs in collar and tie, were atta̶̶̶̶̶̶̶̶̶̶
mother's skirts, thumbs in mouths. Ailsa, the tallest
member of the group, held Nia's hand in both of hers and
bent her head to speak to her. It was clear that the two of
them were communing with their eyes in a bliss of secret
and somehow subversive conversation. Telepathy, Nia
thought: she'd once lived intuitively, able to enfold or
suffuse herself in Ailsa's inner space. They'd understood
one another, without having to speak. Braiding their
thoughts into the one plait. In the photo Nia was gazing up
at her mother with an expression of melting tenderness.

The second picture showed Ailsa and another woman, of
equal height but strikingly dark, wearing loose, silky trousers
and a white, sleeveless blouse. She recognised her, of course:
that woman, Mona, the pursuer of Ailsa's ghost. Arms round
one another's waists, the two of them seemed about to burst
out laughing at some mad private joke to do with the young
man in uniform on their left. And Ailsa looked – there were
no other words for it – radiantly beautiful.

'Poppy and I are off to Egypt,' she told Les. 'On a
cruise.'

'I know – Dad said. Are you sure it's safe to go?'

'Why shouldn't it be?'

'Well, terrorism, for a start. Nowhere's safe in the
Middle East any longer.'

'Not since Bush and B.Liar went into Iraq all guns
blazing, you mean?'

Her Tory brother hated it when Nia went off on one of

political rants. He'd been a member of the territorials in his youth, playing the cornet in the regimental band. She saw him swallow a sharp retort.

'I was thinking more of 9/11,' Les said gently. And then, to defuse things, 'Well, really I was just thinking of your health. You'll come down with something gastric and I'll have to come and fetch you home.'

'Oh, don't be so stuffy. It'll be fine.'

2

They'd just left their moorings at Southampton when Nia, holding Ailsa's skirts bunched in both fists, said she would get off now. She wasn't sailing on this nasty sea, said Nia. She was going home. Home she was going.

Go home Mami! she bellowed. And letting go of the skirts, Nia struggled to make a break for it. Ailsa gripped the child's wrist, shushing her. The wives and kiddies thronged the rail as the brass band played the *Empire Glory* out of harbour. It oompahed through 'Colonel Bogey' and many of the women sang along, their fear lifted, and the conscripts further down the ship whistled.

'Can you see Uncle Archie?' Ailsa cajoled the hysterical Nia.

'See him! See my lovely Archie!' the child shrieked, waving at the receding crowd on the quay.

'We're going to be with Daddy though, aren't we?' Ailsa encouraged her.

Dull old England receded with every moment. *Sailing to*

23

Joe! Ailsa thought. Goodbye to Church Stretton, Archie and everyone. Once she was out of the way, perhaps he'd find himself a nice girl, have children and be happy. Her cousin – once her *kissing cousin* – had shaken his head at the news of their departure and raised one hand as if to brush a moth away. The cryptic gesture said that he was content with his lot. *Knowing you are in the world. So take care of yourself, Ailsa, you are precious to us all.* She gripped the rail tight. She'd always loved Archie. But it would never have worked. Joe of course had no idea. She'd never breathed a word. Her husband could be jealous of his own shadow and, when she'd allowed him to kiss her after that first dance, he sulked at the thought that she might be *fast*.

At home they'd begged Ailsa not to go to Egypt: did she want to take Nia to her death? Consider the germs, the flies, the heat, the filthy habits of the natives. Not to mention terrorists. What was Ailsa thinking of? Archie's parents, socialist to the bone, had mildly pointed out that we had no earthly right to be there: the so-called Anglo-Egyptian Treaty was illegal, the Empire an expensive farce. Attlee knew that, if Bevin didn't. We'd scuttled out of India and Palestine and we'd have to scuttle out of the rest of the Middle East. Scuttling was all we were good for. The War had beggared and bankrupted Britain. Rationing, which they'd largely escaped on the farm, was getting worse, not better.

Ailsa's mother's people, Shrewsbury Tories, said Suez was the Empire's jugular vein; it made us safe in our beds. Protection against the Commies. *The point you have to remember is that Egypt's on Uncle Joe Stalin's doorstep.* And by that token, no place for wives and kiddies.

Go home, Mami, now! Going now!

Nia bolted along the deck to where she thought she remembered the gangplank was. She squirmed through the jam of bodies.

No gangplank. Nia frowned down at the churning grey waters. The brass band drew off and the waving folk on the harbour were getting smaller: to Nia it seemed that the jetty moved away like a ferry, while the great troopship stood still. The lines of weeping families on shore waved Union Jacks and pocket hankies, leaving Nia high and dry.

Oompah, went the band.

Twin khaki men hunkered either side of the child.

'What's the trouble now, dearie? Lost your mum, have you?'

'Mami!' shrieked Nia. 'Lost! My! Mami!'

Nia and her mother were one lovely weave, like a plait. Nia could sense Ailsa's emotions through her skin, and think in her mother's mind. Mostly. But the plait was beginning to become unbraided. It had been coming to pieces for some time. Her mouth squared up and quivered.

'Goodbye! Ta ta! Write!' shouted the women, leaning over the rails, arms outstretched.

The band swung into 'The White Cliffs of Dover'.

Nia hung high in the air, in the powerful arms of a khaki man with a beret, who might possibly have been her father, although he usually wore blue. But he had this same tobacco smell mixed with hair oil and petrol.

'Are you my daddy?'

'I don't think so, Gingernut. Not unless there was a big mistake made.'

He and his pal winked.

'We'll call your mum over the tannoy. What's your name?'

'What's yours anyway, mister?'

'Cheeky. Yours first.'

'Nia Josephine Roberts.'

'Comical little miss, aren't you? Best get them to call for Mrs Roberts.'

But Ailsa was here already. Fierce, protective Ailsa, who snatched her lamb from the arms of the military, and then remembered to be grateful to the friendly-eyed private, who said, 'There you are, Mrs Roberts. No harm done. Gave you a dickens of a turn, I should think.'

Ailsa felt fit to faint in the uproar, and Nia, clamped to her with arms and legs, chin hooked over her shoulder, suddenly weighed like lead, causing her mother to stagger. The band music drifted away, leaving only the frail filament of the women's singing, until they too gave up and watched in silence as their ship drew out.

'Saw my dada,' Nia told her mother, speaking around the thumb she had wedged between her lips.

'You can't have. He's in Egypt. Waiting for us.'

'Did so see him.'

'There you are – get down now. You're too big for Mami to carry.'

Ailsa crouched to straighten the green velvet coat that Nia wore with matching leggings and a darker green bonnet that made her look like a miniature Robin Hood. From the bonnet, excitable tendrils of ginger hair curled.

Now the tugs had led them out into the centre of the harbour. The wives turned away from the rails, drying their eyes, blowing their noses. It was an adventure, after all, leaving behind the stint and dreariness and fog. Something new. No rationing in Egypt: cans of peaches in

26

the NAAFI, as many as you could eat. Sunshine and beaches: almost a holiday camp, they'd been assured. Ailsa winced at the jolly bellowing that passed for conversation as these sensible souls girded up their loins and began to knit the bondings that would make life livable on the *Empire Glory*. She held Nia to her side, watching another troopship, the *Empire Sunderland*, move into port. The troops were all on deck, sailing home from the Far East, cheering themselves into harbour and home.

The women of the *Empire Glory* waved to the men of the *Sunderland*. Five hundred raw conscripts and regulars kept segregated on a forward deck of the *Empire Glory* called out to the tanned and euphoric homeward-bound men, who taunted them about their pale and pasty skin. *White knees! White knees!* they bawled, among other catcalls, more obscene. The ships slid past one another so closely that Ailsa made out individual boyish faces. If they were returning from tours of duty in the Far East, they would have come through the Suez Canal, from the panting humidity of Singapore or Malaya, postings Joe dreaded. No place for kiddies, he'd said. I couldn't have my Nia exposed to that.

Nia stared. The world was too big. Too grey, the sea and the cloud. Her brain swelled, trying to take it in. On the bus the conductor would dingdong the bell and let you off at your stop. Trains, smelling tastily of egg-sandwich, opened friendly doors at stations. In silence Nia laid hold on Mami's body and wrapped her arms round its solidity.

The womenfolk drifted down to nest in their cabins; the troops were tannoyed to their muster. When a white-coated official reminded Ailsa that the time had come to go below decks, she nodded but lingered, taking deep lungfuls of salty air. The ship's engine throbbed up through the one creature that she and Nia made together. The coarse camaraderie of her fellow wives in the bowels of the troopship held no appeal. But they were all right: good sorts. What a frightful snob I've become since my marriage, Ailsa thought, and quailed. Folk who wouldn't read a book to save their lives: what did she have to say to them or they to her? The irony was that it had been *because* Ailsa had read books that she'd disdained the petty and artificial distinctions of class that made Britain what it was – and voted Labour, what's more, in the first election of her life.

Not quite got round to telling Joe yet, she thought, and smiled. Buck up, she told herself. Only a fortnight and you'll be with him. You'll see the Pyramids and other wonders beyond your wildest dreams. 'Go down *now*, Mami,' Nia moaned.

Only two bunks were left: upper and lower beds next to the rasping air conditioning. And when the queasiness came over her, Ailsa was forced to swap with her daughter to take the lower bunk, throwing Nia into hysterics until a Nice Lady in uniform came in and forced another woman to swap her coveted bed with a porthole.

'We shall see the flying fishes, dearie,' the Nice Lady told Nia, as Ailsa lay languishing.

Nia glanced away from the powdered, fragrant face to the porthole. In her mind, goldfish swam across the sky.

'Yes, and you shall see the porpoises! What do you think of that? Nice pretty porpoises playing in the blue, blue Mediterranean Sea!'

The Nice Lady was clearly finding the sceptical Nia hard going. She straightened up, to Nia's relief, for the heavy bosom and the perfume-waft filled her with inexplicable gloom. The Nice Lady asked the time but no one in the cabin owned a watch.

'Well, never mind. The natives will trade you one for a few ciggies. Don't let them swindle you.'

'What else?' asked Nia.

'Pardon me?'

'What else will we be seeing?'

'Oh – well – let's see. We shall see the apes on the Rock. At Gib, of course. Jolly old Gib.'

'That's a posting I would really like,' said one of the women sharing the cabin, and sighed. 'Brean,' she added. 'Babs. Bound for Fanara.'

'And talking of rocks ...'

The Nice Lady mentioned rock buns for tea, at which Ailsa retched.

'I'm hardly ever icky,' said Babs. 'Seasoned vets us.'

Whereupon the ship gave an ironic lurch which had them all except Nia heaving over buckets. She pinched her nose between thumb and finger and wished for a peg. It frightened her to see Ailsa, grey and limp, float off beyond the power of tantrums to control her.

'What's to be done with Tiddler?' asked Babs. 'Aren't you feeling umpty at all, dear?' She spoke as if seasickness would be a convenient playpen into which Nia could be deposited for safekeeping.

The Nice Lady said there was no help for it, she'd take Nia with her and keep her occupied. She reassured the mother that she'd soon get her sea legs, in a tone that told

Ailsa, Buck up, we're not even in the Bay of Biscay yet, you'll wish yourself back in the English Channel before too long, my lass.

*

Going to eat rock-buns, they were, up there somewhere. Well, let them go then and leave Ailsa to die in peace.

The next time Ailsa opened her eyes, Nia was bustling out with her golly under her arm, without a backward glance. She's punishing me, thought Ailsa, oh well. Once assured of quiet and privacy, she felt more herself and propped herself on a couple of pillows, taking sips of water.

But then the door opened again. The officious woman with the chins was back.

'What language does she speak, Mrs Roberts?'

'Well – English.'

'What, all the time?'

'Oh yes.'

'Just checking. Funny little character. Cheerio.'

Ailsa knew what she meant. Nia's carroty hair and grey-green eyes gave her a fey look. Her eyebrows and lashes were so fair that they hardly showed except when she blushed. Blushes were explosions of blood into Nia's pearl-pale face. She looked like an albino and talked back in a mixture of English and Welsh that sounded plain daft. Comical at her age, but Joe set great store by what he called 'well-spokenness'. Even so, Ailsa took umbrage at the woman's saying like that, 'Funny little character', inwardly denying that Nia was a pickle.

From the first Ailsa had melted at the intensities of Joe's Valleys lilt. His first language was Welsh, a fact he seemed ashamed of. *But you're bilingual, Joe!* Oh no, he'd said, blushing, Welsh doesn't count, it's low. She'd made him teach her intimate words to share as the little language of their love. *Ti'n werth y byd, cariad* carried more emotion than 'You're the world to me.' But in Joe's mind his tongue betrayed the threadbare poverty in which he'd grown up and the use of the same tea leaves twice over.

They seemed to be entering, if not calmer waters, a more steady unease. Ailsa fished out Joe's photograph and looked into the wartime face of Joe as he had been in the Western Desert, muscular arms folded, eyes crinkling, his funny buck teeth in that small mouth, a soft mop of hair that was licensed because they had no Brylcreme in the Western Desert.

Whatever was that black thing on the sheet? A dead spider? Ailsa flicked at it with her nails. No, it was not alive: just something embroidered on to the sheets, to stop you filching them presumably, as if you would want to go off with such linen – linen that carried ancient stains neither boiling nor bleach had been able to remove.

One more sip: that's right, stay down. It did. She eased on to her left side and prepared to doze. The ventilator grid snored as if a fat man were sleeping there, some inveterate wife-waker; the ship's engine thrummed through her entire body. Ailsa opened her eyes. Another black spot on the edge of the pillow. It could not be, but was, a swastika.

*

Nia, placed on a seat bolted to the floor and told to show good manners, picked up her bun and brought it down with a thump on the table. Soon a couple of big girls had joined

31

in the din, whacking cakes on their plates. Nia slid down under the table and crawled to the end, face level with a line of red sandals and white ankle-socks. Her cot sheet was clamped between her teeth and her golly was stuffed down the waistband of her skirt.

Bolting down a corridor, Nia felt the thrill of escape polluted by the shock of isolation. Through the tannoy came a male voice instructing all Other Ranks wives and children to attend for life boat drill on the deck aft.

The deck aft?

Nia ran against a tide of women and children forcing their way up the narrow corridor. Pelting back the way she had come, she ran straight into the hands of the Nice Lady. Dragged up to the deck, Nia grizzled quietly and made her limbs go limp and her lips pouty, as the lady struggled to get her into a life jacket. Finally she was handed over to Mrs Brean, who was instructed to keep a firm hold on her, as she was a demon.

'I won't run away,' Nia confided to Babs.

'How do I know that?'

'*You're* not nasty.' Nia, in a tender gesture her daddy often used, cupped Mrs Brean's cheek in her palm, just softly, for a moment, so that the woman went still and gazed at the kiddie, surprised.

'Ah, I expect you want your mum, darling, don't you?'

'I won't be trouble.' Nia shook her head emphatically.

'Course you won't, pet.'

The softened lady melted altogether as Nia raised her arms to allow the life jacket to be slipped off over her head. She held on to the back of Mrs Brean's skirt as she turned to attend to her own brood, mentioning to a fellow wife the

32

possibility of tombola later and something nice to – you know – when they'd got the kiddies to bed. Babs gestured with her hand, pouring a series of imaginary drinks into her mouth at top speed, to her companions' amusement. She did not feel Nia let go and slip back towards the door leading, Nia thought, to the cabins. She ducked beneath a cordon marking off one area of the deck from another. Khaki men in rows further along were being barked at as they struggled into life belts.

Down some stairs, up more. Her sandal-soles drummed on metal as Nia beetled along one passageway and down another. Hand over hand up a ladder. Panic raced along behind but Nia would not allow it to catch up. She burst through a half open metal door that silently closed behind her.

High up Nia stood on an iron platform, with railings, suspended above a gigantic stench. It rose from a room vast as an aircraft hangar she'd visited with her daddy, where she'd marvelled as the entrance was rolled back like a curtain and from the oily guts of the dark building a plane had taxied out. Was there a plane in the ship? Her father loved the oily insides of an aeroplane. Taking Golly out of her waistband, she showed him the sight. He waggled his sticky-outy arms, eyes wide in disbelief.

There was no plane.

The hangar went on for dark, windowless miles as far as Nia could see, dimly lit by lights on the walls. A noise like thunder. Kitbags lay on a net, strung by swaying ropes from iron hooks attached to girders. Nia felt sorry for the kitbags. When her father undid the toggles, you could dig out his wash bag and unroll it, pulling out his comb, greasy from his lovely head. And his razor, flannel and nail clippers, each of which was interestingly dear to her. The kitbags hung above the midget men below. Everything hung from something. For the floor was awash with vileness. Men lay in hammocks, their heads hanging over the sides. Beside each was a bucket with a mop.

Nia pulled out her abhorred ribbon and held it out over the void. Then she dropped it into the dark stink, watching it fall on to a metal table with three enormous kettles on it, their spouts all pointing forward. She sent her kirby-grip after the ribbon and felt the relief that came when your hair stopped pulling tight. But where was the door? It had somehow become a wall. She panicked; pelted up and down on the platform. Even when she found the iron door, Nia was too puny to pull it open.

It opened from the other side. Nia clung to the man, sheltering under the peak of his cap. She would like such an important cap. His lah-de-dah voice marked him as an officer – even she knew that. Everything would be all right now. She rode in his arms away from the noise and foulness. His name was Alex, he said, and what was her name? Was it Monkey?

No, she said. I am Miss Nia Roberts.

Oh, I thought it was Monkey. Are you sure?

They joked and he jounced her up and down and tossed her in the air and caught her, and Nia laughed with a high pitched squeal, looking anxiously from side to side as they navigated the labyrinth.

The Nice Lady, when found, seemed obscurely more irked with the man in the peaked cap than with the stray child.

'It is beyond a joke,' she said.

'Oh, I wouldn't say that.'

When he went away with a wave of his hand, Nia dismissed and forgot him.

'I hope you're well pleased with yourself, madam,' said the Nice Lady.

'Yes, thank you.' Somewhat quenched, Nia clung to the hand that grasped hers.

The Nice Lady looked down sharply, alert for insolence but uncertain of irony.

3

The cabin was empty but for a shadowy girl tugging back the sheets on the only unclaimed bunk. Ailsa passively observed the stranger's movements as she dragged a comb through dark, tangled hair without bothering to look in a mirror, bobby pin between her teeth. Seeing that Ailsa was awake, she came over to crouch by her bunk.

'Feeling rotten?'

'A bit grim.'

'I've got some salts you sniff. Somewhere. Hang on.' She rummaged in her bag. 'No idea why they work but they do seem to help.'

Ailsa breathed in peppermint balm. The stranger's eyes were liquid and dark, iris melting into pupil, beneath the wings of her eyebrows. Terribly intense but arresting and oddly familiar. An ugly-beautiful face with a large mouth and perfect teeth; skin cinnamon-brown. *I know you from somewhere.* Joe would have called her a *darkie*: how odious of him, and Ailsa was cross with her husband and a bit ashamed, although he wasn't there and would have kept quiet if he had been.

'What I do is stay up on deck as long as I can and get the benefit of the air until I've got my sea-legs. Think you could make it if I gave you a hand?'

'Honestly, I daren't risk it. You go.'

'I'm Mona, by the way. Jacobs.'

'Ailsa Roberts.'

'Now, what can I get you?'

Her voice was cultivated, every sound precisely pronounced. Toffs' English. Ailsa lay back against the pillow and craved Lucozade. The girl was no sooner gone than she was back with cherry Corona and ice cubes; ciggies such as Ailsa had never seen before, in a cylindrical tin with its own opener. The ice cubes brought relief. Ailsa's stomach calmed and the ciggies did the rest. And they cost next to nothing, said Mona. Duty-free. Life will look up now!

'Wherever did you get all this?'

Ah, so that was it. An officer's renegade wife, Mona Jacobs was proud of being a misfit amongst *those horrors up there* and clearly ashamed of her husband's rank. They were socialists, she and her old man, and they wouldn't *dream* of living it up in a family cabin, knowing, as Ben said, looking at the lists, that there were pregnant women travelling who were packed in like bloody sardines. Can you believe that? So that's it, Ailsa thought incredulously: you are slumming it with us hoi polloi. You think you're an angel visiting us from heaven.

A prattling angel. This prohibition on fraternising between officers and 'men' was worse than the Montagues and the Capulets, but the visitor didn't give a damn about

37

small-minded idiots, why should she? Not every day you met someone you could talk to. Anyway *they* weren't in the RAF, thank God, were they? *They* hadn't joined up and signed their lives away like mugs, and just because she was some bod's wife didn't mean she answered to his name, rank and number. *You do, you know*, Ailsa thought, looking down, biting her lip so as not to laugh. How did the husband like being referred to as *some bod* or *a mug*? How old was Mona? Mid-twenties perhaps but adolescent in manner, wearing slacks, her loose way of carrying herself a slovenly protest against deportment. She gave Ailsa her full attention, with a close, gentle gaze that only reinforced a tickling sense of *déjà vu*. They stared at one another for a moment.

'Got it! You're the motor bike girl? Aren't you?'

It all came rushing back. The cabin was full of the memory of mad girls in wartime flocking in and out of the flats at Brewers' Green, the dawn chorus of their voices (on the razzle all night) echoing along the alley, their heels clicking (for their shoe leather was the best), the glossy tops of their heads gleaming in the sun. And all spied from above, through geranium blossom with its cool rainy scent.

It was the girl with the hot water bottle. Mona Serafin. The name echoed back from wherever it had lodged. Her surname was now Jacobs *but I call myself Serafin-Jacobs, double-barrelled. Who wants to give up her own name, I ask you?*

They stared, eyes on stalks, giggling, clutching one another. They were back in the war, the party wall breached at last. The women's eyes glistened with the glow of memory.

This was how Nia found them as she was lugged back

in disgrace from her tour of the ship. Out of control, Mrs Grey said – and quite honestly the staff had better things to do than go chasing round after disobedient girls.

'Mami!' Nia cried, bursting into dramatic sobs. 'Where have you been?'

'I hope you're feeling better, Mrs Roberts, because you will have to look after her yourself from now on. You've not been smoking of course, ladies. In the cabin.'

'Oh dear – have one yourself.' Mona offered the carton. 'Please do.'

Mrs Grey reddened. She addressed herself exclusively to the mother. The kiddie would have to go back to leading reins if she couldn't behave properly. Leading reins! How would a big girl like that?

'I've been in the hangar.'

'Did she say *hangar*?'

'A big sick bowl with hundreds of men in it.'

'She's making it up.'

'Hanging. In the air. I was looking for the aeroplane.'

Nia scrambled on to the bottom of the bunk and wormed her way up the gap between her mother and the wall. Stuffing the centre of her cot sheet into her mouth, she tossed the rest of it over her face, a flannel veil, and breathed the moist, self-scented, off-white world that accompanied her wherever she went. Ailsa knew Nia feared nothing once she was in her pod.

Mrs Grey explained that Nia had found her way to the troop deck where the soldiers were housed. Yes, in a state of abject squalor, Mona said, it was a disgrace. They were only young boys, many of them conscripts, and they were treated like scum. Typical British idea of democracy: a few dozen officers swanning around in two thirds of the ship and five hundred human beings living like pigs in the hold. Mrs Grey sat plumb down on a bunk and stared, rhubarb-red, saying she found that a novel view and quite an interesting one. That fighting men should expect the conditions of a luxury liner, well well. However would we have won the war if such a cushy doctrine had prevailed?

'And your daughter could so easily have fallen to her death,' she told Ailsa, gently now, for the mother had gone rather pale. She made it clear that she placed the blame squarely on Wing Commander Jacobs's wife, to whom she referred as a 'visiting officer'.

'Oh, *please*, Mrs Grey – don't embarrass me. I'm just a civilian woman like anyone else.'

'We take our husbands' rank, of course.'

'Oh no, *really*.'

Officers' wives, however out of line they got, could not be attacked from below. She'll go for me when you're not here, thought Ailsa, so shush, do: it's me, not you, who'll be in the dog house. In Ailsa's mind's eye, Nia swayed high up on a platform. She lost footing, she tripped, she pitched down into the abyss. Ailsa wrapped her arms round her daughter's body, warm through the cotton, and hugged her close.

Mona raised the question of the monograms on the sheets. 'They can't be *swastikas*, surely?'

They were, and some younger women had already taken the law into their own hands and snipped the vile things out with decent English nail scissors. Mrs Grey, at last in agreement with the Wing Commander's uppity wife, said something must be done. No doubt about *that*. After the war the ship had been requisitioned, lock, stock and barrel, from the German navy and converted, with the least possible expense, to British use. The *Reichsemerald* had become the *Empire Glory*. She was due to be broken up after this voyage. Mrs Grey left them on reasonably amicable terms. Thank heaven, thought Ailsa.

The Wing Commander's wife patted her lap, inviting Nia to climb up and have a Wagon Wheel and Corona. The child needed no encouragement. She cradled her beaker, smiling over the rim, sipping and jingling the ice cubes. Mona presented her full face, gravely attentive. She seemed to loom, all eyes, at Nia, who stared straight back

'Lady,' she said. 'You need a damn good wash, my girl.'

Ailsa's face flamed; Nia meant, she knew, (but did Mona cotton on?) Mona's dark skin.

Without batting an eyelid, Mona explained that she was meant to be like this. You should be happy with who you are, she explained. Always.

'So let me touch it then.'

'Go on – that's fine.'

Most delicately, Nia stroked the dark lady's face with the backs of her fingers. A beautiful look stole into her eyes, an expression caught from her father. She cupped Mona's chin in both palms and nuzzled noses. Then she gave her a kiss, breaking through every convention into an intimacy that was its own courtesy. Ailsa saw how struck the woman was – the childless woman, who mirrored back Nia's unembarrassed gaze, dark eyes swimming. Mona looked, Ailsa thought, amazed and sad. But she'd have her own kiddies one day. And then this ocean of simple love that blessed them would be an everyday given of her existence

41

too. *The bliss it has been*, Ailsa thought, *to be your mother, Nia*. The thought rocked her.

Tranquil, Ailsa's daughter sat in the stranger's lap, humming to herself, her thin ginger hair and pale skin making a strong contrast with Mona's darkness as she folded a shy arm around Nia's middle. It was an episode of extraordinary peace. Ailsa of course had to spoil it with her nerves. She came in with, 'Nia is the limit, she really is. Oh, I'm so sorry.'

'She can only know what the world tells her.' Mona nuzzled the top of Nia's head with her chin.

'Mona, I didn't...'

'Course you didn't. Unfortunately, Ailsa, you aren't *the world*.'

No, I'm its tannoy, Ailsa thought, ashamed, as they left the cabin to go up to the mess. Its wireless set.

Babs Brean sang out, 'Still green round the gills, Mrs Roberts? Better eat while you can. Wait till you get to the Bay of Biscay!'

She winked at a bleached woman, with whom she'd struck up an instant and intimate acquaintance. Bosom pals they'd become in a trice and it seemed to Ailsa as if the women had all sought out partners in whom to stow their secrets, so that they could anchor themselves in gossip on the lurching world of the *Empire Glory*. They walked about coupled like the animals in the Ark. And just as easily as they'd fallen into step, these sudden little unions would be dissolved when they set foot on dry land.

And Mona and she were the same, but caught up in a past, which lay around them like a strangely glowing mist.

42

It's you, it's really you, Ailsa thought and in her mind the relationship they'd *almost* had took on an aura of mystery and meaning. The memory of the day she'd realised that the next door girls had left the Old Brewery returned with exaggerated significance, as if it had marked an epoch in her life. Oh those girls: their philosophy and emotionalism, their all-night parties and the operatic arias in the bath. They'd vanished – but at first she'd hardly noticed. She'd been married by then, to Joe who was everything. All Ailsa's passion had poured into her only-just-consummated marriage. But when Hitler had thrown the doodlebugs at London, Ailsa had looked up in mid-word, fountain pen in hand, from writing to her husband in Italy – and registered her neighbours' absence.

She'd known then, known for sure, that she was about to die. The rattling rocket halted over her head. A moment of pure evil. You had a few seconds until it blew you apart. Ailsa's mind had flicked sideways to the neighbouring flat. Empty! As empty as it had been for days, weeks. She'd hardly missed the girls' bright presence. No time for any valedictions. Alone, she was alone.

She heard the doodlebug hit – someone else. Oh, thank you, God.

Now she learned that the girls had left the Old Brewery when they'd had enough of being glorified secretaries at the Ministry. Mona and Bobbie had joined the UN Relief and Rehabilitation Administration, resettling slave workers and concentration camp victims. At first Mona had worked from an office in Birmingham; then at the end of the war she'd been drafted to Lübeck in North Germany. Met up again with her old man and married him.

43

'We thought you so glamorous in those days, Ailsa, I can't tell you.'

'*Me* glamorous! You can't be serious.'

'You've no idea how we used to discuss you and speculate on what it was you did and who exactly you were.'

'You're joking.' Ailsa grinned, liking the idea. Obviously they'd glamorised her young isolation, casting her as a figure dauntlessly modern, who went her own way and exemplified some kind of unreal *Zeitgeist*.

'We decided you were a spy! Were you a spy?'

'Oh yes.'

They giggled. A spy was just about it, although what you witnessed from your window was bound to be skewed. As what they'd seen of her was skewed. Perspective conferred mystery – and especially to those ultra-educated types, whose whole minds were occupied with cerebral romance – thinking about Thought, existentially in love with Sartre and de Beauvoir, names she'd caught from next-door and looked up in Marylebone Library. Ailsa's shy solitude had turned her into a storybook girl for those gilded Oxford types, ignorant of the fact that her lack of a single pair of nylons could reduce Ailsa to tears, as she pulled on lisle stockings lumpy with darns or went bare-legged. *They* wouldn't have minded bare legs. Bohemians didn't. For they could have dressed from head to foot in silk if they'd liked. They'd never have fathomed that Ailsa struggled to summon courage to order fish and chips in the Corner House. They'd seen a modern girl who walked alone – and not only straddled a bike but understood its innards, sleeves rolled up like a mechanic and oil to the elbows. They'd heard her

44

whistling perhaps, for at times (and how could Ailsa have forgotten this?) she really had felt like that – a free spirit.

No mother of a dependent child could dream or claim such licence. The Wing Commander's lady wife would soon see through her. For now I am prosaic, she thought ruefully. And yet, accepting a cup of cocoa from the urn, sipping to see if it would stay down, a rebellious spirit spoke up in Ailsa. I am not the common run. Anyone with eyes can see that.

In the reassuring hubbub of women's and children's voices, she chatted to an Irene and a Hedwig, one of the German brides the boys had brought home after the war. The Allies had been forbidden to fraternise with the defeated enemy in his – and her – misery. But how could they fail to fraternise? A word too sexless for what was bound to happen. The boy-soldiers were young and human, and once the killing had ceased, how could they be otherwise than on the side of life and sex and birth – and of pity? Ailsa dreaded to think what Hedwig's married life had been like, stranded amongst the insular, Jerry-hating English. She itched to try out some of her German.

'Chopsticks' echoed from the piano, an out-of-tune grand of all things. Mona craned and said it was a Blüthner, concert grand, the real thing, taken over presumably with the vessel from the German *Kriegsmarine*.

'Do you play?' Ailsa asked her.

'Not nowadays, no, I don't,' Mona said dismissively, and without asking whether Ailsa played. Ailsa didn't like to boast. She smiled down at Nia, who was being good as gold.

Nia snuggled against her mother's arm, thumb in mouth, her admiration and pride unreserved. No one else had this mother, only Nia. And she didn't have to share her. This soft-haired lady, willowy and tall, with the special clean smell even under her arms, the shirt-waisted blue dress decorated with flowers in white circles. This one and only. Nia's, forever.

'We'll have singsongs on the voyage, I've no doubt,' Babs said. 'Look at your daughter, Mrs Roberts. She's eaten up half her bread while you weren't looking. There's a good girl, dear. You see, you *were* hungry, after all!'

Nia glared. She'd been playing a game of pinching the triangles of bread into moist particles between thumb and finger. The rhythm of the game had been soothing and she was put out at the interruption. Having unconsciously fed herself the bread, Nia was annoyed to have her conformity exposed. *Spoilt brat*, women's expressions said. Babs proposed to make tracks: tombola and a drinkie later for the grown-ups. Her daughters whined and thumped off flat-footedly in her wake. Nia's face said, *Bossy*. Then she could be seen to think, *Big Bum*, as Mrs Brean turned to shepherd her flock to the cabin. She grinned over her cocoa. Love for Ailsa brimmed.

'You got cocoa all round your mouth, Mami,' she said, and with a forefinger gently drew a mirroring outline round her own lips. 'A moustache.' She added, thoughtfully, '*Darling*.'

'You have a pearl, Ailsa,' said Mona. 'A little pearl. I'm so glad we caught up with one another.'

Eyebrows twitched as the ragamuffin received this fulsome praise. Ailsa dabbed cocoa away from Nia's mouth, proud that Mona saw her daughter's quality. Not everyone did. To be frank, she didn't always. Nia could be so odd.

But in Mona's world, 'odd' was good, or likely to be. 'Even' was dull and despicable. Ailsa prepared to tell Joe what Mona had said. *You know the lady on the troopship, Joe? She told me Nia was a pearl.*

*

The pearl was put to bed with the others in the cabin. She settled down happily after their whispered prayers, the mothers taking turns to babysit. The released women applied lipstick and left for the deck.

Ailsa watched the pale wake ploughed by the ship in the blackness of the sea. The quiet, nervous Irene stood with Ailsa at the rail, wringing lilac gloved hands as she stared homeward. Ailsa asked how her boys were: two white-blond seraphs who kept close to their mother, attached wherever she went, impeding progress. What an immaculate family they were, all appearing just-ironed. Irene White seemed a woman created out of fear, detecting germs on cup lips, kiddies' fingers, taps. She gazed plaintively at Ailsa and spoke of the worrying state of the lavatories. Christopher and Timothy had gone off to sleep, *rather against their better judgement*, she said, with a small reserved smile. When Mona appeared with her husband, Irene shrank from the towering officer and could scarcely speak.

Ailsa smiled into dark, diffident eyes: the Wing Commander stooped and slouched as if in pathological apology for his outlandish height. Older than Mona, fortyish perhaps? In love with her from the crown of her head to her toes. He deferred unashamedly to his wife. Ailsa liked him for that. Dark rippling hair, very thick and bushy: she could just hear Joe murmuring, *Hair cut, you!*

47

He looked Jewish. Of course, that would be it: Mona must be Jewish too. *Call me Ben*. How did a high ranking officer not know that she couldn't possibly? The Wing Commander was a medic, a psychologist. His unkemptness was truly breathtaking: shirt button open at the neck, a general air of unruly sweetness. Something to do with status, no doubt; no one could call a high-ranking officer to account and demand that he adopt a military bearing.

'Surely you recognize Ailsa, *Habibi*?' Mona said. 'The gorgeous girl on the motorbike. You do, of course you do.'

He didn't and neither did the blond conscript officer, Alex, although both had been frequent visitors at the Old Brewery, among the young men tumbling in and out of love with Ailsa's neighbours. Free love, Ailsa had supposed, fascinated, mildly scandalised. For in those days she'd half expected to settle for poor Archie in the end and go home to her cousin, the Quaker Meeting and the warmly humdrum farm. The patrician young men at the Old Brewery had fascinated Ailsa: they all seemed to upset each other terribly, and to need to discuss it and make it worse. Disturbance rolled round like thunderstorms. It was always the end of the world – or the dawn of a new age. Occasionally a couple of sensitive but combative young philosophers would be heard in passionate debate through the open window, about Plato, as they claimed, but really about some girl they both loved. Their friendships with one another also seemed lived on the level of romance: an eros presumably without sensuality, as in Shakespeare's sonnets to his Young Man.

The bombs fell and the skyline glowed with fire. Houses were reduced to rubble or left standing like shattered obelisks, landmarks on which, as years between the Blitz and the doodlebugs passed, grass and purple fireweed rooted. The high-ranking boy officers went off to be maimed or die in Libya or Albania. And their poetry went with them.

'We're taking turns to keep watch over the kiddies,' Mona told her husband. 'It's first watch now. Then we've got second. So we can't stick around later than nine.'

'Oh but *you* don't have to, Mona,' Ailsa said.

'Maybe, but I want to.'

Winy gaiety sparkled. It was an adventure, a lark, after all, going East. It pepped Ailsa up as if a route had opened up back to the daredevil despatch girl, licensed to break the Highway Code and mount the pavement if necessary. Back then any evening might have been your last. The ruins stank of rotting flesh; teemed with fresh ghosts. So you'd give life a run for its money. What wouldn't Ailsa Birch have given for a chance to sail to the Orient, in the wake of all the Memsahibs and diplomats, civil servants and engineers, pukka worthies and unworthies?

An odd little scene took place in the women's mess, around the concert grand. The Wing Commander coaxed his wife to sit on the piano stool and try out the instrument. *Go on, darling. Just for me.* Mona's face closed up. She sat stiffly and rested her fingers on the keys. Ailsa, aware of a painful pause, saw her lip quivering and thought: *Oh no, she's going to cry*. She slid on to the stool beside Mona.

'Squeeze up, *cariad*,' she said, as easily as if the obscurely suffering girl had been a large-scale version of Nia. 'Let's try a duet.'

Not to shine in the company of a concert pianist,

however rusty, came as no dishonour to the star pupil, Grade 8, of Mr Ernest Beaver at the Abbey Grammar School, Shrewsbury. They romped through a bagatelle and tangled fingers over a Mozart duet with impromptu syncopations. By and by Ailsa withdrew and let Mona storm into Beethoven's *Hammerklavier*: a stunning parody of it, rather, for the out-of-tune instrument boomed and jangled. Through soft passages throbbed the engine of the *Empire Glory*.

The Wing Commander, taking over, thundered out fistfuls of notes in a boogie woogie, standing with a fag hanging from his mouth, swaying from hip to hip, and Alex jived with Mona, then with Ailsa. Then Mona played and the men danced together, a sultry smooching tango that made Ailsa's stomach ache with laughter. Now she was in the Wing Commander's arms. He curled her up, unfurled her, and Ailsa, loose and pliant as a rag doll, fell wherever she was thrown. She twisted and turned, her skirts belled, until she became conscious of women in the back of the room and a scatter of clapping. The room was required for tombola. Sweating and exhilarated, Ailsa sensed the women's eyes on stalks and all the stalks pointing in her direction. So what?

*

Through the pale grid of her lashes, Nia watched her mother and the new dark auntie. She rubbed with one finger the patch of Teddy's hair that had gone bald with kissing. The ventilator went Ooh-Ah.

The two women were sitting knee to knee on the next bunk. Whispering. Nia heard the blessed names *Archie* and

Joe. Saw them touch glasses of yellow stuff like egg shampoo smelling of cough mixture. *Cheers! Iechyd da! Prost!* Mona's big strong hand seemed like her own daddy's hand on the end of a lady's arm. Odd as this appeared, it was also good, and she allowed it. *Call him Habibi, everyone does, it means Sweetheart*. Nia dropped off again, under the spell of the rhythm of the whispering, to and fro, to and fro, until the two voices vanished into the Ooh-Ah of the ventilator and became one voice.

4

Mona Serafin-Jacobs, Nia thought. Stalking Mona. Her stomach turned over. She looked across the aisle to check on her daughter: fast asleep, thank goodness. Poppy, who hated flying, had gone green as the plane took off from Manchester for Aqaba; her magazine lay unread in her lap.

Now Nia was free to gnaw on the bone of Dr Mona Serafin-Jacobs.

Twenty-odd years ago, after mother's death, cards from Stalking Mona kept on coming. She never gave up. She'd apparently written many times every year after they'd gone their separate ways. Ailsa had kept the lot in the box. It had not deterred Mona that Ailsa never responded with a proper letter, contenting herself with a polite annual card. From each card Stalking Mona had sucked all the juice and manufactured extra from her own imagination. She'd reminisced copiously about London in the Blitz. Mona's handwriting was an assertive and characterful italic script, which chased itself across the page, each word linked by a threadlike tie to the next, loops like nooses. It didn't take no for an answer.

Well, it had bloody well had to.

Scanning the latest letter on her stepfather's behalf, a couple of months after her mother's death, Nia had resented the tone of insinuating intimacy with a black dislike that was out of proportion really, but then everything was out of proportion where Nia and Ailsa were concerned. Sometimes Nia had wished her mother dead. But when your mother dies, the sun sets behind the mountain and never rises; the eternal dies that day. Poppy, at eighteen months old, had given Nia the will to live. Against the tide of a profound reluctance whose origin she took care not to examine, and because Archie seemed saddened beyond measure when the letters kept coming, Nia had eventually got round to informing the creature of Ailsa's death.

The creature was a concert pianist of world stature. On her record sleeves one saw a strong, melancholy face with full lips and striking eyebrows. Her dark hair was coloured with henna and kohl rimmed her nearly black eyes. It turned out that Ailsa hadn't kept Stalking Mona informed about her life: she'd not bothered to mention her remarriage to Nia's step-dad and the two boys. So Mona Serafin-Jacobs had addressed her mam all those years as 'Mrs Ailsa Roberts'. How typical of Ailsa to withhold vital information.

Dear Dr Serafin-Jacobs, Nia had written. *I am sorry to have to tell you ...* Something like that.

Dear Nia – came the reply, *I am more grieved than I can say to hear of your mother's death. I had learned (though not directly from Ailsa) of her remarriage and her two sons. May I ask you, Nia: how has your life been? You see, although it*

53

is a quarter of a century since I saw you, I recall you so well
– you are etched upon my memory. If there is anything I can
ever do for you and yours – anything – please let me know.
And I would love to see you again.

She had signed herself: *Ever, Mona.*

Visceral inertia had stayed Nia's hand. Nia had neither
replied with a letter nor responded to the request that she
phone, nor, God forbid, that they meet. She'd left it till now
to get properly in touch. But cards had kept flocking in to
herself, every birthday and Christmas, with a handwritten
note enclosed, as if Nia had somehow or other been
doomed to inherit the burden of her mother's adorer.

The name *Mona* in Ailsa's journal carried a sickening
resonance. Nia had no memories of that woman. But in the
act of reading the name, she seemed to see a dark, dramatic
face emerge from a mist, nothing like the forbidding mask
on the record sleeve: vivacious, reckless. Forcing itself up too
close. Swooping down, snatching her up, breathing on her
face with a licorice scent. Nia had a sense of – whatever was
it? – something she could only think of as *boundless cruelty*.
Even so, Nia had never realised Mona's importance until
Ailsa's journal came into her hands. The existence of the
green notebooks gave her no peace. She read in fragments:
shards that penetrated her heart and stuck there festering.

The young Ailsa was not the mam she knew. Nia
recognised herself all right, a horrid, boisterous, attention-
seeking little madam. Deep down she was still the only child
she'd been then, proclaiming and defending the unique
bond that attached her to her mother's heart, for it could
so easily be forfeit. Had she detected that danger so young?
The leaves of the green journal with its neatly forward-

sloping handwriting imprinted on Nia a fresh signature of loss. She'd rarely felt secure in a relationship. No sooner had she begun to love, truly love, Poppy's father than she'd gone cold on him. *He will change. Something namelessly bad will happen. If I love him. If I let myself.* Yet Jude and she had become excellent friends over the years and that meant something to her and everything to Poppy.

The journal paper had scarcely aged: it might have been written last week. Nia struggled in the web of handwriting. It was like falling in love, she thought, with a thousand misgivings, in love with a fresh Ailsa, hungry for life and craving adventure. More akin to a sister than to the mother she remembered. Actually, Nia thought, as the window whitened with cloud and the plane entered a phase of turbulence, the young Ailsa really was rather like me, wasn't she? *She must have understood. And, if so, she'd have feared for me in my wild days.*

There'd been no question, when the chance of the cruise came up, but that Nia must follow her young mother into Egypt, leaving the older Ailsa in the green shires of the Marches. *I'm coming*, she'd promised her. *Wait for me.*

Mona Serafin-Jacobs was still, at eighty-something, giving rare recitals; she was scheduled to play Beethoven's Fifth Piano Concerto with SOPH, the Symphony Orchestra of Palestinian Harmony. Nia had written to her care of her agent: *My daughter Poppy and I expect to be in Ismailia on 6th October.* She'd trembled as she typed the invitation and dropped it in the post box at Craven Arms. No going back. She'd brought the journals to show to Poppy and perhaps to Mona, for there were questions only this woman could answer. This thought filled Nia with exquisite disquiet.

55

Already she understood things about Mona that Ailsa had totally missed. Politically, the young Ailsa was a complete simpleton. How could her mother have been so naïve? *I was born in Jerusalem*, Mona had said. *What does that tell you?* Ailsa hadn't a clue what she was getting into. Only a year before the *Empire Glory* docked, the struggle between East and West had exploded. The Israeli state had risen at the heart of the Arab Muslim world, and that world could not abide it, not then, not now, not ever. Our modern reality was being born in fratricidal carnage, Nia thought, while you sailed blithely into the eye of the storm, Ailsa, innocent as a babe, your picture-book Bible as your guide-book, as witness your answer to Mona's question, *What does that tell you?* Not a clue.

Poppy opened her eyes and stretched. 'Are we there yet?' she yawned, in parody of her plaintive childhood question. She reached out to touch Nia's hand, across the aisle, and smiled.

'Nearly there, *cariad*,' lied Nia. Through the porthole, she could see the *papier maché* mountains of Italy, silver with snow. They'd be boarding a cruise ship at Aqaba, the *Terra Incognita*, to sail through the Red Sea and through the Suez Canal to Port Said and thence Alexandria.

*

'I was born in Jerusalem. What does that tell you?'

That you're Jewish, Ailsa thought. *Obviously. I've worked that out already.*

The two of them rested *cwtched-up*, as Joe would have said, on the bunk, drinking gin like old friends. Unused to spirits, Ailsa grew squiffy, then dozy. Her head lolled against the pillow and Mona's shoulder. At her throat Mona had a chain with a silver ornament attached; her fingers constantly played with it.

'What's that round your neck?'

'The key to our house in Qatamon. The side entrance.'

'It's pretty. Where is Qatamon, Mona?'

'A suburb of Jerusalem. I was two and a bit when we were driven out.'

'Driven out?'

'In the run-up to the so-called Arab Revolt. Between the Wars, during the British Mandate. I don't remember any of the violence. But I do remember our house, at least I think I do. Do you think Nia will remember things that are happening now? Will she remember this ship? Perhaps it's not my own memory but some sort of composite family memory. Anyway I wouldn't lose it for the world.'

Ailsa learned that Mona's father had been murdered by mistake for another Serafin. Her mother had fled with Mona and her brother. First to Lebanon, then to Cairo, and from there to relatives in London.

'I never speak about this. Even to myself.'

'Don't if it's painful.'

'No, I want to, Ailsa. So you'll know.'

In her teens Mona had been sent to Brussels to study piano, while her brother, the violinist, had emigrated to America. She'd come back to London eighteen months or so before the war, tail between her legs. It had not been a success. But then life had looked up! In a very big way. A year at Cambridge reading Greats, then Brewers' Green and the girls and Ben. And now *you*, Ailsa!

Ashamed of her ignorance, Ailsa let the moment go by

when she could have asked why the Serafins, Jews in Jerusalem, had been driven out of their own city. And why, now that the state of Israel existed, they couldn't return. Israel had opened the gates for massive immigration, Ailsa knew *that*: a thousand Jews a day were flocking home to the Holy Land. From the ends of the earth. The ancient Exodus was at last reversed. The remnant of Europe's persecuted Jews could find a place to lay their heads. So why not the Serafins?

Mona was describing a white veranda: when you stepped out in the morning before the heat got up, its cool tiles were delicious under your bare feet. Her window at Qatamon had looked out on an apricot tree and an orange tree. *Our* tabby and her kittens basked in their shade. Ailsa felt saturated with the light and colour of Mona's memories and with their sadness, as if they constituted a dream of her own.

The cat had been called Petra. A fat, overfed creature, purring like a motor.

We had to leave her there. Under the tree. But I never speak about this.

That meant: don't ask questions. I will tell you what I can. Mona said the women of her family had been strong people. Obliged to be. Resourceful and flexible and inventive. They'd had to learn other languages and customs, transplanting themselves in different soils. Every new language clashed against the others until you absorbed it and each in turn seemed to be Mona's first language, or equal first. Or they bled confusingly into one another. Tower of Babel in here, she said, tapping her head, confusion of tongues. That's how it is with nomads. Never a dull moment. All the borders in the world seemed to run through her like rivers.

But Mona was happy now again. Radiantly happy. She had a pal from a golden time. No mention was made of the piano. What had that been about? Something to do with being a refugee, Ailsa thought. She was squiffy and had to be helped into her bunk.

Next day Mona's bunk was empty. They'd all been sick as dogs in the Bay of Biscay but things were calmer now. Ailsa, with a pounding headache, went over to Mona's bunk and turned down the sheet. Nightie gone. Wash-bag gone. She'd been *taken*. Who had taken her? Don't be silly, of course she hadn't. Ailsa slowly began to dress and made her way up on deck.

Sky and sea were dazzlingly blue, the breezy sun warm on her face and arms. A handful of hardy folk had already clambered out of the misery in the ship's belly and lay on deck chairs soaking up the sun. It was another world, a holiday place. One could dimly see grey-green land over the sea-shimmer. And a white-coated waiter approaching with tea and biscuits.

The German woman lay fast asleep on a deck chair, pale hair tucked under a scarf, a cardigan draped round her shoulders. Ailsa sat down beside her, sipped sweet tea, nibbled a sugary biscuit. The quiet was bliss; the fresh air tonic. A book lay open on Hedwig's lap, its pages whispering as the breeze turned them over one by one, unread.

When Hedwig yawningly awoke, Ailsa couldn't resist exercising her beloved German: *'Guten Morgen, Frau Webster. Ein richtig schöner Tag, nicht wahr?'* Hedwig's eyes were puffy. You've been crying, Ailsa thought, as her neighbour hoisted herself up in the chair and removed her sun glasses for a moment, to rub her eyes.

'*Guten Morgen, Frau Roberts. Sie sprechen also Deutsch?*'
'*Kleines Bißchen.*'

Hedwig came from Hamburg. Her husband had met her in the ruins. He had saved her from bad things. Taken her to safety.

She did not look as though she felt safe. It came out that the ladies in her cabin, all but *Frau* Irene White, had treated Hedwig as if she were personally responsible for the swastikas on the sheets. Hedwig had never been one of *them*, she was blameless, surely that was clear? She was a British citizen, she said. She did not complain that her younger brothers and her best friend had been cremated in the firestorm. For this vile bombing might have been a necessary evil. But it should be known that her parents had been persecuted – *verfolgt*, she said – by the Gestapo.

That was what they all said, of course. Me a Nazi, an anti-Semite, an informer? Perish the thought! But in some cases – many – it must also be true. How could you know? Ailsa, embarrassed, murmured that she was sure no one really thought that, of course not, not in their heart of hearts.

They did, of course. The master race turns on the stranger in its midst. And who was the master race now?

Hedwig, encouraged by Ailsa's mild sympathy, was soon in full spate. The way she talked, those swastikas described British bullying as well as Jerry's. A *Reich* and an Empire: what's the difference? Not that she said this in so many words – but Ailsa heard it. Steady on, whoa, she thought. That cap does *not* fit. We are pretty decent after all. She was glad to break the contact when Irene and her two small sons came up on deck and Mrs Grey arrived with Nia, sucking her thumb and dangling her golliwog. Taking Ailsa aside, Mrs Grey explained that the Captain had had a discreet word with Wing Commander Jacobs. His *lady* had been persuaded to return to the officers' deck, for the convenience of everyone. She felt Mrs Roberts would like to know this, for she had been placed in a situation that was simply invidious.

The women streamed up on deck wearing sun tops and straw hats; there were ice creams for the kiddies. A festive mood prevailed. Ailsa and Nia strolled, tasting the sweet air and so serene in one another's company that they hardly needed to talk. Ailsa was lazily haunted by the thought of the *deutsche Kriegsmarine* sailing in this ship before them. Flaxen boys drilled on the sundeck; culture-loving *Leutnants* read in its opulent library.

The barrier between the officers' and lower ranks wives' quarters turned out to be nothing but a faded red rope slung between two posts. Ailsa stepped over; Nia ducked under. On the officers' deck, they made their way to Wing Commander Jacobs's cabin. It was hardly a conscious decision.

Day by day Ailsa breached the red cord with a growing sense of entitlement. In turn, Mona sauntered into the lower world when she felt like it. Authority dozed in a deck chair, soaking up the sun. The *Empire Glory* became, with every passing hour, its own world. They forgot to look back or forward, moving deeper into warm sunshine over a lapidary sea of blue glass.

Nearing Gibraltar, the tannoy pointed out the Pillars of

Hercules, either side of the straits, and behind you, ladies, boys and girls, is Africa! Tugs led them into harbour; a layer of cloud burned away from the turquoise sky and the Rock rose up before them. Everyone cheered. Ailsa's heart soared as the *Empire Glory* was coaxed through a huddle of rusted tankers to the landing stage. The Greek crew of the *Aphrodite* called to the women and waved their hats. Derricks were rigged; gangways swung out so that harbour officials and dock hands could board.

'Restocking and refuelling,' the tannoy informed them. 'Military supplies to be landed and other material loaded for the Far East.'

Crates, barrels and boxes were swung out of the holds. The tannoy assured the wives of its confidence that their on-shore behaviour would do credit to King and country. Rollicking troops on their deck received their own tannoy-lecture from the Padre, who cautioned them to exercise self-control, bearing in mind that the body was the temple of the Holy Spirit. Wild cheers at this. Ailsa watched the lads swarm down the gangplank in their khaki tropical kit, clowning like boys let out of school, which in a sense they were. They seemed incompletely fashioned, as if the potter's clay had not had time to dry. The ghost of a song lingered in their wake: *Roll me over in the clover, do it again!*

'Ladies, boys and girls, you may disembark!'

As Ailsa took her first steps on foreign soil, she felt her new life begin. No going back. She and Mona, Ben and Alex sat at the table of a pavement café, breathing in the scents of lemons, coffee and spices. They passed the dreamy, exotic afternoon like two couples who'd known each other forever. They were stared at, talked about, of course they were. But how could Ailsa have passed up this chance to live beyond her class? In another, less visited part of her mind, she flinched at her own bravado. Saw Joe's puzzled, kind, shocked face if he ever got to know.

Which he wouldn't. It would all have to end, she was clear about that, when the *Empire Glory* docked. For the time being: why not?

Officers enjoyed luxurious comfort. Easy to make oneself at home in the peace and privacy of the Jacobs cabin. On the last morning before Malta, Ailsa let herself in. Mona, showering in the cubicle, was performing 'Stella by Starlight' at the top of her voice, a one-girl jazz band of improvisations, while she lathered furiously with the salt water soap that raised few bubbles and left you skinned over with a slimy layer when you towelled dry.

Her powder-blue nightie lay in a heap of silk. Ailsa folded the garment, tucking it under Mona's pillow. An intimate action, sisterly. *I've fallen in friendship*, she thought. *And that's that*. And there was a closeness with Ben: his open manner set Ailsa at ease in a way she wasn't used to with men. Was that charm or was it sincerity?

Beside the bed stood a photo of the couple working with the UN refugee unit in Lübeck after the war, repatriating prisoners and slave labourers. In a drab uniform a size too small for her, bursting out all over the place like a schoolgirl, Mona stood unsmiling and workmanlike, sleeves rolled up, beside her husband. Ailsa thought of the two Jews finding their soul mates in those ruins. The marriage couldn't be more than a couple of years old, younger than hers and Joe's, which perhaps explained why there were no children yet. Ailsa was touched by the tenderness of

63

husband and wife, showing their affection as the most natural thing in the world; flattered by their inclusion of her. By Mona's confidences and Ben's gratitude, for he seemed to credit Ailsa with nothing less than restoring her music to Mona's hands.

He told Ailsa more about Mona's musical career. She'd been a pupil of the great Julie Brandt-Simon at the Brussels Conservatoire. Julie had been a second mother to her. When the Serafin family had come to London, the pianist on a visit to Britain attended a concert performance by the fourteen-year-old prodigy; she'd written to Mona's mother: *Bring your daughter to me and leave her until she comes of age: there is still time for me to correct her errors*. That had ended in tragedy. After Mona had returned to Britain, her teacher was taken into custody by the Nazis. Mona's gift deserted her. For Ailsa the thought of having somehow restored it was wonderful. But perhaps Mona had been nearly ready to play already; any catalyst would have done?

No, and he was writing a poem about it, Ben had said. When it was finished, she might like to have a copy?

'Oh, I would. Nobody's ever written me a poem before.'

Who wouldn't have been awed, flattered? At home Ailsa's collection of nineteen records contained three Brandt-Simon renderings of late Beethoven. The record sleeves showed a sharp-featured elderly woman, hair scraped into a grey bun: in her sixties a power house of a woman with pale, unsmiling eyes. You wouldn't want to cross her.

Mona was now into 'That Old Black Magic'. Ailsa shouted to her but she didn't hear through the mad racket of her singing.

Whatever did Mona see in Ailsa, for all her leaven of learning? Nothing Ailsa said ever seemed banal to Mona. *Tell me it all*, she'd order. *Hold nothing back.* Ailsa would laugh: what could there be to hold back? Her life was mundane. The post office, the farm, her war work, marriage and bringing Nia into the world. But she found herself confiding more intimately about Archie and Joe: out it all came, quite private things. As you might with a sister. It was not betrayal.

The singing got louder, then ceased, and the water was turned off. Mona came out of the shower naked, looking for her wrap, dripping all over the floor. Ailsa gasped, blushed, laughed, swerved her eyes.

Mona grabbed her and swept her round the cabin, singing 'Night and Day': *You, only you under the sun!* Mona smouldered and sashayed till Ailsa hurt with laughter. *I think of you, night and day.* She kissed Ailsa softly on the mouth and let her go. For several minutes the trace of the kiss lingered, tingling like peppermint.

*

In the Mediterranean lassitude the women collapsed on the sun deck like a colony of seals. Ailsa lay in shadow wearing her modest two-piece costume, while Nia played with the Brean girls, having been issued with a blanket caution against naughtiness. Closing her eyes, Ailsa tried to ignore a discussion of the alleged smell of Egypt, which the seasoned veterans told the new girls would hit them well before the *Empire Glory* so much as spied land at Port Said. The shittiest pong in the world, they said, and Ailsa felt Irene flinch.

Lying back, she gave her mind – and, in her daydream, her body – to Joe. She imagined herself stepping out of her clothes just as Mona did, chatting all the while. *Night and day, you are the one.* The dark triangle of pubic hair against the paleness of Mona's generous body had shocked her. From Mona's soaking hair, little rivers had crept down her forehead and down the ripples of her spine. Her moistness had been absorbed into Ailsa's cotton blouse, dancing her round the cabin, and when they'd moved apart, she'd carried the trace of Mona. Ailsa had drawn a sharp breath.

Nightly sensual dreams made her blush on waking. Was it Mona or was it Ben who aroused her? Or both? Against her will, Ailsa was kindled by the sensual heat that sprang between husband and wife; the experience they seemed to have of mysteries so far all but closed to the virginal Ailsa. Mona had said something about an open marriage. That if you loved someone, you wanted the fullest possible happiness for them. Didn't you? Possessiveness was *bourgeois*: look at Sartre and de Beauvoir. Ailsa distrusted those two libertine Gallic philosophers. She shrank from such arrangements as likely to benefit the man rather than the woman, unless she was missing something important – which was always possible. Someone would be hurt, it stood to reason. Mona, feeling her draw back, had said no more on the subject. It wasn't just prudishness on Ailsa's part, no, she didn't think so.

Turning away in momentary aversion, she'd seen the Jacobs as carriers of the germs of chaos. They were busily culturing it on a tray. She didn't want to be infected.

And yet they were a picture of married tenderness. It was perhaps with herself that Ailsa quarrelled. Perpetually on tiptoe, she peered excitedly over a high wall. Always with her husband there had been a shy and numb uncertainty, kind and sensitive as he was.

She'd believed that was how sex was, nicer for men than for women, except for the sweet and heart-fluttering moments that led up to the act itself. Always too short. A promise, not exactly broken, but never fulfilled.

It came back to Ailsa now: the night at Brewers' Green when she'd awoken to an animal sound behind the partition, a throaty rasping, a *Go on, go on, don't stop!* A woman's voice that wound up and up like pain. Like birth.

She drifted off.

Half an hour later she was awoken by the sound of, was it, gunfire? Where was Nia? Ailsa sat up, distraught. There were no children at all on deck. Just the women basking, who reassured her that the kiddies had gone below for a game of hide-and-seek. Supervised, of course. The infantry on the mess deck were having some sort of drill. Firing blanks, Irene said, *don't worry!*

'Did you see Nia go down?'

'Oh yes. She was with my boys. She crouched down and kissed you before she went. Rather sweet actually. I always wanted a girl.'

No land for miles around. The sapphire sea, so tranquil and tranquillising. The engine beating up gently through the boards as the ship made for Malta.

*

Nia straddled her way over the red cord dividing off the men's deck. A parade was going on towards the back of the ship: if she were seen, she'd be scooped up and returned to her mother. The lifeboats were a perfect place for a sunny nest. She *cwtch*ed down between the boats and the rails, drawing from her pocket a package of cake and several wine gums, wrapped in a paper napkin. She fed the dry cake to her golliwog and, humming to herself, put a wine gum in her mouth. Enjoying the sensation of the humming against her palate and the back of her nose, she stood up and looked through the railing.

Porpoises.

The creatures were magical. In their speed and shiningness, rising and falling, the porpoises followed and sometimes led the way. She watched them dart through the green water to overtake the ship.

The soldiers at the front were stamping on caps for a laugh: that was her first thought. Wriggling through the gap between the lifeboat and the bulwark, Nia peered out at the rumps of khaki men in shorts. They were killing themselves laughing, as they shot rifles at, she supposed, invisible soldiers on other boats in the sea.

'Got you!' they shouted. 'Get that one there!'

Perhaps there was a war – but why were the soldiers laughing? Were they playing Cowboys and Indians?

And now a fight had broken out amongst themselves. Nia rose slowly to her feet, sticking her thumb in her mouth through the cot sheet, staring in silence.

One soldier launched himself at another, roaring, wrenching him round by the arm. The grabbed soldier, a tall, lanky man, spun on the spot and his rifle slewed right round. He was shouting; the short man pulled at him; he lost his footing.

The gun was pointing straight at Nia.

It went off. Once, twice. The first shot went far wide. At the second crack, Nia fell.

'A kiddie! There's a kiddie!'

*

The women crowded to the rails, craning to look at the water.

Oh no!

What are they doing?

Target practice. Disgusting. Someone should tell them.

Ailsa rushed to the rail. The water was boiling with blood; they were ploughing through blood. What was it? Oh no, not the porpoises. The gun-happy infantry were using them for target practice. Ordered to do so, someone said. Uproar. Barbarians! Oh God, porpoises are only *fish*, get a grip! Don't you eat fish and chips then? Hedwig protested in a high, hectic voice that actually she did not eat fish and chips, neither were porpoises fishes, as it happened, but warm-blooded mammals like ourselves, if anyone was interested; she was a vegetarian. And someone piped up in a loud whisper: *Oh yes, we know, so was dear old Adolf.*

Ailsa watched a wounded creature arch above the racing water. Dark blood poured from a gash like oil from a pipe. Its raised fin vanished. The *Empire Glory* powered on. There was shouting; the shooting stopped and the women turned from the rails. How could it be that we made a slaughterhouse even of the sea?

Now there was a diversion. A sister troopship, home-ward bound. The women read the name: the *Empire Windrush*. They gathered at the side again, waving and calling.

A soldier came running: 'Which of you is Mrs Roberts?'

An accident, the young Lieutenant told Ailsa. He looked about nineteen. Unfortunately, he went on, the little girl had been caught in the middle of it. But no, no, she was not injured, don't be alarmed. Somehow or other she'd found her way on to the troop deck and hidden under a lifeboat. The men had been drilling, doing target practice. A conscript had seen red, one of these Cruelty to Animals people, and tried to stop them shooting the porpoises. He'd caused a shot to fly wide, in the direction of the little girl – which luckily had ricocheted harmlessly off a bulkhead. The idiot who'd caused the accident was a trainee teacher in civilian life, destined for a desk job in the medical corps at Fayid. He'd got forty-eight hours in solitary.

Restored to her mother, Nia sat in the crook of Ailsa's arm, sucking her thumb, Golly in her lap and her cheek against the cosy pad of her sheet. She said nothing. Again I took my eye off her, and again she nearly got herself killed, Ailsa thought, with somersaulting heart. Her own *gallivantings* (for that's what people would call them, *gallivantings*) on the *Empire Glory* came into question. Who had taught Nia to jump over the red rope? Her face burned. It had got to stop. What on earth had possessed her? Ailsa rested her hand on Nia's head, and kept it there. Nia felt up and fondled the big hand with her small one. She wore Ailsa's hand like a cap. It secured her. It held her down to the ground and kept her mind inside her head. Nobody told her off.

'Why were they shooting the creatures, may one ask?' Hedwig wanted to know.

The Lieutenant was courteous but his face said it all:

Bird-brained Kraut. He explained. The troops must be kept at the peak of training: if the enemy attacked, we must be ready to defend our women and children at a moment's notice. The men had left Britain crack shots and crack shots they must remain.

'Well, I am disgusted.' Hedwig's face was brick-red. 'The creatures are innocent and friendly. What have have they done to us, I would ask, to be used for target practice? I for one cannot stand by and witness this *Barbarei, diese Brutalität.*'

And a tremendous row erupted, with the German woman attacked on all sides for her resistance.

'If the kiddies are kept under control ...' the Lieutenant courteously suggested to Ailsa, and didn't go on.

He meant well. Most folk did, when you came down to it, and yet somehow or other the sum of our actions could be arrogance and cruelty. The women savaged Hedwig, who was near to tears but held her own in deteriorating English. Like the scapehen in an overcrowded, squawking roost, Ailsa thought, the gang viciously gathering round to peck the runt to death. Out of the corner of her eye, soothing Nia, she was aware of the German woman faltering away, into a space of deeper isolation. In the war it had all been black and white. Now there was fog everywhere. The woman was outspoken and brave. Qualities that did not endear themselves to the nice, prevaricating English. *Nazi*, they thought automatically whenever they clapped eyes on Hedwig. She might as well have gone around with a label round her neck. And look at me, I'm just standing by.

Ailsa sat with her quiet daughter in her lap. She'd lose all these travelling companions once they docked at Port

Said. Her mind seethed. Who was the enemy we were supposed to engage? The Soviets? Looking out to sea, she imagined a Communist warship bearing down on the *Empire Glory*. After Prague and the Berlin blockade last year, when they'd all thought, *War can come again, worse this time, we are weak, it will wipe us out*, such a warship – a whole fleet of them – was easy to imagine.

From East Germany, the Red Army could march to the western seaboard just like that. What was to stop them? They only needed to pull on their boots and they'd be at Dunkirk, four million men. They needn't even bother to march: one bomb could do for us, now that the Soviet Union was about to become an atomic power. War is normal for our generation, Ailsa thought. It will come back and we'll not be surprised.

It will. There will be war, this year, next year.

She felt no dread: weariness rather. The nearer the *Empire Glory* sailed to Egypt, the nearer it came to Molotov and Stalin. The Soviet backside in the south where their oil and minerals were. The oilfields of Iran and Iraq. And that's what we were doing at Suez, she thought, threatening the Russians' backside to prevent them overrunning civilisation.

And that was why the porpoises had to die! Us and our pop-guns! No sense to it at all. If you asked a Russian woman what she wanted, she would say, as Ailsa did, a better life for our children, security. But the Russian woman was not asked, any more than the Egyptian woman was asked, or she, Ailsa Roberts, was asked, though she ranked as a voter and a citizen.

Ailsa's eyes drifted to a capstan upon which an insect

had alighted. A greenfly? Scooped up on a breeze, perhaps, from Italy or Greece.

Beguiled, Nia reached out and caught the creature on her fingertip; held it close to her eyes and announced that it was her *pet*. She did not smile. What knowledge now rode behind Nia's eyes? Blood boiling in water, porpoises turned to meat. On purpose. And when the conscript went yelling up to the soldier and grabbed his gun ... what did she see and fear? Nia would forget but the knowledge would still be there. The greenfly blew away. Ailsa searched in the glazed green eyes for a comfort the subdued child could not extend. She kissed Nia's forehead and freckled nose and cheeks repeatedly and begged her never to run off again and leave Mami. Nia hummed. She wouldn't go near the railings or look out over the sea with its treacheries. Malta was coming into view but Nia would not so much as glance at it. Malta for all Nia knew might be bad. Or, if it were a good and beautiful island, Malta might be butchered in front of her eyes.

Ailsa would have to withdraw from Mona, delicately, gently detach. No option. She herself had taught her daughter contempt for boundaries and Nia had suffered for it.

Happily the child was safely down in their cabin taking a nap when the ship put in at Malta and sacks of rotten potatoes were distributed to the cheering troops, together with orders to pelt the wogs in bum boats selling their wares, to keep them away from the hull of the *Empire Glory*. For their own safety's sake, as Babs observed to Ailsa.

5

A day out from Port Said, the blazing heat intensified. The time of farewells was nearly upon the women of the *Empire Glory*. A row of prams stood in the shade of an awning, empty of babies, who were being fed below. Babes of the Empire: tomorrow's soldiers and mothers. Mrs Grey said, *Mark my words, the jolly old stork will be paying a visit to your Married Quarters, ladies, nine months from tomorrow night! Oh you may giggle and shake your heads but we can look forward to the patter of little feet in – let's see –* and she'd counted on her fingers, with a chuckle – *end of March!*

And soon Ailsa would be in Joe's arms. She felt as shy as a bride at the prospect.

She made her way down to the library: it was goodbye to Mona and that was for the best. Costly leather-bound books with gilt titles on their spines rose to the ceiling, inherited from the German Navy. A volume of Goethe's *Early Poems* lay on the table, open at *'An den Mond'*. She'd studied a selection at school and knew some pretty well by heart. Ailsa's eyes negotiated its thorny Gothic script. The young Goethe lingering by the moonlit river knew that jests and kisses were things of the past. Some unstated act of betrayal had taken place that had changed everything forever.

Blessed the one who, turning away from the world, without hate, holds a friend to his breast ... The German didn't allow for a woman friend, as the English word did. *Freund* was not the same as *Freundin*. She'd made this point to their German teacher, Miss Quilleashe. Q had replied with observations about the difference between inflected and uninflected languages. Ailsa remembered dear old Q bursting out on some occasion: *Think of our Goethe! our Heine!* when all things German had been brought into doubt and suspicion.

'Hallo, darling, *habiba*, *chérie*, *cariad*.'

Mona bent over Ailsa's shoulder, resting her cheek against Ailsa's hair. And still there was this strange shock of recognition from Brewers' Green. For years Ailsa had forgotten the intense dark girl next door. Never given her a thought. And then the dark girl had sprung from the past, bringing with her the full repertoire of forgotten gestures, usurping a place in Ailsa's life, as if spotlit, destined.

Mona sat down next to her. 'When we get to Ish, I'm going to beg, borrow or steal a decent piano. Do you think you might be able to come and play with me?'

How could Ailsa say, *If my husband lets me. Which he can't and won't* ...? She and Mona had been dreaming on the *Empire Glory*, a shared dream Mona had kindled and they'd both stoked, of equality in friendship. She'd think of Mona, Ailsa promised. Often. Always. They could at least *keep in touch*.

'Don't say that. Please. Don't.' Mona burst into tears. 'How can you, Ailsa? Those are awful, searing words.'

'They weren't meant to be awful and searing,' Ailsa said helplessly. She shrank before Mona's histrionics. Better to end it now than have this emotional excess looming over her. And Mona read this as clearly as if Ailsa had said it aloud. 'I'll lose you. I know I will. I have lost you, haven't I? Just like Julie.'

It all came out then: those had been the last words Julie Brandt-Simon had said, frigidly, to hurt Mona when they parted, *Let us keep in touch*. Moody and headstrong, Mona Serafin in her mid-teens had thought she was God's gift. No sooner was she in Brussels than she was correcting her teacher and laying down the law.

'That's how I was, Ailsa, I was an utter hooligan. I fought my teacher every step of the way. But somehow or other, she got me under control. Julie taught me everything, we worked together for eighteen months, the most amazing time of my life. But then I went off the rails, seriously off the rails – started denouncing her teaching methods, for God's sake, and stole her wallet and ran off with a tram conductor for two days. I had to be fetched back by the police. She was beside herself.'

Julie had got up from the piano and screamed at Mona: *You ungrateful girl, I will send you packing*, and Mona had yelled back at Julie, that she was *nothing but a bloody Yid*.

She'd wept and apologised, but Julie had had enough: an elderly woman, she couldn't cope with these hysterical scenes, Mona had gone over the line and there was no way back. Julie turned away with a gesture of disgust, saying words to the effect: they should keep in touch.

Nothing but a bloody Yid.

'But, Mona, why would you call her that? You're a Jew yourself.'

'Of course not!'

'Aren't you?'

'No. No, I'm not. How on earth could you think that? Surely you realised I'm an *Arab*?'

There was a stunned pause. They both drew back. Mona was a Palestinian Arab who'd been a pupil of the greatest Jewish pianist in pre-war Europe.

Hunter and prey were confounded in Ailsa's mind. To her, pogroms meant Nazi crimes against Jews; to Mona, Jewish crimes against Arabs. Ailsa had emerged from the War seared by the suffering borne by the Jews: it was an obscenity, heinous, vile, what were the words for it? Their suffering was seared in her conscience also. A couple of years back the British Navy had violently boarded the *Exodus*, a ship full of Holocaust survivors, illegal immigrants trying to get into Palestine under our Mandate. They'd been turned back and forcibly disembarked in Germany; housed in the concentration camps they'd left. For weeks cinema audiences had viewed this obscenity on the newsreels, rising and shaking their fists: *Shame! Shame on us!* Rather than arriving at the Promised Land, the refugees had been roughed up by the British, those *gentlemen fascists*, as the Jews called them. Anti-Semitism was rife in Britain: Ailsa detested it; she'd always felt on firm ground detesting it and it was dismaying now to hear the hardness in Mona's voice as she spoke of the *Exodus* as a propaganda coup. How could she say that? It made Ailsa sick to hear it. But she tried to understand the terrible, cloven logic of it all.

77

Cultured, westernised, Christian and affluent, the Serafins had been driven out of Palestine long before the War. Most of her remaining relatives had now been expelled or had fled last year when the Zionists proclaimed the state of Israel. Some had been killed; some were missing; others were refugees making their way from the camps to Egypt, where Mona and Ben hoped to do something for them – perhaps find jobs with the British military in the Canal Zone. They'd lost everything.

'So you can never go back?'

'None of us can go back,' Mona explained, as if to a child. 'Palestine's been abolished.'

Had you not noticed? she implied. *Can you be so blinkered and ignorant, yes, and prejudiced?* Zionists she called fascists. '*Zionists* I mean, not Jews. Of course I didn't mean all Jews, how could I? I'm married to one. Best chap in the world. He's been disowned by his own family for his anti-Zionism and for marrying me.'

For *Habibi*, as for his Arab wife, the newborn state of Israel was *al-Naqba*, the catastrophe.

And yet you sinned against your teacher, Mona, your beloved Julie, Ailsa thought, in the same way you'd been sinned against. Out had spurted venom, *nothing but a bloody Yid*, from the fang you didn't know you had. The music left your hands. And you thought, *I can never go back*.

*

It would be several hours before Port Said came into view. The queue for the last ration of duty-frees stretched right round the corridor. The *Empire Glory* fizzed with excitement, while the Tannoy broadcast non-stop practical instructions and bracing advice. Ailsa hoisted Nia in her arms, reminding her that she'd be seeing Daddy soon, what about that?

She smiled at Irene and spoke to her two little blond boys, but Ailsa's mind still laboured with Mona's story, glimpsing the politics of hate that had exploded in Mona when she called her beloved mentor a Yid. It's what we blurt out, thought Ailsa, that condemns us. It rushes up from underground. But given time, it could surely have been forgiven?

It was impossible to abandon Mona. How could she?

Hedwig came from the head of the queue, cradling half a bottle of brandy like a baby. 'Now he'll be pleased to see me,' she said.

'He'll be pleased anyway, Hedwig. He'll be over the moon.'

'Yes, isn't it wonderful!'

Expectation of happiness and homecoming made Hedwig shed years; she was a radiant girl again. She'll be all right now, Ailsa thought. The queue melted away, allowing Ailsa to buy a large box of Woodies for Joe.

The final packing complete, everyone crowded to the rails. Heat hammered down on the crowns of their heads as they neared land. The White boys, sweltering and dejected in their best shirts, bickered in a glum, half-hearted way. The elder, wearing a tie for his daddy, twisted it savagely to drag it off, nearly throttling himself. Nia stared mutely.

The *Empire Glory* lay poised between the giant stone moles of Port Said and everybody sniffed, with varying degrees of disrelish. A hot smell, Nia thought, sticking one finger up her nose to touch the smell that was pink and lodged in your throat. It rolled out from the shore, which was clouded in a dusty lilac-coloured fog. Nia did not dislike the stink. It was better than the hangar where soldiers had been hung up in hammocks.

Ailsa held tight to Nia's hand. The sound of the city was like the roar of a distant football match. The luminous morning mist burned off all of a sudden, like a curtain not being raised but destroyed, and they all went *Ooh!* and *Ah!* as the skyline of Port Said appeared. Minarets and cupolas, seedy warehouses and blocks of flats. Graceful white buildings with terraced balconies overflowing with greenery, Roman arches, roof gardens and dovecotes. Jewish and French names.

Nia was in ecstasies. She'd spotted Woolworths, her favourite shop, looking out over the jetty.

'Oh look! The Statue of Liberty!'

'What?'

'There!'

'The Statue of Liberty's in New York harbour.'

'Oh. What's that then?'

Ailsa gazed at the outsize statue of Ferdinand de Lesseps, prophet, promoter and digger of the Canal, pointing at his waterway, a sheet of gleaming water that led into and through the city itself. A lighthouse stood at its mouth. With every moment, the world of the *Empire Glory* lost reality. As they navigated in to berth through a crush of shipping from all over the world, a mass of brilliantly painted bumboats nosed out, piled with exotic fruit and vegetables. There was uproar. They could see the faces of the vendors with their wares, shouting up for watches or fountain pens in return for their goods and reaching up little hemp bags on poles.

'*Effendi!*' they called ingratiatingly. '*Effendi!*'

The soldiers bartered, taunting and insulting the vendors, sending down half crowns for fresh oranges, which were thrown up to the deck with change in worthless piastres stuck in their sides. A *howzat!* rang out every time an orange was fielded and a *boo!* for every one that fell wide and dropped into the water.

'Very cheap ... very great bargain!'

Nia was still grizzling to go into Woolworths and buy mixed sweets in a white bag.

'But, Nia, we're going to see Daddy soon. Daddy's down there, isn't he?'

The heat was stifling. There'd be no more sea breezes. How could she stand it? The glare beat up off the water and seemed one with the din as the natives fleeced the foreigners. Ailsa faltered back, treading on someone's toe.

Nia said she was going to take Daddy to Woolworths to buy pipe cleaners. So there.

Ailsa, looking round at the hot, excited faces of the wives and hearing the soldiers singing, realised, with soaring rapture, that this was it! She'd arrived at her heart's desire. Joe was here on the quay, somewhere in the hustle and bustle. To be seen and held and embraced. She pressed forward in the crush, elbowing a stout woman out of the way, and waved her hanky, in case he were down there and could single her out from all the other women.

6

This was the land of the dead, one of the passengers was complaining. It was all mummified corpses and madmen with bombs.

The *Terra Incognita* had berthed at Safaga. Nia and Poppy shuffled down the gangway, hanging on tight to their passports. At last Nia was following Ailsa into the Middle East. Reaching dry land, they looked back at the liner, which towered above them, gleaming white, in contrast to the rusting hulks in the harbour, an opulent, floating island of Britishness. It wasn't the way Nia had toured India and Swaziland in her time. She'd backpacked, working her way round, getting to know people. And the worst thing was, she was positively *enjoying* being cosseted like a colonist, gorged fat on lavish food.

We are the ship's babies, she thought as she and Poppy boarded the Egyptian agency bus. And this is our pram.

'You are all Egyptians now, my good friends!' said Zahrah, their smiling, headscarfed guide. 'Please, be comfortable and make yourselves at home. Egypt is your country today!'

This was the famous hospitality of the Middle East. It was extended even as we bombed their brothers and sisters in Iraq.

'Yes, you are Egyptians now! We welcome you as our family.'

Nia clapped in appreciation with the others. But she wouldn't want to be an Egyptian, not if she also had to be a woman: no thanks. The headscarf and the veil; the leering, jeering males who mobbed Poppy and feasted on her bare arms.

They were to join a convoy of a hundred coaches, for unfortunately although Egypt is your home, Zahrah confessed, there are bad people about who want to bomb our honoured visitors. Never in her life had Nia seen so many soldiers or armed policemen.

'Today we travel to famous and lovely graves,' Zahrah told them. 'You will see the Valley of the Kings. Do not worry about Ahmed,' she added. 'Ahmed is a very nice policeman travelling with us in plain clothes to ensure our safety.' The shyly handsome young man in a dark suit napped the four hours to Karnak. His hands lay slack in his lap; a holster bulged at his groin. Armed men were stationed at junctions and bridges, holding up donkey carts and women with bags, to ensure safe passage to the convoy of westerners.

After the parched, dark desert of Safaga, the bus entered the deliquescence of the green country bordering the Nile. It was a sudden and excessive transition from drought to fertility. Village after village of mud brick houses in earth and sky colours, without running water and sanitation, lined the way. Nia's heart ached for the pauperdom of people whose lot had hardly changed in millennia. What I am seeing, Ailsa saw, she thought. Families shared quarters with animals. From glassless windows multicoloured washing hung like flags. But villages clearly had electricity, for their roofs bristled with television dishes. How come Nasser, whose socialism had promised so much to the *fellaheen*, had delivered so little? Why hadn't he succeeded in reforming the *baksheesh* economy, in which inadequate incomes had to be supplemented by tips and favours? Nia felt ashamed of her plenty; possessive of it too.

This was hardly the way to see the Middle East, spying through glass panes under armed guard. But Poppy, exhausted from teaching, had said when she'd seen the last minute cut-price tickets, hey, let's go for it. Crazy not to.

Do we really fancy it though? What about the Awful People?

Poppy had flinched: *People are people.*

Nia was ashamed. How Poppy could put up with her, she had no idea. In her own twenties, Nia wouldn't have been seen dead on a cruise with her own mother, so stuffy and po-faced. They'd have brought their own frost to the East. Poppy was so laid-back that they'd never quarrelled, even in her teens: her soft robustness issued in a tactful going of her own way. And Nia, child of the Sixties, had been a parent so compulsively liberal that Poppy would have found little to rebel against except permissiveness itself.

Awful People, Nia continued secretly to think. Some of her fellow cruise-guests expressed a surly sense of entitlement, bullying the crew. Retirement had brought an unexpected magic to their first cruises, hard perhaps to recapture as one entered the compromised health and hope of deeper old age. Others were cheerful and adventurous. Poppy chatted to a lovely guy across the aisle who'd been stationed at Tel-el-Kabir after the War. He spoke warmly of Egypt.

Nia kept quiet. It's my father I fear, she thought: he's out there somewhere. With every moment she moved nearer to the time when, on its passage through the Suez Canal, the *Terra Incognita* would draw level with Fayid Cemetery and all that was left of Joseph Elwyn Roberts. His scrawl in the diaries was all over the place, with a child's misspellings and odd abbreviations. Several times she'd opened his book and tried to reconstruct his meaning. A tongue-scramble of impressions that could only be made sense of by weaving in Ailsa's clearer account. Nia had been so painfully moved that, after skimming a page and hearing his voice, she'd put it away for a braver time, leaving him down there on the quay at Port Said eternally waiting for his wife and daughter to join him.

The veteran from Tel-el-Kebir offered them a mint, which Nia accepted with a smile. His lively eyes were pale blue, almost bleached. He might easily have known Sergeant Joe Roberts, and even remember him. These folk were the last of her parents' generation, on pilgrimage to the places of their early lives as National Servicemen. For Nia too this was a pilgrimage. The little she remembered was nonsensical: hail stones big as ping pong balls and screaming her head off between a camel's twin humps. And – this seemed to be her first memory – bleeding creatures in the sea. Perhaps it was some corrupted memory of Mami's hands gutting fish. But the creatures that bled all over her memory were enormous beings with intelligent, expressive eyes. Some film perhaps. She blinked it away and listened to the veteran from Tel-el-Kebir. This was the last such voyage the veterans were likely to make, now that the Middle East was well nigh closing down. Nowhere was safe, he said, after our assault on Iraq.

Luxor and Karnak passed like dreams. They trooped through the monumental temple in smiting heat; then after a picnic lunch ventured underground into the tombs of Tutankhamun and those of various Ramses. All in eight hours flat. The sun was sinking and Poppy's face, arms and neck were gilded by the glorious light. Her child's goldenness was one with the yellow hills of the Valley of the Kings in the dying sun, the splendour imparted to tawny mud villages on rust-red hillsides, the rich patina of sand gilding the mortuary landscape in this vast necropolis on the Nile's west bank.

Poppy remained asleep while Nia disembarked at Memnon, where they were to have a 'photo stop'. The twin colossi were all that remained of a vast temple. Now they sat as sentinels of a portal to – well, nothing. Emptiness. Absence. Faces smashed away, chests weathered, the seated figures preserved in their ruin an intact majesty. They reminded Nia of Henry Moore's statues of father, mother and child, in a Yorkshire landscape. The relationship of triangles and spheres to the rolling land had made sacred space of landscape and figures. But here the statues sat hieratically apart. And of course there was no child. Nothing to link them. The sun gilded and warmed the colossi's intact knees and lower legs. Behind them a rust-red mountain rose with a village on its foothills. New busloads of tourists arrived looking for something to photograph and Zahrah beckoned to her *Terra Incognita* charges.

Perhaps it would be the magnificent temple at Karnak that Nia took away with her. But more likely, Nia thought, climbing back into the bus, it will be the memory of that dog slinking through the ruins, an image of destitution. A ginger bitch with swollen teats, head low, consumed by hunger and exhaustion, had curled up at the dead centre of a vast aisle behind twin pylons, completely exposed. Many feet, in sandals, trainers, flip-flops, lace-ups, moved past her, not so much aiming kicks as shoving at the bitch in passing. She did not stir. Nia later saw the scapebitch, as she called it to herself, like the biblical scapegoat – in the coach park, nosing its way into the stink of hot rubber and oil beneath a parked van.

*

Shy as hell Joe felt, standing on the quay in his KDs, arms folded, wearing a jaunty look. He'd have his two darlings safe in his arms within the hour. The chaos of the quay frazzled his nerves as the towering ship inched in and the ropes were thrown and secured. Petty officials in self-important fezes scuffled among themselves, apparently disputing points of procedure; traders of all sorts swarmed round the ship jabbering; a man in a robe called him Johnnie and wheedled Joe to buy genuine Ancient Egyptian scarabs, straight from the Pharaohs' tombs. In this mess and din and reek, it seemed as if the shore were doing its best to push the *Empire Glory* back out to sea.

Gyppos couldn't organise a trip to the Pyramids, so Dusty Miller was complaining. But Joe smiled and said good-naturedly to the scarab-man, 'Not today, my boy, thanks all the same,' gentle as to a child. He didn't abuse or scoff at the Egyptians to their faces and disliked it that others did. They were childlike, as far as Joe could see, incapable of discipline and reason. Their smarmy ways he didn't much care for but they had a living to get and he bet he'd have toadied in their position. They lived in squalor and owned nothing. And though he'd lived rather too near to the bottom of the heap back home, the Gyppos' scavenging pauperdom made Joe and Chalkie seem like lords.

So he grinned at the scarab-man as he waved him away and was somewhat unsettled when the chap laughed and said, 'OK, right you are, Taffy-Effendi.' Antennae they had like nobody's business, some of them. Hardly ten words of English to call their own but they could nail an accent. Geordie, Mick, Jock: you name it, they mimed it like parrots.

The other blokes awaiting their families had fallen silent and, in the midst of the furore, they took on the attitude of men at prayer, all gazing upwards.

'Not so long now, Taf.' Chalkie was that rare thing, an *old* friend. The two of them had been together in the Western Desert during the war, slept together, messed together. Joe relished Chalkie's quiet presence, his modesty and funny faces. Slightly built but wiry and strong, Roy White was blessed with an understated sense of humour, a frizz of corkscrew curls close to his head and wire-rimmed specs always at an angle. 'Poor things,' said Chalkie. 'They'll be worn out.'

'Aye,' said Joe, 'bless them.' His hands shook as he handed Chalkie a cigarette. Women's faces peered over the rails. The gangways were lowered. An eternal pause. Then he glimpsed, not Ailsa but Nia, a pale sun rising above the railing by the gangway, only to set instantly.

'My daughter! My little girl!'

'Where?'

'There.'

'Ah! The wee gingernut!'

Here they came, shuffling down the gangway, the tall, elegant mother holding the hand of the pale child with her golly in one hand. But Nia suddenly stopped. Stuck fast. Holding up the queue behind her. One of the women, seeing the difficulty, reached back and hoisted her up, carrying her down. Joe tussled forward against the hurly-burly of husbands.

'Ailsa,' he said. '*Cariad.*'

Home.

Nia stuck her thumb in her mouth and thus plugged it, so as to remain neutral. The man plunging at her mother had a great and convincing likeness to her Daddy, but was he the same? She felt Mami rip away from her like sticky tape. This man was crying and so was Mami crying. Nia wanted nothing to do with that. Looking up, she saw them disappear into a knot made of both of them. Only Auntie Mona was left faithfully holding her by one hand, with Golly under one arm. Darling Mona who'd suddenly appeared on the quay in her red dress with a wide-brimmed sun hat, grinning down in reassurance. Quietly, Nia gave herself up to imagining a glass of ice-cold Lucozade, seeing in her mind's eye the rustling yellow paper wrapped around the bottle. She did not look at the Daddy-man but instead secretly uncurled her hand to check that Little Yellow Man was still there and had not changed in any way. Yes, he was the same, exactly, with bite-marks all round his faded face. Having checked, she again mounted vigil, tightening hot, wet fingers around his friendly woodenness.

'Well well, my beauty?' He crouched and gentled her with a well-remembered voice – and seemed to want to sweep her up and perch her on his shoulders, where she'd be able to bang on his head with her fists, like a drum. But his close-up face didn't seem quite right. The one inside her head didn't have such sunburnt skin, as dark nearly as Auntie Mona's. The fleck of bloody toilet paper on a shaving nick under his ear and the chin-stubble were not quite right. Only his blue-blue eyes were the same.

'Say hallo to your daddy, Nia,' Ailsa urged her.

'She needs to get used to me, bless her,' said Joe, with his crooked little smile, as if he knew a joke. He straightened up and took a step back. He was saying that he had some presents for the girlie in his kit bag. Should he give them to her on the train?

'Oh but Mona – I haven't introduced you! What am I thinking of? This is Mona, Joe – my good friend – she's been so sweet to me and Nia. Mona – my husband.'

Joe shook hands cordially. How glad he was, he said, that Ailsa had made a pal on a voyage that cannot have been much fun for anyone. He was grateful to her. Half-caste? Dark as weak coffee and not with sunburn, that was for sure. Seemed a decent type though. And well-spoken. An educated, superior voice if ever Joe heard one. With this thought, all ease and naturalness drained away: he was the tinplate apprentice, son of a furnaceman, the lowest of the low at the South Wales Canister Company.

Joe gripped Ailsa beneath the elbow, to move her on. But the crush of jubilation made movement impossible and the Military Police were nowhere to be seen. Chalkie jounced both his boys in his arms, whilst kissing his wife. The children's hair was white as wheat and their cheeks flushed with heat and over-excitement. Joe was introduced to Chalkie's ladylike wife, Irene, and spoke to a tearful foreigner who could not find her husband. Corporal Webster, RAF Fanara, she said, did he know him? had he seen him? *My friend Ailsa will help me*, she said desperately, gripping Ailsa's arm. *My good friend*. Who wouldn't panic in these circumstances: just off the ship and no husband? With her baby-blonde hair and pale complexion, she looked ready to faint with anxiety.

'Stick with us, Mrs Webster,' Joe said, 'until we find him. Don't worry: he'll be here.'

A moon-faced bloke Joe recognised by sight shouldered his way through the crush: *Hedda!* he was calling, over people's shoulders. *You're all right, I'm here, you're safe now.*

As the crowd parted, he barged though and, taking his wife in his arms, lifted her clean off her feet, both of them laughing and weeping, swung her round, kissed her. 'Thanks, mate,' he said to Joe. 'Norman Webster. And this is my darling Hedwig.'

The Military Police directed the passengers through customs. The crowd thinned. As Joe was about to pick up Nia and follow them, Ailsa said, 'You must meet Ben, Joe, Mona's husband. And Alex.'

As the senior officer and his companion arrived, Joe stood smartly to attention and saluted.

A bad moment, terrible, Ailsa thought afterwards in the train. Joe's hand had shot up, a barrier that put them all in their places. With this signal, all possibility of conversation had died.

The Royal Air Force had semaphored to them through the language of Joe's salute a reminder that fraternisation between officers and Other Ranks could never be countenanced. Fraternisation, Joe's ramrod arm had said, would undo the proper and natural order of things; it would soften military discipline, the foundation of the Empire. Joe had held his arm rigid, quivering, far longer than was called for, blank-faced, eyes staring forward at the officers' shoulders, as if for parade ground inspection. It is a sad day for the RAF, his mute stance had said, when a sergeant has to instruct a senior officer in King's regulations.

'No need for that, old chap...'

Habibi, thrown into confusion, had been left with his hand held out for a handshake. Ailsa saw his sloppy uniform and springy curls as if through her husband's eyes. Alex had had the presence of mind to return Joe's salute, as regulations required, just touching his temple in greeting, a superior kind of *Wotcher, mate*. But Joe, a statue, had remained at attention. Face brick-red; not blinking.

Unbelievably, Joe had carried on saluting, despite his pal Roy White's humorous nudge. Before the barrier of his hand could fall to separate them, Mona had reached for Ailsa and hugged her, pulling her under the brim of her hat, into its dusky, patterned red shade. She'd kissed her on the mouth, while Ailsa pulled back because of Joe – poor Joe, caught in this trap. She wasn't saying goodbye, Mona had whispered, not now, not ever.

'Be happy, *chérie, liebste, habiba.*'

'Oh, Mona ... and you.' Ailsa had had to bite back the words that had so lacerated Mona, *Keep in touch.*

'See you soon. And here's a little something for you, don't lose it. Our address is on it and a note. And something from *Habibi*. I'll wait for you to contact me, OK?'

'You shouldn't have. I've nothing for you.'

'Aha. Wait till you see it. Stolen goods.'

Ailsa had crammed the brown paper package tied with string and sealed with wax into her canvas bag: a book, obviously. She doubted whether *they* would let her see Mona again. Already as they boarded the train, with its shining carriages painted silver to reflect the heat, she could see this friendship going into the past. The *Empire Glory* had been an interlude. Joe was everything to her, Joe and Nia. Of course they were.

Joe said nothing whatever to disparage her friends. The men had maintained their formal smiles at one another across the corridor of rank. Correctly but also with goodwill. The dock had bellowed around them. Alex had slackened the tension with that public school drawl. Ailsa, reading Joe's face, could see immediately what Joe had thought of *him*. Smoothie, nancy-boy, poufter, was the gist of it. Which had taken her aback, for it hadn't dawned on her before that Alex was effeminate. Perhaps he was. She'd seen it in Joe's eyes.

Nia, squirming and whining for Auntie Mona to pick her *up*, had confided, 'Auntie Mona, my botty's itching!'

Frantic embarrassment and hilarity had reigned. Even

Joe had laughed and relaxed. *Habibi*, shaking hands with Ailsa, had wished her well, thanking her for her true friendship to his wife. Ailsa read Joe's appraisal of Ben: *short back and sides*, she read, as clearly as if he had spoken the words. *Joker from Civvie Street, scarecrow in uniform.* Next to Ailsa's impeccable husband, the slouching Wing Commander did look like a ragbag. Nia's fingers had had to be prised one by one from Mona's, to the chorus of Babs Brean, who paused to say, 'She'll have to turn over a new leaf now she's with her daddy, the scamp!'

And here, oh dear, Babs was on the train with her husband, whose arms were round both of his daughters. They sucked sherbet through licorice straws and gazed up at him through eyes silly and beautiful with love. But everyone's eyes wore the same expression. Shy too, as if on a first date.

'Not long now,' said Ailsa to Nia.

'No.'

'And then we'll be home together. The three of us.'

'Yes.'

'What an *adventure* for us, darling,' Ailsa said. 'Aren't you pleased to see Daddy?'

'Yes.'

'Are you tired, lovey?'

'Yes.'

'Put your head down on Mami's lap if you want to drowse.'

She patted her lap, smoothing the creases of her skirt for Nia to lay her head on the intimate place, hers only, where Mami's soft legs and secret body joined. And Mami's hand stroked her hair, quelling the qualms in her head, by holding it still and calm. Nia kept her eyes and ears open, viewing the skewed world from beneath.

As the train drew out, Nia considered the Brean girls' sherbet dabs. She watched the father remove his arms from his daughters to light up a fag. Then he put his arms back round them and dangled the fag from the corner of his mouth, growing a worm of ash that hung and hung. He could talk like that, hardly moving his lips. The girls sucked the licorice, leaving a moist gloss of black on their lower lips.

And his worm fell. It collapsed on to his knees, where the breeze from the open window winnowed it away.

The carriage filled with smoke and chat. Joe and Ailsa lit up. Nia watched from the corner of her eye as Joe struck the match and offered it to Ailsa, who bent to take the light. She saw his hand move from cupping the flame to brushing her mother's cheek. Nia registered the consciousness between her parents that trembled like the plumes of blue smoke the sun revealed as it beat on the glass. She saw that this quivering and pluming had nothing to do with her. She saw the same hand flap the smoke away from her and push the train window further down so that she didn't have to breathe it. But the smoke would not go away and she had no sherbet dab.

She looked over at Topher and Timothy White, fast asleep in their parents' arms, one to each parent. Tim's mouth was open and he was dribbling, his cheeks flushed. The parents were talking to one another with their eyes.

'Don't whatever you do put your heads out of the window, or your hands and arms, even when we're moving.' Babs' voice dominated the carriage as it had the cabin.

'Oh *really*,' grumbled Ailsa under her breath.

'Why shouldn't we lean out of the window?' asked one of the wives.

'The wogs snatch your rings and watches. Just like that. Gone. Don't they, John? They travel on top of the carriage, and snatch your valuables if you put your hand out.'

'Never.'

'Well, don't blame me if you get caught out, that's all. They have blades to slice through watchstraps. They pull off rings. Before you can say Jack Robinson. Never trust them.'

'All the way from Southampton I had that,' Ailsa said to Joe. 'Wretched bossy booming.'

The Brean children looked fearfully at the windows. Their quiet dad grinned at them and took the empty yellow cylinders that had contained the sherbet.

'All gone?' he said. 'Never mind. Snuggle down. Oh *look*! Look out of the window! Soon you'll see a sight! A real treat!'

Nia scrambled up to see a sight. She imagined a circus or a fair like the ones that came summer by summer to Abertawe. The sight turned out to be nothing but a long ribbon of road on one side and, on the other, a procession of ships sailing through the desert.

*

The Suez Canal. So that was what all the fuss was about. The Pharaohs had dug canals to link the Mediterranean with the Red Sea; Napoleon and his engineers, finding traces of these ancient workings, dreamed the same dream, which Ferdinand de Lesseps realized. How many Arab slave

96

labourers had died to dig … this ditch the Roberts family was arriving to defend as – somehow – British, as British as the Manchester Ship Canal? From the train window, overcome by heat and light, Ailsa was seeing for the first time the artery of Britain's Empire. She dripped with sweat; her head pulsed. The train slowed and stopped. It slid back to universal groans, and stopped again. Heat. Searing heat. Godforsaken salt marshes stretched away as far as the eye could see. Ailsa saw a lunar landscape flat as Suffolk and sterile as death. No shadows and no people. A silver liner glided in slow motion towards Port Said, the water of the canal invisible. Light overwhelmed the camera of Ailsa's eye, bleaching out the mineral sands around the stationary train, as heat muscled in to the exposed carriages. Someone spoke the word *terrorist*. *Those jokers have cut the line.* The loco crept forward and stopped dead at a station at the end of the world.

As Ailsa stepped out on to the platform, light intensified into a form of darkness; one eye broke up and spun zigzag shards on a central hub. *Shot, shot*, she cried out, stumbling down on to the sweltering platform. She vomited. The passengers pulled away.

Was there a Medical Officer on the train? The request was shouted along the platform and a medic came running. Migraine headache, he said, like as not. Move her into the shade and let her lie still on a bench. Don't fuss there. Cover her eyes. He'd inject ergot: half a tick. Not pregnant, was she? Ailsa heard it all, magnified to blaring dissonance, like a sheet of tin being shaken with great force. While the medic rummaged in his bag, the wives clustered round. Quietly unlacing her hand from her husband's, Hedwig took Ailsa's head on her lap, stroking her hair. The Brean children were appointed by their father to fan the ill lady, which they did gently and patiently to a chorus of 'Good girls!'

You showed me kindness, Hedwig whispered. Now I take care of you.

Nia's shot Mami lay still. She might be dead. Although there was no blood, that did not mean anything. There was a pool of sick, smelling and black with flies, already drying. Nia felt blank. She would not tell anyone her suspicion, leaving the way open for Mami to come back to life. This closed the path to a darkness as vast as the world.

Reluctantly Joe surrendered his wife to the womenfolk, for according to Ailsa Nia was a demon for running off and had spent the whole fortnight on the *Empire Glory* devising stratagems of escape. She was Napoleon on Elba, Ailsa had said – though where she thought she could run to on a ship was beyond her.

Chip off the old block, you rascal, Joe thought. He hunkered with the child, with whom he felt gauche, uncertain – and halved, for his eyes were on Ailsa even as he calmed Nia. Father and daughter hid with the rest from the deranging sun under an awning. Some device had been detected on the line and was being made safe by Bomb Disposal. It was one of the tricks the wogs constantly played, never realising how dependent on us they were for their very bread. Egypt had gone to war against Israel last year. Now that they'd been trounced by Israel, they denounced the treaty they'd been happy enough to sign with Britain in '36; set their sights on driving us out. So they cut the lines; went off with copper; chucked their grenades and ran: kinder-garten terrorism. You couldn't take them seriously.

A bus was on the way from Ish. Meanwhile there was no danger and nothing to be done but to keep as cool and calm as possible while they waited. Nia consented to sit on her daddy's knee and he thought, his arm circling her, that she was coming round to him after all.

'Mami's only got a nasty headache, you know that, girlie, don't you? Soon we'll be on a lovely bus and we'll be flying away up the Treaty Road and soon be home, isn't it?'

'I'm wondering where we are?' asked Nia in a grown-up voice.

'Ras-el-Esh,' Joe read aloud on the name board. 'That's where we are.' English and French translations were given under the morse of Arabic script.

'And what is the Cheaty Road?'

'The way home. Treaty, not Cheaty.'

'And who are those beautiful men?'

'Arabs they are – off to market in Port Said. Look at their wonderful fruits now – fresh dates, those little green and yellow things, see? And look at those melons, the size of footballs. Ever seen such whoppers?'

Across the platform *fellaheen* stood motionless with sacks of produce awaiting trains to Port Said. In their pale robes, head dresses and stately tallness, they looked like timeless figures from Exodus or Leviticus, as illustrated in the Old Testament Joe had received for Sunday School attendance at Libanus Chapel. At the far end of the platform crouched a group of women covered from head to heel in black, squatting on their haunches, chatting and giggling, so that you wondered what the joke could be. Were we the joke? They displayed baskets of food, to sell to passengers.

'Are they the Arabs we've got to watch?' Nia asked.

It gave you a jolt to realise how much the kiddies picked up, Joe thought. You imagined they'd be absorbed in playing with their toys in their own little world. Mind, Nia was a bit of a prodigy. He kissed her head. The hair radiated from one place in a whorl like the pattern of a fingerprint or a spiral shell. It all came back to him, the heart-storming surprise of her arrival in the world. The comical games of 'Boo' and throwing the rattle which never seemed to wear thin his fragile patience. The scent of her after the bath, the worry over her least cough or sniffle.

'*Are* they?' she demanded.

'Are who what?'

'Those Arabs. Have we got to watch them?'

'Those are nice, harmless Arabs,' he assured her. 'Not nasty ones.'

'How can you tell?'

He was stymied. 'Oh, well, they look nice and peaceful, don't they?'

'Yes.' Nia craned round and said, 'Daddy.'

'Yes, my beauty.'

'Where is my Auntie Mona?'

'Well, I expect she had to go to her own home, didn't she, with her husband.'

'My Uncle Ben.' They get fond of people, he thought. A fortnight at sea and any kind face seems like blood-kin: how could it not? But they forget quickly. He slipped a sweetie to each of the children indefatigably fanning Ailsa. A flock of six now, he saw, including Chalkie's ash-blond boys, two and four years old. Dear little chaps, burly and solemn. Sweet and touching it was to see their solemn industriousness as it was to see how happy Chalkie was, hand in hand with his quiet Irene, his thin face wreathed in smiles, putting his hand up to his mouth as if to wipe away the grin.

The *fellaheen* stood in full sunlight on the plinths of shadows equally majestic and seemed to say: in what way have we provoked or offended you? Please enlighten us. What precisely was the reception you expected when you came to our country? They were looking up the line with patience, as if waiting was nothing; they had been born to wait; had been waiting now for centuries, for millennia. They'd have a long wait yet if they were expecting a train to come down that line, Joe thought. Your terrorist brothers have cut it.

One of the black-clad women looked up and smiled. A ravishing smile. Smiling for me? Joe wondered, reddening. They didn't generally. And you didn't look at them for fear of causing an international incident. But no, he had intercepted a smile meant for Nia, who was waving.

Here came a punkah-wallah, to join in the epic fanning of Ailsa. His large fan and the breeze it made dwarfed the children's. They speeded up, arms beating like insect wings.

'Is he a nice Arab, that one?' Nia asked.

'Shush, Nia. No need to keep asking that. Yes, he's cooling down Mami's face lovely, isn't he?'

He put Nia in the way of benefiting from the breeze and gave her and Ailsa some sips of water. She was reviving; thanked the punkah-wallah apologetically. The old man nodded and his face crinkled up into a map of wrinkles. Ailsa said, 'It is so kind.'

'You don't have to thank the punkah-wallah, dearie,' Paul Brean's wife explained. 'That's what he's for.'

*

'Hallo, lady,' said Nia. She hunkered down to be on a level and became chatty and pleasant. 'How are you today? Where do you live?'

The dark liquid eyes looked back with a small smile. The lady was beautiful, very young, like a pearl on a black velvet cushion.

Nia reached out and touched the curve of the lady's cheek. The lady seemed astonished, almost shaken. She put up her hand and touched the spot the white girl had caressed and, as she did so, the sleeve of the black robe fell back to reveal slender metal bangles that chinked and gleamed a secret song as they slid up her arm.

What had they got in their baskets? Nia asked them, and pointed one at a time to the good things they had no larder for. Bread, she told them: say after me. Bray-eed. Well done! Melon. Cheese. Very good! You can speak English, can't you, now? Flies cruised and landed on the good things, and were seen off by the women's indefatigable hands flapping. Nia contemplated the bare feet they had no shoes for. She asked the old granny next to her lady where her teeth were. Had she lost them? And she peeked at a silent baby shrouded in a black shawl that engulfed both its mother and itself. Was it dead? It didn't move or cry.

A basket was piled with melons like green footballs. One had been cut open: the succulent pink flesh of its insides gleamed in the sun. Nia's mouth watered. She put out one finger to touch the gash where the juice shone.

'Great Scott!' came a chorus of voices, and 'Come away this minute!' and 'Don't put that filth anywhere near your mouth!'

102

Part Two

Ismailia, September 1949

7

That dreamy moment when the helicopter vaulted into the air recalled the childhood passion for flight, when tree-climbing was not enough. You craved more. Wanted it so badly that swan wings branched their quills from your shoulder blades and you rose with a thunderclap above your friends in the street, their envious faces uptilted to marvel at the power of the bird boy, above the slate-roofed terrace, until Trewyddfa Hill spread out beneath Joe and the gleaming Tawe and the belching steelwork chimneys.

Ground staff had all too few chances to fly. Joe, and the young naval pilot sat in the cockpit of the wartime two-seater helicopter, a baby of a creature, the first of the Dragonfly models, beautiful workmanship. Skimming and manoeuvring low above water, you felt how it earned its name. All flight was learned from birds and insects. They were the marvels of creation, not us. *A reward for your night's work, Taf*: a helicopter recce was a joy like no other. A bubble blown into the air, windows all around you, transparent. Thirty-six hours Joe had been awake, testing and tuning the engines of the four Dragonflies they'd grounded for inspection at Shallufa. Checks made, the engine roared sweetly, the rotors spun. Away they sped over the desert sands, tawny brightening to amber.

Dawn painted the Bitter Lake violet and flamingo pink. Travelling north, Joe skimmed RAF Kabrit, where pale-skinned airmen in vests were pounding the runway perimeter in the merciful dawn cool, one-two, one-two; a Lancaster bomber was refuelling on the tarmac and you could see, not just the upturned faces of the guards with their rifles on the command tower, but their grins as they waved. The Dragonfly's shadow billowed to immense proportions in the early light, a crazily comic insect of mighty dimensions.

From a jetty at Fanara a Gyppo was fishing and as they passed, Joe watched the gleaming line twitch as the fisherman hauled in a handsome lute. It thrashed in his hands. And was stilled as the fisherman stunned it on the jetty. Blood-red eyes, silver scales. A beauty that would feed a family for a week.

The Pharaohs had understood the principles of flight, Joe was convinced. At Sakkara he'd spotted what was surely a scale model of a glider, mislabelled a bird (but what bird has a notch for a tail-plane?), made of sycamore light as the balsa models of his childhood, his pride and joy. If you'd launched the Pharaoh's model as Nia threw the paper gliders they made together, the ancient model would have flown yards. For sure. Their engineers knew things we hadn't caught up with for thousands of years. Like us they'd observed birds in flight and studied the principles.

Perhaps they'd got off the ground themselves: who could say? And yet the Gyppos had settled for backwardness and mud. Mushrooms of black smoke rose from the dung fires of a village which was no more than a jumble of mud huts roofed with reeds.

Boats were out, practically a fleet. The white triangles of their sails caught the calm breezes of dawn in gracious curves, stained with carmine from the rising sun. Joe had a sense of the eternity of it all down there: nothing had changed for thousands of years. Nothing would change. The desert kept everything pristine – buried trucks from the Great War that, with some minor repairs, could be fuelled and driven; oil cans with the faintest gold sheen of rust after forty years. Bedouin with their camels and their ancient, secret knowledge: something eternal about them. In his bubble of freedom, he saw poverty obscured by distance, conflict disguised as peace. The lake was a mass of ripples as dawn released the thermals. The Big Flea and the Little Flea, the only features you could call hills in a landscape flat as a pancake, blazed an extraordinary red-gold.

They flew on over the hospital and camp of Fayid and the bright turf of the military cemetery, where regiments of pale stone lozenges and banks of carefully tended flowers marked the resting places of soldiers and airmen from two wars and too many British children whose dads (so Joe put it to himself) had failed to keep the eggs in a basin of vinegar. Germs coated every surface you hadn't attacked with Dettol. In the heat, the filth, the flies, the merest graze went septic in an hour.

The Dragonfly crossed the colossal arms dump at Abu Sultan. Suez was the greatest military installation in the entire world. The sheer scale of it all: the centre of the empire. You had to be proud. Near Deversoir with its great hangars and tented encampment, the Dragonfly lingered over the swimming hole of jewel-clear water, thirty feet deep, where he and Chalkie had once dived, finding the sea horses and baby octopi. Never would Joe have expected sea horses to be so tiny. And the males carried the young, a detail that tickled him. For wherever he was, he carried Nia, cradled to his heart. As Chalkie did his boys – and that was part of the bond between him and his pal: the unashamed tenderness for their little ones, that rippled out in reverence for the creatures of the earth. Both Joe and Chalkie had been filled with wonder that such animals as the sea horses and octopi should exist and that they – common boys from the pits and steelworks – should be privileged to see them. The water was a gleaming oval of turquoise: a cyclops eye staring back up at him.

Now Joe could see the officers' houses at Kensington Village, brick bungalows with corrugated iron roofs, the saffragi out with brooms, their white robes pink-tinged as they levelled the Memsahibs' sandy compounds. Over Red Flannel Alley the helicopter passed, the mansions of the top brass, with their emerald lawns and trees.

As the lake narrowed and the Dragonfly hovered above the canal, the bloody sun popped out of the horizon like a sac from an egg-yolk. Now the furnace heat would get up. Poor Ailsa would be melting. Joe looked down on the split world: Asia on one bank, Africa on the other. On the canal's eastern shore lay the Sinai Desert, a bleached universe of sand where nothing could live; the west, irrigated by the Sweet Water Canal, throbbed with a lustrous green that saturated date palms and pastures. Wales might be equally green but the homely grey skies dulled it. In Egypt colour was reborn in wild intensities of ruby and gold, emerald and topaz.

The canal opened out into the dazzle of Lake Timsah, Nia's heaven. Joe made out the north-western beaches with their demarcations: the officers' beach being the most southerly from Ish, then the French Beach, and finally the troops' beach, nearest to the point where that open sewer, the Sweet Water Canal, emptied its obscenities. Nearly home now. Passing over the vast army garrison at Moascar, the Dragonfly arced east above Ish, whose white tiered houses resembled wedding cakes with sugar icing, each flat roof an intimate world of parasols, chairs and tables beside roof gardens. On the harbour front built by de Lesseps for the Canal Company administration were the mansions and ateliers of the very rich, surrounded by French ornamental gardens. Yachts flew colourful flags. Beyond the mansions Joe could pick out the geometry of the city's sectors, as if in a diagram: the French and Greek quarters to the east, and the old Khedive's palace, and the dark squalor of Wogtown to the west. And the canal flowing onward to the Mediterranean at Port Said.

Looping south-west, they hovered above El-Marah, where new quarters had been thrown up by Egyptian workmen in two months flat. Lazy he had always called them, downing tools at eleven and picking them up again at four, but Joe had to admit they did the job and did it well, and to time. He pointed out his little world to the pilot: Palmerston Row where Ailsa's pals the Websters were quartered; and branching from it Disraeli Street. He gave the pilot a thumbs-up as they hovered over his own roof amongst brick-built semis that could have been anywhere in Britain except that they were surrounded by a sea of sand and builders' rubble.

A woman who must be Irene White was out in the garden already, pegging up at crack of dawn bleached and starched sheets, immaculate flags of surrender.

*

Planes droned as they circled above the houses. Ailsa didn't bother to look up, standing at the window peeling a potato and dreaming of Shropshire rain. Part of her mind floated far away, to where the heavens had opened on herself and Archie Copsey as they peddled their bikes like billy-o in their sou'westers, water pouring off their yellow waxed capes on to soil that drank till it could drink no more. She thanked her stars to have grown up mantled in a fine net of drizzle under rain clouds that acted as an umbrella against the sun. She recalled the water-logged fields along the Severn in the great flood of '47. Rowing boats navigating the aisle of Shrewsbury Abbey between drowned marble knights and bishops. Such rain – any rain at all – seemed a fantasy.

The window framed Nia crouching to play in what you could hardly call a garden. Sand pit, maybe: Nia's Eden. She was as good as gold these days, having settled beautifully with her parents in El-Marah. It had only been Joe's absence that had made Nia so cranky and wayward on the crossing. Now Ailsa could be proud of her daughter, modelling sand castles with Christopher. She smiled to see Nia wearing a halo – the disc of her yellow sun hat – beside the next-door-but-one neighbour, in thrall of course to little

110

Miss Roberts, doing as he was told, she did not doubt, and now trundling the miniature wheelbarrow to – over *there*, Nia was pointing, *that* sand there, Topher! To the children their new home was nothing but a bucket-and-spade playground. The heat hardly bothered them, slathered from top to toe in calamine. It had been good for Nia, in every way, coming to Egypt.

The Roberts had spent a couple of months in a temporary home in Fanara, by the Great Bitter Lake, waiting for new quarters to be built. So this was Ailsa's first real married home, at the edge of the desert. From the back windows stretched a plain of sand. It played strange rainbow tricks under the rising or setting sun, turning into pistes of mauve or orange; reared up on itself in the midday heat haze that foreshortened distances and made you see a milky pool rising into the air. The desert filled Irene with fear, imagining terrorists on camels galloping up with blades and pistols; it lured Ailsa like a magnet. Open spaces always had. She hankered to walk out into that splendour of emptiness. Come winter's cool, she'd give freer rein to her wanderlust.

Yet Ailsa was content with her lot, patient with her limits. When had she been as happy?

From the kitchen window she could just see the fascinating pale silhouette of Ismailia, dominated by water tower, mosque and Coptic church, with blocks of modern flats painted in pastel shades. She and Joe delighted in exploring the lakeside city. At the eastern side the town glistened, its French and Greek quarters maintaining a grandiose nineteenth-century dream of heroic commerce. All drenched in luxuriant greenery. Westward lay the filthy

111

huddle of the so-called native quarter, known to the troops as Wogtown. It stank. The townsfolk had neither plumbing, sewerage nor running water. How come then that the women were able to hang a bunting of freshly washed laundry from their windows? How come the men's *gallabiyyas* were so white and crisp? The people rose proudly above their conditions: she could see that even from this distance, God knew how the poor souls managed it.

Ailsa had given Joe a straight look on the one occasion he'd referred to 'Wogtown'. He'd apologised immediately: women were entitled to their nice sensibility, was the thought she read in his eyes. But he was gentle with the Egyptian vendors, as long as they kept their distance. He made sure to put out leftover food for the Egyptian dustmen and their malnourished families. He'd stand aside, respectfully averting his gaze, from an Arab lady hurrying along the road in her black shroud.

Ailsa started on the second tatty. She'd carve the peel off in one loop again, so help her. It had been the letter from her aunt, with a postscript from Archie, no doubt, that had set her hallucinating rain. She kissed the precious air-letter whenever one was put in her hand. These blue wafers said: *we are here; you are there: not so very far is it, from there to here?* And it's just pouring here, wrote Archie, tipping it down, and I have to put on my galoshes just to go down the path.

The *Empire Glory* seemed another world. Passing the signpost to the officers' exclusive bungalows at Masurah near the *Bois des Fontaines* in Ish, she'd peer down the boulevard: no Mona. But they might bump into one another. Leave it to chance.

Ailsa tapped on the window for Nia to see that she had nearly, oh so nearly, got the peel off whole!

Nia turned her head, busy palms still patting the fortress under construction, and grinned approval. Ailsa finished the potato, halved it and dropped it in the saucepan, then picked up the twin tails of peel and held them either side of her head as ear rings, bouncing up and down like springs. Nia and Christopher ran to the window and stood craning and giggling through the wire netting. In they rushed to claim the peelings and out they ran again.

And in the wood at the Wrekin with Archie, Ailsa, a girl of sixteen, had sauntered through green gloom over the spongy give of beach mast and held his hand as rain pattered through the branches. Would Archie ever marry? She thought of him working the family farm under the Long Mynd. Drops had fallen coldly on their heads as they kissed. It was odd how, separated from her cousin by a continent, Ailsa thought of him more than she'd ever done at home. For 'home' was what Archie represented. She turned on the Baby Belling and crowded the saucepans on to its single hot plate. 'Miracle-worker, you,' Joe always said in wonderment. Today they had fresh cauliflower from the Egyptian market; she had the knack of simmering it till it was just this side of soft. Not the king himself feasted on better meat and three veg, Joe said: that was for sure. Well, Ailsa had replied, it is not likely we'll find out.

She would not say that the Primus was her enemy, though it smoked and stank and exerted a senseless will of its own. Knowing its temperamental ways, she kept a lookout for a tongue of flame to flare up and scorch her eyebrows. The creature's square head accumulated soot.

Ailsa had to pull this off and clean the clogged hole in its black neck with a pipe cleaner. But she made little of all this and spoke back to the treacherous Primus with hilarity. She rigged up a grill for Welsh rarebit by upturning a two-bar electric fire on a row of bricks.

Genius! Ein Meisterstück, Ailsa! Hedwig in nearby Palmerston Row had scurried off to build her own grill. Now they all boasted upside down electric fires. Pregnancy and her husband's doting love suited Hedwig. Ailsa was glad to brush up her German and, now that the Englishwoman was the one mangling a foreign tongue, the poor soul didn't put her back up half as much. There was a little German community in Ish, men who'd stayed on after the prisoner of war camps had closed. Why would they want to go back to their ruined, starving homeland? Nazis, Joe called them. But he took his watch to the German watchmaker's shop off the *avenue Impératrice*, knowing Fritz would do a good job of mending it, and was not disappointed.

Ailsa glanced out to check on Nia. And, oh dear, she was burying Christopher. With his permission, no doubt, the goose. If Irene came round to collect him, only to find him buried in his best red shorts, there'd be frosty looks, possibly words between them, which Ailsa very much didn't want. Irene was a good enough soul: kept herself to herself and wouldn't be seen dead with a headful of curlers in the NAAFI. Irene never came wheedling to 'borrow' a cup of sugar, in order to bore you to the teeth with inane gossip. She took her boys to the library and read to them at night. And Chalkie, Joe's pal, was the salt of the earth.

Checking the Primus, Ailsa went out to the children:

'What are you doing, Nia?'

'Mami!' In rapture Nia left her prey in his temporary grave and launched herself at Ailsa, embracing her thighs with abandon, as if she hadn't seen her for a week.

'Got sand in my eyes,' Christopher lamented. 'Mrs Roberts!'

'Don't bury Topher again, Nia,' she said as severely as she could. Disentangling herself from her daughter, she released the lad, who was only covered in a thin layer of sand. Nia's powers of excavation didn't stretch much further. Ailsa dusted him down and ran her hands through his white-blond mop. His eyes were dark brown, creating an odd effect in the albino face.

'Can Topher stay for tea, Mami?'

'No, I don't think so, Nia. His mummy wants him, doesn't she? Play nicely for another fifteen minutes and then come in and wash your hands because Daddy will be home for tea, and Christopher's daddy too.'

'My dad's on guard duty,' Christopher said in a lugubrious voice.

'My daddy's in the sky,' said Nia. They both looked up.

Ailsa went in and turned the control on the Primus down just a touch. Expecting Joe home so soon gave her heart a lurch, a pang of joy. It was still the first time ever. Because he'd gone away to the war and come back, and gone on ahead to Fayid and she'd followed, and because their life would be a rhythm of such absences and reunions, their love had the quality of – what would you call it? – perpetual romance? A weak word for the passion that moved her when she opened the door to Joe. A word too secular for her repeated sense of homecoming, her rush to the magnet of her husband. And her knowledge that he was the same. The raw emotion on his face. His ability to laugh and dance, so light on his feet, it was a scream, with her in his arms, all round the flat; his brimming tears at the height of their lovemaking. His skin was thin. He was transparent.

She went to lay the table. They had no easy chairs at all. The great brown Marconi wireless stood on a box, beside a lamp, serving the purpose of a hearth. They grouped themselves around it. But their life was luxurious in comparison with the austerity they'd left behind. To see tinned pears stacked on the NAAFI shelves along with the delicious cubed fruit salad with cherries for Nia still made Ailsa dizzy. Not even rationed! Ailsa had put on weight and was more rounded (which she was glad of at the French Beach) with all the good eating. But where were her wedding and engagement rings? A short tizzy. Ah, good, there on the sudsy side of the sink. Naked without them.

*

Joe itched to be home. Just to check: is this really you? My Ailsa with me in this wilderness? Her milky skin that mustn't burn. The straps of the petticoat which she had informed him was 'ivory, not grey, Joe, if you don't mind'. The silky texture running over her flat stomach and hips. Something sizzling in the oven, scenting the kitchen with an overpowering sense of home. On the table, as soon as he had washed, as much as he could eat.

Instead of this, he and Chalkie found themselves detained at the offices of Fayid Hospital waiting for a document to be typed by the sand-happy corporal who acted as head clerk in the general office. As he touch-typed, the clerk murmured to himself, 'Shufty bint! Shufty bint, oh aye!' A harmless, superficially unflappable bloke, he could type at a phenomenal rate and talk to himself at the same time. Should have been sent home a long while back but somehow had got stuck here in the sand like a Jeep with its wheels spinning. Been in Wogland, he said, since the beginning of the war.

Chalkie said he knew how to put Joe in the way of half a ton of spare socks if Joe was interested. Interested? said Joe. I'd kill for them and so would Ailsa. She spent her whole time purifying his appalling socks. *They stink*, she said, *in the nostrils of the Almighty*. Fallen off the back of a lorry, had they? Call them liberated, said Chalkie with a grin. He'd done a bit of bartering with one of the stores-wallahs, ending up with several gross – more than even he could use with his sweaty feet. And Irene was worried about having such a mountain of liberated socks in the house.

'What are you asking for them?' Joe asked cautiously. Socks, a unit of exchange, were worth a fortune. In the furnace heat underwear turned to damp rags and dis-integrated, steeped in sweat and fungal rot. The Air Ministry judged sock-rations by temperatures at Whitehall.

'Free to you, Taf. I'll sell the bulk of the stuff, of course.'

'You sure, Chalkie?'

'Course I am.'

'What did they sting you for?'

'Oh well.' He coloured up and picked at a hangnail. All his fingernails were bitten down to the quick. 'The Tiger. And fifty in cash they're paying.'

'*No*. You'd never give up your bike, boy. I don't believe you.'

'Well, you know, I couldn't get the petrol.' Chalkie paused. 'And of course my Irene isn't keen.' He blinked and looked away: the bloke was prepared to give up his pride and joy for his wife's peace of mind. Petrol could be found, if you wanted it enough. It wasn't that.

A heap of rusty tin the Tiger had been when they'd first got hold of it. More like a bomb waiting to explode than a vehicle. Chalkie had ridden it with the seam of the petrol tank leaking petrol. One spark and up she goes! Joe had helped him knock, weld and polish it into shape. By the time they'd finished, the Tiger was a beauty. They'd rigged up a garage from a packing case and Joe had designed a makeshift alarm. Now the 350 cc Matchless was to be turned into socks.

'Shufty *binties*!' the head clerk broke out. 'Not long now, lads,' he told the men. 'I wouldn't mind seeing them, I can tell youse that,' he said to himself. The office fan was placed on his desk, as if for brain-calming purposes. No one mocked him or took notice of his monologue. Wants his mam, thought Joe. Needs a wife.

The loss of the Matchless got to Joe somehow. He hadn't given it a thought since his family had joined him but now it reared up in his imagination. He could feel it between his legs, the engine he'd tuned vibrating against his thighs. The snarl as he or Chalkie accelerated away, ploughing up dust. The roaring thrill of it. Been to the Pyramids together they had, on the Tiger. Climbed the Lesser Pyramid at sunset and drank a Stella at the top.

'Give it her, boy, give it her good.' The clerk pulled out another page, separated the carbon copies and inserted new paper. 'Oh, I will, matey, don't you worry, I surely will,' he replied to himself. 'Good *and* proper.'

'Is that nearly ready?' Chalkie asked him. 'I don't want to mither you but we're officially off-duty.'

'Coming up to the boil she is,' said the corporal. 'Wait your turn. As the Bishop said.'

Joe shrugged, raised his eyes to the ceiling, where flies roved round naked light bulbs. 'Knock down the price, Chalkie, and I'll buy her. We can still run around on her the same.'

Chalkie's eyes behind the thick panes of his specs looked as round as the glasses. He licked his lips nervously. 'Well, but how could you afford it, Taf, with your family and all?'

Joe wondered at his own rashness in making the suggestion without OK-ing it at home. As a married man, he ought to be beyond such irresponsibility. The root of his dependence on Ailsa twinged as he tugged on it.

'In any case,' said Chalkie. 'Wouldn't the missus object?'

'A few beers, a laugh, the odd game of football, a bike ride – a man's got to have the right to that. Why does Irene mind so much?'

'Tell you the truth, Taf, she's afraid of everything pretty much. She's afraid of the poor old char wallah. Thinks he wants to kill her. I have to search the bed for spiders and snakes every night. Pity to add to the list if I can avoid it.'

Joe thought with pride of Ailsa's strength of mind, her plucky refusal to be daunted by smells, cockroaches, dirt, whatever Egypt could throw at her, and her interest in what she called *the real Egypt*, beyond the confines of camp life. At the same time, he was visited by a quick, poignant view of Irene, so dignified and pleasant, walking with her sons to the bus stop, in a creamy pleated skirt that swayed this

119

way and that, and white high-heeled shoes. She'd never be good-looking, though he supposed she was to Chalkie. But Irene was well-groomed and held her head high, all the while fearing a trip-rope.

'Brave she is, boy, to cope. No one would ever guess she felt like that. Her bearing it is.'

'Look through there,' said Chalkie. 'Hey, take a shufty. For Pete's *sake*!'

The sand-happy corporal twisted his head and peered through the open partition into the neighbouring office, where laughter had broken out. He grinned and the grin widened into a beam, the first smile Joe had seen on his poker face. 'Oh, that's nothing!' he said. 'Just Wing Co Jacobs from N-Division. *Habibi* we call him. Bringing light relief sorely needed.'

'N-Division?'

'Neurotics as opposed to Psychotics.'

'*Habibi*?'

'Arabic, mate. For Sweetheart. He calls us *Habibi*. And we call him *Habibi*.'

A growing audience clapped and sang along. The tall, gangling Wing Commander waltzed a bluff staff sergeant from Burnley round the office. The officer's mop of black curly hair flapped up and down as he whirled his partner. The waltz turned into a tango, the men clapping. The stout sergeant, playing the lady's part for all he was worth, allowed himself to be bent back, pouting and smouldering.

Oh yes, I know you, Joe thought with a smarting pang. The Jewboy whose wife had latched on to Ailsa on the voyage out, with the blond poufter hanging on his every word, smarmy, charming. Joe listened in disgusted

120

fascination to the joshing as the laughter peaked in the office next door. Everyone was dancing now. A broad-shouldered clerk took up the tune of 'Making Whoopee!' on a paper and comb. *Habibi*! caterwauled the men. *Ya Habibi*!

Joe could hardly help grinning and tapping his feet. He was sorely tempted to whisk Chalkie in and play the fool with the rest. It was something he did at the drop of a hat, childish excitement welling up, his pals egging him on. But for God's sake. No. Officers did not, could not, behave like this. Only once a year, at Christmas, did they descend from their high horses, to serve the men their dinner, a one-off ritual that confirmed the order of things. This loosened it. These bad eggs, public schoolboys left over from the war, Commies, with no more than a month's training at Cranwell, knew that very well.

The sergeant from Burnley, after a final canter round the desk, was whirled into a flat-footed arabesque and released. Applause. They called for more. *That's it for now, lads! But I shall return. Now, what the dickens did I come in for?* The officer scratched his head. The laughter waned and the men dispersed. Someone handed the Wing Commander a sheaf of papers, speaking with respect. Joe heard him enquiring kindly about someone's wife and kiddies.

He remembered the way his own wife had looked up at the fellow, meltingly. The courteously familiar way the Wing Commander had spoken to Ailsa. He'd have kissed her goodbye if Joe had not been there.

And yet at the same time Joe thought – *knew* even – that the officer was queer as a coot. There was something effeminate about him: soft gestures, affected talk. The jag of jealousy persisted. Joe turned away before he could be buttonholed. Sweat prickled in his armpits, for all that he'd been standing in the stiff breeze of the fan.

As they left the building, they talked of the terrorist taken last night just inside the perimeter with a can of petrol. Of course Irene was afraid. She was right to be afraid. With the war over, the RAF was marshmallow at the centre. Handling the wogs with velvet gloves. A new breed of cut-throat terrorist was cutting railway lines, stealing the blankets off the camp beds of sleeping soldiers in their tents, setting tripwires on the Treaty Road. The soft types in high places would not allow the Forces to retaliate in the measure required.

'You're right about the Tiger,' he told Chalkie. 'Dead right. It wants getting rid of. Heap of old scrap.'

'Oh well, I don't know, Taf. You almost had me convinced.'

Perhaps Ailsa is afraid too, Joe thought. Terrified all the time and too proud to show it. He was ashamed at his wish to have something of his own that he did not share with her. Anxiety stirred in case she had the same impulse. There'd been boyfriends before him, he knew. He'd seen the adoring way her cousin Archie looked at her. And perhaps memories of Archie and the rest of them still stole through her mind, the very thought of which was intolerable. Share Ailsa he couldn't.

Chalkie was urging a weekend outing to Lake Timsah. The kiddies got along like a house on fire. For Christopher it was always Nia this and Nia that. They had a little play-world, he said. It was sweet to see.

'Right you are. Let's do that. Ailsa and Irene should see more of each other. Good pals they could be. Well, I'm off home, boy,' Joe said and laughed, 'to shufty bint.'

'Right behind you, mate. Whoa, no. Guard duty.'

*

The thought of Ailsa doing or thinking things behind his back had stuck in Joe's mind at an angle. He was discomposed but kept forgetting, as he made his way home, what the heck he was nettled about. He thought of *Habibi* kicking up his heels. This led back to the memory of the wife passing Joe's wife a package at Port Said, amid all that extravagant hugging and kissing and swearing eternal faith: where had Ailsa put that? What was in it? Why would she have hidden it? Looked like a box of some kind or a book.

But when he saw her at the window, the whole question was closed: Ailsa waved and jumped up and down, pleased to see him. Joe admired Nia's castles and bridges in the yard. Works of engineering they were, so careful and precise. Clever little hands.

'Oh,' sighed Ailsa. 'I've missed you.'

He held her delicate waist contained between his hands. Her solid, honourable and reassuring self. 'Tell me you love me,' he said.

'I do love you. All and entirely and, oh, stop it, your tea's so nearly cooked, Joe.'

Calamine-anointed Nia sat with her golly at the laid table, humming to herself. He stole up and placed his hands over her eyes: 'Guess who?'

'It's you, it's you, naughty!'

'Come and see something, Nia.'

'What?' She scrambled down from her seat and put her hand in his. He drew her to the window.

'Nia, someone's been building fairy castles in our front yard! Who can it be? Was it Mami? What do you think, girlie?'

'Me and Topher did it.'

'Never! I don't believe you!'

'We did.'

He uncurled her fingers and laid them over the back of one of his hard hands: 'Artist's hands,' he said, admiring the shape and length of her fingers.

Ailsa called them to the table. Braised chops, very tender, with carrots and onions cooked in the gravy, cauliflower and peas. As he poured a pyramid of salt on the edge of his plate, Joe told her all about the poor old Shufty Bint corporal, skipped the Wing Co and the riotous dancing and went on, when they got to the pears and custard, to the sock saga and the sale of the Tiger. He made the tale extravagantly comic, inflating it like a balloon, playing all the parts including the Tiger's, giving over only when Ailsa begged him to: she had a stitch from laughing.

Joe tempted Nia's slender appetite with teaspoonfuls of Daddy Bear's custard. He poured a hill of salt on to the table cloth for her and, with intense concentration, she created a world of tiny dunes and lanes. Foreigners the size of pinheads would wander down its sculpted lanes admiring the peaks and slopes of her white invented world. Watching their quiet daughter, while Ailsa removed the pudding plates and made tea, Joe wondered if he could ever bear to have another child and dispossess Nia of the unrivalled love that embraced her.

'I say, Aily!' He leaned his chair back on two legs and called into the kitchen.

'Hallo!'

'Whatever happened to that package the woman – the *lady*, beg pardon – on the ship gave you? Did you open it? What was in it?'

*

Nia got out before the trouble broke. She picked up Little Yellow Man and removed herself from the unease that might or might not give way to hurt silence, raised voices, a burst of tears.

'Oh, you never said,' her father had said to her mother. 'Didn't I?'

The buzzing in the air was not caused by flies: there were no flies in the room.

Standing on her bed, Nia looked out of the window, her vision criss-crossed by wire netting. Behind her the voices ebbed, then eddied again. No one was shouting, in fact there was laughter, but still the sound was not quite right. Now one of them was turning on the wireless, saying the dreadful word 'News', which preluded shushings and 'Keep still'. Probably they had switched it on to hide their row because it was clear that they were not listening. Nia wriggled. The wireless came down on her like a net, trapping her boredom in her head. She ignored it until it was nothing but a humming, tuneless murmur.

An Arab was walking, on his own, out and out into the desert. In a straight line. No camel. Wearing a pink headdress.

Today she and Topher had buried a doll. Hester had yellow hair and eyes that opened and shut. Joe had paid the earth for her. A baby for you, Nia! A *merch fach* of your very own to look after! Nia had no heart to explain how much Hester disgusted her; how she wanted to spit on her. Each night when her parents left the bedroom, after the story had been told and the Lovely Words had been spoken, she'd shoved Hester under the bed. But she'd wake in the night, disquiet. Smeary shadows roved the walls. A body under the bed.

Today Topher and she had dug a pit and buried Hester with all her grave-goods: feeding bottle, change of clothes. They'd erected a complex fortress on the site.

Nia's Arab man was still walking with measured pace, on and on, in a straight line. She closed her eyes. Each time she peeped through her lashes he was tinier. Who was the Arab? Who? Where could he be going? As she stared, the dazzling heat-haze troubled her obscurely. Her mind swung and her tummy felt sicky. She was surrounded by something huge of which she could only say that it was not herself.

Later they would enquire about Hester's whereabouts. They'd never guess and she wouldn't tell. One day Nia knew she would forget. The forgetting went on always, and you had to hold on to anything you wanted to be sure of, in your hands where you could see it, like Little Yellow Man and her rag of cot-sheet: that she knew. She could already feel forgetfulness nudging in towards the doll.

Nia jumped down, opened the door a few inches and listened.

'Thought is free!' she heard her mother exclaim, apparently in fun but with an undercurrent of unease.

The Arab was now as big and small as one segment of Nia's thumb. As she pondered him, flies batted against the grid of thin wire mesh and fell back. Fat they were and well-fed. Flies fed on donkey-turds and dog-turds and every kind of Egyptian filth. Then they flew to English houses to try to make you blind like Egyptian children. Mami chased them with a swatter in a frenzy of hygiene. Flies' graveyards hung from the window: sticky ribbons blobbed with black. And yet you could see them altogether differently. Nia watched a bluebottle, perched on the sill to soak in sun. A visitor like a jewel, its surfaces emerald and sapphire. A creature of jet-black light.

*

Oh how tedious, he's in one of his moods, Ailsa thought. Unless I'm very careful, we are going to have a blow-up.

She was parched. 'Let's top our carburettors up!' she said playfully, pouring glasses of water for herself and for him. 'There you are, my lovely.' He didn't drink. He looked, she thought, using words not in Joe's vocabulary, *lugubrious, lachrymose.* Ailsa turned her mind away. Once at the Wrekin after rainfall she and Archie had drunk rain from a leaf. She thought of grass blades bent back and beaded with pearls. She drank off a whole glass of water but it failed to slake her thirst. And still Joe was maundering. Telling her about how wretched poor Irene was in the desert. What had that feeble-minded female to do with Ailsa Birch?

'But, darling,' she broke in, 'I don't feel lonely. I honestly don't. I'm very self-contained.'

He met that with silence. Did not know what to make of it. She watched him swallow the word 'self-contained' and have trouble digesting it. I should not think of myself

127

as Ailsa Birch, she thought. Why did I think that?

'Don't you miss me then?'

'Of course. But I know you'll be back at a certain time and I suppose I look forward to it rather than lamenting. Frankly, that's not my way.'

She spoke coolly and robustly, and made herself think of starch. Petticoats that stood up like a white tent that didn't need tent-poles. That crackled when you tried to sit down. But I don't want to turn into a starched petticoat, Ailsa thought. She made herself speak more lightly and tenderly. 'Joe, sweetheart, you wouldn't want me to be unhappy in my little corner of the world, would you?'

'Of course not. But. Doesn't the day seem long? Do you find it frightening to be here on your own?'

'Frightening? There is Nia to look after and the cockroaches to whack with a broom. And, well, masses to think about.'

'Like what? What are you thinking?'

'For goodness' sake! I mean: thought is free!'

'What the dickens do you mean by that, woman?'

She rounded on him. 'Nothing. Stop being childish. And don't call me woman. I won't be called that. Don't you think things and then forget what it was you thought? Do you tell me absolutely everything that goes through your mind?'

'Pretty much.'

'Well, you shouldn't,' she flashed. 'Everyone needs to call his soul his own.'

Joe flinched as if struck. His face darkened. He got like this and it was so silly: he had to be jealous of someone and, if she did not see anyone outside the family and the

NAAFI girls for a whole day, he had to be jealous of her own relationship with her*self*, for heaven's sake. What did he want her to be: a puppet?

'I can only be me. Can't I?' she pressed.

He swallowed. Ailsa quite clearly saw the moment when whatever switch it was that turned on this mood flicked it off again. She observed it every time but could never predict the moment or locate the form of words that would do the trick.

'Yes,' he said. 'Yes. Oh heck, Ailsa, what a bloody ass I am.'

And the best of it was, Joe soon got over it. Sorries and kisses. A walk, arms round one another's waist, into the yard, to see the stars hanging like lamps near to the earth. Or, contrite, he'd go out to bring in the washing, stiff with sand and sun.

It was true, she'd kept Mona's precious book to herself, feeling she had the right to open it, in her own time, when he'd gone off to work and Nia was lying down for a nap. It was a volume of Goethe's poetry stolen from the library of the *Empire Glory*, with an italic inscription on the title page. *Ach, du warst in abgelebten Zeiten / Meine Schwester oder meine Frau*. In some other world, you were my sister or my wife. Light-fingered Mona had pinched it from the Allies, who'd commandeered it from the German Navy, who'd thieved it from the world. Hardly a legacy to share with Joe.

In it Mona had enclosed the final version of *Habibi*'s poem: *Her hands on the keys, your hands on her hands* ... The poem unlocked his heart for Ailsa: his love for Mona was infinitely tender, unassuageably needy. He identified with Mona as a mother with her child. A strange

129

comparison, Ailsa knew, but, yes, that must be it. *Habibi*'s need to cherish was more powerful than his desire to be cherished. He'd willingly share Mona with anyone able to bring her peace. *He loves me*, Ailsa thought. But such love conferred a burden. Only if his wife was happy could he be happy and how, in such a world as the one in which Mona Serafin had grown up, could that ever be the case? Once she had the poem by heart, Ailsa had ripped the draft into confetti scraps and thrown it away.

Well, Joe's rages were only ever hiccups. Over now. Ailsa heard Nia speed from her room, telling Joe off, saying that he must be spanked, driving him before her into the sitting room with a rolled up newspaper.

The air cooled suddenly here. When Ailsa went out into the back yard, her arms came over all gooseflesh. The quarrel had left her, as always, off kilter, with a sense of being obscurely in the wrong. Yet how had she offended? She knew Joe couldn't condone any relationship with the Jacobs family. The humiliation of watching him salute his superiors on the dock at Port Said stayed with her, making her own cheeks burn when she thought of it. Knowing his sensitivity, she shared the quick of his embarrassment, and in the moment of seeing how ... what was it? ... *small* he looked, she'd broken the tie with Mona like a zip wrenched undone.

Now that he'd raised the whole thing, Mona rushed vividly to mind, rousing a wistful sense of loss. And a stir of impatience with the narrowness, the strait limits of this so-called married quarter. Never having a proper conversation with anyone. Ailsa knew where the toffs' bungalows were at Masurah. She'd bloody well go and see Mona, if he went on like this. Why not? Ring the doorbell. Here I am, Mona. Remember me? If Joe only knew how he provoked her to do the thing he feared. Standing in the lozenge of light outside the kitchen, Ailsa became conscious of silence around her. It rang in her ears like the tacit messages in phone lines strung from pylon to pylon. So quiet that the barking of wild dogs and the roar of planes hardly impinged. The stars hung large and close, like lanterns.

Joe came and mantled her shoulders with a cardigan, reminding her of the mosquitoes. He'd rolled down his sleeves and buttoned them, to set her a good example.

'Listen, Joe. You can't hear a thing, can you? It's totally silent. Haunting really, isn't it? So lovely. And the moon.'

They listened together to the silence of the desert. Then they sauntered to the end of their yard. He'd wondered, he said, whether it was very selfish of him to have wanted them out here, where life was not easy. And his mam would gladly have kept them with her.

'I'd have died, Joe, *died*, if you'd left me behind.'

His jealousy was appeased. As she spoke these words, which were nothing less than the truth, Ailsa was aware of yielding her husband total reassurance. At some level she knew quite well that Joe's jealousy somehow pre-empted hers. Sensual love exposed the quivering heart of you. She could have been jealous of every woman on the camp, except that he, the more openly emotional character, got in first and made it unnecessary.

'Joe,' she said. 'I *ought* have shown you. I'm at fault. Mona Jacobs gave me a book of German poetry. I just put it away. Would you like to see it?'

131

'Oh God, no. Please. Stupid fuss I made.'

'Don't you miss wet weather, Joe? A nice bit of drizzle. Cool and pleasant. Your body having a drink. We've got cooked minds out here. What wouldn't I give for a deluge and no brolly.'

8

'Culture!' exclaimed Hedwig, pushing forward to join Ailsa and Irene in the NAAFI queue in Ish. The wives were not pleased with the German woman's contempt for the decencies of Saturday queuing; they stared and muttered. Ailsa heard the word *Kraut*. Hedwig, oblivious, went on, '*Hochkultur*! At last we get a chance to hear some real music! Believe it or not! Beethoven in the desert!' Her voice pronouncing the word *Beethoven* took on a note of reverence. She handed Ailsa a leaflet advertising a concert at the De Lesseps House. Under the auspices of the Anglo-Egyptian Friendship Society, she read. In aid of refugees. Hedwig had been given it by her countryman, Erich Stolz the watchmaker. 'And look who's playing!' She pointed at the name that had already leapt out at Ailsa. 'You remember her, don't you? From the *Empire Glory*?'

Ailsa blushed scarlet. She wanted to cry.

Hedwig was saying they must wear evening dress to the concert. Pearls and gloves. Unfortunately she had no pearls

133

and, alas, no decent gloves any longer, for her lilac evening gloves had gone astray in a previous move, no idea how, since she'd wrapped them in tissue paper. Her evening gown she had made herself in pink silk, hoping that no one could tell it was home-made. Bigwigs would attend the concert. High-ranking Egyptian ladies wearing gem-encrusted dresses. Cultivated, educated people would attend, Hedwig said. She pointed to the name above that of Mona Serafin-Jacobs: *Oum Koulsoum*. An Egyptian lady who would be singing classical songs. Erich had described her as the most famous woman in Egypt, a national hero. Erich had been interned as a prisoner of war from Rommel's first desert campaign. Now he'd learned Arabic and lived and worked among the Egyptians. A highly civilised man, Hedwig said, and no mean violinist.

It was so important, Irene remarked, ignoring questions of high culture, to include the right amount of onion in mince, chopped up nice and fine, as on its own mince was so bland. Didn't they think so? And plenty of seasoning. That had been how Irene's mother had cooked mince. Also one must be careful not to over-cook.

'But, Irene,' Hedwig said, 'minced animals are not what we should put in our mouths, so I feel.'

'Well, they are not precisely *animals* ...'

'What in heaven are they then?'

Irene began half-heartedly to distinguish pig from pork. Common assumption was with her but reason had deserted her and she faltered.

'Oy – why are you pushing in, you?' one of the women in the queue demanded of Hedwig. She'd covered her curlers with a floral scarf for a do at the airmen's mess. The faces of the sergeants' wives all said, *Vulgar*, and the woman read the message. She prodded Hedwig. 'Wait your turn like we all have to.'

'Excuse *me*,' Hedwig rounded on her. 'I am not here for these sausages but to talk with my friends. I would never queue-jump in my born days. Could you kill a cow?' she asked Irene. 'You yourself? Bludgeon her with a mallet or slice her throat? Are you happy to employ illiterate men to do this for you?'

Ailsa turned away, leaving them to wrangle. She steadied herself against the counter. Whatever it was that had sparked between herself and the Arab woman belonged in another world. A shipboard romance. Without the romance. So she'd told herself. But the name on the leaflet – the *prestige* of the name – brought their friendship out of hiding. Mona seemed to turn and look Ailsa straight in the eye, saying, *See what you have enabled me to do, habiba. And what you have turned your back on.* That characterful oval face, the changing weather of its moods; her hands. Hands that had been paralysed since Mona left her teacher but whose music Ailsa had somehow, by luck or grace, wakened.

Would there be Forces people at the concert? How would she broach it to Joe? For certainly, without the shadow of a doubt, Ailsa would attend.

Still parrying arguments about the legitimacy of mince, Irene told the woman in the queue, 'She's with me actually and she's not in your way,' and to Hedwig, 'You have your ideas, I have mine. Let's agree to differ. Oh look, there's my Roy. Roy! Coo-ee!'

Roy – Ailsa had to be careful not to call him Chalkie in front of his wife – appeared, beaming, and took his wife's basket as if it were an honour she bestowed. He escorted the three women out. As they emerged into the *Place de la Gare*, the heat seemed to Ailsa stifling, the street clamour deafening. She looked round the square.

A tall woman was walking away. A dark head wearing a red beret at an angle.

'Sorry,' Ailsa said. 'Go on without me.' Chasing full pelt after Mona, she ducked and wove through squaddies and black-gowned women. Stumbling into a portly Egyptian in a tarbush, she hurried down Empress Avenue, past the *Voyageurs* Hotel and the *Bon Goût* restaurant, where the person in the red beret crossed the street with long strides. But as the woman twisted her head to check the traffic, Ailsa realised it wasn't Mona. Nothing like.

Pace slackening, she stopped, awash with sweat. Men in *gallabiyyas* flowed in all directions and a stately, whiskered official in an elegant suit carrying a fly whisk was forced to step out of her path, flashing the bare-armed white woman a glance of intrigued rebuke. Men's faces leered. Clapped-out cars and an army Jeep rushed past; bells rang on bicycle rickshaws and a donkey bearing the deep red stripes of many beatings was dragged past her on a rope, a boy lashing its rump with a cane. Ailsa stared. She smelled the donkey's stink as it gargled and foamed at the mouth. The eyes were huge and melting, but sticky with pus and beset by flies. Ailsa stood near enough to hear its harsh breathing as if its lungs were full of death.

And then came the boy.

'Death to the British!' the youth shouted. Burly military policemen bore down on him.

'Evacuation with Blood!' He bawled this slogan in

136

English straight into Ailsa's face. For a shocked moment, she thought of menstrual blood. His mouth seemed to come at her; she smelt garlic breath; saw milk-white teeth, the pink interior of an open mouth. The whole face seemed to rear at her, a colt stampeded (for he was young, in his teens). She saw the whites of his eyes. And then he was taken. One towering military policeman at either side lifted the lad sheer off his feet. At once he went limp in their hands, still close to Ailsa on the surging pavement, where a new pandemonium had ensued, one he took no part in. She saw that his eyes were beautiful. Dark brown pools of sudden serenity, with long, curling lashes. His lips moved silently, as if praying, and this quiet at the eye of the storm seemed to go on for an age, which in reality could only have been the seconds it took for Ailsa to step back.

When the policeman's fist slammed into the young man's stomach, he bent double and cried, *Allahu Akbar!* God is great!

Scattering in all directions, passers-by cried, *Allahu Akbar!*

Ailsa's hands flew to her own stomach, in sympathy. She'd never seen, never imagined such violence. When one is struck, we all are. No man is an island, entire of itself. She whimpered out a cry like a cat's mew.

'Are you hurt, Madam?' Another khaki man held her gently by the top of one arm. The boy gushed blood from nose and mouth. They were searching him, shoving their hands between his legs, lifting his *gallabiyya*. The boy's blood spattered Ailsa's blouse. Two front teeth hung from his lips on strings of bloody mucus. They'd beat him to a pulp in jail, she knew.

We'd beat him rather.

Both her hands reached out to the young man, as to a child. But he shrank back in a way he'd not done from the military policemen. To be touched by a woman. A foreign female without modesty, an infidel. Pollution. Taint. Infection. Defiling his perfect martyr's moment and blocking the path to heaven. The knowledge flashed through Ailsa in a second that there was no sign she as a woman could offer that she abhorred these injustices, this occupation. For to them she was of no more worth than an army's *impedimenta*. Chattel. Breeding stock.

Brakes squealing, more Jeeps arrived, and an army truck. Rifles sprang up everywhere. The young man was lugged away and tossed into a truck, from which another boy in white was gazing out, eyes wide with terror. She glimpsed her boy for a fraction of a moment, before they slammed the doors.

'Did the bastard molest you?' asked the tender policeman.

'Not at all.'

'Thank goodness.'

'He's just a child. He wasn't armed, was he? What was he supposed to have done?'

The word terrorism was spoken. But anti-British slogans constituted the extent of the schoolboy's trespass apparently. That was our justice and democracy, Ailsa saw. A bitter taste flooded her mouth. We are thugs. We take our thuggery all round the world, calling it civilisation. But it hurt her to think this. She did not want to think it. We were the civilisers, the educators. Recoiling, Ailsa said she was perfectly all right now; she would walk back alone. When she was ready. Not before. Thanks very much. The policeman wouldn't take no for an answer. Should they alert her husband? *What, to come and round me up too?* Certainly not. She would go about her business. Ailsa turned on her heel, head high. But shaking from head to foot. As she turned, a man with a moustache, bowing his head, introduced himself as proprietor of a nearby pavement café: he had seen what had happened. Would *Madame* care to step inside and rest, take a little refreshment, as his guest?

He was Greek, all crinkly smiles, his hair raven black, oiled close to his head, his moustache a work of art, its ends rolled to points. The café in *rue Hussein*, beside the Grand Hotel, spilled out on to the pavement, where men in *gallabiyyas* rested in dusty sunlight with half empty cups and others in shirt sleeves chatted over a board game. As she stepped under the awning and walked through to the back of the shop, Ailsa was aware of the stares. An unaccompanied British woman was fresh meat displaying itself on a butcher's slab. She held her nerve and her dignity, back straight, head high.

What a relief to sit down in the most private part of the café. The air, blue with smoke, was bitterly fragrant with the scent of coffee. The proprietor brought a silver tray with an elegant silver pot, above a methylated wick-burner. Presently he poured a thick brew into a tiny painted cup and stood back, a white cloth over his arm. *Merci, monsieur! C'est très bien*. Ailsa held an intense sip in her mouth, savoured its sensuality. Cheeks burning, she settled the delicate cup back in its saucer. *Mrs Ailsa Roberts*, her compatriots sneered in her mind, *is drinking black faecal sludge from the bottom of the Sweet Water Canal*.

Thoughts of Mona confused themselves with the violence she'd just witnessed and with which she was stained. As she arranged a silk scarf over the blood-speckled bodice of her blouse, Ailsa again saw the blood gush from the protester's mouth – and the teeth he'd lost, hanging from strings. It was sad for the young man that he'd had his beautiful milk-white teeth knocked out. As had happened to the little conscript on the *Empire Glory*, when he stood up to the common-or-garden violence of his pals. The men who shot the dolphins. And Nia had seen the dolphins die. But the boy who'd cried *Allahu Akbar!* would take pride in his stigma; he'd parade it when we eventually freed him and say: *The filthy British imperialists did this to me*. He'd have lost them for Allah's sake.

Ailsa took another sip of coffee. The shaking calmed. Dangerous to wander off the beaten track. You might bump into reality. The chain reaction might go on forever. But for all her foreboding, it was in Ailsa to wander. She'd do it again. Yes. It wasn't even a matter of the will. Yes. Seeking Mona now was hardly a choice; it was a compulsion. Oh in some past life you were my sister or my wife. *Verboten*: the relationship was forbidden – which tempted you to enter a maze of dreaming and poetry. *Your hands on her hands* … A mirror-world crazy and dark and mystical, where all roads might lead to dead ends. But still you had to try.

Male eyes roved away or challenged hers. The voyeurs taking leisurely drags from Turkish cigarettes were handsome characters many of them, with green or tawny eyes, looking like rotters because of their mustachios. One Adonis lounged with an elbow round the back of his chair, head turned, leering at Ailsa with the frankest lechery.

In his rather splendid English, the hovering proprietor enquired whether *Madame* was happy with the coffee? The service? Could he offer her some of his home-made sweets or pastries?

Going to shake her head, because she truly was not hungry, Ailsa smiled, yielded and looked at the delicacies on the offered platter. *Baklava*, he said, and *Ma'amoul*. She took a tartlet and placed it on her plate.

'These are works of art,' she said. 'Too good to eat.'

'*Madame* must try them before she passes judgement. Are you feeling more yourself? May we telephone anyone to come and fetch you?'

She shook her head. Filo pastry, crisp and delicate, ambushed Ailsa's mouth with almonds, melting on the tongue. Another exploded with dates.

A tall, pale Britisher in shirtsleeves two tables away caught her eye. Officer class – though they didn't normally visit native cafés, let alone banter with Egyptian companions in what must surely be Arabic, sharing a joke.

Song poured from a loudspeaker. Ailsa sat back and listened to an Arab woman on the radio. Singing, obviously, of sadness. The café stilled. Men swivelled in their chairs towards the loudspeaker, looking up with devout, innocent expressions. It was not a music Ailsa understood. No clear shape, no sense of progression. All melismas and sobbing ornamentations, repetitions with variations of long complaints, so it seemed, expressed with luscious melancholy, in waves that rose and broke upon one another, soaked with desire, until the unseen radio audience cried out in frantic rapture and the men here in the *Café Grec*

141

joined them, addressing compliments to the loudspeaker. And again they fell into a trance, as the powerful voice took up where it had left off. The unseen Arab woman flaunted her ache. And perhaps she was saying, this is how things stand behind the veil, perpetual longing: how would you like to share it? Heartbroken, abandoned, the voice asserted the sensual desire forbidden by Muslim culture between man and woman. Which all the men in the café heard with unembarrassed ecstasy.

Within half a century, Ailsa thought, I don't suppose there'll be any more veils or head scarves in Egypt. Or in the world. Women will be full citizens, they'll enjoy equal rights just as we do, she inwardly informed the patrons of the café. They'll walk free and proud as I do, a citizen, the peer of any man. You can't stop us.

The prow of the coffee pot appeared at her elbow. No, oh no more coffee, thank you! She ought to leave now. Well, just a smidgeon. And why not? The Air Force would do its best to prevent her straying again over the line into the real Egypt, if only in the persons of Joe and Nia, her beloved policemen. She'd linger just a little while. Nia was spending the whole day at the kindergarten: plenty of time. Ailsa felt, whether rightly or wrongly, that the European proprietor protected her, veiled her, with his impressive, civilised courtesy, against the insolence of the other diners.

The Britisher, scraping his chair back, took his leave of his Egyptian companions, who lavished on him many courtesies and insistences that he stay, repaid by promises on his part to return and enjoy their company longer next time, *Insh'Allah*. You could read it all in the extravagant gestures. She couldn't help smiling. There was all the time in the world here and friendship between man and man was everything. Ailsa had seen young men walking hand in hand or with arms loosely embracing one another's shoulders. As he neared Ailsa's table, the Englishman smiled and paused. 'Enjoying the coffee? Ah, and I see you've been trying the sweets. Frightfully good, aren't they? What do you think of our Oum Koulsoum?'

'I'm sorry?'

'The singer. She's a legend here. The voice of Egypt, they call her.'

'*That* is Oum Koulsoum? Isn't she coming here soon? To the concert?'

'She'll be mobbed.' He perched on the edge of a chair, offered a cigarette. 'Oum Koulsoum is what the Arabs call *asil* – the real thing, authentic. Child of the *fellaheen* – a *bint il-riif,* daughter of the countryside – that means, true Egyptian, the deep Muslim values of Egypt, singing in the ancient, traditional music. It's very intricate, technically difficult – no printed score, it's all improvisation.'

It was a love song, he said: *Come here my darling and see what havoc your eyes have wrought.* That kind of thing. But more than that. What they were hearing was the slow burn of Egypt's wrath with the West.

'How, if it's just a love song?'

'Well, I suppose it's *Egypt* that's betrayed and scorned and enslaved.'

'I thought Egyptian women were supposed to be not seen and not heard in public.'

Oum Koulsoum was the exception that proved the rule, he said. And sat down: 'Nobby Bowen.'

Joe wouldn't like this one bit.

143

Nobby had gone native. He lived in the Greek quarter, in a flat rented from his widowed sister-in-law, Leila, who with her little girl, Heba, occupied the ground floor. He'd married a Cairene, a Coptic Christian. A renegade toff with a social conscience, a yen for adventure and a distaste for protocol, Nobby had insisted on joining the lower ranks when he was called up, learning Arabic and following in the footsteps of his hero, Lawrence of Arabia. He wanted to live amongst *real* people, in the *real* Egypt.

She couldn't help herself. She said, 'Oh, so do I.' And immediately regretted it.

He was impressed and showed it.

So men could dodge the system, Ailsa thought, as he talked. A few were prepared to go their own way, in broad daylight, living in two worlds. Men could but not women. A big talker, Nobby hardly needed to be fed with questions. He was pals with several chaps who'd gone native: two older NCOs had been here since the end of the Great War. They'd married sisters – and there was Jim, a Guardsman.

'But don't the British authorities object? Doesn't it breach their protocols?'

'To tell you the truth, they've been jolly decent and fair-minded about it. Basically there's a hands-off attitude. Of course it would be different for a woman. Unthinkable.'

'Everything's different for women. And what about your wife?'

He had six glamorous sisters-in-law. Imagine him stepping out with seven gorgeous ladies on his arm! And all but one in search of a British husband. He had to admit, it was sometimes a pleasure to escape to the RAF and his pals, and then escape back again to his family.

And the food! Out of this world! He advised her to try *Melokhia*, soup traditionally made by peasants but the Pharaohs had dined on it. The most fragrant bread in the world. Stuffed grape leaves – cold fried fish with anchovy sauce – roast pigeons with cumin and lime. Apricot pudding – *samak* and sherbert. Simple food made mouth-watering with spices. He mocked the British with their condensed milk and canned peaches. For them food could only be wholesome if it was tasteless. Not that he looked down on his countrymen.

Oh, but you do, Ailsa thought. Especially on the women. You can't help it. Your public school arrogance. His face was boyishly eager, with china-blue eyes that darted here and there to make sure he missed nothing of the life around him. 'Yes, well,' she said primly, 'we're conservative because we don't want dysentery, or worse.' He caught the mild reproof in her voice. But in her heart Ailsa was thinking she'd go to the market in Ish: sample these luscious foods.

They spoke of the boy demonstrator. The British would be chased out sooner rather than later for we'd made common cause with the Pashas who bled the *fellaheen* dry, Nobby said. Bevin counted on the Egyptian factions cancelling each other out – the Wafd government and the Islamic Egyptian brotherhood, the Commies and army officers and the pashas. But the writing was on the wall. And the reason for that – the precipitant – was Israel. Wave after wave of upheaval had hit the Arab world with the creation of Israel. It was reinforced by the Palestinian refugees flooding the Middle East. They made the injustice impossible to ignore. Nobby had a friend in Ish, a remarkable woman, who'd made it her business to find jobs and digs for them. These exiles had nothing. They'd been driven out of Haifa and Jaffa and from hundreds of villages liquidated by the Israeli army. Their families had been murdered or dispersed. The refugees spoke to their brother Arabs without need of words. At the same time, the British were keeping bloodsuckers in feudal power in Egypt – those same leeches who'd profiteered from the war against Israel and ensured that the army had useless out-of-date weapons. The treaty Britain had forced on Egypt would be torn up. If not this year, next.

Ailsa told him what Nia called the Treaty Road: the Cheaty Road. He laughed aloud.

'Well well,' he said, 'it's good to meet a free spirit, Mrs Roberts. I hope we meet again. *Bukra fil mish-mish*. Have you met that phrase? *Mish-mish* means apricot. Or apricot-tree. *When the apricot comes into flower*. Which it never does, of course. So: tomorrow never comes. A relaxed attitude to time is taken here. Europeans need to adjust. But I'd best be on my way even so.'

Ailsa let Nobby escort her to the French Square, where he met his sister-in-law and her daughter, about the same age as Nia. No time to speak to them. No time to ask Nobby, *Do you know Mona Jacobs?* Ailsa caught the next bus back to El-Marah by the skin of her teeth.

Irene came haring out of her house. There'd been an incident, she said, taking Ailsa's arm. They'd been so worried. Had Ailsa been caught up in it?

She shook her head; smiled.

Irene yelped: 'What's that blood on your blouse? Have you hurt yourself?'

'No, I'm fine. Just a tiny graze on my finger but it kind-of got everywhere. Would you mind picking up Nia, Irene, when you fetch Christopher from kindergarten? I need to … wash my blouse. And would you mind perhaps not mentioning to Joe that I went off by myself? He'd only worry, quite needlessly.'

Irene smelt a rat, of course she did. Luckily Chalkie had gone off to the camp as soon as he'd put Irene and Hedwig on the bus, so he'd have no idea how long Ailsa had been absent without leave. Irene knew far more than she let on and one felt her disapproval though her face maintained its politely neutral expression. Disapproval, or was it fearfulness? Irene had never misbehaved in her life, not out of integrity, Ailsa thought, for the woman was an awful coward, but from fear of consequences. But she surprised Ailsa by saying, just before she went off with Tim in his pushchair, to fetch the other children, 'Did you catch up with the lady? Was it the person you thought?'

There was some itch in Irene that made her curious to know about deviancy. A gossipy streak that gave her insight.

'It wasn't Mrs Jacobs, was it?' she said. 'No, I thought not.'

The first thing Ailsa did when she escaped was to pull off the blouse. The boy's blood had dried brown. The armpits were drenched in sweat. Ailsa stood in her petticoat and washed the garment out, rubbing and rinsing till the stains didn't show. She hung it on the line, where in the furnace heat of mid-afternoon it would dry in ten minutes. All the while she cudgeled her brain for ways to get to the concert either with or without Joe's knowledge and permission. Why not just come out with it straight;

147

take him along? Tell him the Websters were going: make it a foursome? Joe had a passionate reverence for classical music. She could explain that it was for the music that she was going, not for the musician. I'll see you, Mona, she said aloud, and that's that.

9

Nia sat beneath a sunshade in the lido, a glass covered area with tables and chairs on bare wooden decking at the top of the ship. A combo played old-time melodies on a raised area – a silver-haired Perry Como look-alike slackening the passion in songs that had always struck Nia as scintillating: 'Under my Skin', 'Making Whoopee'. Poppy, with a tranquil, dreamy expression, swam round a small pool sunk in the deck. A kitschy green statue of a mournful nymph drooped over the water.

Poppy looked up: 'What time is she coming? Should I be getting out?'

'Oh, not for ages. Go on basking.'

The phone call had come late yesterday evening, just as Nia was getting ready for bed. The *Terra Incognita* had berthed for two days at Sharm al Sheikh, where Poppy and Nia sunbathed on the private beach of a luxury hotel, taking countless dips in the warm water of the Red Sea. Most of the recliners were vacant, the war in Iraq having emptied hotels of tourists and hoteliers' pockets of profit. Monumental hotel blocks stood empty, their dark windows facing the turquoise water. Impoverished staff mobbed the few guests, competing to offer service likely to attract *baksheesh*. Sharm, which would be empty of tourists for as long as convulsions lasted, felt like the end of the world. Armed soldiers patrolled the beach perimeters, where barbed wire had been laid to protect the bathers.

By and by, despite the apocalyptic desolation of the place, Nia had allowed herself to lie back, drowse and dream. All too soon they were rounded up and bussed back to the *Terra Incognita*. Nia had promised herself another such soporific day tomorrow and perhaps a cruise in one of the glass-bottomed boats that took you to view the exotic fish and corals.

After supper, she'd stretched out on her bunk. Lassitude from the heat and relaxation had been broken by the phone call. An elderly, grating voice over a poor line. Mona Serafin-Jacobs here. How are you? (No pause for an answer.) Let's keep this short. No point in waiting around to join you in Alex when I can board at Sharm. All arranged. Expect me tomorrow latish afternoon. Suit you?

It had to be all right, didn't it? The peremptoriness of Stalking Mona's manner had put Nia's back up at once. No time had been granted for response, for the caller hung up abruptly, leaving Nia silenced, ears ringing, receiver in hand. Little chance of sleep after that.

By morning she'd all but blanked the whole thing. Nia was good at that: sand sifted down over memory and threat, while she affected the neutral public persona Poppy called her po-face and didn't like one little bit. The carapace, which had stood her in good stead in all sorts of painful situations, was the legacy of her mother. Not the Ailsa of the diaries, whose skin was scarily thin and whose heart lay nakedly open, but the older woman who'd taken unspecified deadly blows and been forced to build a fortress on the instability of her losses, sinking her soul down into herself.

Passengers came and went with coffee and tea. Nia vanished into her book.

She'd missed the arrival of a woman in sunglasses under the sunshade at a neighbouring table. *Is this you?* Nia's heart beat hard.

But no, too young surely even for a vigorous old age. The stranger's build was monumental, her face craggy and striking; her cropped dark hair (dyed, surely) was oiled close to her head. She wore three-quarter trousers and an embroidered and beaded tunic, tawny coloured. Pushing her sunglasses up on to her head, she took a sip of coffee, looking over the cup to where Poppy lay becalmed in the water. Her eyelashes were thick and curly, with kohl round her eyes, strong eyebrows pencilled in. And yes, dashing and distinguished if frail (for she walked with the aid of the stick Nia saw resting against her chair), here was their guest, Mona Serafin-Jacobs.

Mona's eyes in the light filtering through the sun roof were just as Ailsa had described them and as one saw on her record sleeves: deep liquid brown, troubling. Nia stared, then swivelled her head away, but looked back again. It was up to the visitor to say the first word. Nia felt paralysed.

Going to take another sip of coffee, the stranger caught Nia observing her. For a long moment they held one another's eyes without smiling. Mona was the first to rise. She advanced without the aid of her stick, holding out her hand to take Nia's in a firm grip. Nia caught a waft of expensive perfume.

'I knew you at once,' said Mona, choking on the words. 'Believe it or not. How are you, Nia?'

Nervous agitation gripped and shook Nia; she was a quailing child. She summoned hypocritical pleasantries, polite formulae. So glad to meet you after all this time. How are you? Is your cabin comfortable?

'Yes, yes, fine, it's fine.'

Was the woman going to cry?

Poppy's head appeared over the parapet of the pool. Beaming. 'Mona!' she cried. 'Hey, it's Mona, isn't it?'

Dark hair plastered down her head and back, Poppy scrambled out and rushed to their visitor, stopping just short.

'I won't hug you,' she said. 'Unless you want to be drenched.' So much more naturally than Nia, Poppy reached across and kissed Mona with her cold mouth on both cheeks. And watching Poppy chattering away, wrapping a towel around herself, Nia felt as if she were observing her own self – herself as she ought to be. She was conscious of her own profound reserve.

They would go into the pool! cried Mona. Now! What about it? Why not? They could all be wet together! And really the sun was so roasting! What was it Milton called clothes? *These troublesome disguises which we wear!*

Mona began to peel off down to her dark underwear.

And this too was just as it ought to be. One should live without stiffness and self-consciousness. But Nia's face

152

flamed with embarrassment as she followed suit. And this stripper-off of wrappings was Mam's bosom friend? It was unimaginable.

But how much easier it was bobbing about together in the cool lassitude of salty green water. Poppy was telling Mona about Aqaba – how it had been a ghost town, no visitors at the hotels; echoing space between the bare red hills and the premonition they'd had there of catastrophe, at the borders of Jordan, Israel and Saudi Arabia. Men with guns.

Mona lay on her back and basked, dark hair raying around her head. '*Plus ça change,*' she said. And now the West had brought another wave of *Shock and Awe*, not just to Iraq, but to the Middle East and the world as a whole.

'It's the Suez crisis all over again,' Nia said. 'But on an incomparably vaster scale – apocalyptic. It's as if we can't learn.'

'You surely don't remember Suez?'

'I remember it clearly. It politicised me. My Welsh grandparents sitting more or less on top of the radio, ears glued to the Nine O'clock News. Nasser nationalises the Canal. Eden plots with France and Israel. Our glorious troops sent in murdering and bombing. Plot detected. We all run home with our tails between our legs when the Americans tell us to. Suez was probably the first time I realised our leaders were asses.'

'But you can only have been about ten.'

'Age of reason. It's all downhill from there.'

Mona laughed. A sense of what the two of them had in common slackened the tension. They spoke of Clem Attlee, the postwar Labour Prime Minister, and how, if he'd had his way, Britain would have pulled out of its colonies before we could make further mischief.

'Might have beens,' Nia sighed. 'Counterfactuals. Silly game really.'

It occurred to her that, if the Brits had packed up their guns and gone home after the war, she and Topher might still have their fathers. And Mona might have her husband. What had happened to the Wing Commander of the diaries, the lovable *Habibi* who'd so upset Joe Roberts by his friendliness with his wife – the anti-Zionist Jew who'd married a Palestinian refugee? The desire not to know had been nearly as sharp as the yen to know. Whenever Nia opened the diaries she'd reread what she already knew, unable to bring herself to read on. Her mother was young again, complex, radicalised and reckless – and her father, well, Joe was no saint but she felt a sweetness in him. He'd loved Ailsa, he'd loved Nia. But had Joe loved her as dearly as Archie did? She doubted it. If Attlee had had his way, Joe and Chalkie and Ben Jacobs would have come safely home. There'd have been no stepfather. Archie would be nothing but a distant second cousin – unbearable thought. Of course you wouldn't know what you'd missed.

And Chalkie, who seemed a lovely guy, might have saved the world from the prolixities of Topher's poetry.

'So what else did you see in Jordan?' Mona asked Poppy. They floated on their backs, bodies swirling with green water, rippling with sunlight.

'Oh, the ruins of the original Aqaba. The Citadel where the British ships lobbed cannon balls at the Turks, wasn't it, in the First World War and jolly old Lawrence of Arabia stormed down from the mountains.'

'And an aquarium,' said Nia. 'We were the fish – or rather Poppy was. She was mobbed by guys with their eyes on stalks.'

'Well, if you will look like Nefertiti, what can you expect?'

'That's a rather nice compliment,' said Poppy. 'I'll buy you a drink for that.'

'I speak as I find, my dear, as you will no doubt discover.'

It was a rather quenching remark, though delivered in jest. Nia could feel the power in Mona to annihilate you if she chose – or if the cause she espoused, or the agenda she favoured, seemed to require this.

Yet Mona, when they'd hauled themselves out and dressed, was clearly overwhelmed with fatigue. She sat quietly with tea and a scone under the turquoise shade, sipping and nibbling, and failed to look particularly formidable. When from time to time their eyes caught and held, for no more than a moment, Nia was conscious of a search going on that cost their guest dear. Mona sat as if collapsed into herself, looking like an old lady. No different from the humming throng around her. She's searching for my mother in me, Nia thought, but she'll have her work cut out to find her. Ailsa Roberts had been a young woman in her heyday; Nia was getting on in years. And Mam had been astoundingly beautiful, with that heart-shaped face, high cheek bones and green-blue eyes. The nearest Nia had ever got to that was an expressive and eccentric feyness that had made people stare. Years ago.

She in her turn searched out Ailsa in Mona. The two survivors had come through life looking for the one elusive love. And if Ailsa did not somehow endure within both these women, she was nowhere.

Poppy seemed to see it all, without the need of words. She kept the two older women balanced with her naturalness and warmth, until she judged the time right to leave them in one another's company. If it was OK, she said, she'd go and chill out in the jacuzzi. She bent and kissed each on the cheek. Taking Poppy's hand, Mona looked into her face with a beautifully soft expression.

'I've got all your CDs,' Nia told Mona. 'Every single one. I inherited Mam's collection of your records, of course. And everything since. And there's a DVD of a concert in Ismailia with Oum Koulsoum. That was amazing.'

The concert had been filmed by the Egyptian television service, focusing on the legendary singer, with Mona Jacobs on the margins. People had fainted with emotion at that concert – and then the fight or scuffle had broken out later. None of this was explicitly shown on the black and white DVD. Nia had watched again before coming on the voyage, frame by frame, pausing and staring, after learning of Ailsa's presence in the audience. The cameras panned the packed auditorium during the intervals when the Egyptian men got to their feet to applaud their heroine, weeping, calling out her name, reaching out their hands. The young Mona stood tall and willowy in a simple, closely fitting black gown with pearls at her neck. A most poignant look on her face as she rose from the piano stool and held out her hand to the Egyptian singer. A shyness no longer remotely apparent. Pianist and singer had come forward and bowed together, over and over, while the Egyptian half of the crowd went wild, to the buttoned-up consternation of the British auditors. In one frame, you could see tears gleaming on both women's eyes. The concert had been in aid of the Palestinians, the refugees of *al-Naqba*, the Catastrophe of 1948, some of whom were in the audience.

The pianist's publicity photo on Mona's record sleeves had changed over the decades, as hairstyles and outfits altered, until with the early 1980s there'd been no portrait of the artist, just a frozen Alp or a view of the Sahara. Nia had listened intently to Mona's interpretations of Beethoven's late sonatas, hailed by critics as powerful, with 'colossal intellectual grasp' but a suspect reckless virtuosity. A subtext occasionally appeared to the effect that Mona Serafin-Jacobs was too formidable for a woman. The pianist was on record as distrusting what she derided as mere beauty. The Dvorak piano quintet she had condemned as 'too beautiful and sensual for me', as if such music were a temptation to an aesthetic of sybaritic surrender. All art was political. Nia herself had grasped that easily and early. She could share the underlying puritanism of a Palestinian exile who'd seen too much too young, ever to forsake the political forum. And yet here they were on the *Terra Incognita*, in the lap of postcolonial luxury.

Nia had also inherited her mother's collection of Julie Brandt-Simon's records. Two women had laid their hands over Mona's musical life, passing on power and inspiration. She blurted, 'My mother was in your music, Mona, wasn't she?'

It was the presence of the longing the Welsh call *hiraeth*. A sense that someone vital has just been present, but now is absent. Someone *Mam-gu* would have called *werth y byd*. Nia had heard this quite clearly as she tracked the pianist through her recordings. The search for a woman worth the world.

'Your mother was remarkable. Once known, never forgotten. She restored my music, Nia. Ailsa was a great person, a great human being. You should be so proud to be her daughter.'

How could that electrifying spirit have dwindled into mere Mam? The increasingly dowdy and correct bourgeois *Hausfrau*, as Nia had once called her to her face – and Ailsa, turning, had lost her footing, as if slapped. She'd steadied herself with one hand on the sideboard; then she'd realigned the ornaments and vases and left the room without reprisal. Nia's unsparing tirades had demanded: come out and face me, show yourself, show you care about me. Ailsa would rarely riposte, never raise her voice. Infuriating, guilt-inducing.

'Your mother was a pearl,' said Mona. 'That's all we can say. A pearl.'

'Yes.'

'When I'd lost my confidence, she gave it back to me. I mean, in my music. But just tell me this, Nia, if you don't mind. You have done so well in your life and professionally of course you've reached the top of the academic tree. But was your childhood a happy one? Your stepfather – was he kind to you?'

That was easy. 'He's always been good to me, Mona. More than good. I was an absolute pest and a brat, but Dad persevered and always saw that I had everything I needed. He's still alive, you know. I'm very close to Dad – but not in a wordy sort of way. He just is. Like, you know, a landscape.'

'I cannot tell you how glad I am – relieved – to hear it.' Mona sat back in her chair and closed her eyes, a burden lifted.

'Archie had been Mam's childhood sweetheart, you know.'

Mona's eyes opened wide. Evidently Ailsa had not told her friend everything. 'That I ... well, didn't know. Well. She never exactly said. I knew they were very close. And your mother – was she happy?'

Happy was hardly the word. Ailsa had appeared content with her husband, devoted to him. Eternally grateful to him, watchful over him. Archie wasn't one for singing and dancing. Nia remembered Ailsa patiently explaining the jokes in Christmas crackers, the table heaving with the children's laughter at their dad's perplexity. And he was the best-ironed husband in Shropshire, Nia used to say. Even his farm clothes were in a state of outrageous laundering perfection. Nowadays he just slouched around in baggy old cords, content to be a comfortable old ragbag, as he said. Nothing of Archie's ever seemed to wear out, at least according to him.

'He was a good husband to her in every way,' Nia said. 'She liked the farm – and they had a market garden which she more or less took over. Green fingers she had.'

'I didn't know that. How lovely. Thank you for telling me.' Mona was like a child being told some marvellous story. Sucking on the details like sweets. At the same time the lines of her face folded in fresh sorrow.

'Dad doesn't have much sense of humour.'

'Ah, and Ailsa did, of course.'

'Did she?'

'Oh, she was a serious person, thoughtful and enquiring, but she could also be such a giggler, once she got going, couldn't she?'

'I never saw that side of her. I can't honestly pretend we really got on. Sorry. We quarrelled a hell of a lot. Not at the end, when Poppy was born. But earlier. Well, when I say quarrelled, it was totally one-sided. I yelled; she just looked daggers.'

'Well, of course. You were mother and daughter. What did you quarrel about?'

'Politics, miniskirts, women's rights, the lot. Her views were a bit fossilised, even to the point of claiming that she didn't have political opinions. She left those to the menfolk. See what I mean? Politically incorrect to the n'th degree. She had this godawful friend, Irene, who came to live near us. Ghastly woman. I think they egged one another on. They'd always be in and out of one another's houses and they'd complain over their knitting about their children going to the dogs.'

'Ah, poor Irene White!'

'I don't know about *poor*. She was a complete tartar. She died only last month, in fact.'

'Her son was named Christopher.'

'Yes. Tôpher White the poet. He spells it with a circumflex to show he's Celtic. He isn't Celtic, as far as I know. Poor guy, he never had a chance with a mother like Irene. And this portrait of his saintly father smirking down on him from over the fireplace. Topher turned out a bit of a sociopath. Still, at least he has his very weird poetry. I get on with Topher. But Irene's other boy, Tim, was the favourite: he could do no wrong. Except that he grew up a complete creep and he'd steal from Irene's handbag to pay for the drug of choice.'

'Irene's husband was your Daddy's closest friend.

They'd fought in the Western Desert together – and then they were your next door neighbours in El-Marah. Good-hearted, decent people. I don't know how much you know, my dear, about those times? I hope you could forgive your mother. Dear, lovely Ailsa – she was so deeply hurt.'

Deeply hurt. Suddenly Nia couldn't go on.

'No more, Mona. Don't.' She stumbled to her feet, clattering the crockery and toppling the chair back so that she had to pick it up, rummaging for the clothes and bag she'd hung on it.

Dear, lovely Ailsa. Deeply hurt. Something terrible and eerie was in the offing – knowledge Nia had been holding off for many years. It would not have been so bad if Mam were still alive. The terrible, smiting blow would have come as a relief. Nia could have made amends. She could have gone to Mam and said, *I get it now. I do understand, oh please let me love you and try to love me back. Tell me your side of things. I'm with you every step of the way.* But there was no way back.

'It's all right, Nia. It's all right. Let's talk again when you feel up to it. Or never. We don't need to talk. I'm so sorry. I'm just very pleased to see you. I got ahead of myself. Just seeing you is so thrilling.'

'Later, Mona. Not yet.'

Her tears streamed down. It was the way the old woman had said *your Daddy*. The echoes rang round the emptying lido, where the band was packing up and the guests were removing themselves in twos and threes to shower and change for dinner. Mona had Nia in her arms and was rocking her, going *shush, shush*. Holding, rocking Nia, not now, of course, no. But at some time far in the past when

161

the unthinkable thing had happened.

'But don't go away, Mona,' she pleaded, blowing her nose, fiddling in her pocket for her cabin key. She was going nowhere, Mona said, unless ordered off the *Terra Incognita* by Nia. They both grinned. And after all, there was so much to be experienced of this almost colonial way of life they had on the ship. Mona was fascinated: it brought back the gracious living of the Shepheards Hotel and the dear old Mena House at Giza. And apart from all that, she'd been welcomed aboard by the Captain as a VIP and agreed to give an hour's recital in, apparently, the Admiral Nelson Room, whereupon the cost of her journey had been waived.

'You missed Remembrance Day,' said Nia. They got into a conversational stride again. She told Mona of the veteran with the black beret and blazer displaying his row of medals, videoing the occasion. The junior officer dipping the flag, the padre, the vanishing pieties of her parents' generation, remembered deeds and places that soon would all be gone. The ballroom dancing and the bridge. The deck quoits and the indoor golf championships. The final feast swallowed in the dark.

*

The pianist raised her hands slowly from the keys; held them suspended, head bent. Piano and pianist separated into two. There was silence. Her hands returned to her lap, head still bent, in a posture that quenched the glow of her pearls in the darkness of her hair and her black high-necked evening dress, fashioned like an Arab *gallabiyya*. The silence in the auditorium lengthened out like a long-held breath. Not a cough or a rustle. From the passionate intensities of its centre, the subtle minor key had led the sonata to the verge of the grave, the music laying down its life to eternity. There was no more to say. Fertile land gave way to the desert.

Silence, stillness.

Then the storm of applause. The Egyptian orchestra raised its hands to the pianist, clapped and cheered. Mona got to her feet, her balance unsteady for a moment, looking oddly shy and unnerved. Standing by the piano under the spotlights, she bowed. The audience rose. More, more. But Mona would give no more. This was all she had to say. It was her first public performance since her hands had got their music back. Ailsa, sitting three rows back from the stage, understood that Mona could not supply an encore. She tried not to look at Mona's husband and Alex at the end of the front row, clapping wildly, but saw them anyway out of the corner of her eye. She breathed shallow, carried by Beethoven's music into the aching recognition of another and higher world altogether, for which she was homesick. A perspective from which one saw the larger picture, the earth from the air, where the banal doings of everyday were inconsequential. It was a feeling Ailsa had experienced on the one occasion she'd flown; when she walked the Long Mynd massif, or saw the stars from the desert. She yearned to belong in this world of Mona's. For Mona to take her there, fly with her high above it all, the stupidity, the trivia. Her heart twisted, to think she'd been the one to restore Mona's power. *I'm good for something then*. And yet at the same time her husband's hand stole across and cherishingly brushed her bare arm, so that the hairs stood

163

up: the music also had to do with the love-without-end she shared with Joe.

Hedwig, sitting next to her, wept without restraint, Norman concernedly clasping his wife's hand in both of his, fearful perhaps for the baby, not understanding that these were good tears, art-tears. Ailsa glanced at Joe. His face looked, she thought, stricken, as if he'd seen something at once terrible and wonderful.

Whatever was he thinking and feeling?

The audience rose to its feet. Mona held out her arms for a moment, with a sort of shrug; then returned to her place at the piano. Ah, she is going to give us an encore, the audience concluded. Murmuring and exclaiming, they settled down. They were mistaken. It was now time for the Egyptian singer. Closing the lid of the instrument, the pianist yielded place. She was to remain on-stage through the virtuoso's performance.

The Egyptian members of the audience, out of respect to the European custom of deferential silence to musicians, had applauded decorously. But for them, as Hedwig was now explaining to Joe, murmuring across Ailsa, silence implied dislike or lack of interest. Egyptian music was full of improvisation, it was participatory, she told him: it was something shared between the musician and the listeners – like love, she said. Their *Kultur* is so very different. They think we are cold eggs, Hedwig explained, no, cold *fish*. She had to raise her voice as the Arab audience took over the auditorium, calling out with passionate abandon for their singer to come on stage. Many of them were up on their feet.

Ailsa stole a glance at Mona, gazing now towards the

wings, along with the Arab orchestra, waving their violins and tabors, their drums and lutes. They all smiled and beckoned, in sign to the audience that the beloved was at hand. Not showing herself. Immanent.

Joe's head swivelled and he glowered across at the noise-makers. *Pipe down, you wogs, for Pete's sake*, his look said. At this moment Mona's eyes locked with Ailsa's. Fingers at her lips, she blew Ailsa a kiss.

'Joe, it's all right,' she whispered to her husband. 'It's not rudeness. It's their own kind of courtesy.'

'If you say so.'

Expectation mounted; soared. The auditorium was a scene of uproar. Nothing happened on stage except that the orchestra beckoned the unseen singer with yet more flamboyant gestures. Hedwig, excited, grabbed Ailsa's hand and squeezed. Her face looked exalted. Ailsa, for an unpleasant moment, had a vision of blonde Hedwig at some dreadful rally or other, in a crowd high on mass emotion. And always there came this query about Hedwig – but where it came from, from reason or prejudice, Ailsa did not know, for after all Hedwig was ready to embrace another culture, the antithesis of her own. She squeezed Hedwig's hand in return.

Embarrassed at the antics of their Egyptian counterparts, the Britons smiled and raised their eyebrows, tucking in their chins, nudged one another or pretended to ignore the whole thing.

'All that's part of the performance,' Ailsa said to Joe, her hair soft on his cheek.

'What, like a pantomime?'

'Well. Oh – well, perhaps. In a way.'

She heard what his tense posture said. Why can't the wogs control themselves in a public place? They were making this exhibition of themselves just to nark us. She wished she hadn't brought Joe. Why did he have to make these faces? But it had been preferable to invite him. Ailsa had kept quiet about the incident of the arrest in Ish and the *Café Grec* and Irene hadn't said a word. Ailsa preferred to be straightforward. Was it actually true that any relationship with Mona must be carried on behind Joe's back? Now that he'd heard her play and knew how serious – noble – Mona's music was, perhaps he'd turn a blind eye to their meeting up occasionally, not too often and discreetly. What could possibly be wrong with such a friendship?

The artist walked on to the stage, wearing a simple white dress, black hair parted in the middle and drawn back into a chignon, jewels hanging from ears and neck. Oum Koulsoum was entering her middle years, inclining to plumpness, her features dramatically dark. She carried a decorative handkerchief. As they greeted one another, Mona looked slight and girlish, though she was the taller by six inches.

It began. The desert gave way to fertile land.

And this is ecstasy, Ailsa thought. She knew now what had roused the faces of the men in the *Café Grec* into rapture, dreaming awake as they listened to the wireless. The living voice was flagrant in its abandonment; it was nakedly powerful. The voice of Egypt, as Nobby Bowen had said. Ailsa grasped the principle now: the words of the poem to be sung were sacrosanct. The words drove the music. But the music was endlessly virtuosic and where they went together depended on the singer's improvisations

166

in response to the promptings of her audience, in mutual obedience to subtle and ancient rules of which Ailsa knew nothing. Over and over Oum Koulsoum repeated some phrase, evoking its meaning in variation, melisma, voice-breaking. She flirted her handkerchief at the audience, made love to it with long-lashed eyes. Ailsa lost all sense of time. There was no awareness of beginning, middle and end. She forgot to worry what Joe was thinking, or Mona. After each ascending phrase, the audience replied, urging the singer to repeat, shouting compliments.

Joe fidgeted, crossing and recrossing his legs. He sighed. Ailsa glanced at her watch. An hour and a quarter had passed.

'And now Ahmad Shawqi's *Salu Qalbi*.'

Sudden silence. Which became a mounting roar as Oum Koulsoum moved into the song's climax.

Later Ailsa would be told that the phrases that lit the touch paper were 'Demands are not met by wishing; the world can only be taken by struggle.' A revolutionary message. The Palestinian Arabs had been slaughtered and driven out by the Zionists; Islam violated; Allah ridiculed. Egypt had been trampled. By its own corrupt rulers. By the hated British occupation. By Israel. Egypt would rise. Ailsa felt she had understood this in the moment of hearing the uncomprehended Arabic. Shared the impulse to be carried up on the music's religious passion and erotic, revolutionary abandonment.

The European audience shuffled from its seats, stiff and yawning, but in disagreement on the merits of the evening.

'Bit of a racket.'

'*Mais sa voix, c'est si belle.*'

167

'Thought it was never going to end, didn't you?'

'Meeting of East and West.'

'The old girl's got a bit of meat on her.'

'Herrliche Musik, oder? Aber was bedeutete ...?'

'Thank God that's over, I thought I'd pass out. The hysteria. The smell.'

Europeans and Egyptians filed out through two separate doors but were forced to mingle in the hall, under brilliant chandeliers. They hit a bottleneck at the exit, where a group of young men chanted, *Salu Qalbi, Salu Qalbi!*

The Europeans pushed forwards. The Egyptians withstood them. Minor officials, excitable and voluble, tried to usher individuals into gaps that weren't there or to steer them back against the press into the auditorium. As the mass of people swayed to and fro in this bedlam, a lady in a blue silk evening gown stumbled and fell. Screams: someone's being trampled underfoot!

A flash photograph was taken.

Someone was laying into the Egyptians with his fists.

'Back! Back!'

Ailsa called to the people behind her, still struggling to leave the auditorium, to give way, move back for pity's sake. They took no notice. Ailsa put her arms round the pregnant Hedwig to shield her from the crush.

Orders were barked by a voice of authority – some Major in civvies, to judge by the handlebar moustache. The crowd began to shuffle back into the hall, relieving the crush. Joe and Norman Webster pressed forward to a scrum of Britons and Egyptians blocking the entrance. Wrenching the men apart, they cleared a space round the fallen woman: *Dusty, whoa! Not worth it, boy.* Ailsa had heard tales of Joe's hot-tempered pal, Dusty Miller, a pigeon-chested pugilist with a brick-red face and the light of God in his eyes.

'My specs! I've lost my specs!'

Ailsa heard the wail. Bruised and shocked, her gown torn at the bodice, the lady in blue stared round with the naked eyes of the myopic. Joe's head disappeared from Ailsa's view. He groped round for the spectacles; fished them up wrecked.

The panicked woman struggled to fit on her mangled spectacles – one lens missing, the bridge cracked. Her husband appeared. Order was restored. Military Police materialised and marched the demonstrators away. Balked of battle, Dusty disappeared into the crowd.

'You did well there, Joe,' Ailsa said. Her husband had kept the peace. He'd restrained the wog-haters, showing the decency that in the end was the core of his character.

Norman, beside himself about the fright his wife had suffered, wanted her to see a doctor. She was not so weak as to faint in such a *trivial* situation, Hedwig said. This is nothing, nothing. A small scuffle. But, yes, she would sit down for a moment.

The Wing Commander crouched beside Hedwig, taking her pulse, asking how she felt, speaking reassuring words to her and her husband. *Habibi*'s big, plain face, not glimpsed by Ailsa for months, seemed ridiculously familiar. He smiled and greeted her affectionately. She resisted the impulse to hug him hallo, wanting to say something about how wonderful Mona had been tonight, share some of the magic with him before it drained away.

But when she saw the look on Joe's face, Ailsa said nothing of the sort. Taking her husband's arm, she leaned heavily on him, pretending to feel faint. 'I've come over a bit funny,' she said. 'Oh gosh, I'm queasy. Could you take me home now, Joe? I need to go home.'

Soldiers from Moascar had cleared the hundreds who'd assembled to greet and celebrate their adored singer. Ailsa, supported by Joe, walked through an Ismailia emptied of native inhabitants by summary curfew, its mansions lit into creamy glamour by a three-quarters moon. She was fine now, she assured him. Honestly, fine. Just needed a breath of air. The two of them walked dreamily, arms round one another's waists, heads tilted inwards. The silence was broken only by the muezzin's call to prayer.

10

Something in Nia's yard had been forgotten. She rested back on her heels and looked round. What could it be and where? Sand drifted into the yard from outside, compromising her castles. Whenever Nia turned her back, the desert reached out its hands. It enlarged her monuments but blurred their outlines and finally all her empires slid away into its softness.

Good! Because you could begin all over again.

Nia forgot to look round for traces of whatever it was she'd forgotten. She couldn't keep her eye on everything.

Ali, the bony boy who collected bottles and cans, stopped outside the garden with his handcart. He waved to Nia and pointed to her door: would she get her mother? Ali had lost one eye and yet he was one of the most beautiful children Mami had ever seen, so she said. The remaining eye was green, like Nia's but with thick, curly lashes. The dead eye was nearly closed. His hair was a mass of dark curls. Ali stood at the gate, in a short, ragged night-gown. His skin was very dark, almost black. He wore no shoes.

Nia's father came out rather than her mother. 'What is it, girlie?'

'It's Ali for bottles.'

Nia knew what he would say: *'Imshi! Yallah!'* with *that* look on his face. Ali would be sent packing with no bottles, guilty of germs and dirt.

Her father paused.

'Bot-dee-lee-yay, Mr *Effendi* Taffy sir?'

Her father frowned. Bobbing back into the kitchen, he returned with two lemonade bottles and a plate of scraps left over from lunch. He bent and smiled into the boy's eyes. At once Nia, jealous of the boy, scowled. Ali took the bottles and added them to his collection: *thank you, thank you, Effendi.* He emptied the scraps into a hemp bag and signed to Nia's father to wait. Rummaging in the same bag, he brought out a piece of bread.

'*Pita.* For you, *Effendi.*'

Nia trailed her spade over to the gate and stood watching to see what her father would do now.

The boy wanted to give the man his lunch.

'No, no.'

'*I-wah.* Yes yes, *qaiis.* Take.'

Nia could smell the bread's deliciousness. It had just been baked. But she could see the germs from the flies' feet wriggling on the crust.

Her father accepted the bread. She knew he'd chuck it away once he got indoors. He'd go, *Ugh! Filth!* For a moment Joe seemed lost for words. He held the bread in one hand, slightly away from his body, and thanked the boy as politely as if he had been an English boy. Feeling in his pocket

172

amongst the jingling change, he brought out a few piastres, which he handed to the child. Ali lived in a mud house with mud furniture, so Mami had told Irene, who'd murmured, 'Poor things, they don't know any better.'

But Ali refused the money. He looked shocked; took several paces back, shaking his head. Baffled, Joe also shook his head. Nia watched her father into the house. Ali waved goodbye to Nia and pushed his cart round the corner. He was a stunted twelve- or thirteen-year-old, Mami had said.

Irene had wondered if the natives ought to be encouraged to come round the Married Quarters scrounging; wasn't it dangerous? They might take advantage of our kindness and rob us, the menfolk being on duty.

Nia returned to sifting the caramel sand for a cake. She would pour water on this delicious flour and harden it in her bucket like bricks. The sun would bake the cake. She'd cut it into slices with the bread knife, which she had hidden, and share it out equally.

Daddy cast his shadow over her, creeping up behind.

'Wotcher, Joe *bach*,' she said without turning.

'You little monkey.'

'Wotcher cock.'

'Now now. You can be clever but you mustn't be rude. How did you know it was me?'

'I just do.'

'What are you making?'

'A cake. What did you do with that bread?'

'Oh well, we couldn't eat it, could we?'

'No.'

'Make the most of your sand pit, *cariad*. We're having topsoil delivered.'

The yard would be transformed, he said. Into a garden! What did she think of that? Seeing Nia's defiant pout, he explained that he and she would rake the earth and water it. They'd plant seeds and watch wonderful green plants come up and flowers of all colours, pink and purple and white. Jacaranda. Bougainvillaea. Just us, the two of us. You and me together, isn't it? With your baby wheelbarrow.

'And, you know, there's plenty of sand,' he added. 'Out there. And most of it in my ears and nose and mouth.'

'Orifices!' said Nia.

'Nia!'

'What?'

'Where did you get that? Say it again.'

'Why?'

'Well, *cariad*.' He crouched down. 'There are some words...'

'Mami said it.'

'Ah.'

He had no answer to that. She intuited his distress.

'She meant *horrid faces*,' she reassured him.

'Anyway, I've got something for you, girlie. In the market. Couldn't resist it. Just for Nia. Do you like it?'

'Golly likes it,' Nia said, and he had to be content with that. She reserved judgement, for the inside of the fez smelt funny and you had to balance your head to keep it on.

*

The black, open-topped sports car drew up at the kerb several houses down. Again. The secret lady behind the wheel had swaddled her head in a navy blue silk scarf covered in tiny silver stars, tied round her throat. She wore dark sunglasses and bright red lipstick. Her skin was like caramel. Nia stared at the lady, who pretended not to be staring back.

'Come in and have your nap!' Daddy called from inside the house.

She dragged in, whining that she didn't want a nap. In her bedroom Nia stood on the bed and looked out through the wire netting. The lady had driven off. She'd come again. Nia knew who she was, although she was supposed to have forgotten. Her name was not supposed to be said. It was a secret between the two of them.

*

'What's that on your head?' asked Topher. 'It's red.'

'It's a fez.'

'It's got a tassel.' He fingered the silky tassel with reverence.

'I know.'

'Girls don't wear fezes.'

'They do.'

'Don't.'

'English girls do.'

In Ish the Egyptian merchants walked down the spacious boulevard of *rue Sultan Hussein* with oiled black moustaches, flicking fly-whisks, their heads topped by a fez. How dignified they looked, how tall and impressive. Daddy said they were a big fat joke. She couldn't see it.

'I want a fez,' Topher moaned.

'Give it me back, all right, if I let you borrow it?'

The cake was nearly baked. She would cut it now. But where was the knife? She had lost it. Buried it somewhere.

It was boring digging around for a knife. Nia began to disbelieve in the knife. Instead they sloped round to the shady side of the house and Topher, still wearing the fez, said he would show her his if she would show him hers.

A chipolata sausage, she thought. Well. She raised her shirt and pulled down her knickers. They examined one another.

'My botty,' she said.

'That's your botty round there.'

'No, it's all my botty. Does yours sometimes itch?'

'No.'

'Mine does. Sand in the orifice,' she confided.

They were married, according to Topher. They stared at one another. Nia did not know if he was right – but something had happened between the two of them, she wasn't sure what. For once Topher was master of the situation. He poked his head forward and puckered his mouth, shutting his eyes; pecked at her mouth with his dry little beak. He seemed pleased and satisfied. Gravely removing the fez, Topher restored it to Nia's head so that they could go in and see whether there were any cheese straws.

'You are so sweet with Ali,' her mother was saying to her father.

'Of course I am, poor dab.'

'How touching that he gave you his bread. His mother would have baked it.'

'Oh aye.'

Nia heard her mother put on her teachy voice, telling her father that the villagers would think it wrong to sell their bread; they'd think it shameful. Bread was sacred and communal. And out of hospitality they kept water on their

176

window sill, if they had a window sill, for the thirsty passer-by. And we called them greedy! Well. She bet the *pita* would have tasted delicious.

'Great Scott…'

'Keep your hair on, Joe, what there is of it! I know we couldn't have eaten it. But – Joe, have you seen the bread knife?' Mami was rummaging in a drawer.

'In the drawer?' came from the other room.

'I've looked there.'

'Well, don't flap.'

'What do you mean, don't flap? It's a sharp knife! Joe, will you come and help me look? Nia, you haven't been touching…?'

'No, Mami.'

'Have you been baking at all, Mrs Roberts?' asked Topher.

'You'll have to ask Irene if you can borrow hers,' came Joe's voice from the other room.'

'You go, Joe. No, I haven't been baking.'

'I'm busy,' called Joe, with a yawn that seemed to come from his belly.

'Oh yes – doing what?'

'Putting my feet up.'

'Well put them down, my lad, and march them in to Irene. Will you two children get out from under my feet? Out! Both of you, vamoose until I call you in.'

'I like your mince pies, Mrs Roberts,' said Topher as they left. 'They are savoury.'

Out by the sand-cake Nia fished around for the knife. Nothing. Joe went grumblingly in to Irene and didn't come out for a while. They could hear laughing from in there. He came out waving a bread knife and Ailsa said, all very well, but where is ours?

'Your daddy has shown my mummy his pork sausage,' said Topher. 'Probably.'

Nia did not reply. How could she know? Then all of a sudden Nia's back and fezzed head were peppered with ping pong balls. From the sky, a thrill of ping pong balls. Whopping hailstones slammed down all around them. They rushed to gather them, never mind the pain, in a bucket and began to suck them. Sky ice. A wonder in a world of wonders.

Irene was out like a flash.

'Chris! Come in this minute!'

And Topher was gone. Just like that. Nia placed one hail stone under each armpit and wriggled her entire body in complicated bliss and anguish as they melted.

A blade showed from the sand. Nia reached for it and could not grasp, once she had feathered it free with extreme caution, how this thread-thin line had appeared on her palm, seeping scarlet beads, a shock she greeted with a paroxysm of silence.

11

Joe lay spread-eagled, his arms and legs a star, in the shade of a wicker fence. Sabbath at Lake Timsah: everyone was on the beach. For the second week running he'd skipped chapel in the hut at Fanara provided for dissenters. Mam would not be pleased, but then Mam would not know. His face was draped with a month-old local paper she'd sent out, containing mention of a Morriston Orpheus concert at Libanus: *if only you'd been there with us*. Last night, reading the article over a few beers, it had come over Joe to sing '*Cwm Rhondda*, Bread of Heaven', which had led to 'O love that wilt not let me go'. Ailsa was left sobbing, until Nia flung her arms round her mother to comfort her, asking her father in a droll, rational way not to sing please if it upset Mami. They'd both burst out laughing and Ailsa had explained that she was not sad but moved, in her heart. But don't sing any more, if you don't mind, Nia had insisted.

That had been a strange affair at the concert in Ish, where the lady whose husband had kissed Ailsa had played so beautifully that it had been all Joe could do to restrain tears. And ever since that night he'd found himself breaking into song at the drop of a hat or whistling the tunes from *Aïda* and *La Traviata* he and Chalkie had heard at the Rome Opera House during the war.

Just a sec: the woman's husband had *not* kissed Ailsa! Joe had made that up in his own imagination. He'd have liked to though: any fool could see.

Or perhaps not, since the fellow was a queerboy with his poufter pal at his elbow.

Which should reassure Joe but somehow it didn't. And whatever the reason for his revulsion, Joe felt sick to the stomach about any association between this shambles of a British officer and his Ailsa.

Yet the Wing Co had been nothing but kindness and courtesy to Hedwig Webster. Joe spoke to himself calmly: *chwarae teg*, let Ailsa see the friend if she wants to. His wife was well-spoken and educated, unlike himself, and the equal of any toff. Ailsa was a person to be trusted, whoever else was not. The love between them held tender and true. Thinking in these terms reassured Joe and restored balance. Still, he'd mull it over again before bringing it up with her.

Removing the paper, Joe peered to check that the kiddies were safe. Chalkie was with them at the water's edge, directing an operation to empty Lake Timsah with their buckets into an irrigation system he'd helped Nia, Christopher and Timothy construct. Fine – and she was wearing her sun hat. Lovely bloke is Chalkie, Joe thought, leaning up on one elbow. Heart of gold, do anything for anyone. And they'd both benefited by Ailsa's idea about the Tiger. She'd sort it with Irene later today and set the poor girl's mind at rest. Ailsa had a head on her shoulders, that was for sure. He lay back in the Joe-shaped resting-place he'd hollowed out for himself in the hot sand.

The concert obsessed him. The piano had transported Joe to a world so intensely pure that he'd forgiven the musician for her madman of a husband. He'd perfectly understood why Ailsa should have been drawn to her. How could she not be? This lady was exceptional: he'd experienced a reverence which only grew when she rose from the piano at the end of the piece, shy, childlike, infinitely touching.

But then when the Egyptian, whom he nicknamed The Oom, had begun to sing – howl, rather, a cat on heat – Joe had found himself seething with unease, shocked. *I want, I desire*, The Oom had warbled. Good grief, you didn't need a translation. He'd twitched around in his seat, leaning one way, then the next, sighing, with a rhubarb blush. Tweaked his trousers to conceal his erection. Rasped his palm up his chin, until Ailsa's eyes signalled to him, *please* stop that fidgeting. The wogs had got to their feet and brayed at The Oom: a brothel audience. Ailsa hadn't had a clue of course, in her innocence, that the place was a bristling forest of pricks, all pointing one way.

Strait-laced? Aye, but the chapel boy was not sorry for that. He'd never joined in with his mates' blue jokes and filthy songs.

The Oom had not even been a good-looking woman, but greasy and plump, past her prime. The whole sordid act had reminded Joe of the belly-dancers in Cairo in the war, prostitutes, girls in their teens. Of the smutty postcards sold by leering vendors at Port Said showing sluts displaying

181

childishly half-developed breasts and grubby tangles of hair, smirking at the camera. Which made you sad for them in point of fact. Their flesh was cheap; little choice but to sell it. But it was in their blood, the hot lack of control.

Oh, and the bird-brained little Jerry woman yapping about *Kultur*! Solemnly explaining in her know-all way that the Orientals had a different *Kultur*, which we Occidentals must study and respect. She'd sat back with a 'now-I've-enlightened-him' nod, ringed fingers cradling her pregnant belly. The baby might so easily have been lost when the wogs stampeded, obeying the dictates of their sickening *Kultur*.

Ailsa waved from the beehive bathing huts, her face a pattern of sun-stencils through the straw of her broad-brimmed hat. He waved back. Bad thoughts ebbed. She was pleased with his behaviour to Ali and with the way he'd helped sort things out at the De Lesseps House. Good: for he was not putting it on. As individuals the Egyptians were easy to love, especially the kiddies, who had nothing but their smiles – and the gift of bread that shamed us. Joe had not intended Ali to think that he was offering to pay for the bread. How did you take such a gift from such a giver?

He could learn from Ailsa about so many things. He saw that clearly.

Just think, she'd exclaimed, we're pitching camp where the Children of Israel pitched theirs. He'd thought about it. Sunday School at Libanus came into focus with RAF El-Marah and the desert. Yesterday Ailsa had stopped in her tracks and looked out over the sand towards a stand of date palms in a circle of green. It might be a well, she said. Angels met humans at wells. In those days.

He'd looked along her eye line, for the intensity of her gaze had created the illusion that Ailsa had spied something out of the ordinary. The heat had created the usual reflective haze you'd swear was a lake in the middle distance and the mirage of a shimmering castle with towers and battlements hovering near the horizon. He'd told her then about the Wells of Moses, twenty miles or so north of Suez City. A dozen wells in one oasis, supposed to be filled with water shed from the rock Moses struck with his staff.

'Oh Joe, I should so love to see them.'

He determined that she should see the wells, even if they turned out only to be a few mosquito-ridden mud-holes. She should visit the Pyramids. Even Jerusalem, if that became safely possible in these dangerous days. Ailsa should drink her fill of knowledge. He kept his trap shut when she hesitantly aired the lefty, liberal views she'd picked up about our having no right to be here.

We would always be needed in the East. If the Gyppos knew what was good for them.

Stuck out in the Western Desert in '42, Joe had never expected to find himself back in peacetime. Although he'd thought seriously of demob into Civvy Street at the end of the war, Joe loved Forces life: the comradeship, the safe hierarchy, travel. Even the war-torn desert. The strange glamour of the Western Desert had mesmerised him: starlight haunting a moonscape made ghostly by the clawing shadows of tamarisk and saltbush. One day, out on salvage operations in graveyards of Allied planes, they'd come across an ambushed Great War patrol car, half-buried, bullet-riddled, its rubber and metal preserved as new. It was a converted Ford, stripped long ago of its Lewis machine gun. A skeleton wearing rags of uniform had remained in the passenger seat, all but his skull, which lay in the back. The boys had clustered round, fascinated by this relic of the Light Car Patrols of the Great War, in which their dads had fought. With a bit of tinkering, the vehicle could have been driven off. Frederick Ash, aged twenty, the lad's service book had said. *Fred*, Joe had thought, *or Freddie*.

Rubbing off the fine golden glaze of rust from the steel of the antique Jeep – rust that acted in the desert as a preservative – Joe had thought with an intense pang of his young dad. You came here. Now I've come here. A breath in between.

While the boys brewed chai, Joe had scanned the endless sand, violently white and shadowless in the high sun, littered with silica glass, shards of Roman pots and ancient flints. An acre of relics. Turning over fragments in his palm, Joe had imagined his young dad crouching here before him, fiddling with the jigsaw of remains. Time and space were a knot: no decay, a queering of distances. Beside the car, orange peel dropped thirty years back had dried to a dark brown, nut-hard curl. Sniffing the peel, Joe had been penetrated by its thin, original scent.

Dad had come home murderous, alcoholic and silent from what he'd seen, what he'd done out here. The children lying in bed had trembled hearing Dad lay into Mam. Mam who was the bread of life. Once Joe had rushed between man and wife, a slight boy of seven: *You don't do that to my mam*. He'd shrunk before the certainty of a punch that would knock him into kingdom come. Dad, turning away without a word, had slunk off. *But, cariad, don't cross him*, Mam had said later. *I will deal with him, have no fear*. And she had. Something in her contemptuous, pale blue stare had gradually quelled him. Dad had become a beaten, coughing man, afraid of his shadow, minding his manners at table, except when he relaxed with his pals in the womb-like fug of the Duke's Arms.

Yet once they had cycled down from Treforys together, singing and laughing, for Dad had been quite a comedian in his time, the boy perched on sacking tied round the crossbar, the man's arms guarding him either side, his iron hands on the handlebar grips. Out across the brown mud of the bay they'd padded with a sack for cockles and winkles. How did it happen, that change? No one knew. First you had one dad. Then a stranger wearing his mask.

Sabbath on the French Beach: this was the life. Families picnicked, splashed around, rowed in kayaks, swam out to rafts anchored in the lake. Some looked like darkies, tanned earth-coloured. Ailsa was keeping cool in one of the beehives, being chatted to by Irene. He heard a great deal more of Irene's voice than of his wife's. All the men on the beach must be aching with envy of me, Joe thought. Ha!

He loped over the sand to join them in the hive, playing the fool as he went, high-stepping, the sand burning his insteps. Parking himself, Joe laid his arm lightly round Ailsa's waist. The lightness of his touch secretly reminded her of last night. What we did then we shall do again, it promised. She rested her bare, sandy back against his chest, and almost imperceptibly pushed back against him.

'What's that you're knitting, Irene?' he asked.

'A three-ply jersey for my Roy,' she said fondly, passing him the pattern. He found himself turning over a single sheet containing a list of instructions to k. this and p. that.

'It's for when the winter comes,' she said. 'We can't be too careful when there are sudden changes in temperature. And the nights can be simply freezing, don't you find, Ailsa? The temperature *plunges*. It's not normal.'

'Well, it's normal for here.'

'Yes. But.' Irene paused. '*Here* is not normal. Roy says I shall get used to it. But I don't think, between ourselves, that I ever will.'

The burden of what Irene had to say was a prolonged wail. And yet the tenor of the knitting needles, click-clicking, was rather calming.

'I heard you singing hymns,' she said to Joe. 'It was *lovely*.'

'Dreadful racket,' Joe said. 'Nia told me off.'

'I cried,' Ailsa said.

'So did I,' said Irene. 'I came out of the back door when I heard the singing. Thinking it must be a broadcast. I'm afraid I listened in to the whole concert, Joe.'

Joe was touched at the thought of their neighbour listening in the cool stillness, arms folded, midges swarming like fireflies in the pool of light.

'Joe, you ought to be flattered,' Ailsa said.

'Oh I am. Really I am. Blushing actually.'

'You're not,' Ailsa said.

'You just can't see it through my handsome tan.'

'Where did you learn to sing like that?' Irene wanted to know.

'No learning involved, to speak of. Everybody sings in a choir where I come from.'

'I heard you and Nia clapping,' said Irene. 'And I clapped too. I hope you don't mind.'

It seemed a cue. Chalkie and Irene must come in of an evening for a drink, he suggested. Ailsa's smile looked brittle. Irene retreated into her shell. She didn't tend to go out in the evening, she said, because she found she got worried about her quarter. In case it wasn't safe to leave her babes in it, even with a baby-sitter.

Ailsa said simply, 'I'm sure we're very safe. It sometimes takes a while to feel safe though. Everything's so strange at first. I thought I was going to be plagued by migraine. But, touch wood, I've not had it again.' She tapped Joe's head with her knuckle. 'Or, I should say, *insh'alla*, shouldn't I? Arabic. If God wills. By the way, Irene,' she went on, 'Joe and I have been putting our heads together about that motor bike. I wonder if you would allow us to buy it from you – perhaps at half price? – and then the two boys can go on using it to go to work? Having their own transport is an advantage – and Joe has faithfully promised me to ride safely. Of course you wouldn't get the socks thrown in if we did it this way.'

Irene looked fit to cry. It was not the money, she said. Of course not! She didn't begrudge Roy *anything*. And it was certainly not the *socks*. If the Air Force would just allow the men to wear other socks than Air Force issue, there would be no problem at all. She was perfectly willing to knit Roy's socks. Irene's mouth turned down; her face twisted. The thing was, it was not safe at all for men to ride alone. She was sure Joe was a careful driver and would take care of Roy. But the Egyptians were so dangerous. They hated us, she said with a tremble in her voice. They were blowing men up, a few here, a few there. Opportunists. Terrorists. The men who were murdered were people's husbands and fathers and sons.

'Do you know what their slogan is? *Evacuation with Blood*. They come up behind with knives,' Irene said, 'and cut your throat. I know they do. No one tell me they don't, because they do.'

'Well now, dear,' said Joe in a gentle voice, 'I can't deny it has happened in the past. But it is not a regular thing. If it were, and if we were really in danger, you know, the Forces would never allow the women and children out here in the first place. Would they?'

'Wouldn't they?'

How did Chalkie put up with this perpetual bleating? It got on his wick. After half an hour of the sorrows of Irene, Joe was glad to leave her to Ailsa and go and call the children for a siesta in the hive. He did feel for her, of course he did, and she was an excellent sort of woman. Look at how she'd admired his music. But what a misery-guts. He felt damn sorry for Chalkie. The bloke should put his foot down. And wouldn't that be more reassuring for Irene in the long run?

The water of Timsah lapped around his ankles, tranquil and homely. The green woodlands that fringed the shore could easily have been growing in the Gower. Arms crossed, fists in armpits, he waited for Chalkie to hire a skiff and bring it round. He glanced down at what Ailsa called his *pelt*, the forest of dark fur that covered his chest and arms, which he had once been afraid (knowing nothing of women) would revolt her smoothness. *For Esau thy brother is an hairy man!* she'd said, taking delight in what he deplored as crude. Even now it was sometimes hard to believe she could love the physical specimen he was, child of steelmen and miners, and looking and sounding every bit the part.

In the beehive, the kiddies were now in their shorts. He watched Nia wind her arms round Ailsa's neck and give her cheek a tender kiss. Then, not to leave Irene out, she did the same for her, and Christopher followed suit because he would always do what Nia did, even act like a girl. Although Ailsa always said, *Ah Joe, she gets these winning ways from you.*

Chalkie paddled the skiff in close to shore and leaned over to balance Joe as he climbed on. Joe settled behind him, holding one of the double paddles.

Chalkie asked, 'Did you bring it up about the Tiger?'

'Ailsa did. Leave it to her, I would, she's clever like that. She used to ride a bike herself, you know. Courier in the war.'

They paddled sleekly out towards the centre of the lake, taking it easy, leaving the shore chatter and activity behind. Chalkie had had a bit of a turn on guards last night. Dusty Miller going on about shooting a Gyppo. Sick of the velvet gloves approach to the wogs.

'Shoot me a wog! Is what I want!' A moderate dose of Dusty went a fair old way. Joe privately thought it was the wartime desk job that had left the chip on his shoulder. But, fair play, Dusty was an uproarious drinking companion.

Chalkie lamented the weary work of sharing a duty with a bloke like Dusty, when you just wanted a smoke and a brew. 'And he's looking out for wogs the way normal blokes sniff for skirt. Come three in the morning, Dusty hears a suspicious noise behind the wire and a sort of cracking sound – and he's up with his revolver – fires two or three times and we both hear a snort and a thump – dead body falling, Dusty's first kill. Nothing else. So we both spend the rest of the night three feet from a corpse – and Dusty's ecstatic, died and gone to heaven: *I've got my first wog!* Going on about being blooded. Kissing his revolver. At first light we see the body lying just beyond the fence, and Dusty's going, *A donkey! I've shot a fucking donkey!*'

'Jesus Christ!'

Chalkie stopped paddling and turned to Joe. The boat rocked slightly in the water. Odd look on his face.

'Taf, he was inconsolable. *Oh my God, mate, what am I going to do, I've killed a poor donkey!* Yes, and he's over there with the donkey, and the donkey's throwing this whacking great shadow, and, you know, the flies are out in squadrons, and there's already a stink, and Dusty's got his head down with the donkey's head ... and blood all over his hands ... and he's on his feet and throwing up.'

'Not told Irene about it, have you, Chalkie?'

'Best not, eh?'

'Best not.'

Joe wondered if Dusty would have thrown up if the donkey had turned out to be an Arab after all. You didn't know how people would react when it came down to it. Thinking of bullnecked, loudmouthed Dusty, he smelt fear, the kind of fear that screws itself up into aggression, aggression that must get a climax somehow, and the moment it does, turns to a shambles of squeamishness. Death is real then? Half-baked, slow-witted recognition. Oh, I never imagined.

*

If there was another moaning, drivelling word out of Irene, Ailsa would grab her knitting needles and plunge them into her heart. There was no excuse for it. Someone should tell her. Instead of that, the husbands were polite – and then sloped off, down to the boats and the inviting water. She got to her feet and brushed the sand off her shorts, slapping it away.

Looking down at Irene's nest of light brown curls, Ailsa thought: oh but she's a good sort, she really is. She has been keeping it all in and now she's allowing herself to let it out.

But what am I: a sick-bag? Was this all her life amounted to? Torpor of tedium in a horror of heat?

The water gave a shout. It called.

Nia and the boys had attached themselves to a vast Irish family that had taken over two of the neighbouring beehives. The kiddies played leapfrog. Nia was joining in beautifully, nobody could say: *spoilt only child*. Nia went flying over the back of a big bendy boy. She was taking very little notice of Ailsa. The vaulting girl, in mid-air, seemed the picture of happiness.

Irene had turned the topic of conversation to the difference between shortcrust and flaky pastry.

'Sorry, but I want to go in,' Ailsa interrupted her.

'In?'

'In the water. You don't mind just keeping your eye on Nia for a few minutes?'

Irene's mouth gaped. Ailsa skedaddled without waiting for the answer. Had Irene cast a veto, she'd have slapped her, hard, across the anxious mask of her face that refused life, refused life itself! Ailsa ran down the searing sand, glimpsing her daughter look up as her mother mutinied. Inwardly Ailsa begged Nia to let her be, let her go, just this once let her hop, skip and jump into her own world. I can't stand it. Don't ask me to. This is me now. Cheerio!

Not a bleat out of Nia. Oh good girl.

Ailsa waded past squealing small fry in the shallows. Past men in boats. She freestyled out beyond the reach of all but the strongest swimmers. Timsah grew colder as its depth increased beneath her; she couldn't tell exactly where she'd come from. The lake, spinning on its axis, had come to rest in a new alignment with the woods and sky. Matchstick folk along the sands were indistinguishable: which was the officers', which the men's beach?

The rafts were nearer at hand than the shore. Using the wet ropes strung round the base, she dragged herself to the edge of the nearest, kneeing and squirming her way up. The raft rocked slightly and a shrimp-pink young man who'd been sunbathing took fright and, mumbling an apology, slid off the side into the water. Ailsa sat down on the edge. The bone-dry, bleached boards took no more than a second to absorb footprints. The salt water drying on Ailsa's skin in the suspicion of a breeze gave cool sensuality beneath a veil of godsent cloud.

A mile across the water, near the eastern shore, ocean liners and trading vessels paused in patient convoy, waiting to pass north from Africa, India, the Far East. The queue would stretch back through the Bitter Lakes, until the pilots allowed passage into the canal's last leg before the Mediterranean. Great silver birds. She watched in fascination. Their stillness, power, direction. Behind the picturesque serenity lay the endless, disputed deserts. Sinai, bleached yellow, the prettiest honey-colour, stretched into shimmering distances towards Nazareth and Galilee.

Places where Jesus's feet once trod; places now of murder. *O little town of Bethlehem, how still we see thee lie*, Nia had lisped last Christmas. No village or town in Israel remained untouched by the slaughter and evictions. Over there, across the canal and the picturesque sands. Ailsa saw in imagination Mona's violated home at Qatamon. The abandoned apricot and orange trees in the garden of Mona's childhood, *our cat* with her kittens basking abandoned in the shadow forever. Mona had belonged to an earlier wave of refugees, Christian Arabs caught up in the so-called Arab Rebellion of the 1930s. If she were to venture back now, she'd find a Jewish family in her home.

Ailsa hadn't understood, hadn't wanted to understand, what Mona was telling her about the crime against her people. Jewish suffering; Zionist crimes: the mind staggered before the twistedness and treacheries of the postwar world. How did you gain a true perspective? Ailsa had spent her life so far cocooned in the sticky threads of received opinion whilst flattering herself she was free.

Invisible guns ensured the dreamlike passage of ships through Suez – guns held by us, the folk larking on the western shore of Timsah. The leading vessel had evidently been given the go-ahead. It slid forward slow-motion towards Ish, where it would carefully penetrate the narrow opening of the canal. Smoke poured from the funnels; from this distance one could not hear the engines. Its gliding motion was soft as a swan's.

After the concert Joe had not raised the subject of Mona and Ailsa hadn't pushed him. But he'd been so moved by the piano music that she'd been half expecting him to withdraw his objections. They were balanced, the two of them, in a loving equanimity she shrank from disturbing.

Joe wasn't going to budge though, was he? Ailsa swished her feet in the water. The silver forms of fish basked below in the clear green depths, water-ghosts.

*

Ailsa lumbered up from the lake, thigh muscles gone to jelly. And there they loitered, Nia, Christopher and Timothy, with Irene under a pink parasol, held by a tall black man in a pure white *gallabiyya* and a red cummerbund.

'Oh you're *here*. Thank heaven,' Irene said. She waved the black man away. He bowed slightly and withdrew, shutting the parasol. Irene looked fit to faint. 'Don't worry, I shan't say a word,' she whispered.

'Pardon?'

'I won't mention it. But I can't keep doing this.'

'Mention what? To whom?' Ailsa, bridling, scooped Nia up and held the little body tight, feeling through the cotton the pit-a-pat of heart against heart. The woman was a policeman, a spy.

'Mami, did you have a nice swim?' Nia asked.

'I did, lovely. I went for miles! I'm fit to drop. Thanks for keeping an eye on Nia for me, Irene. Perhaps you'd like a dip now and I'll take care of the little ones?'

'Oh no.' Irene jumped back as if she'd seen a nasty stinging insect.

'Fine but, if you change your mind, just say the word.'

'Topher, your mami can't swim, can she?' Nia observed, looking down at him from Ailsa's arms.

'No.'

'Mine can.'

'Well, mine *can* if she *wanted* to,' said Christopher, crestfallen. 'But she doesn't want to.'

'Are you scared of water, Mrs White?' asked Nia directly.

'No, dear. Not as such.'

As the child turned her face back towards her mother, Ailsa saw with relief that she had rejected the impulse to call Topher's mami a scaredy-cat. Her mind and Nia's mind seemed to braid, beneath the level of words. Irene marched them all back to the beehives with such a glower on her face that Ailsa thought, *Poor soul, her day is wrecked.* Irene had thought she'd found a pal, but no such thing.

'I'm ever so sorry,' she said to Irene. 'I didn't think you'd mind.'

'I looked for you everywhere and I couldn't see you at all. And the lake looked enormous. Like a sea. I wondered if I should report you missing. And what if Joe had come back?'

'Irene – it was just a dip.'

'And I was looking for Roy and Joe and I couldn't see them either. The last I saw of them they were sculling out in one of those green boats. And there wasn't anyone. Only this big black man who insisted on holding a pink umbrella over me. Where did he come from?'

'The Sudan probably. Or from Nubia – in Upper Egypt.'

'The point is, poor dear Nia got into a bit of a panic while you were away.'

'I didn't *so*.'

'Well, darling, you did, a funny sort of turn. She looked at me and went all shivery.'

Caught a whiff of your anxiety, no doubt, thought Ailsa.

Because she's fine, look at her. She lay down, salt-crusted, sand-coated, in a semicircle round her daughter, with their heads on a towel, in the grateful shade. Spoons they were, she told Nia, one lovely darling spoon inside the other; and Little Yellow Man, Nia whispered to her, was also a spoon, the tiniest spoon of all in her hand, but who knows, Ailsa murmured, perhaps he has a minuscule spoon of his own which we can't see, and within that spoon...

When they woke, Joe was back and Irene had been reunited with Roy. She kept her eyes on her husband, trailing his every move, and drinking reassurance from his presence. Roy was the kind of man who could not keep still. He busied himself building a sand crocodile for his boys, for Timsah, he said, meant 'crocodile', what about that then, lads? What if a daddy croc came waddling up out of the lake now this minute! Up and up the beach going *Araagh! Araagh!* looking for his dinner? Well, we'll have a croc of our very own to defend us, won't we?

And he tirelessly performed the drama of a croc-fight until a mob of kiddies had assembled, out of their minds with laughter, stuffing their fists in their mouths, falling down in the sand and popping up with a gnashing roar, until even Irene allowed her face to mist over with a wan smile.

'Oh Irene, he's such a sweetheart, isn't he, your husband,' Ailsa said.

Irene gave her a hands-off look. 'I know,' she said. 'And that's *why*.'

She did not say why what, and Ailsa did not ask.

'I swam out to one of the rafts,' Ailsa mentioned to Joe, within earshot of Irene.

'Oh aye?'

He had a cigarette stuck behind each ear.

'Fun was it, my beauty?'

'Oh aye,' she said, parodying him. She felt kindled and aroused.

'Cheeky.'

'Parrot. *Oh aye* means you aren't listening to me, are you, Joe Roberts? You want to be careful what you say. Never know what you're agreeing with.' She pulled out one of the fags from behind his ear, said 'Finders keepers' and hung it from her lips, pouting forwards for a light. He supplied the flame, chuckling.

So there, you see, Irene, spoilsport, she thought childishly, he doesn't mind, not a bit. Ailsa stroked Joe's furry back as he sat smoking contentedly, and thought how lovely his body was, his flanks and wrists, she would have liked to have caressed the place there, between his legs, which was hers and hers alone, and which no one else might see, at least no woman, and make it stand up tight and when it did so, the blue in his eyes would ache, ache, so that she would have the impulse to comfort him for this joy that was power and also loss of power, and the rage of hunger that was its own satisfaction.

'Can you read my thoughts?' she asked him.

12

They dragged the sacking off the Matchless, their pride and joy. The bike represented a friendship dearer to Joe's heart than any since childhood, formed in the Desert War where they'd literally shared their last drop of water. Something so innocent and likeable about Chalkie, with just a dash of mischief that Joe delighted to bring out of him. They'd give the Tiger an overhaul, polish it up and ride off into the desert with the rest of the boys who'd managed a day's leave. They'd imagine themselves back at Cyrenaica or on the never-to-be-forgotten coastal run from Tobruk to Alamein and Alexandria, the desert sand bone-white, the glimpsed Mediterranean bluer than any ocean he'd seen or imagined. Tomorrow would be Chalkie's thirty-third birthday. After their jaunt they'd fetch up at the Victoria Bar in Ish to celebrate with a couple of drinks.

Marriage is one thing, Joe thought, and the men's world another. Immediately he was beset by a bewildered sense of his own treachery. Ailsa was the air he breathed.

Closeness grew with every day; sometimes he could read her thoughts without a word being said. And, fair play, she begrudged Joe nothing, agreeing with hardly any hesitation to the release of the better part of their savings as a payment for the Matchless. He'd seen Irene's embarrassment and silent fury, when Ailsa engineered the transaction. The poor creature had flushed to the roots of her hair. She'd rather have Roy safe and sound than all the tea in China, she let them know. *Oh, but Joe is such a safe rider*, Ailsa had purred. *He will take the best care of Roy, he truly will. Won't you, darling?* Ailsa was too clever for Irene. Too clever for him, come to that; she could wrap him round her little finger.

His wife was all in all. What in this world could compare with the joy of being taken in Ailsa's arms, taking Ailsa in his?

Even so, Joe could hardly imagine a good life without the comradeship of men and their shared sense of purpose, knowing – even when they larked and joshed one another, cursing the bastard officers – the importance of their presence in the godforsaken, flyblown desert, keeping the oil flowing, the Soviets at bay.

Men needed adventure as women didn't, a need Ailsa understood and respected. A bit of fun couldn't come amiss, in the absence of the womenfolk in Ish for a lazy day's shopping at the NAAFI and lunch at the services club. And the kiddies, for Nia and Christopher had gone on a mystery expedition. He'd been half proud, half sad, to see the little ones, hand-in-hand, clamber aboard the bus with scarcely a backward glance.

The Tiger was freed from its tin den. The metal scalded

to their touch and the rubber stank, soft with heat. As if it had been cooking in that furnace, the Tiger's feral smells were released, pungent and exciting, a delicious reek of grease and petrol.

'Tyger tyger,' Joe recited. 'How does that go on?'

'Not the foggiest. What is it when it's at home?'

'A poem, boy. Burning bright, in the forest of the night.'

'Burning's the word, mate,' Chalkie said. 'Fry an egg on the bugger.'

They lubricated, then wiped the oily parts with rags. Finally they polished up the Tiger with soft dusters filched from Ailsa's drawer.

'What immortal da-de-da,' Joe chanted, crouched at the axle. 'Learned it at school. Never forget that stuff, do you? Fearful symmetry.'

Chalkie had found it easy to forget what he never knew. All above his head, apparently. He left all that sort of thing to the ladies. Ten, fifteen years younger today than their alleged age, Joe and Chalkie polished their gleaming darling to new heights of perfection. Nothing fascinated Joe more than machines, and it hardly mattered whether it was a pre-war can of junk like the Matchless or a sophisticated modern plane, the delight was the same. Chalkie was clearly enjoying his escape from captivity. Not that Irene's husband, fiercely loyal, would ever admit that she sometimes gave him the pip.

They'd pick up Dusty from the mess, and whoever else fancied a run out in the desert. Then roar back to Ish to quench their thirst.

*

Sauce for the goose, my boy, Ailsa thought.

Escape had been child's play. When Babs Brean had appeared at the club and wrapped herself loudly around Irene and Hedwig, Ailsa abandoned her knife and fork and half-drunk shandy and made for the lavatory. *I'm off*, she'd mouthed to Hedwig and liberated herself smartly from the building, as she'd got used to doing.

Sauntering along the *Belle Époque* boulevards, Ailsa relished the sweet taste of freedom, knowing exactly where she was going, along eucalyptus-lined avenues, where palatial colonial houses with flaking stucco glowed white. Easy to imagine herself back a century to the canal's ceremonious opening: the flotilla at anchor, the Empress Eugénie and the Khedive Ismail, pennants waving, guns saluting, the brand-new city festively decked out with freshly cut greenery. Escaping the British enclave, Ailsa always had the impression of entering another time-zone, where, beyond clocks and barbed wire, the ancient people and their gods had only just that minute vanished round a corner.

Insh'alla, she thought, we'll all meet and talk across the great gulf fixed between us, Egypt and England. Why not?

Without hesitation, Ailsa took the path indicated on the British sign: Masurah Village. This morning Joe had set the seal upon her quest by informing her that he and Chalkie were going to tinker with the Tiger and head off for a little jaunt. OK by you, *cariad*?

Quite OK, she'd said, and meant it. Go ahead. Fine by me. But a thirst and an itch of resentment had come over her when she imagined the two men on the bike. Why not Ailsa with a pal of her own riding pillion? Why the hell not? It had never been suggested that she take a turn. Joe had quietly forgotten that she'd ridden a bike twice as powerful as their puny Matchless during the war. Never had a prang. A trained mechanic.

She found herself in a square of white bungalows encircled with verandas whose slender columns formed a rhythm of Roman arches. Jacaranda, bougainvillaea, and flowers whose names Ailsa didn't know – purple, orange, a pulse of white – starred the bushes of lush gardens. The children were presumably all at school or indoors for the mid-day siesta and the only person visible was an indigo-robed Arab saffragi watering flowers, releasing a scent of almost excessive sweetness. *Salaam aleicum!* The gardener bowed, smiled and returned her greeting across lawns and bushes saturated with rich greenness unknown in dusty El-Marah.

It was like stepping into a dream. Mona sat hunched over a trestle table in the shade of her balcony, a fan blowing back the hair from her forehead. A burble of wireless noise spilled through the open glass door. Her head was down; she was writing. Latching the gate behind her, Ailsa advanced until she stood under the balustrade, close enough to hear the page rustle as it turned. *I can still go back.* The saffragi leaning on his rake next door observed her silently.

Breeze from the whirring fan, rocking on a wobbly base, caught Ailsa's hot forehead. But the sound from within was not the wireless: no, it was the murmur of people talking with lowered voices. Visitors. Idiotic not to have foreseen that Mona might not be alone. As Ailsa hesitated, Mona sensed her presence.

'Oh my God, it's you! *Habibi* – look who it is – come out!'

The trestle table and papers went flying, the chair tumbled back.

'Where've you *been*? I swear I'd given up.' Mona's arms were round Ailsa, rocking her back and forth. The urgent expressiveness of her oval face seemed to spring at Ailsa, pouncing forward out of memory into the sensuous world. 'How are you? How is Nia?' and without waiting for an answer, Mona hollered through the door to her husband, '*Habibi*! Come out! She's here.'

'Now she'll be happy.' *Habibi*'s hug lifted Ailsa off her feet. She was dragged indoors.

The Jacobs bungalow had been converted to a giant waiting room. Waiting for what? Pallid faces massed in dim indoor light, fixing suspicious eyes on the newcomer. Every space seemed accounted for, chairs and chair-arms, a long sofa with a crammed row of elderly women and one elderly man. Sombre cross-legged children had to be stepped over and a toddler slept in her mother's arms, flushed head thrown back, hair raying out.

Palestinian refugees. Of course. Mona was trying to find them lodgings and jobs. *Al-Naqba*: the Catastrophe. It was Mona's Thursday At Home, she said. Please wait. Ben, she's come, she's here at last, I knew she'd come, give her a drink, keep her here, you swear not to go, don't you, I won't be long, make her wait.

*

They sped over the burning plain, out into the Sinai, eleven boys on six bikes. All of them high as kites as they drove abreast over primrose-yellow sand, as if flying in formation. An illusion of take-off as speed generated a cool wind.

Joe revved; shot forward, hands hot on rubber, knees clenched to the body of the Tiger which, like a woman, responded with all she could give, so that they hurtled madly in the general direction of Israel. They passed relics of military materiel presumably left behind as the remnant of the Egyptian troops and tanks had limped home beaten and humiliated from last year's assault on Israel. Litter everywhere: personal items like fag packets, a water bottle, as well as webbing and cartridges. The bikes headed for the only landmark, a clapped-out joke of a tank, a mammoth that looked as if it dated back to the Great War. The beast had evidently given up the ghost on the retreat, almost within sight of home – the only puzzle being how it had ever succeeded in shuffling along in the first place. Joe began to circle the crock, which lay atilt in the shallow hollow of a dune and resembled nothing so much as a ditched tin can whose contents had long ago been extracted. Its hatch was open, just as it had been when vacated by the fleeing soldiers. It would still be there in a hundred years.

Joe picked up speed, spraying sand; Chalkie's hands rested lightly on his waist, their two bodies leaning in, balanced as one. The six bikes now described a circle, equidistant as spokes on the hub of a giant wheel.

The wheel slowed and came to rest. Bottles of Stella appeared from panniers. Laughing and joshing, they swallowed the tepid Egyptian beer, distilled from onions, yellow as urine and potent as death. The superannuated tank had its gun trained in the general direction of Ish, as if to signal yet another own goal for the local team. Sun inflamed the men's faces to a fiery red. In roaring high spirits, Joe swigged back the last of his bottle and tossed it away.

Back for a quick one. Your birthday tomorrow, Chalkie. She'll never know. Joe kept peppermints in his pocket for every eventuality.

*

A mood of estranged sorrow filled the room, palpable, as if the air were viscous. Not sorrow: despair. Horror. Something that could not be spoken. Each one in his private prison. *Habibi* chivvied a silent youth out of an armchair. Ailsa must sit. What could he get for her? Oh, nothing. Please don't let her interrupt. She shouldn't be here; why didn't she come back another day? Mona's husband perched on the arm of the chair and looked at Ailsa with affection so frank that, had Joe come in at that moment, he'd have known for sure that the man was in love with his wife, and wanted to knock him down.

'My life wouldn't be worth living if I let you go. Really, you'll buck her up no end. She's been so stretched. A one-person bureau. It takes it out of her and she's missed you horribly. She cries a lot.'

Ailsa gathered that Mona held these consultations on a Thursday, spending the rest of the week wheedling and bullying people sympathetic to the victims of the Palestinian exodus, for rooms and jobs.

'She's a force of nature,' Ben said with pride. 'Isn't she?' Mona's voice could be heard from the veranda, where she conducted the interviews.

'You understand,' Ailsa heard Mona caution an elderly couple. 'I can promise nothing.'

'Oh no, we recognise that. But dentists are always in demand. You can surely see that. People's teeth don't stop decaying, do they? I know you can do something for us, dear. I have every faith in you,' the wife insisted.

'Huda, it won't be the kind of work Uncle is used to. Portering. Hospital orderly. At best, office work. That kind of thing. If I can get it. You have to accept that.'

'I will do anything,' said her husband. 'Anything at all.' His hand patted his wife's knee, as if to say, *do not grumble. Don't upset Mona. She's our lifeline. We only have this one chance.*

'But what about the British? Surely they require skilled dentists? The young soldiers I see in town, their teeth are a disgrace. Some of them have lost all their front teeth. Eating sweets and smoking, and not brushing.'

'Auntie, their dentists are in uniform. They don't use civilians.'

'Or *foreigners*, is that it? Tell your niece where you were trained, remind her. Edinburgh and Washington DC: does that count for nothing, Mona? Do they imagine we will saboutage their teeth? My husband is a consultant back home.'

'Please, Huda. I have been retired for seven years. Our niece is doing all she can. There are so many of us. You can see that, *habiba*.' Small-boned, birdlike, he sat bolt upright in the folding chair; his shabby suit hung loose on his shoulders.

'Very well. Then I shall go out cleaning,' the wife said. 'Don't look at me like that. *I* am not ashamed of honest work, whoever else is. I still have use of my hands and knees.'

Mona was on the phone. Ailsa heard her voice syrup-sweet, requesting a clerical position in the Stores. Manipulating someone to do something against his will. In the nicest possible way not brooking refusal. Pulling rank. Part-time? Then part-time it must be. Thanks. You will not be sorry.

Ailsa watched as Ben escorted the couple into the blaze outside. Oh no, they didn't want a lift; they would walk, she heard the lady say, gallantly flourishing her stick like a baton: they liked to walk, walking was so healthy – and, lucky as they were to have the room all to themselves in town, there was no point in shutting themselves in before they had to. The Jacobs lounge began slowly to empty.

'Excuse me, *ya Habibi*, but she's burning,' said the young woman with the toddler, in a resonant whisper. 'She's ill.'

Ben laid his big palm on the child's forehead and, finding it hot, said they should put her to bed. 'You can sponge her to cool her off, Yasmin.'

'But I'll miss my turn!' the girl burst out. She was dressed in black, with a long white headscarf. When she spoke, Ailsa realised she was younger by far than she had appeared. Fourteen or fifteen at the most.

'Of course you won't. No, no. You must both stay here with us until we find a place for you. Our guests, no, don't cry, shush, all will be well.'

Helping to put the sick child to bed, Ailsa thought with a pang of complicated guilt of Nia. *I hope it isn't catching. Don't breathe in her germs.* She was ashamed of her selfishness but you had to put your own children first, surely?

These children's entire family had been murdered. The sisters had been out at the river drawing water when the soldiers came; they'd crouched in the reeds until the men had gone. Yasmin had walked all the way to the border with

Lebanon, carrying the younger child, who'd caught an infection in the camp. Not typhus, *Habibi* said, don't worry. Ailsa's guts knotted at the unspeakable word. No, no, typhus doesn't present like this, *Habibi* reassured the elder sister: don't panic, Yasmin. For there was typhus in the camps. It had gained a hold in the insanitary, crowded conditions. But this was not how typhus displayed itself. *Habibi*, to comfort his wife's niece, had quit his genial role as everyone's darling for a medic's authoritative calm.

'But are you sure, Ben – definitely not typhus?' Ailsa whispered.

What if it had been herself and Nia? All comforts stripped away; everyone you loved slaughtered. Ailsa was used to thinking of the War as over; of extermination camps as an obscenity the Allies had cleaned up. But how could the survivors ever feel safe? Zionism had turned Jewish fears of a second Holocaust into the mother of fresh violence; fratricide had just moved on, a chain reaction that was never over. Arabs were paying for a European crime. Leaving Yasmin and her sister, Ailsa sat dismayed in an atmosphere steeped in absent hope, which contrasted strangely with the room's opulence. In one corner stood a glossy concert grand, beneath a portrait of Julie Brandt-Simon. The red fire of Julie's silk dress glowed against a dark green background. Such an interior, with its cultivation and taste, must bring home to this exiled Arab intelligentsia the extent of what had been lost.

Mona peered through the open door, wrinkled her nose and grinned. Ailsa pointed at her watch. Mona shut her remaining visitors in the living room for half an hour, leading Ailsa to her study.

A fan at the centre of the ceiling turned slow arms. Between the slats of closed shutters, threads of light glowed, picking out the emerald and turquoise colour of carpets hung on three of four walls. A bed was covered in a white cotton counterpane woven with gold lettering: verses from a Sufi poem, Mona said, as they negotiated the sudden shyness between them. Very beautiful ones. When you next come, I'll translate them for you. And you will come. You will, won't you?

'Yes,' Ailsa said. 'Yes I will. Of course I will.'

'That's all right then.'

'It's wonderful, what you're doing, Mona.'

'No. But better than nothing. Nobody wants to know.'

'*I* know now. Or at least I'm beginning to understand. I didn't really, before, Mona.'

'Dearest,' Mona said and gazed wonderingly at Ailsa. 'Dear Ailsa. Oh love, you came. At *last*. I came to your house. Several times. But I hadn't the courage to ... in case Joe ... and I knew I hadn't the right, no right at all, to disturb your peace. I thought perhaps you'd forgotten me?'

Ailsa shook her head. She let Mona take both her hands and turn them over, kissing the palms. She shivered. The thought of Mona spying was disquieting. And yet it seemed the most natural and inevitable thing in the world to be here with her friend.

'Oh, I've missed you, Ailsa.'

'I missed you too.'

'Did you? Well, that's something,' said Mona. 'Nothing more lonely than missing someone who doesn't miss you, is there? You wouldn't know, of course, how could you, Angel Ailsa? It's been, oh, just a bitter time. Apart from

Habibi of course. Trying to do something for people but it's so little. They have *nothing*, Ailsa. People from my childhood in Qatamon, they stood all round me, they held up the sky, they were my rock and Mama's rock, now look at them, destitute. And our neighbours here, what can I say? They are, oh my God, ghouls, gorgons. Apparently they object to the "bad foreign types" *Habibi* and I entertain. Our friends and family might be "Arab spies working for the Soviets" apparently. We had this high-up geezer with ginger moustaches come round to haul me over the coals. *Habibi* made me promise not to tell him where to get off so I was as nice as ninepence, nearly killed me. Oh sorry, I said, I'm so *frightfully* sorry, they are just a few relatives down on their luck. But hang on, here come the kids. Quick, Ailsa, come and look.'

Ailsa peered down from the window at schoolgirls scuffing along in uniform and cherry red sandals, speaking over one another in a high-pitched nasal drawl. The two in front, Mona explained, were the offspring of a Brigadier. The others, whose pa was only a Major, had been told to walk two paces behind. True. This was their mental level.

'But tell me about you. How are *you*, my love? And Nia? And Joe? I saw him at the concert.'

'Joe loves music, he was so moved.'

'Was he? Does that mean...? My playing was your doing, it was your concert really, you know that, don't you?'

'Don't be silly.'

'It was. Without you I doubt if I'd ever have risked going back to playing, Ailsa. Perhaps I would, ultimately, who knows? It was one of those godgiven moments when someone comes along and just changes the lights and shades without a second thought. The lousy Air Force has forbidden me to give any more concerts for the so-called *native population*. The bastards will let me play in the Officers' Mess to the Memsahibs. Can you believe those people? *Habibi* reckons we'd better toe the line or they'll send us home. Anyway I want to play for you. With you, rather. Beautiful, amazing Ailsa. Look – stay for supper. You will, won't you?'

'You know I can't.'

'Then we'll meet in Ish. When? Tomorrow morning? Please say yes. You can't say no.'

*

The boys burst into the Vic. Not much doing in there, just a few lads who'd been propping up the bar for several weeks by the looks of them, slowly raising glass to lips, keeping themselves topped up, pickled boys who spoke little and slowly to the super-courteous barman, an oily foreigner capable of seeing no evil and hearing no evil, who would agree with whatever was put to him by a thirsty Briton on pay day. Pocketing the change, for like all his tribe he was a thief. And stab you in the back on your way out.

There was a battered joanna in the corner, like an old bloke with stained gnashers and not a full set at that – a seedy instrument with nicotine-brown keys, missing several. The innards had been fixed with elastic bands. Never seen a tuner. The boys positioned themselves around it and – one, two, three! – broke into song, Lofty Hill sketching a rough and ready melody on the piano while Joe let rip his powerful tenor.

Rounds of drinks. Not much in their stomachs. Toasts

to the birthday boy. Speech by Chalkie, chiefly *erm erm*, Joe filling in for his tongue-tied pal. Dancing. The Dashing White Sergeants. The Campbells Are Coming oh ho oh ho.

An influx of already inebriated Salford lads from the RAF Regiment. The racket so uproarious that you had to yell at the top of your voice to get heard.

Jokes. Blue jokes Joe didn't generally appreciate which nevertheless struck him as being so bloody funny he bent double. Dusty Miller on top form. No ladies in the room to be upset, in any case. Joe was a shaken bottle of pop with the cork pulled out. Chalkie chuckled to himself, looking down into his beer, fishing out a fly. A winged creature, said Dusty, drowned and meant you no harm, boy. Not joking this time.

Another? Make that a brandy.

There was a Scotchman, an Irishman – but no Welshman. Hammering of fists on tables. Beermats skimming to the four corners of the bar. The patient head waiter picking them up. The more he fielded the flying beermats, the more the lads felt bound to skim, perfecting their aim, for instance, at the chandelier. The head waiter's bent back was turned; the *gallabiyya* rode up nearly to the back of his knees, exposing spindling and for some unknown reason hysterically comical calves. What does a Scotchman wear under his sporran?

What does an Arab wear under his skirt, hey? Hey? Give up?

*

Ailsa accepted a lift as far as the station. By the skin of her teeth she managed to catch the second bus of the day, which would get her home in time for tea. She sat panting and scarlet, collecting her scattered self. Too late to cook for Joe and Nia but at least she'd be in time to meet the returning busload of little ones and to hear all the doings of the day. She hoped there'd been no cases of sunstroke or prickly heat, and no small boys throwing up on the back seat. Doubtless Babs, who had accompanied the trip wearing an armband, would have had it all in hand.

Ailsa wrestled to readjust to the world of El-Marah. To be interested in the doings of the menfolk and kiddies. And yet it all seemed tediously irrelevant, a theatre in which Ailsa Birch played a menial role as Mrs Joseph Roberts. Her arms had caught the sun in that dash through Ish. Her fair skin scalded easily and would need lashings of cold cream when she got home. They could just have Spam for tea, or corned beef, that would be best. Nia wouldn't want much. The youngsters, who'd have feasted on fish paste and jam tarts, would probably be content with a long drink and a digestive. Joe, bless him, never grumbled about his food.

Where had the time gone? The bus was drawing in to El-Marah. The jewel colours of Mona's carpets still glowed in her mind's eye. The girl in the headscarf carrying her sick sister, saying, *No, Habibi, no, I'll lose my place in the queue.* The soft kiss, lips brushing lips as Ailsa and Mona parted. My sister, my wife. But never mind all that. She must seal in all these fizzing thoughts and not pull out the stopper until she could be on her own, Nia in the land of nod, Joe asleep beside her. And when she was quite sure those two dear ones were completely out of it, she'd allow herself to think of Mona. Slip out of bed and sit close up to the fan in her nightie, to go over it all again and again. But blank it off now.

When Ailsa saw the Military Police Jeeps, she sprinted. Nia! Something had happened to Nia!

Rushing in, she ran full tilt into Joe hurrying out of the back door. His face white to the gills.

'Joe – is it Nia?'

'No. No, my beauty, not Nia. She's still on the bus.'

'What then?'

Joe wrung his hands. She'd never seen a man wring his hands before but, she observed, this was what he did. She gripped his hands to hold them still, and tears brimmed before she had the least idea what she should cry about. Ailsa smelt the booze on his breath. But he wasn't drunk.

Something had happened, he said hoarsely. In Ish.

Oh my God, she thought. I've been in Ish. He's been in Ish. What if she'd been seen in the passenger seat of *Habibi*'s car?

A crowd of blokes had gone on bikes into the desert. Just for a laugh, Joe said with tears in his voice.

'But I thought you said you were in Ish?' she said stupidly.

13

Nia and Mona had taken to one another, no doubt about it. There seemed no avenue their conversation could take without intense interest. No avenue but one, and Mona made no further move in that direction. The bad thing, whatever that was, was unnamed. After dinner, Poppy interrogated Mona about her life – and she talked easily, comfortably, as they sauntered on the upper deck, the sea ink-black, moonlight trailing a path of mercury on the water. Nia felt the powerful attraction of the woman, the grandeur of her manner balanced by self-deprecating humour. And a hungry intensity that, if it set its sights on you, would never let you go. Whatever power it was she had exerted over Ailsa, she was now levelling at Ailsa's daughter.

Mona had never remarried after Ben's death and had no children of her own. She doubted if she'd have made even a 'good enough' mother, too selfish, too taken up with her own concerns. She couldn't imagine summoning interest in a small person's socks. Whenever it had come over Mona to be broody, she'd tried the litmus test of sock-washing and the prospect held no magic for her.

They turned in early. Nia, lounging on her bed with a final glass of wine, thought how close Mona's bed was to hers, through the membrane of the party wall. When she turned over, Mona turned over on the other side and when they lay face to face, their thoughts of one another flew into the partition like birds. The comfortable thrumming of the engine blanked off any sound from an adjacent cabin.

Red wine did funny things to Nia's mind and didn't agree with her, for she'd inherited a tendency to migraine. She had the sudden idea that it was snowing outside the porthole. But of course that was in another country. In Wales, where she remembered the winter of their return from Egypt, staying with *Mam-gu*. Nia in a green snowsuit, mittened and scarfed, was chucking snowballs with the other kids in Pleasant Street. Never seen the stuff before. Ignorant of what it was, but feeling that it was very like the desert, she'd crouched to pick up a mittenful and suck it; leapt along from boot to boot making a pattern; bent to study a robin's footprints. Nia had been in heaven. The big boys and girls, whooping and squealing, had rolled a snowball all the way from the top to the bottom of the steep street. When it had reached the bottom, the ball was as big as Nia, thrillingly bigger even. They'd given him eyes of coal and a stick for a nose. He had a coal sack for a greatcoat and held a wrecked umbrella under his arm. Nia was in awe of him, in love with him. She'd stood still beside him, her face scalding, hands chilled in their sodden mittens. Then Mami had come out of *Mam-gu*'s house, with folded arms, looking down at the children's excitement.

And she'd smiled.

That had been something lovely and miraculous: Mami had smiled. Waved. And Nia, beside herself, had legged it towards her, whereupon something a bit funny happened.

She could not say what this had been.

This was Nia's first winter memory. She'd never understood why it ended in that peculiar way that still made her tummy squirm and tickle. And feel she'd spoilt something good and sweet. But how? She saw now: they must have been just back from Egypt, where the Terrible Thing had happened. Ailsa's face had become a mask from enduring the Terrible Thing. She had become a machine-mother who performed numb, necessary tasks and no more.

But then Mami had smiled. Which showed she could smile. Which released tension like an elastic band snapping. Which meant Nia could be forgiven for something very bad she had done in Egypt. Which could not be named.

But thereupon, when Mami smiled, Nia had done or said something that wiped the smile from Ailsa's face. Whatever this had been, it was unintentional. But bad. She'd brought her badness home with her from Egypt to Wales.

Still, she was and remained used to being bad; Nia had put a brave face on it and returned to her game. She and her cousins raced in full cry out on to Trewyddfa Hill and tobogganed on tea trays or made angels by falling backwards in the drifts, flapping their arms up and down.

Having showered, Nia switched on the bedside lamp; picked up her book. She put it down again. Slowly Nia got up and put her face up to the black porthole. She stood motionless. Nothing to see: no light, no land.

Where is my Daddy, Mami?

Those words, or others like them, were what Nia had unforgivably said.

In the night she awakened after weird dreams, feeling an infinitely comforting and at the same time threatening presence. I could just reach out, she thought. I could say, come in to me, Mona; talk to me. Please be with me. I could do that now. This recapitulated something very far back when, turning over in her crib, the child had seen through the bars two women in one another's arms, swaying to and fro, to and fro. Such a solacing but at the same time anxious sight.

Nia sat up and found herself in tears, knocking on the party wall.

She waited. After a while, she seemed to hear tapping coming back. But the *Terra Incognita* was bucking and racing along like a mad thing. You couldn't be sure that any sound wasn't the engine.

The tapping came again. Immediately Nia cringed back into herself. Why did I do that? For goodness' sake.

There was a pause. She heard, or thought she heard, Mona Serafin-Jacobs's door opening. And her own door being knocked on.

Nia didn't answer. But she slid out of the narrow bed and went to the door, listening to the other listening for her on the other side. The terrifying comforter breathing through the door, one who could not be heard, only intuited. If I just wait, Nia thought, she will go away. She mustn't be let in. Whatever the Terrible Thing might have been, now after all these years Nia could not yet bring herself to ask.

At the port of Suez she woke early after a reverberating

night in which the ship's speed had risen. She'd been carried bareback on a racing horse like the child in *Erlkönig: Wer reitet so spät durch Nacht und Wind?... Es ist der Vater mit seinem Kind.* The stench of petrol permeated Nia's cabin and, when she looked out of the porthole, she could see little but a pea soup fog over the port of Suez. *Who is riding so late through night and wind?* Ghostly cranes, derricks and towers rose out of this murk. *It is the father with his child.* Far too early: five in the morning. She'd go and grab a cup of tea at the lido, bring it down and read.

An elderly man by the tea and coffee urns turned and asked anxiously, 'Was it happening before this?'

'Sorry, was what happening?'

'Exactly. What was?'

'I'm not with you.'

'Were there cups of tea?'

'I think cups of tea are available all night, aren't they?'

Confused as his words were, they resonated oddly with Nia.

'But how do you know?'

'Oh, the tea-making things are put out on this table for us, don't worry. We can have as much as we want, any time we want.'

'You do surprise me.' His face was venerable, worn, with deep folds and wrinkles which suggested weary bafflement. 'How do you know that you know?' Without waiting for an answer to his increasingly abstruse questions, he smiled and said, 'Hot chocolate is my favourite.'

'Come on then, let me make you a cup.'

'Oh, can you do that?'

'I'd be delighted. How do you like it?'

Nia took his cup to a table and was just refusing a tip when his family appeared, chivvying gently: 'Oh, there you are, Dad.'

A few wan folk sat in the lido, in grey-violet light, chatting over cups of tea. Sea mist was burning off, leaving a pink haze on the horizon. Liners lay at anchor just beyond the mole and yellow buoy markers bobbed like toy ducks. Dockers bent to their work on the quay, loading and unloading sacks in an unhurried rhythm, calling to one another, joking and chatting.

Nia sat and watched as low light gilded her fellow insomniacs' faces into transient blessedness – half the face, rather, for the other lay in shadow.

*

Bit of fun, nothing out of the ordinary. No call to give him the evil eye. Dusty Miller, Lofty Hill, Chalkie, Taf Thomas and the boys, the usual culprits. Just riding up and down really over the canal in the desert. Pretty damn fast, letting off steam. Good God, no – no danger, boy. You only fall on sand, after all, like a pillow. They'd had a race or two. Got a thirst up.

Then off into Ish and a singsong round the joanna in the Victoria with the boys and a drink or few, there was, well, a bit of a shindig. And Joe seemed ashamed. What kind of a shindig? Ailsa asked, as lightly as possible, so that he wouldn't clam up. Oh, you know, *bach*. All in fun, mind. High spirits. There were some lads from Abu Sueir, plastered, well away, been there all day, they got into a bit of a rough and tumble, our gang just sat on the sidelines and laughed. Honestly, Ailsa. Honour bright. Came out of

220

there a bit the worse for wear and got on the bikes and suddenly Chalkie wasn't there. He didn't come. I waited around a bit. Went back into the bar. Completely empty. The whole bastard lot had scarpered, except the wog with a fez behind the bar polishing glasses.

Joe has done something in Ish, Ailsa thought, that he's ashamed of. Something violent. And maybe Chalkie had been disgusted and just took himself off.

Perhaps Joe was more drunk than he seemed. For he sat slouched forward looking at his hands, turning them first one way, then the other. He began to pick at the dirty nails of his right hand with those of the left one.

So where was Chalkie now? she asked Joe. 'Joe! Where is he? Stop picking your nails. Use a file if you need to.'

Two Military Policemen were coming out of Irene's. She was in there on her own, with her worst fears confirmed. But it would probably be all right, Joe assured Ailsa. Chalkie would turn up. Most likely he'd passed out and was lying in his own vomit down some sordid alley way, or perhaps he'd wandered off into the foreign quarter, Ailsa imagined, and got himself thoroughly lost, and even now was sitting in some pavement café ... except that Chalkie was totally unadventurous and incurious, as far as she knew. A timorous man, who stuck with his own type.

'Shall I go in to her?' she asked Joe. 'I should really, shouldn't I? Joe, what is it? Are you tight, or what?'

'Course not, *bach*. I'm a bit shocked.'

She could see now that he was quivering from head to foot. Ailsa knelt uncertainly, stroked his forearm; he was out in a cold sweat. She brought him sweet tea and coaxed him to drink. His blue, baffled eyes met her gaze and she forced herself to smile encouragingly. Joe bucked up. They would go, he said, go and talk to Irene. She'd need them with her.

But it was clear when they knocked that Irene wanted a man with her. Joe might stay, if he didn't mind, and if that was all right with Ailsa. Irene made a coy joke of the borrowing of Ailsa's husband. Oh, and would Ailsa mind taking Timothy and picking up Christopher from the bus stop, and perhaps keep them with her until Roy came home? She had not been crying, Ailsa saw. Hadn't given way at all but preserved an uncharacteristic calm, her pale eyebrows raised and forehead furrowed, peering over their shoulders the whole time, so as to spot Roy the minute he came into view. She looked and sounded a bit mad.

Ailsa bedded down the exhausted children in her and Joe's big bed, pulling the balding blue candlewick bedspread up to their chins. They thrashed their limbs about in excitement at the strange linen and sleeping companions. She heard Topher whispering to Nia that now they were *married*, weren't they, they had had a *wedding* actually, and Tim was their *best man*, that was why he was allowed to share. Then they all three slipped their thumbs in their mouths and dropped off. Easy as that.

Several hours later Joe came home for his shaving tackle. He'd stay over, kip down in the chair. No news, he said. No, nothing yet, *cariad*. He'd tell her the minute they heard anything.

'How is she?' Ailsa asked.

'Fast asleep. The MO came and gave her a sedative.'

'How are you managing?'

'Fine. It's the least I can do. I'll kip down in

Christopher's room if I need to. If that's all right by you? How are the little ones?'

'Good as gold. Out like lights.'

Why did he say that, *the least I can do?* Did he blame himself? The atmosphere between them was stiff and polite, as if some mutual concealment were being practised. Which it was not in Joe to do for long (it is in me, Ailsa thought, oh yes, but it is not in him, he is so open and emotional).

When she came back downstairs, Joe was sitting hunched with his back to the front window, by the open curtains. From the blind darkness beyond the window, a barrage of insects butted against the pane. The moon was up, a blade-like crescent, the stars pouring phosphorescent light on the sands. Joe rocked himself, his dark curly head in his hands. She went and crouched beside him, briefly fondled his hair. She should not believe the worst of him. Give him a chance.

'Joe. Sweetheart. What?'

'It was my idea.'

'What was?'

'The Tiger-ride. If I hadn't egged him on, he'd still be here. I don't think!' he said. 'I just don't *think*, do I? I never *think*!' And he struck the side of his head with the knuckles of his fist.

'How could you have known how things would turn out?

'I know now.'

'No, you don't, Joe. He may be back any minute.'

'That's what she says.'

'Well, she's right.'

'You've caught the sun,' he said, meeting her eyes and

223

drawing tender fingers up her arms to the hot skin at the top. 'Whatever have you been up to?'

'Nothing important. Oh, the sunburn – yes, I'll put on some calamine.'

'Let me do it for you. Do be careful, Ailsa. You're so fair. You're going to peel.'

'I'll not do it again,' she promised, touching the smarting skin with her fingertips. The *Habibi* household, like Brewers' Green and the *Empire Glory*, seemed a theatre of illusion. Nothing that happened there had weight or relevance. 'And don't you reproach yourself about the Tiger, Joe. Chalkie's a grown man, after all. You didn't make him go with you.'

'No.'

'Well then?'

'You're so good to me, Aily.'

'What happened in the bar?'

It all spilled out. The boys had arrived with a thirst on them like nobody's business. The blokes there were legless. Even so, it had only been meant as a bit of a laugh. Practical joke. They'd been teasing the darkie waiters, he said, his cheeks hotter than her sunburn. Taunting the Gyppos to show what they'd got under their skirts. You know the old kilt-joke, he said.

'But not you, Joe. You weren't a part of that.'

'Not a part of it, no.'

'What then?'

'On the sidelines.'

He and Chalkie had just been leaning on the piano, he said, if she wanted to know. They were the audience. But Dusty and Lofty joined in, parading up and down wearing

224

table-cloths. Killing it was. Well, seemed so at the time. He was reading her expression greedily.

'Oh Joe – *honestly*.'

And she saw it all. Joe clapping and singing along, swaying his beer glass as he lolled at the piano. The life and soul of the party, so easily carried away. The head waiter's humiliation as men in table cloths mimicked his robes and demeanour. Uproar. Squaddies diving at the Arab's pristine *gallabiyya*, calling him a nancy, asking him where his sporran was, snatching at the hem of his garment, threatening to raise it and peek. Insulting Arab manhood. Insulting therefore his religion, the strongest loyalty he had. For the Prophet would be more dear to him than mother or father. And the infidel men and women, whose lewd behaviour scandalised the bar-tender at the best of times, would by their present actions have entered into a depravity that belonged to Satan.

And for all Ailsa knew, they did not stop at threatening to raise the hem of the robe. She saw them fulfilling the threat, stripping the modest middle-aged man stark naked. To his terror and shame. Throwing glasses maybe. Tussling with the other waiters when they came to his aid. Beery tempers souring. Spilling out on to the *rue Negrelli*, bawling their raucous way down the pavement arm in arm, straddling the bikes, but sudden sobriety hitting them hard between the eyes: no Chalkie. *Where's Chalkie? Isn't he here? Nah. Thought he was with you.* They'd be calling his name. Then retracing their steps. Nobody in the bar except the one bar-tender. So what did they do to him? Roughed him up to make him speak?

She saw and heard it as if she'd been there in the flesh,

recoiling from her husband and the spaniel eyes that implored not only understanding but wifely complicity, unqualified by intelligence and insight. What was your part in all this? she silently demanded. For you, Joseph Elwyn Roberts, were never one to remain 'on the sidelines' of any prank – you'll always be found dead-centre, having the time of your life.

The memory of Mona swiftly passed before Ailsa's vision, dark circles beneath her eyes, surrounded by human need, fending for those who had nothing. Setting Mona against Joe in the scales, she judged her husband. Worthless behaviour, she thought.

Worthless.

'Aye, I know: it was childish,' he wheedled. Hardly the word Ailsa would have chosen. She drew a deep breath and held it.

Sharp as a knife, Joe caught and read her look, then turned away from her, picking up the bag she'd packed. Her expression, that called him *worthless*, as clearly as if she'd spoken the word aloud, cut him to the quick.

'No fucking sense of humour,' he murmured, 'the golliwogs.' Then he added, 'Dusty says.' Looked sheepish. Clearly wished he had not blurted these disgraceful excuses. 'Well now, look, Ailsa. It was not meant to offend. It just got out of hand. I'm telling you.'

'Not meant … to offend? What if Egypt had colonised the West, then, Joe, and a gang of drunken Arabs came into a bar in Wind Street and pulled the Taffies' trousers down for a laugh? Your dad, say. To see what you and he had got in your pants?'

'Don't be disgusting. My *dad.*'

'So how is it different?'

'You know very well how. You can't make that comparison.'

'Why not?'

Not worth answering, his shrug said. If the wogs had harmed Chalkie, his look told her, she would have to change her bloody tune.

For a moment she took a dislike to him. She thought: you are stupid, Joe Roberts, and a little bit despicable. But you are mine.

14

Officials brought chitties for signing, information to be absorbed and messages of condolence. Bigwigs visited in limousines. Irene sat like a queen, receiving ambassadors from some strange land whose language was scarcely intelligible. It had been necessary to perform the autopsy with great haste, since corpses decomposed rapidly in this heat – and Chalkie must be buried soon. Joe helped the widow as best he could.

'You're such a comfort, Joe,' she said. 'I don't know what I'd have done without you. I honestly don't. I hope Ailsa can spare you. And that, you know, she doesn't mind.'

'Of course she doesn't mind.'

'She's been wonderful with the children.' Irene spoke in measured phrases, master of herself, and even picked up her knitting. She wanted Joe to have the jumper and he felt bound to agree to this inheritance. She'd been forever measuring poor Chalkie up, embarrassing the bloke as he offered his somewhat puny torso as the model to her calculation. Joe could see him now (and 'henpecked' he had thought) on the French Beach kneeling in the sand for Irene to decide on the hang of this very piece of knitwear.

And now Joe must think of his friend, with whom he'd survived the Desert War and the push into Italy, dredged up from the foetid Sweet Water Canal in this phoney peace. His body bloated and running with slime, throat slit from ear to ear, genitals sawn off and stuffed in his mouth. Of course Joe had not witnessed the salvage of the corpse. No need to see it to imagine it. He had identified Chalkie. They'd cleaned him up by then, of course. One eye was not quite closed. It seemed to be trying to peep out and make sense of all this, a ball of glazed jelly whose light was dimmed. The other eye was missing from the ruined face. Still you could make out that the features belonged to Chalkie.

*

'Let me make you a cup of tea, Irene,' Joe said. He wanted to turn his face to the wall and weep. How did he deserve this trust and gratitude from Chalkie's widow, who had known from the first that we were unsafe in this hell hole, who had seen the assassin before any of them, and had lost her Roy over and over again before the event.

Out there in the other world, he could hear a child in a torrent of tears. Nia in a paddy, no doubt, because she couldn't get her own way now that she had to share her space with two blond boys whose lives would never be the same. But they did not know their loss. He went to the window and squinted sideways to the Roberts garden, where his daughter, purple-faced and raving, was punching the air with her fists.

229

Irene joined him with the tea-tray.

'I've put out custard creams, in case we feel peckish.'

'Nia's off again,' he said.

'I expect she misses her daddy,' Irene said, and then her mouth fell open and became a hole in her face, which her hands flew to cover, as she realised what she'd said.

It should have been anyone else but Chalkie, Joe thought. If there was any fucking justice in the world. He patted her quivering, convulsing back, saying, 'That's the way, Irene lovely, cry.' Her shoulder was soft to his hands, much softer than lean Ailsa's. Irene was a harmless woman to whom those bastard wogs had dealt a blow that, as the RC priest had said, was *heinous,* it was *an impiety*. And of course it should have been himself or Dusty fished up from the Sweet Water Canal with his throat cut, since they'd led milky-mild Chalkie into the dark place. Chalkie had not taunted the Arab. He'd sat with his pint cradled to his chest and chuckled quietly on the sidelines. That was Chalkie all over.

'I mustn't,' said Irene. 'Got to stop this. Once and for all.' She wiped her hot, blubbered face. 'I can't start relying on you, Joe, I can't. It isn't right.'

She had to tread her own path from now on, she said, stanching the flow of tears with his handkerchief. Plough her own furrow: was that the phrase? She must guide Roy's sons through life under her own steam. The first hurdle was the funeral. And Roy's elder son would be there, standing to attention. Christopher wanted to attend, she said: nothing would stop him, although of course it was none of it real to the child. Even so, she and Christopher would so bear themselves – this was how she put it – as to make her husband proud of them. For Irene felt Roy was watching over them, from up there. Yes, she would bear up, even though it was hard, so hard.

Egypt killed him, the widow said. It was a fearsome thing. Every native was our enemy, even the *dhobi wallah* and the *chai wallah*, yes, and the urchin she gave piastres to because he had only one leg and a pleasing smile, such very white teeth, she said, quite unlike the English kiddies, their teeth rot so young, it is a disgrace – not Nia and the boys of course, we know how important it is to ration the sweeties that get into their mouths and how vital it is to ensure a thorough cleansing of the teeth morning and night, it is vital.

Her cup rattled as she replaced it in the saucer. Her spoon dropped to the floor and Joe retrieved it, substituting his own,

She begged him to have a care to his back, whenever he was in or near Wog Town. How right she had been to distrust the wogs. And everybody thought her silly and timid, including Roy – but *you* understood me, Joe, didn't you? I know you did, though even you did not realise the extent of their evil. She had not been silly. She had been right. So mind your back, she urged him. I shan't be here to warn you, Joe, dear, and Ailsa is so reckless.

Whatever did she mean, he wondered? But Irene swept on with what she was saying and probably she had implied only that Ailsa was not of a fearful temperament. Irene was saying that *even the women in their yashmaks were not to be trusted*. The black-gowned shepherdesses she'd seen in the fields from the train tending their sheep and goats, whom Ailsa had called *bucolic*, who seemed so mild and harmless, what did they keep up their robes? Blades. Ailsa is so good with words, she said, and I'm such a twerp, I have to have a translation! *Oh, Irene, they are not perfidious, they are just people like you and me who want to live*, that's what Ailsa said! Whereas in fact they were all enemies and would stick a knife in the back of an innocent Yorkshireman just like that! – poof! – gone! – so that you would never see your husband again as long as you lived – which was unthinkable, and she kept seeing Roy come whistling round the corner with his cap on the very edge of his head, it was a scream and always quite a puzzle how it did not fall off, he was the Leaning Tower of Pisa as regards headgear. She must learn, Irene said, looking at the palms of her hands, that these people were not him. They were just ordinary bods, she said, who happened to be alive.

Later Joe read Irene to sleep, perched on Chalkie's side of the bed in the glow of a lamp. Strange and wrong it felt, trespassing in his pal's private world. He peered round at the light and shadow and imagined being Chalkie. He saw how huge a thing it was to lose your marriage bed, the intimate core of your life, and be evicted from your own heart, leaving your side of the bed a dead white sheet. As Irene's breathing deepened, he gave over the reading and lapsed into a doze. When he awoke there was a gecko on the wall taking advantage of the lamplight to lick up insects with its long tongue. It looked fearsome, like a baby dragon. He let it be. Doing a good job, as long as it didn't give Irene a turn when she came to.

He could imagine Chalkie, who took so much care for his wife's peace of mind, and who was such a gentle bloke, trapping the baby dragon in a shoebox and putting it out of the back door.

*

'Topher whacked me in the night,' Nia complained bitterly.

'No, I didn't.'

'You did. You were bawling. You wetted my Mami's and Daddy's bed and made it smell, you boobybaby.'

'Stop it, Nia.'

Mami looked faded and almost rubbed out like a drawing. Nia frowned over Topher's and Tim's heads to her mother as she fed the younger boy rose hip syrup. Tim was off his food and Ailsa had resorted to feeding him milk through a dropper. More dribbled out than stayed in. Ailsa gave a huge yawn and said for the fiftieth time, 'Open wide like a birdie!' Topher and Nia crunched toast spread with condensed milk. They had pushed away bowls of prunes to keep them regular.

'Don't be beastly, Nia,' Mami went on. 'Be patient. I don't know what's got into you. You and Christopher used to get along so well.'

Nia could not remember such a time.

'When is it going to be just us?' she asked.

No answer.

'*When*?'

'If you don't stop being nasty, I will send you to your room. I'm sick of it, Nia, do you hear, *sick* of it!'

She jounced the heavy boy on her lap, eyes reassuring him that her rage was not meant for him.

'Are you tired, Mami?' asked Nia.

'Very.'

'I'm tired too.'

'And I am,' Topher joined in. 'I'm done in.'

233

'Well fuck off, boy. Just fuck off.'

'Right!' shouted Ailsa. 'That's *it*!'

Tim howled where she dumped him as she rose enormous over Nia and loomed there. Before she could come down on Nia, Nia had thumped Topher for good luck, with venom. He roared; and she roared as she received the hard slap on the top of her arm, the first of her life.

After the storm had blown itself out, Nia stood on her bed, where Mami had been spending the night, leaving a delicious smell of talcum between pillow and sheet – a smell that was now so blighted that Nia could not sniff it more than once. Nia looked out at the desert where men ran about pretending to shoot each other.

Mami crept in, ashamed. She said, 'Christopher and Timothy are going now, darling. They want to say bye-bye. Sorry I lost my temper.'

Immediately Nia's feeling turned right round. She flew to Topher and attached her arms like tentacles, so that Joe said she'd throttle the poor lad, let go now, my beauty, Christopher is to go home with his own mummy. He peeled her off the silent boy and reattached her to himself, carrying her around their newly orderly and quiet house like a baby. He would not let her go, even when she asked to get down and wriggled in his arms and suggested he needed a nice fag, could she hold the match?

*

Joe packed the cups from Irene's delicate china tea service in socks, nestling the saucers in newspapers. Nia and Christopher, now reconciled, helped in this work, their neat fingers wrapping the nice things with care. Nia admired the pink roses on the cups beyond anything she'd ever seen. Christopher took his new status seriously, for he was now 'the man of the house'. There was something grotesque about this, Joe felt, looking at the child's narrow shoulders and imagining Irene trying to rest her heavy head on them.

He looked up at Irene, who was perched on a stool knitting like crazy.

It must be finished, she was saying. It is for our dear Joe. I must hurry and finish it like a busy bee before we vacate. Mustn't I?

Christopher's eyes swerved from his mother to Joe. He stared. With a sock over one hand, ready to pack a cup, he put out the other to touch Joe's forearm.

'Hallo, dear,' said Joe, taking the hand. 'How are you getting on there?'

'Are you coming with us, Uncle Joe?'

Joe glanced up at Irene. How far did the children comprehend their situation? But Irene just carried on with the knitting, as if her world depended on finishing the piece in accordance with the pattern. Joe thought: she isn't coping at all. She *has* gone mad. Someone had better keep unravelling that jumper, or else all the king's horses and all the king's men...

'Uncle Joe can't go home to England just yet,' he told the child with Chalkie's ingenuous eyes.

'But you will come?'

'Oh aye. One day.'

Nia was watching him fumble with the white lies. 'I'd like some cups like these please, Daddy.'

'Ah!' said Irene. 'Bless her! When Daddy brings you back to England, precious, you shall have a cup of hot

235

blackcurrant juice out of that very cup!'

She shot Nia a bright look that made Joe queasy. Irene hardly knew or believed that it was over; it was over forever and she would not see Roy's face again on this earth.

And there is no other world, he thought. This is our ration. The door of Libanus Chapel seemed to shut in his face.

'You will come and see your Auntie Irene, won't you, cherub?' Irene went on, wooing Nia, in whom she'd never taken much more than a cursory and occasionally appalled interest.

'Yes, I will come, probably tomorrow.'

Irene laughed. 'Ah but you'll have to wait a little while, Nia. Christopher and Timothy and I are going on a long, long journey.'

'*Is* my daddy going with you?'

'No,' Joe butted in, 'of course not.' He watched her stumbling towards the terrible gaping questions: where have you hidden Topher's Chalkie-daddy? Why is my daddy doing your packing?

The quarters were stark with cleanliness. All the intimate touches had been erased. Irene had scoured and polished till her hands were raw-red. Everything was ready for the hand-over and the checking of the inventory. Going upstairs, Joe glanced into her bedroom. Chalkie's uniform was spread out on the bed like a man taken to pieces. His khaki drill was starched and pressed so mathematically that it could have stood up. The brass of his dress uniform had been buffed by Irene to a shine Chalkie would have been proud of. Joe sat on the bed beside the tunic, picking up the empty sleeve and inserting his fingers an inch into the cuff. In a

236

week's time some other bugger would be wearing it.

The bastard Gyppos did for him. It had not been Joe's fault. Back alley darkies had tracked Chalkie in all his … what could you say, innocence, honest decency … covered him in a sack (such terror), gagged and bound him, shut him in a car boot and ran him out into the desert, slit his throat and hacked off his balls and dumped him in the Sweet Water like offal. What do you expect? Joe demanded. What do you expect of these cesspit subhumans? And he wanted to kick the hell out of a wog, any wog, for – whatever Ailsa said – they were all the same. He understood how Dusty felt, the revulsion against the whole ant's nest of them, the murderous colony, with its blind hatred of all things civilised – the smell of them, the smiles of them.

Of course they would not be caught. Three men were said to be on the run. He'd seen the 'Wanted' posters: useless. How did you tell them apart, with their fawning faces? There ought to be some sort of crackdown but, oh no, it was the 'kid glove' approach, bloody public school nancy-boys, play it down. The British were afraid of the whole powder keg going up. Every other day there were riots and strikes and demonstrations in Cairo. Spies freely wandered the streets of Ish, men dressed as women, the so-called *fedayeen* freedom-fighters with their rifles up their skirts. Israel had shamed their effete army. So of course they bite the hand that feeds them. Rather than clamping down, we soft-soaped them. There'd been a slap over the wrists for the eleven airmen, *letting the side down*. And the Air Commodore saying, *The matter is viewed as a criminal rather than a political offence.* Joe had never been in a room with so many high-ups, and an Army General flung in for good measure.

237

The Whites' packing was almost complete. Joe made Nia and Christopher sit on the trunks, where they bounced their small behinds and giggled, while he secured the brass locks and buckled the straps. He attached labels, more than were strictly necessary because you could never be too careful, and he wanted to be sure, he told Irene, that everything would be as comfortable and trouble-free as humanly possible in transit. At least you're going by plane, he said, all of you, on a nice big York, what do you think about *that*, son?

'He's going to look after his mummy on the plane, aren't you, my young man?' Irene purred. Maybe when they arrived home, Irene would start to grieve. Perhaps her apparent confusion was necessary to tide her over until her husband could be laid to rest. And when you are grown up, he thought, looking down at the little blighter who was destined to look after his mummy on the plane, you will realise all that she went through for her country and for you.

*

They were to tow the coffin behind a Jeep on a flatbed trailer. Six sergeants were to bear the coffin, Joe being one of the first pair, at the widow's request. Glad to do it, of course, more than glad, honoured.

The cortege of Jeeps left the mortuary at Fayid Hospital on the brief run to the cemetery, creeping along potholed roads.

Six bearers would hardly be enough, he foresaw. By no manner of means, for Chalkie had needed a lead-lined coffin, in case he had to be dug up and re-examined at some future date. In the heat bodies soon stank higher than hung game. *She* did not know that of course. Dusty, who

238

partnered Joe, reckoned they were going to be dealing with a couple of hundredweight in furnace temperatures. Dusty, poor sod, did not look in good shape. Puffy red eyes. Tremble in the fingers that accepted a fag. Mushy sort of bloke, Joe thought. How he had cried over the donkey he'd shot. *Milk-white it was, Taf. Poor harmless creature. I took it for a bleeding wog.* Couldn't eat meat since then, apart from tinned. Careful about where he trod in case there was life there. Going on about Jesus entering into Jerusalem. Unhinged. And old Chalkie had said, *Come on now, Eeyore, you're getting to look like a poor old donkey yourself.*

And if they stumbled under the load, Joe thought, how disgraceful, what an offence to the honour that was owed to Roy White. But that would not be allowed to happen. And, bless him, Chalkie was scarcely a big man. Not an ounce of spare flesh on the bloke. *Thin as a whippet*, he'd say: *and by George, Taf, I can run like one!* Chalkie's mild, lopsided grin came back to Joe, and it was impossible to believe that his pal was inside the box.

At the cemetery gate, they took off one shoe at a time and stood on one leg to buff up the other shoe with the sock, hanging on to one another for balance. Falling in, they heaved the coffin up to their shoulders.

The six sergeants stood motionless in the furnace of midmorning heat.

Something was badly out of order. No birds. Not one tweet or chirrup. Just a hawk wheeling round by the stand of eucalyptus behind the rows of white lozenges that made Joe think of a draughts-board in which all the black counters had been captured. Which was as far from the truth as could be imagined.

A sweet stink stole up through his nose, into his brain. It seemed to coat his mouth and throat. Chalkie's corpse. The stench came through a gap in the coffin by Joe's left temple into which, great God alive, Nia could almost have wriggled her pinkie. At the other side, Dusty gagged and uttered a whimper. Joe could not see him. He fought his own urge to retch, heave, spit, run. Murmured, *Get a grip, Dusty my boy*. The bastard Air Force skimped on the coffins, leaving them presumably to the Gyppos to bang together, leaving gaps round the screw fittings, and he would like to know – as he would say to Dusty afterwards in the mess – if the officers were buried in bodged coffins. No prize for correct guesses, boy.

But of course they enjoyed a better standard of dying altogether. Buried by their own kind in the company of their own kind, with flags and bugles and full dress uniform.

Sweat pooled in the little dip you had under your nose and above your mouth that Nia called your *tosie*. No way to wipe. Therefore, duty to ignore. Hope not to sneeze.

The blabbermouth RC padre approached, ambling; the bluebottles beat him. Smelling out Chalkie's whereabouts, they crawled in to him between the loopholes and, crawling back out, made for the lips and eyes and noses of the six sergeants.

Come on, you bastard biretta. Chuck your fucking incense and be done with it. Joe stood quivering and nauseous in the heat, making faces and snorting air at the flies, for both hands were occupied and there was no way to bat the devils away. The burial party swayed alarmingly under two hundredweight of lead. With an intuitive shuffle, they righted themselves. Joe's eyes watered from the smoking incense, which at least had the advantage of driving off the flies. Half the squadron took flight. The rest disappeared into the coffin.

Oh and holy fucking water now. A faceful of that. Thanks, I needed a cool-down. And more mumbo jumbo, such that Mr Mansell at Libanus Chapel would have risen to denounce the idolatrous tricks of the Purple Whore of Rome. Slow, slow, the priest led off. The party followed, perfectly in step, the lead weight digging down into their shoulders, sharp-edged, and Joe thought they must all have been pulling the identical face, a teeth-gritting grimace.

Through the heat haze, several hundred yards away across the green, a knot of black-veiled women wavered, waiting round a hole.

At the end of the priest's palaver, all delivered in broadest Irish so that you could understand hardly one word in ten, the time came for Irene to scatter a handful of earth. She scooped it into Christopher's hand instead and gestured for him to throw it. He was a man. Took precedence. Christopher narrowed his eyes with astonishment, peering at the dirt in his palm, though it had all been explained to him beforehand. Full of germs, he had been told Egyptian soil was: Joe had many times heard her warning the little chap not to touch dirt. Now Irene mouthed, *Throw it! On your daddy*. And Christopher obeyed, starting back from the edge as he heard its dry clatter on the coffin-lid. The widow threw hers then.

Finally, the order for the firing party to give the salute. Joe brought himself smartly to attention. The volley of three shots rang like cracks of thunder. So close the riflemen stood that Joe was deafened. He saw Irene reel, as if she

241

had taken a hit, but she collected herself and, looking down at Chalkie's boy, smiled without any blood in her lips. And Ailsa, darling Ailsa, was there, standing behind the pair of them, supporting them, tears coursing down her face. Beside her stood Hedwig Webster, face half hidden behind the dark net of a mourning veil, like a spider's web.

The third rifleman was a darkie or a half-caste rather. Indian bloke from the RAF Regiment. Was it beyond anyone's gumption to have found a white rifleman?

Part Three

Luxor, January 1950
Ismailia, 1950–1952 & 1978

15

At the tomb's mouth stood twin sentinels, an elderly Egyptian ticket-collector in his *gallabiyya* and a soldier with a rifle. The flanks of the hills shone in the low afternoon sun, amber-yellow beneath a turquoise sky. A shaft led deep into the body of the hill. And I am here, Ailsa thought, and Mona is here, and we are together at the mouth of the underworld. The peaks of the Valley of the Kings were ochre in shadow, golden in the winter sun. Ailsa stood in a place of quietness and immensity. The tawny colours reminded her of autumn at home: copper and rusty-yellow leaves and bracken that always seemed to hold a remnant of the sun, a vestige and promise of light. She waited for Mona to come from the Jeep, incredulous but serene as she had been since they'd escaped together. Two women in one dream.

In the end, it had been so easy. All Ailsa had had to do was to ask Joe if he minded her going on the sergeants' wives' excursion to the Valley of the Kings, to Luxor and Karnak. Do you mind, darling? Hedwig's going. I'd really love to. But I won't if you mind. Just say the word.

Of course he didn't *mind*, Joe assured her. However could she imagine that he'd begrudge her this opportunity? He'd take a few days' leave and have a special time at home with Nia. They'd try not to tread egg and bacon into the carpet as they'd somehow managed to do that time she was ill. This winter had been a hard time for Ailsa, what with one thing and another. And he'd been a right old so-and-so, a pain in the neck, he knew that. Go, please do, I want you to go. Sign up for it before all the places are taken.

Since Irene and the boys had left for England, directly after Chalkie's funeral, Joe had been quieter, darker. Once he'd awoken in the night, his own hands at his throat, making choking noises. She'd snapped on the light, peeled his hands away from his neck. Propped on one elbow, Joe had stared at his hands, shaking. Embracing and kissing him, Ailsa had whispered reassurance. *Forgive me, Ailsa. Please, please forgive.* She had insisted that there was nothing in the world to forgive. He'd slept again but she had not. Some veil that should never be tampered with had been twitched aside. She wanted it put back but perhaps it could not be done. Joe would occasionally come out with ugly words against the Egyptians, filth and barbarity. He'd see her flinch back and would immediately silence himself – but it was as if a patch of vomit lay between them, reeking, staining the intimate fibres of their marriage. Its ghost would never be washed out of the sheets.

Lately he'd calmed right down. She'd allowed herself to get in touch with Mona again; to meet in the *Café Grec* and at the bungalow, a forbidden home-from-home. Mona was working on Beethoven's piano sonatas: Ailsa received private recitals. One day she would tell Joe and bring it out into the open – but, for a complex of reasons, not yet. Most of the refugees had either been accommodated or had moved on to Cairo, leaving Mona space for herself. And now Joe seemed genuinely delighted for Ailsa that she had a chance of an adventure, even though it excluded him. He'd be turning over a new leaf for the New Year, on his honour. Take some photos, he'd urged, inserting a film in the precious Kodak and handing it to his wife.

The two of them had been so blissfully and tenderly close then, in the subsequent week, that Ailsa hadn't wanted to come away from Joe, even to be with Mona. He'd had to argue her into going but – *no, I'd rather stay with you* – she'd clung to him, deep in the intimate warmth of their bed. It's only for a few days, Joe had insisted. She'd torn herself away from him. Yet at Luxor she'd hardly given her husband a thought.

Mona came bounding down from the Jeep, oil on her hands, looking, Ailsa thought, like a girl soldier in her khaki shorts and grey shirt, athletic and rangy, sleeves rolled up, a safari hat on her head. On a whim she'd had her hair cropped close to her head, as it had been at the Old Brewery, giving her face a naked, boy-girlish look. For each of the three days of the tour, Ailsa checked out of the group activity and was swept off by the Wing Commander's wife, who just happened to be on holiday, staying at the Luxor Hotel. Hedwig, seven months pregnant, turned her eyes away. She wandered round temples and monuments under a pink parasol, at the tail of the group, and kept her own disappointed company. She'd only come along because Ailsa would be there, she

247

let fall. And Norman had not been keen. She'd seemed too low-spirited, when they met over breakfast, even to mention the word *Kultur*, though excess of *Kultur* lay all around. What was Ailsa Roberts thinking of? Reckless behaviour it was, Ailsa knew – but the chance of a lifetime, and she seized it. There'd be time to devote to Hedwig on the last night, when they could talk German to their hearts' content. Hedwig missed her homeland. With the birth so near, she craved the comfort of having her mother near at hand. *Mutti* had been so practical. You felt so safe. Ailsa knew that Hedwig's mother and brothers had died in the Hamburg firestorm. And her father was missing, presumed dead, in Russia. A hell of fire and ice cut her off from her home. I'll spend lots of time with her until the birth, Ailsa vowed.

All the same she went skipping off with Mona, like big girls in the school playground.

Linking arms, the two women walked up the path to the opening of the tomb.

'*Salaam aleicum*,' Ailsa greeted the ticket-collector, raising and opening her left hand in token that she brought nothing insidious with her, in the rather beautiful gesture of Arab greeting Mona had taught her. They smiled into one another's faces.

'*Shokrun*,' she said. 'Thank you.'

'*Aleicum salaam!* Welcome, *mesdames*, welcome, *bienvenues*!' he said, beaming, head on one side. His eyes were an amazing green, surrounded by smile-wrinkles.

Meeting those eyes, Ailsa felt freed from chains, able to recognise the other for the person he was. *I exist, and you also exist*, her eyes told him. *I have a right to live, and this*

248

is also your right. There were ways of ducking under the fence her tribe erected against other tribes, a criminal barrier made of fear, greed and guilt. A rare moment in history was transacted in every personal meeting. Such open, friendly people Ailsa found the Egyptians she encountered in Mona's company. She loved their dry sense of humour and wished she could converse properly with them in their own tongue, eagerly absorbing the fragments of Arabic Mona taught her. To welcome the white invader as an honoured guest: why ever should they stoop to do so? Ailsa was seeing hospitality where before she'd seen – or apprehended – veiled hostility.

Perhaps, she'd said to Mona, friendship will do the trick. Every meeting between persons of good will is political. Each one closes the gap.

I need you, Mona had replied. *You help me hope.*

The duty soldier at the tomb did not return Ailsa's smile. He stared without blinking, chin raised so that although he was not a tall man, he managed to look down upon her. His glance said, as clearly as if he'd spoken aloud, *Brazen British whore, cover yourself up*. Ailsa faltered, bunching up her collar at her neck. She was aware of his cold rifle butt pointed at their backs, as they made their way down the slope into the gloom, gripping the wooden railing worn smooth by many hands.

No wall decorations: how odd. In other tombs they'd visited, the walls had been alive with gods and goddesses, pharaohs and queens. Painted deities with hawk or cobra faces, terrible and still, had towered over them every step of the way. No such murals decorated the passage or antechambers to Tutankhamun's resting place. The boy king had suffered sudden, untimely death; a lower-caste tomb had been requisitioned to accommodate his hasty funeral. So their pre-war guidebook told them. Holding tight to one another, the two women edged downwards, the air muggy and stale.

At Cairo Museum they'd viewed the exquisite chairs, bed and chariot the young man would need to equip him in the next life; the life-size black and gold sentinels who represented his soul, his *ka*. The three magnificent coffins that had nested together around the precious cadaver. The gold canopic shrine housing his guts, lungs and liver, round which four tutelary goddesses stretched their arms in a gesture of protection so tender and gracious, so human and motherly, that Ailsa's bowels had gone to water. With a pang she'd thought of the frailty of the thread from which your child's life hung. At Fayid Cemetery on the day of Chalkie's interment she'd noticed the graves of children who'd died of some trivial ailment that could have been treated back home without a thought. The dead had to be buried immediately and abandoned by the Great Bitter Lake when the parents' time came for a home posting.

But why worry about Nia? Why feel tugged in the region of your navel, by the invisible cord that bound you to your child? Nia reared in Ailsa's mind's eye and stared past her, implacable as a baby god. *Shan't be long*, Ailsa had wheedled, lingering in the doorway with her case. *Have a gorgeous time with Daddy.* But the child, who was your judge, weighed you in the balance and, finding you wanting, averted her head. *You will only have me for so long. You know this and yet have shortened the time left to us.* The airlessness of the passage made Ailsa light-headed. Why go on? Because you couldn't go back. Mona led the way into the passage forking right.

But, oh no, here he was, the American archaeologist, Mr Bothmer from Brooklyn, who'd talked them round a series of tombs this morning, until their heads had pulsed and their legs ached. In subterranean chambers, some like cathedrals, he'd interpreted paintings, commenting on the preservation of the colours, praising the cutting of reliefs, solving hieroglyphic enigmas. Not that she'd have missed it for the world: such a privilege to be instructed by one so cultivated and knowledgeable. The last tomb they'd visited belonged to Tuthmosis III. The electric current being switched off, their route had been lit by a paraffin lamp held up by a *ghaffir*, as Mr Bothmer called him. They'd climbed a steep mountainside and descended into a crevice hand over hand down a rickety iron ladder; then negotiated rock steps, deep, deep into the mountain side, to penetrate halls and corridors of vast dimension. When they'd emerged, soft-spoken and courtly Mr Bothmer, a handsome, suave man with a leonine head of hair, went off with the guard to share a cigarette on a rush mat in the guard's stone hut.

Now he swept his hat off to them and murmured something about destiny.

The three stood together at the wooden rail, looking down at the chamber Howard Carter had unsealed thirty years before, discovering the nest of caskets, like Russian dolls, that for three thousand years had housed the boy's corpse. The removal of the treasures had left on display only this central emptiness. At the base of the pale stone room lay a modest coffin containing the boy-king's mummy, surrounded on four walls by pictures and hieroglyphs.

Mr Bothmer was scathing about Tut's tomb. 'So disappointing for you ladies,' he said. 'Nothing to be seen. An inferior tomb.'

But he perked up when Mona asked about the meaning of the monkeys on the west wall. He had much to say about baboon symbolism in Egyptian resurrection mythology. The ancients had observed, he said, that when baboons awaken in the morning, the first thing they do is to turn themselves in the direction of the sun. To Ailsa, half listening, the rows of identical baboons looked endearingly like the pattern of a child's nursery wallpaper. She would tell Hedwig about this. Hedwig would be touched; her eyes would swim. For here the truth of human life was laid bare for all to see: mothers' immortal tenderness for babes beyond saving.

A chest of board games had been found here with ivory counters to amuse the young man in eternity. The paintings on the north wall showed his mouth being opened, to restore his senses for use in the afterlife: Mr Bothmer took them through the symbolism at a gallop, for time was pressing. Dark Anubis, the jackal god, led the pale Pharaoh on his journey through death, a quest fraught with terror and danger. Over the river of death. Into the presence of the most terrible gods in the pantheon. The boyish heart was weighed in judgement. Into the sky he ascended, the living image of the god Amun.

'Do *you* believe in life after death?' Ailsa asked Mr Bothmer.

'Oh, well. As a Christian, naturally,' he said, shuffling backwards, giving a high-pitched cough, which he covered with his hand.

It was as if an impropriety had been committed. Shortly

Mr Bothmer said he would leave the ladies for now, as he had an engagement with Miss Natacha Rombova of the Bollingen Foundation and her little dog, which accompanied her everywhere, even into the tombs, where it barked the place down.

When he'd gone they stood in silence, hands on the railing. For ages the murals had been sealed unseen. They were painted for the gods' eyes, Ailsa thought. The gods' eyes see in the dark. But now we come along and breathe on their eternity, defiling them with many-times re-breathed carbon dioxide and sulphur and bacteria. She peered from the side of her eye at her friend: two silver chains on Mona's throat picked up threads of light, the ankh Ailsa had bought her at Karnak and the key to the house in Jerusalem.

Love for Mona suffused Ailsa. I'd risk anything for you, she thought. I don't know what will come of it. Or what it's all about. And immediately the tenderness was streaked by perplexity, a dark slick tainting the clear water of friendship. But what could adulterate true friendship? And theirs was true. Why should their affection feel compromised, aside from its necessary secrecy? Mona's hand reached for Ailsa's and clasped it. Or was it secrecy itself that contaminated what they had, Ailsa thought, at the same time as it kindled excitement and transformed fellowship into something hot, ardent? Dangerous, even. If they could just be ordinary, low-key, this passionate glow would fade. Did she want that? Did Mona? There was something more than life-sized about Mona: a spirit that burned to live on the heroic scale. It had chosen Ailsa as its partner. This force carried Ailsa along, racing dreamily down the current of another's desire.

253

The chamber was almost domestic sized; not magnificent at all, but bare and simple. It impressed her with neither peace nor calm, but with stasis, final changelessness. She thought of Chalkie. Of how there was no time in his world, only a boundless waiting. But how Sergeant Roy White ate away at the living. Was consuming Joe, his comrade, infecting him with spores of death.

'Well, we'll have to love you and leave you, Tut my dear old pal,' Mona said at length.

Wings fluttered in Ailsa's chest; butterflies agitating for freedom. She couldn't wait to get out into the fresh air.

Then, confusingly, there was Chalkie White with the head of a hawk, face turned away, eyes fixed on some sight in another world, turned away sternly and forever. The jackal god had him by the hand and was leading him back down into the tomb, back the way they had come.

Ailsa allowed herself to be supported up into the light of day. Passing the gatekeeper's nod and the soldier's sneer, they climbed into the Jeep and drank thirstily from their water bottle. The sun was setting behind tawny peaks of limestone with their patina of gold from the silted sand; the air had cooled and the swift Egyptian twilight was imminent. Vestiges of sunlight gilded the tired faces of the few tourists who'd followed in their footsteps into the valley.

'I shall always remember that we were here together,' Mona said. 'Always. Are you all right?' She leaned over and placed cool fingertips on Ailsa's wrist, as if to take her pulse. They held and kissed each other. It seemed altogether the right thing. Mona drove through biblical hills with scattered mud brick villages. Black-robed women tended donkeys and goats, or carried petrol cans full of water on their heads. A boy with a cart heaped with palm leaves was thrashing a donkey.

*

Their last night: they laid out a picnic of delicious bread, goat's cheese and tomatoes, and sat cross-legged on the bed eating, drinking, talking. About *Habibi* and his anti-Zionism and how he'd been disowned by most of his family in Manchester as an anti-Semite and a traitor to his blood; then he'd topped it all by marrying not just a *goy* but an Arab woman. *Habibi* could understand why they felt as they did, only he couldn't share it. It was his decency that lay at the bottom of it and common sense, Mona said: his clowning around was his way of tilting at a mad world. He'd put himself in the firing line, every imaginable firing line. *H*e gave people their best estimate, as witness her good-for-nothing self.

'Look, let me show you something.'

From her wallet Mona took a pencilled poem by one of Ben's psychiatric patients, jotted on a scrap of ruled paper above a sketch of the Wing Commander dancing, wearing a ballet tutu over his KDs and boots. Mona carried it around in her bag. Wasn't it the spitting image? She kissed it. She'd wear it away, wear *him* away, she said, with so much kissing.

And yet you can bear to be away from him and spend time with me, Ailsa thought.

'Shall I read it aloud, love?'

'Yes, of course, go on.'

> *Gentle Gentle Wing Co Jacobs*
> *the marchpast the flypast the flytrap*
> *the sad ones are coming for us*
> *voices voices voices the sad ones*
> *butchers knives at Sakkara*
> *the chameleon on the black wall*
> *moths coat his tongue*
> *but Gentle Gentle Wing Co Jacobs*
> *I will join the dancepast in your footprints*
> *through warmer sand.*

'Almost as if Gentle Gentle were a rank,' Mona said. This was how *Habibi* was. He found it difficult to hate. It wasn't in him. A bit of his brain was missing. The young man who'd written the poem had been suffering from psychosis, 'sand-happy' they called it; he'd tried to kill himself several times. Touched by *Habibi*'s kindness, he wrote the first and possibly last poem of his life.

'What happened to him?'

'Sent home, I suppose. Or he killed himself. Many of the boys Ben sees have seen too much. The War, Palestine.'

It wasn't always easy to live with *Habibi*'s sweetness, she admitted, for Mona of course wasn't like that, she was a bit of a bruiser. But he took people for the best in them. When they had met in Lübeck, he'd been with an American, Abe; she had imagined *Habibi*, well, could not love a woman. But that was wrong.

Ailsa tried not to stare. She blushed, breathed short; was aware of Mona's arm, brushing her own. Don't tell me any more, she thought, edging fractionally away.

Someone screamed. A woman in pain or terror or both.

Hedwig's baby made its presence felt. Time to be born, the child announced. Ailsa scrubbed her hands and arms; offered soothing words. The labouring woman clung to her. Two months early and far, Hedwig wailed, from civilisation and clean hospitals and her husband. Don't let me be taken into one of the native hospitals, she begged, raising her white face from the pillow, forehead beaded with sweat. Don't let a foreign doctor get his hands on me. They don't understand about germs, she said, and hygiene. Promise me, Ailsa, promise. And also Mrs Brean. That old battle-axe is not to come anywhere near me.

The baby was not taking its time. It was speeding down a helter skelter and would plunge out into a dirty and unready world if they didn't get a move on. Mona was set to fetching disinfectant, a bucket and a rubber sheet.

'Now clean the sheet with the disinfectant,' Ailsa told her. 'Slosh it everywhere. And your hands and arms. Thoroughly. No, like this.' As the belt of pain slammed tight round Hedwig's belly, Ailsa murmured that all was well, breathe, breathe. There was nobody to refer to. Mona seemed to be plain useless under these circumstances. And Ailsa herself was tiddly.

'If you're going to puke, toddle,' Ailsa told Mona with an asperity she didn't try to hide. 'I mean it.'

'No, I'm not, I'm not.'

Mona scrubbed the red rubber sheet. They laid it on the bed, just in time, for Hedwig's waters broke. Is it a haemorrhage? Mona asked in alarm, stepping back. No, you idiot, it's the amniotic waters. Ailsa told Hedwig this was normal and natural and showed that things were progressing just as they ought. She had no idea if this was so.

Then everything stopped. Hedwig seemed to have lost her way. Get some more water, Mona. It must be boiled for three minutes and watch them do it. Mrs Brean had phoned Ish and Norman would certainly be on his way by now. And they were sending a team of medics. Not long now, Ailsa reassured Hedwig.

'In a strange, hot land,' she heard Hedwig say.

'We're here, your friends,' Ailsa reassured her. 'You're not among strangers, are you? Everything's fine.'

Hedwig fell into a light doze. What was the time? Ailsa consulted the disc of Hedwig's gold watch. A quarter past two. The light bulbs faltered and recovered. A power cut was all they needed. Ailsa called for a torch.

Mrs Brean yoo-hooed round the door. She would take over now. Babs was the one to get this little squeaker born. Her abominable cheerfulness made Ailsa want to scream. No thanks. But I insist. And I insist you won't. Ailsa assured her that everything was progressing in a calm, orderly fashion, and Mrs Webster expressly didn't want anyone round her she didn't know – but get hold of a torch, or preferably two, before you go.

'Oh, but, lovey, everyone knows *me*.'

Mona, returning with torches, saw her off, Ailsa had no idea how, for Hedwig awoke with a shriek. Her nightie rode up as she tried to scramble off the bed, revealing the twisted ridges of old scars from thigh to knee.

'Is *she* still here?' Hedwig asked. 'Don't look, don't look, just tell me. Over there. *Die Jüdin.*'

A Jewish woman? Ailsa soothed her: there was nobody

there at all. Just the three of them and the baby would make four when it came. Did she mean Mona? Or was she seeing things?

Hedwig closed her eyes. Her lips moved; she was muttering or chanting. Was this how people were when they were dying? Was Hedwig dying? Ailsa had to bend to catch the words. What was she saying?

Die Bombenflieger! Mutti burning.

No one is burning. Wake up. You're dreaming.

The bombing of Hamburg, of course. Her mother and brother. Ailsa took Hedwig's face in her hands and stroked it. Let's get this over. Ailsa caught in fragments her hoarse whisper: *Jüdin. Sara. Dort drüben.*

'Hedwig, stop that. Stop that instantly. Now wake up.' She shook Hedwig's shoulder.

'What? What is it, Ailsa? What have I done?'

She was clearly innocent of what had come out of her mouth.

'You were dreaming. And delirious. Never mind. It's all over now. We have to get this baby born. But by the way, Mona is not a Jew. Just for the record. Not that it would make any difference if she were.'

'But, Ailsa dear, I know that,' Hedwig said, puzzled. *'Warum sagst du das, liebe Ailsa? Was meinst du damit?* Why do you say that?'

'I must have misheard something you were saying.'

The belt of pain slammed tight again. The baby was coming now, fast. Contractions almost constant. Ailsa looked between the quivering legs. Darkness was crowning there. I can't, I can't. Yes, yes, you can. Cupping Hedwig's knees in both palms, she created resistance. Just one more push – one more – there.

The bloody head was driven out into Ailsa's hands; the narrow body flopped out after it. Its little willy baptised them with an eccentric arc of urine. Ailsa sucked the mess out of its nose; spat; welcomed the mewing protest. The baby was removed from her hands; Mona wrapped it in a torn-up sheet. Ailsa awaited the afterbirth. Cries pumped out. Good, well done. Over now. But Hedwig moaned, whimpered. Here you are, Hedwig, your little boy, he's perfect. No! Take it away! All was not right. The mother had begun to toss again, and Ailsa, straightening up, realised that labour was continuing. Ailsa said, there's a twin, a second baby, Hedwig, now, when you want to, push, that's the ticket, push. Nearly there.

The head was out and it was the wrong colour. Blue-black. The embryo had died some time ago; its bloodied face bunched like a fist. Another boy, less than half his brother's size. Ailsa could not think what to do with the corpse. She held it in convulsively trembling hands, sheathed in its brother's black slime of meconium. Keep it from the mother, wouldn't that be best? She shouldn't see. Poor Hedwig. Scissors were brought, Babs was there and Ailsa was glad of her. She made way for Babs and left for her own room.

'God, my *God*, remind me not to have children,' Mona gasped. 'How did you manage that? Coping like that?'

'No choice. You have to cope. At least she's got one,' said Ailsa tonelessly. 'One healthy boy. It's all she was expecting after all.'

Mona's hand shook, pouring out the red wine they'd been drinking, what seemed a lifetime ago, sharing their private confidences. She looked at Ailsa in awed apology for not having been more use.

Glass in hand, Ailsa opened the shutters and stepped out on to the veranda. The last violet moment of sunrise burned away; men below rode bicycles with panniers of new bread; a Land Rover drew up on the opposite side of the road, four doors opening, men springing out. The medics rushed into the wrong hotel, the Luxor Star. Ailsa called but none of them heard. She shrugged. Babs would sort it out. Blood flecks stained Ailsa's blouse, honourable blood. She thought of Hedwig's fire-scarred legs. No wonder she wouldn't be seen dead in shorts or a bathing suit, however sweltering the sun. She'd been hurt by us, hurt beyond all bearing, yet she'd picked herself up and agreed to live. It was brave. Yet Ailsa couldn't like her.

On the bedside cabinet lay Joe's Kodak, the film not quite used up. Mona had taken endless pictures of Ailsa and the obelisk at Thebes, Ailsa eating a sandwich at Memnon, Ailsa beside the Nile. Picking up the camera, she went in to photograph Hedwig's baby.

'Such a bouncing fellow-me-lad!' Babs was exclaiming. 'Had you thought of names? I found my girls' names in *The Reader's Digest*.'

'No, he has no name. Where have you put the other one?' Seeing Ailsa, Hedwig held out one hand, with an expression of relief. 'Oh, thank you. Thank you for everything. Whatever would I have done without you?'

Ailsa got rid of Babs by telling her that the medics had arrived from Ish and gone into the wrong hotel. She soaked a flannel in warm water and bathed Hedwig's face; passed a comb through the front of her hair, so that the fair curls

261

sprang up. They both gazed at the child in his mother's arms. The Ancient of Days, thought Ailsa, come out of hiding. A nativity. And it seemed in some measure her child, the boy she herself did not have – yet. The baby's mouth against Hedwig's breast rooted sideways in its sleep. Its hand, a closed bud, was held between its mother's finger and thumb.

'A beautiful boy,' Ailsa said.

'Yes. But what about the other one?'

'Hedwig, it had not grown. It had died in the womb.'

'I see. Where is he?'

If the mother chose to see him, that was her right. Perhaps the baby corpse could be made presentable. Ailsa went out to see. But Babs had ordered it burnt in the hotel incinerator. Ailsa stepped out into the back yard. The heat had risen, though the shadows were still long. Chickens scratched round in the stony sand; a small boy was relieving himself against a wall. Black, rancid smoke eddied from the incinerator. Too late. Perhaps it was just as well.

Hedwig turned her face away. The successful twin had starved out the weak one. Fratricide. Law of nature, Ailsa thought. The nameless survivor had fought for the space and won.

'Ailsa.'

'Still here.'

'Did I say something before – to upset you?'

'No. Of course you didn't.'

'I had the impression –'

'No. Really.'

'That's all right then,' said Hedwig doubtfully. 'Only, you know, one is not oneself at such a time. Where is your friend?'

'Mona? I don't know. Shall I get her?'

'Please.'

When Mona came in, Hedwig took her hand and wouldn't let go. She thanked her warmly and appeasingly for everything. Please sit down here beside me. I am so grateful, I cannot express my gratitude. Would you like to hold the baby? Mona was embarrassed. She'd been a hopeless duffer, she confessed. No earthly use at all. It was Ailsa who was the midwife. She gazed, fascinated, at the boy her friend had delivered, as if she could never gaze her fill. Ailsa used the last few pictures on the reel of film, to photograph mother and child, before Norman and the medics arrived and the room was full of looming men, experts, taking over, ruling the roost.

The wee man was a good size, said the doctor from Fayid. He congratulated Ailsa on sterling work. She took him aside and told him about the dead foetus.

'Often the way. Happens more frequently than people imagine. Mother didn't see it? Good. Not trained, are you? No, then you did jolly well, Mrs Roberts. Good show, congratulations. Plenty of pluck, eh, and a dollop of good old female intuition?'

17

Ailsa simply could not resist it. She hitched her skirt over her thighs and straddled the Tiger. My turn now.

Sleepy Nia at the bedroom window nodded her sage head. Put up a finger to her lips: *Secret!*

Ailsa wrapped her hands round the grips, breathing in the exciting scents of hot rubber and oil. The Tiger sat molten between her spread legs, despite having been parked in shadow. Joe's pride and joy. With the Whites gone, he could display the beast openly, the guilty beast, without fear of upsetting poor mad Irene – not that anything Joe did could have disturbed Irene's piteous attachment to himself. However was she coping back home in Birmingham without Ailsa's husband to simper over?

I'm getting rather nasty, Ailsa thought. It's because I'm champing at the bit.

'Turn the key, Mami! Turn it!' Nia shrieked. 'Go on – roar!'

Joe would not be amused. He would say, *But Ailsa fach,*

it is too dangerous. He'd mean (she'd wave her advanced licence in front of his eyes, he could hardly quarrel with that) it is so immodest, ladies don't, and at the back of his mind would be the songs the men sang about getting your leg over.

'I shan't tell!' Nia called, bouncing up and down.

You say that now, miss, but when you've extorted a sweet cigarette from him, and you're cuddled up for a bedtime story....

Dismounting, Ailsa resentfully unpegged the sun-stiffened towels. Since Luxor she'd felt stalled and stale. Chores were irksome. Egypt had struck her senses a reeling blow: its colours, scents, tastes. For all that she had winced away from Mona on the night of Eric's birth, now she dreamed of Thebes and Memnon, wandering there freely with a friend, the mind opening to wide vistas impossible in this cage. As they left Luxor, Mona had suggested a jaunt to Giza, to see the Sphinx and the Pyramid of Cheops. They could stay a night at Mena House, an old hunting lodge that had been turned into a hotel, at the very foot of the Pyramids. How would Ailsa like to wake up in the morning and pull back the curtains, to see old Cheops blazing in the sun? Wander the Mena gardens together? Ride camels or horses maybe, side by side, into the desert?

Ailsa had the impression that what happened there would change her life.

But how could it possibly be managed? Luxor had been a one-off. Joe was intuitive. His antennae had radar sensitivity. Already her husband seemed to have detected some shift in her, a change he couldn't put a name to. Galled, Ailsa daily resorted to the meanness of using

265

Hedwig as an alibi. After sitting with her for half an hour, she'd skedaddle to Ish, under cover of an errand for Hedwig. Tempting the gods. It had got to stop. The baby Ailsa had delivered thrived but its mother sat listlessly peering out of the wire netting into the desert. *Which way is Luxor?* she'd asked that morning. She wanted to face towards it. Luxor was Hedwig's Mecca, where, Ailsa intuited, the dead baby called her from the other world. And perhaps she seemed to hear it crying – along with all her other dead.

Baby blues, the MO reassured the anxious husband. Quite normal – and all the more to be expected in view of the difficult birth. The doctor was gentle and sympathetic, a youngish, sunburnt man in his thirties, with a surprising head of silver hair. Young mothers come out of it when they're ready. Your wife is tired out, he said to Norman. Give her all the help you can; make much of her. As long as Hedwig was caring for the baby, not attacking it or anything? No? No cause to worry then. But keep an eye out. Give her Guinness for the milk. Does she seem to love her son? Norman was unable to admit that his wife showed no more than a dutiful affection.

If necessary, the doctor had said, we can speak to one of the consultants at Fayid: one of the psychologists. Very good, very humane people. Relating this to Ailsa, Norman had looked shaken, out of his depth. The doctor assured him there was no stigma associated with mental problems these days, nothing out of the ordinary. But *still* – the shame of it.

Habibi, thought Ailsa. *Habibi* would help her. She'd ask Mona if something could be arranged.

266

Hedwig took Eric out in the pram only when it was unavoidable, and then always within school hours. Otherwise a rabble of kids would follow her, chanting, *Adolf! Adolf!*

'Which is not his name and never could be. So why do they do this cruelty?'

'Pig-ignorance. Our "superior" culture,' said Ailsa. 'Try not to take it to heart. Now then, Hedwig, what can I do for you? I've got half an hour. Why don't I wash the nappies?'

'You will do no such thing. I am perfectly capable of my duties.'

'Of course you are, but we could all do with a hand from time to time.'

'You are so good to me, Ailsa.' Hedwig had relaxed her rigidly watchful gaze. 'I know I'm a most frightful bore.'

'Nonsense. It's natural. You had a rotten time in Luxor. Bound to take a while to settle your mind.'

'May I confide to you something?'

An assimilated Jewish girl, her name was Gudrun, had been in Hedwig's class at school, before the Jewish children were expelled. A clever, original girl. She'd been in hiding right under everyone's nose throughout the war, sheltered, as it turned out, by a Christian group called the *Bund*. She'd moved between their homes, not just around Hamburg but all over the place. Gudrun had been conspicuous, a redhead with such terrific cheek: she'd ride the trams around the city and flirt with the SS-men bold as brass. Towards the end, she'd dropped out of sight.

On the night of the fire-bombing, Hedwig ran for her life, she was on fire, her hair was on fire, look, there is the bald patch, it never grew back, you have seen the scars on my legs. Running between towers of flame, choking with smoke, Hedwig sees this girl streaking past. Gudrun, having kept alive for six years, escaping every deportation, breaks out under cover of the fire.

'And did you ever see her again?'

'I don't know if she got away. You have to hope. But then I wonder if I was seeing things.'

In favour of the story was its absurd implausibility, although Ailsa knew that a few Jews had survived even in Berlin. Gudrun was hardly a Jewish name. If Hedwig had been making it up, she'd surely have called her Sara or Rachel.

'That's all behind us now, Hedwig.'

But Hedwig had bleakly replied, 'Penalties are required. To the twentieth generation.'

'No,' Ailsa had insisted. 'No, they're not.'

Eric's crying had interrupted them. He'd batted his arms around, trussed up in hand-knitted blue woollies. Picking up the bulbous boy and handing him to his mother for feeding, Ailsa had thought, What a weight! And far too hot in all that clobber. She felt a singular interest in him. The mother, glancing at her watch and unbuttoning her blouse, had put him to the breast. Her heart was elsewhere. It was with the dead. Eric's unblinking violet eyes were fixed on her face but she rarely looked at him when he fed. The most natural thing in the world and yet Hedwig could not do it. From Eric's angle his mother's face must have looked featureless as a third udder, a planet beyond his ken. She performed all her tasks because she was *verpflichtet*. Duty was a great comfort,

268

she'd explained, looking past Ailsa out of the window to where sand pelted like hail against the glass.

'For goodness' sake!' Ailsa, who found not a crumb of comfort in duty, had burst out. 'Honestly, Hedwig. That's absolutely Prussian!'

'My father is Prussian! Of the highest integrity.'

'Well, sorry, but *Pflicht* is piffle. Look where it's got us. You're bloody lucky, you know, to have Norman and Eric. They love you. Why can't you just be happy with what you've got? Nothing else is real.'

For a moment, Hedwig's canny expression and indrawn breath had suggested something about the pot calling the kettle black. She knew very well that Ailsa was no more satisfied with her lot than she was with hers. Less, perhaps. But she'd said nothing of that.

A pause. Hedwig had patted the baby's back, holding him against her neck, where he bubbled posset into her hair. Then she'd let out an odd little giggle and said, 'Thank you, Ailsa. You are a tonic. Norm does not like to cross me. And I am a bit of a wallower.'

Ailsa had missed the bus to Ish. Mona would have waited at the *Café Grec*. She'd have watched the door, biting her lip. Giving up, she'd have called it a day. Mona had worked after the war with the United Nations Relief and Rehabilitation Administration in Germany, hadn't she, resettling displaced persons? She might know how to trace German soldiers who'd disappeared in Russia. That would be something. But Ailsa hadn't spoken of this to Hedwig. She'd walked home thinking, I'll ride that bike if it's the last thing I do.

Nia screamed, 'Get back on! I won't tell!'

269

'Lie down now, my beauty,' Ailsa called up to her daughter. 'Siesta!'

The new woman in Chalkie's flat was whacking the mats. Ever since she'd arrived, Mrs Wintergreen had given those mats hell. Not that they'd needed beating, for Irene had kept everything immaculate. But nobody trusted her predecessor's cleaning. A Warrant Officer's wife, condemned to slum it amongst sergeants, would naturally assert superior cleanliness. On arrival she'd said – brayed, rather – that after Singapore and Aden, this posting was a doddle, her name was Hilda Wintergreen and was there a Guide troop on camp? She'd do her bit as Arkela. Something of a Memsahib Hilda seemed: everything wilting Irene had not been.

Poor soul, Irene was wandering like a displaced ghost, so her frequent letters testified. Ailsa felt nothing but relief that the unnatural closeness of the two families had been severed. And not only because Irene wanted what Ailsa had got – Joe – but because she did no good to Joe. Something in Ailsa's husband was coarser, harsher. Irene reinforced a ranting prejudice in him that Ailsa could not melt away. It reminded her of his crude dad in Treforys going on about the Paddies and bred moments of sheer abhorrence. Her husband saw it, and was hurt and soured.

The Khamsin season hardly helped. Sand in the bud of your eye, up your nostrils, between your teeth. The Egyptians thought the hot desert wind commemorated the fifty days Cain carried the murdered body of his brother Abel on his back, looking for a place to hide it. A sand blizzard cast Ailsa and Nia down and whipped their faces, so that her daughter cried out in pain before Ailsa could fumble her into a kangaroo pouch made out of her full skirts. A wretched, turbulent season.

Dumping the washing on the kitchen table, Ailsa marched straight back out. Climbed on to the Tiger; started up the engine and rode down the path, on to the waste patch behind the buildings where the kiddies played, which was now deserted. The knack returned, as long as you didn't think about it, in a rush of reverberation that shuddered through your frame. Ailsa's back remembered how to lean and balance. Her shoulders reasserted their strength. The Tiger told her exactly what to do.

Just one lap. For a lark.

She roared off. Was Ailsa Birch again in tunic and trousers, with a bag of letters strapped to her shoulder, a heavy belt around her middle. Ailsa Birch dodging and weaving through London traffic, as she had at nineteen, when you were invulnerable. All dazzling, charismatic ego. Young men had been dying all over the world. Death was the dark angel Ailsa had given a run for his money. She gave him a run now, slewing up sand as she cornered, and picking up speed in the return.

She could fetch Mona and clear off with her into the desert, leaving behind these contemptible barracks. Sauce for the gander was sauce for the goose, why the hell shouldn't it be? And why should Joe be *narked*, as he sometimes illiterately complained, with his wife? In that mood he'd twist everything round until she, who bent over backwards to avoid blaming him, must be the scapegoat for the evil his tomfoolery had unleashed upon his friend.

Enough. Checking herself, Ailsa brought the Tiger stammering home. Joe would spot the tyre marks at once,

271

of course, and know his darling had been tampered with. Too bad. She ran upstairs to check on Nia. The child lay asleep under the mosquito net, flushed, thumb half in, half out of her mouth, tongue intermittently lapping it. Ailsa sat and flicked through a magazine. Nia beneath the net looked like a little white bride, the golliwog a comical wide-eyed groom, whose black moon-face peeped sidelong at Nia with a simpleton's smile. A swelling on the inner part of her daughter's elbow caught Ailsa's attention: a mosquito bite presumably. She must remember to dab it with disinfectant when Nia woke up. No sense in disturbing her now.

Ailsa's world had finally burst out of the frame of Joe's narrow picture. There was so much she could never broach with him. She kept her mouth shut. Yet not one of these concealments could count as a guilty secret, not in any halfway decent world. No, Ailsa didn't think so. Not at all! What was she guilty of? Just getting out of line. Being, not even a black sheep, but a piebald sort of sheep in a field of whitish fleeces.

It's not *me*, she thought, should feel ashamed. It's you lot. *Baa*, she thought, *baa* to the bleating lot of you.

*

The apple tart was safely in the Belling. Ailsa saw, twisting round, her hands covered in flour, that Joe had let in the makings of a colony of flies and was swatting at them with the door still ajar. He didn't kiss her. She crossed the kitchen and nudged the door shut with her hip.

'A parcel came,' she said. 'For you. I didn't open it.'

The sweater had been immaculately pressed and packed in tissue paper. Ailsa heard him rustle the leaves apart and

272

glance in briefly; then replace the lid and leave it where it was. Presumably Irene's devotion embarrassed him, although he had lapped it up, as far as she could see. Was that fair? Obscurely, she wanted him to be in the wrong.

She smelt beer on his breath. She didn't like that. The sky was filmed with a dusty pall and the sand looked grey and shifted around in the desultory breeze.

'Don't start drinking at this time of day, Joe,' Ailsa said. 'I wish you wouldn't.'

'Nag, nag.'

'Oh now, come on. That's not fair, Joe. I don't nag.'

'That a fact?' He locked his teeth over the mouth of the bottle and jerked the top off, against the enamel. Ailsa winced. He would do that once too often and crack a tooth. Then he'd be sorry. That was what louts did, bite tops off beer bottles, men without even a veneer of civilisation or manners. Joe bore the bottle and a glass into the living room. Ailsa remained at the table, quietly gathering together the pastry edges left over from the apple pie and moulding them into a ball to make cheese straws.

'You don't know what nagging is, Joe Roberts, if you think I nag. So don't you dare say so.'

'All right, I won't *say* it.' *But it's still true*, he murmured.

'I beg your pardon?'

'Didn't speak.'

'I distinctly heard you.'

'Not a blinking word, mate.'

'I did.'

'Couldn't have done.'

'Joe,' she said, and put her head round the door, 'please put the beer away. It's not four o'clock.'

'So?'

'Too early.'

'Or too damn late,' he said, meaning nothing in particular. 'Wrap up, Ailsa, for God's sake.'

As she went out again, tutting with exasperation, Joe switched the wireless on high. She heard him kick off his slippers, so that one flopped against the wall and the other landed on the mat. Now he'd be raising his feet and resting them on a coffee table they had agreed in a more temperate hour was too slight to bear the weight of a man's size nines. He drank deeply and smacked his lips in an idiotic way he knew jangled her nerves.

'Any crisps going, Ailsa? Too early is it for crisps?'

She sent a packet of crisps flying through the air at him and again she disappeared.

'Are you not speaking to me?' he roared.

Silence. She heard him open the crisp bag and rummage out the blue screw of salt. He shook the bag up and down.

'*Why* are you not speaking to me?'

'Don't yell, darling,' she said, putting the cheese straws in the Belling with the nearly cooked pie and washing flour off her hands. She came in to him, wiping her wet hands. 'I can hear you without your yelling.'

Joe put out a hand to her and she took it gladly. He pulled her towards him and sat her on his lap, offering a crisp.

'No thanks. Spoil my tea. It's all right,' she said, kissing the top of his forehead where it met the curly black hairline. 'You're upset. Only don't blame me, Joe.'

'Blame you for what?'

'For ... I don't know, Chalkie, I suppose. And don't blame

yourself either.'

He knew, he bellowed, who to blame! The fucking bastard Gyppos! Want someone to geld? Geld them!

Ailsa leapt free of him, staggered and stood with her back to him, quivering from head to foot. It was like watching a man vomit.

Geld the dirty bastards! he bawled and Ailsa's whole body gave a start, as if on the verge of sleep.

He brought his fist slamming down on the chair-arm. The deep qualm Joe was suffering clearly did not abate. He could not shout it away. The louder and more grating his voice was, the more she saw that he sickened himself.

Nia, she mentioned Nia. Not good for Nia to hear her father losing his temper.

'Then don't set me off, woman,' he growled.

'I don't need to. You set yourself off. And don't call me *woman*. I'll not be called *woman* by some illiterate bloody Welshman! Listen to yourself. You have so little – dignity, I'm ashamed.'

She stood up, a schoolmarm, with folded arms, looking down upon her husband, as he upended the bottle into his mouth. Leaving for the kitchen, Ailsa was ready to storm out of the door, but paused to open the oven door with steady hands, remove the tart and twiddle the knob of the Primus.

*

Never heard Ailsa lose her temper before. Joe wanted to say, *You shouted at me, Aily!* With a kind of wonder, almost hilarity, because, ah ha! *illiterate bloody Welshman!* she gave herself away there. Gutter talk if ever he heard it. What

275

would her plummy-voiced pals from the other side of the track think of that?

He could not get out of his mind the photographs she'd brought back from her trip. Who'd taken them all? Someone completely obsessed with Joe Roberts' wife, that was for sure. Joe's wife starred in every one except the three of Hedwig Webster with the newborn baby. The Websters had no camera so he'd given the snaps to Norman. Next to the proud, weary mother sat a bare-armed female, wearing a very expensive watch, with a tiny black face and a gold strap. You could only see a portion of the face but he would know the Jacobs woman anywhere. And this morning Norman Webster had confirmed it. Yes, the officer's lady had been a great support. She'd been staying there then, at the hotel? And the Wing Co with her? Not as far as Norm knew. Mrs Jacobs had been touring in a Jeep apparently. On her own? No idea, mate. And just happened to be at Luxor when the wives fetched up there? Bit of a funny coincidence. Why do you ask? Oh nothing.

Joe kept going over and over it. Ailsa had never mentioned her. Be fair though: she knew he'd hit the roof if she did and opted for a quiet life. Lighting up a fag, he observed the tremor in his fingers. What had he said to her just now? Oh aye, that and that. Well, but she should know he didn't mean it. And she should be careful what she said.

How could he make things right? Small Joe felt, and humiliated. And as ever the heat that had flared up in him had so completely dispersed that he was at a loss to know what had ignited it. He'd been caught up in some stupid pranks that had left Chalkie dead and Irene gone and two boys fatherless. The cigarette jittered in his hand. The world had opened up and swallowed them, without warning. Lovely, decent folk. The best. What was to be said about that? He sat and stared at the whitewashed wall.

Presumably Ailsa was seeing to the tea and giving him a chance to calm down and sober up, not that he was not sober. She at least had a bit of sense in her noddle. It took more than a few pints of Stella to make him tipsy. Still, he would not drink any more. She didn't like it and she was right not to like it.

Illiterate Welshman!

You asked for it, boy, he told himself, and by Jove you got it! In the cinnamon-scented kitchen, an apple tart had been removed from the oven and left to cool on its enamel plate, covered by a sieve in case of insects. He looked at the clove sticking out of the crust in the centre. The sugar-sprinkle. One of her works of art. Ailsa's blue apron lay neatly folded over a chair-back.

Some crazy bugger was out there roaring round on a motorbike on the waste ground.

Nia perched on the table in her knickers, beside a basin of water, milky with Dettol. She swung her legs, cradled in the murmur of concern that passed between her mother and father, to and fro, until it was woven of both their voices, a hummed hymn of anxious cherishing.

The explosions and rampages were all over now. They would not come again as long as Nia held the two in thrall to her bad arm.

'I blame myself,' said Mami.

'Don't be daft.'

'But I do. I should have acted as *soon* as I saw the mark. She looked so peaceful in the land of nod, didn't you, Piccaninny? I didn't want to wake her. Oh *dear*, Joe.'

Ailsa's face appealed: lost child and old woman, for, with her forehead furrowed into deep lines, she looked to Nia like her *Mam-gu*, mapped with many wrinkles.

'It's quite all right, Mami,' Nia said in a grown-up way. 'It's only a mozzy-bite after all.'

'There you are,' said Joe. 'Babes and sucklings.'

As they continued to dab with cotton wool and to discuss her, Nia sat content to queen it, settling and centring her world around her. She craned to get a look at the spot, which was angry and inflamed, weeping green nastiness. She murmured the words *Illiterate Welshman!* bubbling them on her lips and rolling them round her mouth. The festering wound on her arm did not bother her. They would take care of it, even though she knew from their contrite whispers that a girl of nine in Fayid Cemetery had died of an insect bite. One day she was right as rain. Three days later she was dead. But Nia's parents had the power of life and death. Her eyes followed their faces, one speaking, then the other, like a game of ping pong.

'So much pus,' said Ailsa.

'Iodine?'

'Yes, maybe. Definitely.'

'The MO?'

'I think if it's no better tomorrow...'

Topher had had iodine on his cut shin. It had been purple, he'd said, and stung like heck, but Topher's dad had told him he was a brave little soldier. The iodine had dried brownish-yellow and it killed the germs stone dead, he said, like this, and he fell down on his back to show her how dead the germs were, his tongue lolling out of his mouth and his eyes rolling. Topher had shown her his chipolata.

From the sky a large hand came down on Nia's forehead. It was hard and cool. It took the heat from her forehead in its cool span. Daddy's face came down and asked her how she felt. And Mami's face came too.

Mami had hit her once, towering above her, when Topher was there. Hit her hard! Slap! Smack! Nia had curled into a ball like a spider in her bed. Daddy had never hit her, he was good. Another Mami did that. Her face in a red rage had been dark as sausage, her cheeks meaty slabs.

Now the good Mami's fingers were tender on her shoulder. Both of them were here together, balancing the world.

*

The pus had death in it. They both saw that. The greenness of death. And Nia was not eating. Her arms and legs were thin. There was no weight to lose. Sharp shoulder-blades jutted from her ribby back. What was more important than to keep her healthy and happy? How had she been allowed to get so skinny? Father and mother wove back in together, a single seamless mind that braided the little girl into its weft.

He would simmer the plaice for her in evaporated milk, Joe said to Ailsa. Of course he knew how to do it! He'd watched her often enough, hadn't he? And the two of them were *cwtch*ed up so cosy and nice in the lamplight.

He watched from the doorway as Ailsa read their daughter her bedtime story. Two stories she was having tonight, two! Ailsa said – because of the nasty iodine. Mother and daughter sat like one being, Nia's eyes huge in wondering concentration on the page, her bud-mouth slack as she breathed deeply. It was Mrs Rabbit, her daughters, Flopsy, Mopsy and Cotton-tail, that Ailsa was reading about, and her naughty son, Peter. They turned a page. Joe watched Nia's engrossed eyes move to the top of the page, follow the words one by one, for Nia was clever, no doubt about it, she could read, she was destined for great things, university, the law, medicine.

Joe tried not to think of the infected wound. There was so much you could do for this kind of thing nowadays. Jabs you could have.

He went back to the kitchen and checked on the plaice. Simmering gently, the juices flowing out into the milk. Just two mouthfuls, if he could get her to swallow them, three even: strength for her body as it tried to heal itself.

The story was finished. After a scolding, Peter Rabbit had eaten blackberry jam for his tea, round the fire. Nia drew a deep sigh of satisfaction. She stretched and squirmed on her mother's knee; then settled again for the second story, reaching up with her good arm to stroke Ailsa's neck and chin just under the ear, where a dewdrop earring hung.

'Open wide, my beauty!' Joe said, crouching, eyes crinkling. 'Look what Daddy has cooked you.'

On a teaspoon, he inserted two or three tender flakes of fish into her mouth. Watched for her to chew. She did. And swallowed. Not looking at him but gazing rapt at the first picture in the next story.

'There,' he said.

'Isn't that wonderful?' Ailsa fetched Joe such a smile that his heart clutched itself as it had on the dance floor in Peckham, when she'd swept by him in uniform, fox-trotting with another airman, whom he'd lost no time in tapping on the shoulder to claim her, for it had been a gentlemen's excuse-me. Ailsa was saying to Nia, 'Well! What a treat! We didn't know Daddy could cook, did we? Watch out, Joe, or you'll have to be our cook and we'll be ladies of leisure.'

'Mami have some, go on,' Nia insisted.

'I don't mind if I do. Delicious! Mmn.'

When every scrap was gone, Joe whirled round the room with an imaginary Ailsa in his arms, singing 'Don't Sit Under the Apple Tree'. Then he jitterbugged, hurling the phantom partner here and there. And finally when Nia had calmed down from her giggling fits and consented to go to bed, he took Ailsa in his arms for real and they danced their way through the rooms, her hand open on his open hand, his fingers lightly resting on her waist.

*

281

He can turn, she thought, her face against his face, moving slow-slow to the music he sang. And then he can turn again. Without any warning. This is how he is.

For she had been sure, stopping the Tiger on the common, as he careered towards her, red in the face and shouting something she couldn't catch, that he would strike her, in front of the windows of all the neighbours. He would deal her a dreadful blow. The panes held the flame of the setting sun like bloodshot eyes. And in the moment before he reached her, where she straddled his bike, she had time to imagine the new Warrant Officer's wife catching sight of those Roberts ruffians next door brawling on the common. Gutter people, low and brutal.

No time to dismount: it had been as if Ailsa were pinned to the bike. But in those seconds she'd conjured a scene of wives in aprons feasting on the shameful spectacle of a drunken Taffy beating his hoity toity wife. Time to ask: why have I done this? Provoked him when it would have been prudent to coax and cajole? Lied to him and gone behind his back, held him cheap, judging and blaming him? Joe's rushing figure seemed to pause in mid-stride to give Ailsa time to take in her situation.

There he'd been, face too close to her face. She'd thought, *Oh Joe, your hair does need brushing*. She'd been aware of the wristwatch and the dark fur on the arm he had raised. Holding on tight to the Tiger's handlebars, Ailsa's body had thrust forward, skirt riding way above her knees. After the roar of the engine, the silence had been intense.

Ailsa had heard in advance the crack of Joe's fist on his wife's jaw. That was where it was aimed. And he was a powerfully built fellow, he would down her with one blow, she was helpless, would bruise, and bleed maybe, her nose might be broken as he slammed his fist into it and he'd have robbed her at one stroke of her good looks, and what about Nia? Nothing in the world would ever be the same again.

But instead of flinching and cowering, Ailsa had grinned and said, 'What ho, Joe. Coming for a ride?'

He'd wavered. Knots had slipped undone in slackening ropes. His eyes had melted. There'd been a soft, brushing kiss on her lips. For, yes, he had turned again. The violence was all gone, the threat, if there had ever been any threat, and perhaps there had been none, she'd imagined it. For Joe would never hit Ailsa, she saw that now. He would and could not do so, and still be Joe.

He'd mounted the Tiger behind her. Placed his hands lightly either side of her waist and all he'd said was, 'Right you are.'

*

Don't sit under the apple tree, Joe crooned. *With anyone else but me.*

His hands scarcely needed to guide her. Her body knew which way his body intended to move before he knew himself. So they had always been, from the first time he had taken her in his arms, so that he'd felt at ease with her before they had spoken half a dozen words. *Before I knew you, I knew you*, he thought, and they wheeled round together.

Joe had climbed on the pillion, in Chalkie's place, behind his wife, and looked at her tapering back and the nape of her neck, taking her body softly between his legs. Ailsa's back had been a field of blue flowers, her waist caught in a belt of the same fabric. He'd laid his hands gently on her

283

waist and, looking at them there, thought, *I have not hurt her.* They had looked together over a cliff edge and seen the drop. Having taken it in, they'd drawn back, and not just a foot or two either, but a mile.

*

Her parents were the two wings of one dove that brooded over Nia deep into the night, as she lay scalding, the bad place on her arm swelling up so that if you looked at it you could see the abscess fester. Sometimes they murmured over her and sometimes their shadows danced together on the wall. Then the faces came down again resting over her but she had trouble sorting the muddle of four eyes and two mouths. A hand dipped a flannel in cold water and laid it smoothly across her forehead. There was a dark auntie on a boat. Cowboys were shooting porpoises. She cried out that they were shooting the creatures! Stop it! Topher ran away from the hailstones because he was only a boy. Custard had been poured for her into a Mickey Mouse bowl, deliciously, except that the surface began to churn and curdle.

The khaki doctors forced her down on the khaki camp bed. Nia roared out in terror and flailed at them. When the needle went in, the light went out.

'All better,' said Mami. She could not have sat closer without taking Nia into her pocket. 'All the nasty's gone now, isn't it? Oh,' she said to Joe, and yawned hugely, 'thank *God*. Another day, the MO said, one more day, and it might have been too late. We must be so careful, Joe, mustn't we?'

Nia was in her element with a new teddy named Penicillin, with a wide, soppy face, black button eyes and

284

a sewn-on smile from the NAAFI. They were travelling in a *royal car*, as her father said, a black purring giant, a limousine fit for a king! And a chauffeur too, we've got our own chauffeur, shan't we just swank?

'You don't mind being called a chauffeur, Paddy, do you?'

'Course not,' said the driver. 'Honoured.' He rummaged in the vanity cabinet with his free hand and found some Licorice Allsorts to treat the poor peaky little patient.

Sucking, Nia thought well of everything that had been laid on and the arm they had lanced throbbed hardly at all. It was covered in an important dressing that must not be picked at with your fingernails.

Their voices rustled like leaves in a bright tree canopy.

So much care, Joe.

We shall, don't worry.

No diversions.

A warning to us, cariad.

Yes, a warning.

Not take our eyes off her.

Nia looked out of the window at the sprawl of sand and the bump of the Big Flea, the sole hill against the flat horizons. The Flea was being climbed by tiny stick men. Above it black-winged birds hung. And there was wind up there, air currents, said her Mami. Nia turned away to the quiet ecstasy of the world inside the body of the car, a mass of human pillows and cushioning toys. Glutted with comfort, she smiled into Penicillin's furry forehead. The world radiated out from Nia and around Nia it turned. And that was that.

No one else matters.

No one at all.

Do you want to take her home?

How do you mean, home?

England.

Oh no, I couldn't.

But is she safe here?

*Joe, don't suggest it again, don't even think it. Where
would we be without you?*

Over there lay the Great Bitter Lake with a reed bed
spiking up beside the road. A flat plain of silver water. Nia
pressed her nose against the pane and thirsted to be in the
water.

Paddy the driver was saying something about blue
waters, purple hills and a crimson sun. He had a feeling for
the Bitter Lakes, he said, a feeling as strong as his feeling
for Ireland, and of course the blokes laughed at him but,
you know, perhaps it *was* his feeling for Ireland that came
out in the sadness of any glorious landscape. For this, he
said, was the land of Exodus in the Bible, did they know
that? Nia knew that something in what he said and the way
he said it might have made people scoff. Her parents did
not scoff. They listened attentively.

'Is that Ireland over there?' she asked.

'No, my beauty – this is Egypt, isn't it? Ireland's just
over the water from Wales.'

'She doesn't remember, Joe.'

'Ah but she remembers her *Mam-gu* and *Tad-cu* in
Treforys? And the aunties?'

Nia cast the net of her mind. There was *Mam-gu*
hanging out clothes in a back yard with a dank smell
containing black soil and shadow, with a wedge of

sunlight in one corner, and a coal hole Nia relished. And four aunties, Betsi, Gaynor, Mair and Magdalen, with uncles to match. And beside *Mam-gu* and these aunties in the world of her memory, but along a corridor in another room, was a tall, dark lady wearing a silky emerald scarf and trousers that swished as she walked, who smelled of almonds and took Nia on her knee and she felt the generous give of breasts inside her sweater, and heard her low, strong voice, very close.

'Auntie Betsi, Auntie Gaynor, Auntie Mair, Auntie Magdalen and my Auntie *Mona*!' she recited.

She felt her mother and father flinch, as they did sometimes when she showed them up in public and they had to whisper sharply. But they did not whisper.

Paddy the driver half turned and asked, over his shoulder, if she had ever floated in the Dead Sea.

'She hasn't actually,' said Ailsa. 'No.'

Well, he went on, you can't really swim there, don't expect to swim, but you can't drown either. The water will buoy you up, he said. It's thick with minerals. Bitter, he explained, that's from *marah*, bitter waters, the waters of desolation.

'Why can't I say *Auntie Mona*?' Nia burst forth.

'Shush, dear.'

Not everyone knows this, the driver said, but the bottom is covered with millions of empty spiky shellfish, millions and millions! Napoleon saw them when he invaded. And these nasty spiky dead creatures have been there thousands of years, millions even! And no one knows how they got there. And if you tried to walk out, your soles would be cut to ribbons. And before the Canal was dug through – over there in the middle, marked by those buoys, can you see them? Before that, the Bitter Lakes were completely dry, did you know that? And down the middle was a vast bank of salt hard as brick, seven miles high, I'm not joking, I swear. Lot's wife, you see – that must have been the origin of the story of Lot's wife in the Bible.

Her mami was holding Nia's hand in hers, a bit too tight. Pouting, Nia burst out, '*Mona's* wife! *Mona's* wife!'

Mami bent her head and asked how was the poorly arm? There was jelly for tea, she said, and Golly was waiting at the window making funny faces for when Nia came home. And all the neighbours walking past (she bent lower, so that her lips were touching Nia's forehead), well, they would see Golly peering out of the Roberts window waiting for Nia and her new chum, Penicillin, wouldn't they?

Nia sighed with renewed contentment. She poked Penicillin's head up to get a sight of the sails of the feluccas and dhows, plying to and fro, slow and magical. She had forgotten to be cross, enveloped in the blissful love that gathered its force again and radiated towards her from both sides. An ocean liner passed softly across the water, dwarfing the feluccas.

*

Up in a balloon? Yes, why jolly well not? Sign her up for the full junket, Mona insisted. Seize the hour! This would be a first!

It would mean an early start for the balloons must take advantage of the precious dawn breezes by the Nile. They'd see the Pyramids and the Sphinx from the air. Poppy said she might pass on the balloon ride as she had no head for heights. But she'd definitely want to see her mother and Mona sail up into the air.

And what were the other treats on offer? Mona wanted to know. She scanned tomorrow's itinerary. Ah, lunch in the Mena House. Not been there for half a century. She wiped her lips with her serviette and sat back.

'I've brought the photos,' Nia ventured. 'Of Mam with Poppy. If you'd like to see them.'

Mona turned over the photographs without comment. There was neither a tremor in her hands nor a change of expression until, replacing them in the envelope, Mona handed them back and rose to her feet. Stuffed them into Nia's hands with rough impatience. She swayed, reaching down to steady herself on the table. She would rest now, Mona said gruffly. An octogenarian balloonist-to-be was wise to take siestas. She would lie down in her cabin. She'd be fine, don't *fuss*. *Anno Domini*, it creeps up on you. Later, later. With a peremptory motion of her hand, Mona waved Nia and then the assiduous waiters away, using her stick to support herself to the lift. *Madame! Madame!* they pleaded. But no one dared intervene to help the old woman against her will. All eyes watched Dr Mona Serafin-Jacobs totter into the lift and a momentary hush fell on the surrounding tables in the lido.

'She'll be all right,' said Poppy. 'Don't worry, Mum. She must have loved Gran so much, mustn't she?'

'Yes. She did.'

Nia shuffled the photographs in her hands. Her mother's dewy eyes glistened in the gaunt face as she cradled her grandchild. Ailsa had rarely bestowed such blissful looks on Nia. Not as far as she remembered. But then, why would

289

she have? Nia was not proud of her theatrical adolescent rages. Storming around, crashing doors, denunciations. Ailsa had been made to represent everything Nia abhorred, a handy target. Antediluvian attitudes! You're a fossil! Marriage is legalised prostitution! What's this rubbish you've kept from my childhood? A fucking *golliwog*! You should be ashamed of yourself! Giving a little girl a *golliwog*! Racist filth! Whatever were you thinking of? What do you mean, *I loved my golly*? For Christ's sake! What choice does a child have? Anyway what have you ever done with your life? Only Archie had known how to restrain Nia's outbursts.

When a person had gone, it was forever; a forever lived from hour to hour, day to day. Looking back, it was hard to credit how much time Nia had disdainfully wasted. She'd chosen Cambridge University partly for its distance from Ailsa's twinsets and pearls and the visits of the abominable Irene; and when she'd embarked on her postgraduate degree, visits home had been rare and phone conversations difficult. Ailsa had been aghast, in her subdued way, at what she called Nia's antics and especially when she'd been in prison for her CND protests. *You fucking well ought to be proud of me that I stand up to these murderous bastards!* Silence. But the birth of the illegitimate Poppy eighteen months before Ailsa's death had altered the balance between them.

Into Nia's mind swam the memory of that day she'd had always seen as set in silver. After Poppy's birth, she'd been gripped by a needy, weeping compulsion to be with her mother, whatever the cost to either of them. She'd driven up from London to Shropshire with her daughter and the further north-west they got, the greater the purity of frost and mist on the landscape. Uninvited and unannounced, she'd driven into the snowbound farmyard of her childhood. Poppy had been six weeks old when Nia crossed the threshold carrying Ailsa's grandchild.

The light in the Copsey home had been blanched, a sap-spitting log fire in the grate. Archie had been off in the far field with Les, freeing the stranded ewes. A clean smell of heated linen lingered in the kitchen, mingling with a scent of fried onions. The ironing board was still up and a pile of folded towels lay on the kitchen table. Everything was exactly as it had always been, as if waiting with held breath for just this moment. Taken by storm, Ailsa's eyes had brimmed with tears. She had not known about a grandchild.

How heartless of me, Nia thought now, not to have shared it with her. Despicable, outrageous. And she never reproached me.

When Nia had passed her mother the little one in her holding blanket, saying, *Her name is Poppy*, Ailsa had looked down with tremulous wonder and joy into the speedwell blue eyes and turned away, the bundle in her arms. Nia had thought: *oh yes, you've got what you want now all right. And it isn't me.* Ailsa had bent down with her light burden. She'd straightened up without it. For she'd turned aside only to lay the child on the couch. Her mother had reached out her arms to Nia, in the most expressive gesture Nia could remember. She'd rushed into Ailsa's tenderness, weeping. They'd both sobbed wildly.

The intensity hadn't lasted. How could it? No, but it had happened. A window between worlds had opened, never

291

fully to close. Perhaps if Ailsa had not been ill – and Nia hadn't realised how ill her mother had been. Archie had not let on. Tall and willowy, with only a sprinkling of grey hairs, Ailsa with her peachy complexion, perfect teeth and beautiful blue-green eyes had seemed robust enough. But even then she had been dying. In truth the photographs they'd taken of grandmother and granddaughter betrayed gauntness and frailty. Mona must have seen both the melancholy remnant of Ailsa's beauty and the signs of death in her face.

The truth of it was that some eternally tender mutual wound had lain between mother and daughter – if you touched it, it would bleed and never be stanched. Obviously this was to do with her father, lost in action. A war hero but the government had for long denied that the violence in the Suez Canal Zone after the War constituted a war at all. And here was an odd thing: learning of the successful campaign for a medal for the Canal Zone veterans, Nia had found herself cynically applying for a posthumous gong for Joe Roberts. If there was one going, why shouldn't she have it? Nia's motive had been subversive: she had in mind to wear the thing on anti-Iraq War demos with his row of World War II gongs. Back had come the answer: regrettably her late father was ineligible for this medal.

Now Nia startled herself with the thought: Ailsa's silence was meant to protect me. Her silence was a curtain of love.

*

Nia and Mona hung lighter than air beneath a house-high bubble of blue silk. They rose together, to float beside a stand of palms. Nia reached out to the rustling fronds of the treetops, cool to the touch and emerald in the red disc of the sun. Stillness and motion seemed the one state.

The scarlet peony blossoms by the trees were veiled girls in red robes, seated cross-legged as they baked early morning bread in a brick oven. You could see that one batch of bread was already baking; dough for the next was being pummeled. Suspended in a yeasty cloud, Nia breathed in the scent of fresh bread mingled with the bitter smoke of a dung fire.

Salaam aleicum, the balloonists called down.

Aleicum salaam. Smiling faces tilted up; the girls got to their feet and waved to the folk above.

By imperceptible degrees Mona and Nia drew away, making their weightless way fifty feet into a dream of blue air; they were birds or clouds, silently euphoric. The minarets of Cairo's many mosques pierced a blue-grey fog, the Nile curving its green ribbon through the city.

A red-gold flush burnished the desert to its horizons. But from moment to moment colour altered, until, when the women looked down at the complex geometry of the Sphinx and the Pyramids, the sands had turned yellowish-brown, like the quartzite-tinged colour and texture of female skin in the statues of the Pharaoh's wives. The desert itself seemed to Nia like the skin of a face, too great for its features to be made out or its expression guessed.

18

'Where were you in the night, my sweetheart?' Ailsa asked Joe, once they'd settled on the Liberty bus for the Saturday shopping trip.

Last night they'd made love but it had left Joe wide awake, as if someone had taken a can opener to his ribcage and exposed the throbbing heart of him. Throwing on some clothes, he'd gone out and hauled the ground sheet off the Tiger, walking the bike up the moonlit road before he mounted, so as not to disturb Ailsa.

'Couldn't sleep. I thought you hadn't heard. I tried to be quiet. Sorry, love.'

'It's all right. What was the trouble, *cariad*?'

He liked to hear the Welsh endearments in her mouth. The love in her voice assured him that she was his home, he hers, wherever they lived; no quarrel was final and no bad words unforgivable.

'Oh, you know. This and that.'

'Chalkie, was it?'

'Aye.'

Ailsa said nothing but he felt her sympathising care mantling him. She no longer blamed him, thank the Lord. But he blamed himself. The grief and remorse did not abate. With every day his friend seemed more present, not buried safely in the cemetery at Fayid but burrowing like a maggot in Joe's body. He clutched his pounding chest and wondered, should he see the MO? Was he building up to a heart attack? Perhaps it was some physical illness he was mistaking for grief. Fingers plucked his emotion like a catgut string; adrenalin rushed in his belly and exploded in spasms, as if to warn of some ambush about to be sprung. But the calamity was in the past. And he was fighting fit.

'Where did you go?' Ailsa asked gently. She enclosed his hand in both of hers.

Joe had ridden towards Ish, looking over the canal towards the black world of the Sinai, qualified by moon and starlight, where there were no electric lights, no people, nothing human. Icy cold. The sterile realm of death where nothing changed. Bodies buried there thousands of years ago had desiccated in the sand that leached their liquids and purified them of bacteria and rot. They'd work their way up again with mummified faces recognisable.

In Ish, he'd ridden through glimmering, nearly empty streets. At the Vic no lights had been showing. Back to the Sweet Water Canal where Chalkie's mutilated body had been tossed by assassins into the filthy flux. Back to the wall of darkness surrounding Fayid Cemetery. Nothing to see, nothing to feel. Weary now, hearing wild dogs howl, wondering what the heck he was doing here, Joe had turned for home but paused beside Lake Timsah. Leaning the Tiger against a tree, the cone of its light trained on the bank, he'd crouched beside the water, lighting up a fag. Insects had sparked in the nimbus of the Tiger's single eye. Turning away, Joe had gazed out over the inky water, taking a deep, satisfying drag.

Pure peace out there. Beckoning.

The lake had lapped softly at his feet. The triangular sail of an Arab boat sliding silently past, like a great pale bird, had carved a white wake in the moonlight. A man's dark head showed against the sail. So close had the vessel passed that moonlight was visible on the lens of the sailor's eye. In a dream the two men had observed one another, from their separate worlds. No sound except the ripple against the vessel's bows – and across the still sheet of water the call of night fishermen.

He'd felt, for want of better words, obscurely blessed. Momentarily he'd heard a sigh breathed out and sensed, as if in a dream, the presence of his pal at his shoulder, saying, in his friendly way, *Steady on, mate.*

'I went out for a ride.'

'Did it help, Joe?'

'It did, in a way.' She knew, of course. She read him like a book, as he could never read her.

He took her hand. 'You weren't scared without me, were you?' Soon he'd have to go into the desert for three weeks' exercises, leaving her alone. The situation was worsening, everyone was aware of it. Endless student demonstrations in Cairo, lynchings, theft and strikes. Anyone could have lynched him last night, Joe reflected. Idiot. What had he been thinking of?

'Course not.'

Nia nestled on his lap, Penicillin on Ailsa's and Golly on Nia's, as the bus nosed its way through heavy traffic. Breeze through the opened window played on their foreheads and fanned Ailsa's newly washed hair. I nearly struck her, Joe thought.

Aye but, fair play, I didn't.

He'd promised himself, bargaining with God, to keep a tight rein on his anger. Nia's illness had unnerved them both. Clinging to one another in an ecstasy of fear, they'd wept and Ailsa had said, *My fault, all my fault.*

In his imagination Joe kept seeing the bastard mosquito on his daughter's arm, rear legs and posterior raised, head lowered, plunging its dirty needle into Nia. A child's life was frail. And she'd called out 'Auntie Mona! Auntie Mona!' in the car on the way home from hospital, making Joe realise he'd cut off not only his wife but his daughter from something that meant one hell of a lot to them. Of course that couldn't have been helped. But had he needed to be so brutal about it?

Joe had not struck his wife.

Instead we've got this tempest of passion, night after night, he thought. It was a new thing for them. Joe's chapel upbringing had never prepared him for this rapture of desire, whose satisfaction only increased desire. He didn't want to be away from her, he told Ailsa, and she smiled, no, not for a minute. Though it would be a rest from you-know-what!

Nia piped up: 'I don't know what!'

'Quite true, you don't,' said Joe.

'I want to know what.'

'Too bad. Don't go sulking now. Think about what we'll buy for Mami in the market.'

'Where are you going anyway?' Nia asked sternly.

'On manoeuvres, girlie. In the desert. That is what daddies do, isn't it?'

He watched Ailsa's fingers stray to the love-bite on her throat. She caught his glance and turned to look out of the bus window, tweaking up her collar to hide the mark. He'd have liked to lower the collar and put his lips to the place.

'BRITTISH OUT! UNITTY OF THE NILE DELTA! AL-GALA BI-L-DIMA!' some illiterate clown had written on a wall. A ragged boy with a bucket and brush was earning a few piastres by scouring off the graffiti. So-called 'spontaneous' mobs were rioting in Cairo and Port Said. The Egyptian so-called government was threatening to abrogate the Treaty and declare war on the British as an enemy army on its soil. They'd promised to cut off the supply of drinking water, fresh food and labour. They'd be cutting their own throats – as the new Tory government at home would show them.

If things were less tense, he'd have got Ailsa a jalopy. You could pick them up for a song. A car would have kept her from coveting the Tiger, which she now seemed to accept was off limits. Lately Ailsa had retreated into herself a bit. Didn't venture out as much. She hadn't wanted to come out shopping today in Ish; Joe sensed her concern as to how he'd be with the wogs. Irene had had more grasp of political reality, in her fears, than Ailsa in her grammar school idealism. That was odd: Irene had been afraid of wogs. But Ailsa feared *her husband* with the wogs. He knotted Chalkie's sweater round his neck as the bus rounded the final corner. Irene had been right all along.

We're here to prevent or fight World War III, he thought. And it will be an atomic war. The Ruskies are atheists. No more mosques and minarets for the poor old Arabs when the Ruskies fly in to this ready-made arsenal at the gateway to Africa and the Persian oil wells. And the flabby playboy King Farouk: no kings on the other side of the Iron Curtain, hadn't the Gyppos noticed? But the obvious never struck them. We are your friends and protectors, he told them. So you murder us. And perhaps the simpletons were natural fascists. They'd welcomed Goebbels to Cairo in '39. To the Gyppos, Hitler had been a heroic corporal who'd defied the British Empire to make his country great – a model for Arab officers. With his own eyes Joe had seen these asses swaggering through wartime Cairo sporting toothbrush moustaches, shaven heads and monocles.

Chalkie had been killed by fools who could not identify their true enemy. Thinking of Irene still upset him. He'd been speechless with relief when she'd gone. Joe felt (and it was a bit mad) that he owed her a life. Chalkie had been far and away the better man.

A peaceful, smoky Saturday atmosphere filled the bus, everyone in civvies, with shopping baskets on their laps; small girls flaunting best pink ribbons and boys in their Sunday shorts with low side partings. Two Military Policemen sat at the back, with holsters full and eyes vigilant. He didn't like needlessly to frighten Ailsa by pointing them out. Perhaps (it was a light going on) she was more timid than she let on. And proud: she'd hate to show fear. After all, his wife was bright and kept up with the news: she could read the signs of growing tension. Joe laced his fingers with hers and stroked the back of her hand with his thumb. Every time they touched or looked, each knew that the other remembered. The passion of their nights. It ought to be more than enough to sate his longing and settle his jealousies. Too much, boy, come to that! He didn't understand where the storm had come from. Was it normal to want your wife again as soon as you'd loved her? The moment your climax had exploded, an empty ache.

But did you ever reach a woman fully and finally? In each act of passion Joe possessed and lost Ailsa.

What did she write in that notebook? He knew where she hid it. One evening, he'd taken the pretty green notebook in his hands, turned it over, felt the texture, opened and closed its brass clasp. He'd not read a word. That would be a shameful intrusion.

But perhaps it was a journal of Ailsa's fears. Women had terrors men couldn't imagine. This might well be the truth of it. How stupid never to have guessed it. Such a clod he was.

They drew into the *Place de la Gare*. Joe carried Nia down the steps of the bus. Soldiers with guns strolled near the bus stop, with a casual, off-duty air. Under the surface, the Canal Zone seethed with unrest.

'See you at the Club for lunch?' he asked Dusty.

'I've got a thirst on me already.'

'Oh no you jolly well have not,' said Dusty's missus, a bird of a lady: *petite* Dusty loyally called her and Ailsa looked like two of the midget. She hated to be seen next to *petite* ladies.

'Sah!' said Dusty, saluting his other half.

'See what I've got to put up with,' Caroline chivvied, and led him off.

Joe handed Ailsa down the steps.

'Hey! – Joe!'

Here, in civvies, was Nobby Bowen, a bloke perpetually off-side, chatting in some foreign gibberish with, oh no – a coal-black nigger wearing a suit, a trilby and a bow tie, carrying a string bag half full of packages. With his shiny skin and broad smile, he was the spitting image of Nia's golliwog. *Thicklips*. Must be one of the officers' saffragis. Nia looked up, fascinated.

As Ailsa turned, Joe saw Bowen's face light up. Ailsa frowned, shook her head and strode away, head down, across the square.

'Ailsa! Hang on, will you? Where the heck are you going? Nia!'

Without turning, his wife motioned impatiently with her arm, *oh do come on!* But Nia was not budging. She held out her hand to Black Sambo, to shake it. He crouched to her, smiling in her face, and Joe squirmed at the contrast between the golliwog's shining blackness and Nia's red-blonde hair. The two Military Policemen stood watching, po-faced.

'You've met my wife, Nobby?'

'Thought I had. Not so sure now. Must have seen her somewhere.'

'At the concert?' Joe helped him out. He called out again to Ailsa. Bowen was telling Nia that this gentleman was his very good friend and a prince in his own country. Nia's eyes were quite round. Bowen was one of the toffs who'd gone native and married a duskily luscious girl, hourglass figure, sashaying along in a figure-hugging costume. Wearing

301

pillbox hats with bits of veil.

'Pleased to meet you, my dear little person,' the black man said to Nia in polished, lah-de-dah English.

'And what is your name?'

'Nia Josephine Roberts.' Nia put out her hand and stroked his shiny face, beaming. 'What is yours?'

'My name is Kassay.'

'How do you do, Kassay.'

Ailsa stood with her back to them, way across the square, while a woman in black offered her something from a basket – figs perhaps – and an ambling squaddie paused to eye her. Joe dragged at Nia's arm. She resisted, slipped her hand out of her father's, slapped at him and ran round behind the golliwog's legs. She danced from foot to foot, making naughty faces up at her father.

'Now then, Joe,' Bowen said. 'We've been discussing the politics of oil. Which do you think is more important, oil or water?'

Nia thought water.

'And where does water come from?'

'Up there.'

'No rain falls here though, does it? The water Egypt gets to drink comes from Ethiopia. Through the Sudan. And that, in the future, will be power for Kassay and his people.'

Aye, if and when they get the know-how, Joe thought. *When the sky rains pears*.

Kassay straightened up. He showed little of the obsequiousness of the Egyptian servants but looked Joe straight in the face, through eyes of extraordinary beauty, large and dark with long curling lashes. A melancholy look to him when he was not smiling. He must be well used to slights from the Arabs. Egypt laid claim to the Sudan. For them the black Africans were savages. Wogs, in other words. Every wog had to have another wog further down the ladder. Joe had seen the Gyppos follow the dapper black servants of the officers, wiggling their hips in mockery of their Europeanised fancy dress.

When he'd managed to tug Nia away, they caught up with Ailsa. Husband and wife linked arms.

'The coloured chap comes from Ethiopia,' Joe said, keeping his thoughts about golliwogs to himself. 'Is that the same as Abyssinia, or another place?'

'The same. I hope you were polite, Joe.'

'Course I was polite! Honestly though! What a comedy!' He laughed.

'What is?'

'Well, Nia and the coloured gentleman. She has a *thing* about them. Do they look lovable, you know, sweet, to a child?'

'She doesn't know she's supposed to despise them, does she?'

'Oh, come on. You know I didn't mean that. Give me some credit, Ailsa.' He changed direction, to shut her up: 'Bowen was taken with you. Nearly had to knock the bloke down'

'Don't be silly. What did he say?'

'Thought he knew you.'

'Oh?'

'Mind, he claims to know everyone in Egypt so why should you be an exception? Gone native he has. Thinks he's Lawrence of Arabia. Knows a hell of a lot about Pharaohs though, so *chwarae teg* I don't condemn him.'

Later, in the *souk* at Fayid Village, she made for the spice street. Tiny cupboard-like stores displayed pods, seeds, translucent resins and freakishly shaped knotted roots, fragments of edible bark. Roasted, pulped, pounded and crushed delicacies. The eye and nose – somehow the soul – were drunk on spirituous plenty. Ailsa admired lemons preserved in salt and rose buds from Damascus. She haggled for and bought several cones of black cherry kernels, musk and ginger, bargaining in an ungainly mixture of Arabic and English.

Beyond the spice street she breathed in a hot stink of rottenness. The smell of everything. Compost and petrol and spices, sun on offal and ordure. The ferment penetrated Ailsa with a pang, not unpleasantly, reminding you that life was planted fair and square in mould. Like the goodness of manure or the intimate blood-smell on your sanitary towel, which you raised to your nose and sniffed without disgust. Curdled milk and crumbled Gorgonzola. The smell of Joe and Ailsa, their skins slick with sweat, attached at the root.

The passion of their nights would kill him, her husband swore! No more! Sleep, he absolutely must sleep! But if they decided to sleep, he'd turn to her again because whatever they had found must never be allowed to slip away. Never, never. Hold, enter, have me. Again. Their eyes did not close when they loved. Joe saw her and Ailsa revelled in Joe's seeing. And that felt dangerous. Dangerous was exciting. This, she supposed, was marriage. But wasn't it excessive? Would it go on like this, at this intensity, till one of them died? Was it that Joe had felt something elusive in her depart from him and he must have it back? And she in turn, having almost forsaken him for Mona, rushed in panic for home. Since Nia had nearly died, Ailsa had withdrawn from that other world. Mona had let her. She made no motion to reach in and try to claim Ailsa. Thank goodness Nobby had had his wits about him in Ish and managed to deflect Joe's suspicion. Good thing he'd been out and about without his ladies. They'd have mobbed Ailsa like brilliantly coloured butterflies. *Ailsa chérie! Comment va?* How would she have argued her way out of ambush?

Ailsa paused at a treasury of fruit. Piled melons, green and yellow, with a few gashed open to expose the glistening sunset-orange of the juicy inner flesh.

Carpets now. Their jewel colours sang in shafts of light. In the ruck of bodies, Ailsa's eyes tasted the deep claret of her chosen carpet, against a pattern of ochre or gold, how would you describe it? Autumn trees on Wenlock Edge or walking with Archie under the bronze tree canopy at Pendlebury. Her mind felt faint with the colour's sensual purity. It made her think of Mona's carpets on the wall like tapestries. Ailsa reached out now and stroked the pile: unimaginable luxury. She wanted this. The carpet-seller had his genial eye on her. He sidled nearer, smiling.

She shook her head and took a step away from the stall, backing against a hot jostle of bodies. The noise took the top of your head off. Her memory reached for the sombre twilight of the public library at Shrewsbury, with its familiar chill. Recoiling from this heat and squalor, she imagined herself a cool vestal again, with a virgin page and a full fountain pen, in a high gallery of the library. The chaste enjoyment of working for university entrance. If she'd become a scholar, Ailsa could have lived unto herself, not given her body over to the passion of a man and the parasitical need of a child. They used you up. To them, what were you but an udder? They could never let you *be*. They were always nuzzling up to probe and taste you, and prying into your brain to try to handle what was there. She thought of her green notebook; she'd write about the scent of the salted lemons.

Three weeks, she thought, *I've three weeks of privacy.*

And yet she didn't want Joe to go, not for a moment. He's my life, she thought: nothing less.

Traffic bellowed; men shouted *Pri-ee-mus! par-a-fin!*; wirelesses attached to lamp posts blared and an organ grinder with a tambourine in his free hand and half his face and one eye missing seemed to be following her around. There were flies sticking to pus on the good eye. Beyond or beneath this racket shimmered an echo, like a radio signal, a bass note to bedlam.

A soldier with a rifle strolled through the throng. The crowd parted. She read the chill watchfulness on his face, the mute masks of the faces he passed.

Grief and guilt thrilled through her. She couldn't stand it, the grasping hands, the reek, the need. How is it my fault? she asked them all. How can I help it if you live in mud huts and have bilharzia and your babies die and you can live on a tithe of a tithe of what I possess, and yet I think of myself as poor? For a moment she saw them – smelt them, rather – as presumably Joe did, a dirty, lousy, contagious rabble. They hated and resented her, for all they fawned and for all she tried to feel, and did feel, love and concern and contrition. The carpet-man came up too close, with his desperate eyes, big and brown and melting: '*Madame* Lady like the car-a-pet?'

Ailsa looked round for her husband. Beside a stall selling brass pyramids and camels, Nia on Joe's shoulders cried out that she had spotted a goat, a real live goat, look there, Mami! It was going, Ailsa supposed, to have its throat cut. And oh! Nia cried, she had seen a rooster, a lovely golden rooster with a big red crest, in a cage, over there. As the crowds parted, Ailsa beheld the creature in all its beauty, the coxcomb a plume of red flesh, the lens of its eye a flake of gold.

Joe's watchful look. His gaze embraced her and all her longings. Is there something, anything you want? I will give it to you. I and only I will satisfy you. In the overpowering heat, she felt herself sway and jerk, as if on the edge of sleep. She had three weeks promised.

'Seen something you like?' he asked.

'Too dear. Anyway where could it go? What could go with it? We've got nothing that won't be made to look, well, a bit dull.'

'No, but we shall have. One day we shall, shan't we, *cariad?* When we've a home of our own.'

Joe quietly noted the carpet. Smiled with his eyes at the seller. Haggled a little.

Quais giddan car-a-pet, effendi!

Mafeesh faluk! said Joe. 'Not a bean! *Shufti!*'

He patted his pocket and shrugged. That endearing smile he gave to the carpet-man, Ailsa thought, was sincere. He forgot to hate Egyptians when they came one by one. Away from Mona's influence, Ailsa too often slid on shit in the region of Joe's prejudices. The communal prejudice, rather, the lawless prejudice that brought us here, self-righteous gangsters, and kept us here.

And there was reason in that, she thought: *I have to live with him. I can't afford to be contemptuous of my husband.* And Joe was not as bad as his prejudices.

The carpet-man saw them depart. He let out a wailing cry over his lost sale. As if they had cheated him, stolen his livelihood.

'Sorry, *cariad.* Can't possibly afford it unless he halves the price.'

'Of course you can't. I really didn't expect it, Joe. I was just interested. You can read Egyptian carpets. They are legible.'

*

At home they bumped heads, reaching down for the blue air letter on the doormat.

'You seem so frightfully far away, Joe,' ran the letter, 'and I wondered as soon as we arrived if I'd done right to come home and leave my Roy all on his own in the earth at Fayid, unvisited? But how could I have stayed, as things were? It buckets down with rain here, the rain is full of smuts, my mother-in-law is patient with us but I can't help feeling in the way in such a cramped house, rationing is still dire, it's so damp, we all came down with colds and Christopher is playing up, he wets his bed, the naughty boy. I feel he needs a man's discipline.

'But now, I want to put a plan to you and would you please advise? There may be a way I could return to Egypt, Joe, and I need to be completely practical about this, I have no one to advise me. I asked the RAF about a filing clerk's job somewhere in Ish – I have secretarial training you know. And it seems they are desperate for the *right people* at the NAAFI – and, to cut a long story short, I expect to fly out in the near future. You were such a pal to me, I feel there is a little portion of my Roy wherever you are, is that mad? I feel I may be mad sometimes.'

'It looks as though she's angling to come back out,' Ailsa said. 'In fact she *is* coming back, look.'

He didn't want Irene, it was as plain as a pikestaff. He'd turned a corner into this new happiness: she could read it on Joe's face. Their one ewe lamb was well again and their marriage restored. Irene was trouble.

'That's insane,' he said, handing the letter back. 'I mean, she loathed it here. Afraid for her life she was, every minute of every day.'

'She's just lost, isn't she, Joe. Shall I answer?'

'Aye, you answer, that's best. Look, I need to go out.'

'What, right away? I thought you were cleaning your kit? Do you want me to do it?'

'No, it's fine. Leave it there. I'll just tell Nia where I'm going.'

He leapt upstairs three at a time and she heard him talking to Nia, who was supposed to be asleep.

'Dear Irene,' Ailsa wrote, 'Joe has asked me to reply for both of us...'

She suspended her pen above the paper. Imagine if it had been the other way round, she thought, and Joe had been killed. Imagine that the hole at Fayid had been dug for *my* husband and that Roy White had helped lower a coffin containing the remains of Joe into the earth. And in some way been accessory to that death. How come Irene not only withheld blame from Joe but turned to him as her mentor? Mad was the word. 'We both feel your loss acutely,' she wrote. 'Never a day goes by but we think of dear Roy and you. How we hope that the dear boys ease your pain in some measure.'

She felt almost guilty at having Joe, while Irene had nobody, in a stricken world where rain fell full of soot and you were on your own.

Irene would come: she would come and try to take Joe away. She hadn't a chance in hell. Too intense, their sensuality. Joe unpeeled Ailsa; Ailsa opened to Joe. But what were they trying to do, consume each other? As she pictured him rearing there above her, and herself moving on his sex, dragging her softness against his hardness, awakening now the secret sensation between her legs, she wondered if this could possibly be normal and right?

Perhaps it was not normal. But how could it not be right? They were married, weren't they? Everything they did was sanctioned. Their bed felt anything but chaste. Something was waiting to happen between them, a breaking open, a rupture. Something violent and obscene that did not happen to nice girls from Church Stretton. She would not be able to avert it, for she liked Joe's licking tongue, his stumbling fingers on slick places; enjoyed the smell of their salt and sweat among the rucked sheets in the morning. But her abraded body was beginning to feel as if it were enduring an assault.

A couple of hours later, cooking smells filled the house. She'd flavoured the chicken with ginger from the *souk*.

'I'm back!' Joe yelled and bounced in. 'Shut your eyes!

Shut them! Go on.' Something was being unloaded from a van parked outside; it was hefted into the quarter.

'You naughty thing! Honestly!'

A magic carpet, Ailsa cried, and burst into tears bcause it was too heavenly; the kind of thing Ailsa Birch could never have owned. They took off their shoes and stepped on to it. She crouched and paddled her fingers in its colour.

'But, how can we afford this, Joe?'

'How can we not? When we have our own home, all our things will be as good as this.'

She was afraid to step on it, shy of its glory. All afternoon her carpet glowed at Ailsa, as she walked round it or just came in to stare, absorbing colour, like light through stained glass.

Later when Nia was sound asleep, Joe laid Ailsa down on the carpet in her slip. She didn't want to. One day she would wince and twist in his arms: *Oh for God's sake! Leave me alone! Yallah! Imshi!* The moment she gave way to her need to be herself, and love became a duty, Joe would detect it instantly and interpret it as desertion. And what then? The stress of it all, the strain of it, the bother, she thought, and tears squeezed through the edges of her screwed-up eyes.

He began to tune her, relieving her of choice. She went along with that. Instead of tearing herself away, she let the knots loosen.

'Wait a tick, *bach*,' he said. 'We'd better put a towel under you.'

She groaned as he left. Was soon back. She lifted her hips for the towel to be spread beneath them. The lifting of her body was sensationally exciting. Their eyes were open.

311

She allowed her spine to arch, splay-legged. Joe delayed and delayed. Sprawled on the carpet, with Joe kneeling above Ailsa, the pads of his fingers skidding on her secret places, there was a building, bittersweet ache. Too like pain. She opened wide her eyes. Failed to say *Joe, you're hurting me*. Reared, shuddered and let out an ugly cry which, as she pulsed, went on and on, filling her with shame.

Could this be right? Ailsa lay quivering. She did not know the word for the sensation. Normal? How could it be? What would he think of her, now he knew she was *that kind of woman*? He slipped inside her and climaxed at once, his cheek against her cheek, his palms flat against her palms, both of them weeping.

*

When he'd gone, the house was still and quiet. Ailsa hardly knew what to think. She missed him immediately, and yet she embraced the peace.

Nia was round the corner playing with the Websters' baby – Norman's idea, to cheer his wife up. And he'd be there to supervise, for Hedwig just sat like lead most of the day. She'd given up nursing the child herself, in case, as she said, her milk was bad. She didn't want to poison Eric. Her milk had a fishy smell, Hedwig insisted: it was compromised. The father mothered the baby whenever he was at home and did it tenderly and with evident pleasure. Nia had accepted his invitation, not because she liked babies but because Mr Webster had promised Coca-Cola *with ice*! The promise of ice had overridden any anxiety about her father's absence. *Right-o! Ta ta then!* she'd said casually as Joe bent to kiss her, his eyes dewed with tears.

Ailsa tidied the house until everything was in its right place. Then she stood at the window with her arms folded, humming dreamily to herself, rocking on the balls of her feet. There would be no more of that dreadful rutting like beasts on the floor. When Joe came home, she would have to tell him: *I am not that sort of girl. It's not how I was brought up.*

Ailsa took off her pinafore and hung it up. She sank down in Joe's chair, her head in his dent, leaning on the cover that saved the chair from his hair oil, though the whole chair smelt of Joe. Oil and tobacco and the sweat of him that was acceptable and savoury, like no one else's. She reached down a heavy library book from a pile on the table and opened it on her lap. Not a lot of call in the desert for Victorian translations of Dante, the librarian had remarked, glancing her over appraisingly. There were facing texts, the mysterious and beautiful Italian on the left, the English key on the right.

'Do you know Italian?' he'd asked.

'I have some Latin and I think I may be able to work it out on the page. I'm hoping so anyway.'

It had been a manifesto. There is more to me than all this.

The print was large and ornate, according each word its sonorous authority. The pages were a sombre khaki, speckled with mould, and smelt deliciously of libraries, her mind's home. Ailsa read slowly aloud in Italian, entering the dark wood of this world with Dante, glancing over to the English to make sure of her path. It led, of course it did, to the book under the bed. She ran upstairs and hefted out the shoebox.

313

19

Quiet mornings, just the two of them awakening together, often in the same bed, for Nia liked to creep in with Mami while her father was away.

Nice cool Shropshire weather, Mami said, opening the curtains. After they'd washed, Nia watched her pull the newly pressed dove-grey dress over her head and then wriggle, her face hidden, hands waggling out of the cuffs.

'Help me, Nia! I'm stuck!'

The waist of the dress was catching on Mami's bosom. And she seemed to be all elbows.

'Mami, for goodness' sake breathe small. Go into yourself!'

Ailsa giggled and obeyed. Her head popped through the dainty white collar as her arms threaded through the cap sleeves.

Nia helped smooth the soft mothery fabric down over the silky sheath of Ailsa's petticoat. She laid her head against the flat belly; breathed in the scent of ironed cotton, combined with talcum powder and shampoo. It was hard to believe, what Topher had once told her, that she had once been inside there, like an egg, he'd said, in a nest. You've seen an egg? You've seen a nest? Well, like that, one in the other. There's a chick in every egg, he'd said, a fluffy yellow chick. Surely you know that? It seemed to Nia that Topher had told her this only yesterday.

Nia went round the back of Ailsa and gently pulled down the hem, to lie evenly. Then she wound her arms round from behind, head nestled sideways against the small of her mother's back. They rocked, the two of them as one creature, back and forth, as she'd seen Mona and her mother do. Together Nia and Ailsa shuffled to the mirror, where Nia peered round her mother's body to assess how they looked. Though Mami's expression was odd, Nia understood it. Ailsa had caught sight of a stranger in the mirror, as Nia herself sometimes did when, skipping into an empty room, she met a mocking mimic. It froze when you froze and stared, and sprang to rude life behind your back.

'It's all right, Mami,' she reassured her. 'Put your eyebrows down. I'm here.'

Mami's eyebrows were strong wings over the greenness of her eyes. But when she was worried, they rose up and crinkled her forehead. Now her face smoothed; she brushed her freshly washed hair and said Nia could do up all these fiddly buttons for her if she would be so kind, with her small, expert fingers.

While Ailsa perched on the pouffe, Nia fastened mother-of-pearl buttons one by one, her heart tickling with a fussy sort of pleasure.

'How do I look?' asked Ailsa.

'Nice.'

'Good. Now, what about breakfast.'

Nia cupped a brown egg between both palms, to coddle it. Ailsa allowed her to lower it on the spoon into bubbling water and to cut her own soldiers. The butter melted deliciously into the soldiers and she hummed as she chewed. They would see Auntie Mona today, as they did every day. It made Nia feel calm and still inside. She felt Mona's presence all around them. They'd bumped into her by pure accident the day after Daddy left – *Well! What a surprise! How are you, my dear?* – as if it had been necessary for her father to go out of one door for her auntie to come in through another.

But first of all the Roberts girls would read their books. When the breakfast table had been cleared and the washing up done, mother and daughter would remove the table cloth and sit at angles to one another with crayons, pen, books and paper. Daylight fell on their open books, each page like a pale, absorbing face. They'd read snippets aloud and sometimes remain so quiet that the steady pulse of their breathing would hush Nia into a half-dream.

'What are you writing now?' she'd ask when Ailsa opened her fountain pen and began to scribble in a special green notebook. And Mami would read aloud beautiful things, such as the way in the Nile Valley the strong, clear sun would pile the colours on top of one another in layers: lifting the blue sky on to the yellow cliffs, on to the green land, the black bank, the blue river. The sunlight in Egypt is different from anywhere else, Mami had written. It shrinks the distances so that the colours all walk forward.

This formed a picture in Nia's mind, which she drew for her mother, with herself standing between Mona and Mami next to a tiny pyramid and a big camel. For the three of them had been to Cairo in Mona's Land Rover and viewed the Pyramid of Cheops. They'd stayed the night at Mena House, before motoring home to the bungalow.

Nia had run around with nothing on her feet across Mona's cool marble floors, soles slapping on cold surfaces, and perched on a red cushion with the pussy cat, Isis. A feral cat – a wild, mangy tempest of a creature from the streets, so Mona had said. Isis would never be really tame. Nia had ordered the two women to make room and then to *cwtch* up round her, and settled herself between them, safe as houses between two lots of bosom and two sets of skirted thighs. Auntie Mona had carpets on the walls, nearly as nice as the carpet at Nia's home.

Mona had no child, only Nia.

Mona had no country of her own. She would like to go to Jerusalem again, she said. It was her dearest wish. But she was *persona non grata*. It was a bad thing to be. Nia knew this, though Mona said it briskly and cheerfully.

Habibi was a big, funny man whose legs were like stilts. He'd tossed her high in the garden till she screamed; he'd danced with Mona and Ailsa, his arms round both their waists. His fair-haired best pal, Alex, had sometimes crouched down and played jacks with Nia. Presently the two men had been sent off in their turn to exercise in the desert.

'*Salaam aleicum!*'

'*Aleicum salaam!*'

Mona's friends would wait for them in a room in Ish

bright with brass, hangings and tassels, and a chandelier. They were the Palestinians who'd been thrown out of their own country. Not Mona's relatives who all wore normal dress and went to church on Sundays but friends who were Muslims and covered their hair because it was too lovely for men to be allowed to see. She remembered an oval platter in the centre of a low table containing meatballs; there were salads, rice dishes, fried potatoes. Everyone reached to take what they wanted in their fingers. Nia's meal had been an uncontrollable mess, her chin and hands running with sauce. Afterwards Ailsa and Mona had drunk thick coffee out of baby cups and Nia a glass of sherbert. Polite murmurs of conversation had swollen into passionate discussion.

'We call our home our own,' one of the women had said, with unimaginable sadness in her voice. 'We must believe we shall return. Otherwise there is no life.'

Nia, bored, prowling the edge of the room, had discovered a cage covered in green felt. Lifting the edge and peeking, she'd seen a sleeping bird, lime-green and yellow, head under wing.

Later Nia had overheard Mona telling Ailsa of a shocking, obscene thing that was done to girls of six.

'The *dawa* comes. To cut it out at the root. She buries it in a hole. It is of the devil. Girls often bleed to death.'

Ailsa's face had been twisted and ugly, her arms crossed over her breasts.

Mona had played rippling rivers of notes on the three-legged piano. Creeping underneath with Isis, Nia had enjoyed its gentle boom and sweet throb. She'd watched Mona's beautiful bare feet, with dirty soles, working the pedals. She'd stretched on her tummy, eyes close to the feet, enthralled by their fleshy pushing of the metal. Thrill had flipped into shock as a roar erupted from the body of the piano, thundered into Nia and split her head wide open. Purple in the face and screaming, Nia had shot out and so did the cat.

Oh little *habiba*, did I give you a shock?

Not one drop of shampoo did Mona get in Nia's eyes when she bathed her. She sleeked the soapy hair up in a wet pixie peak. The two women bundled Nia in a thick towel and Mona sat on the lid of the toilet and sang. Nia had two mothers.

'That's enough of my yodelling,' Mona said.

The two mothers washed one another's hair and combed it out, taking turns to sit in front a big gilt-framed mirror in candle light. Mona bent to kiss the nape of Ailsa's neck and when Nia copied her, she smelled blossomy shampoo on clean, moist skin and saw Mami's silver teardrop earring gleam in the soft light.

Nia had basked on the exciting little bed with Isis, whose pelt shone like coal. Eyes half closed, vibrating with purrs, the creature had stretched back over the pillow and given herself up to bliss, Nia stroking her belly. They were staying overnight.

In the officers' quarters, Nia thought. *Ha!*

She'd thought about Daddy in the desert when the waft of roast lamb and gravy and roast potatoes reached her from downstairs. Which Daddy loved. His plate was always a mountain range of potatoes. A lake of gravy. Second helpings. The dad-pad will be getting fat! he'd say, patting his middle. Mustafa had been cooking a Sunday dinner, even though it was not Sunday. Mustafa was not a servant. He was a respected friend, a chef from Palestine where he had owned a restaurant. Palestine was not Israel. That was a lie. The smell had roused juices in Nia's mouth, sickishly.

In the slatted, mothbally wardrobe along one wall of Mona and *Habibi*'s bedroom, she'd found a row of crisp shirts and ties, blazers and suits. And two full robes of dark material with a bodice, back and panels of intricate rich red embroidery, a wide silken belt to go with them. The pattern and colours told people which village you came from. Mona was selling them for the Palestinian women friends who'd made them. Ailsa had said she longed to buy one but didn't think she could take it home. *Keep yours here with me then*, Mona had offered. Inserting herself into Ailsa's kaftan, Nia had drawn the cool folds round her face. Then she'd sat and played with violet mothballs that hung on strings and tempted her appetite like sweets. She'd put out the tip of her tongue and tasted one. Dry and cool, not at all minty.

Leaving the wardrobe, Nia had sat on the edge of the big bed and bounced. Feeling under the pillows, she'd touched a nightie. She'd peered in the drawers of the bedside cabinets at either side and sniffed small private smells. Among Nivea jars and nail clippers, had been a rubbery thing in a packet, with an interesting shape, which she put in the pocket of her shorts to look at later.

'Nia! Din-dins!'

Scooping up the bulky cat, she'd lugged her, squirming and spitting, downstairs.

Awakening in the night, Nia had heard women's voices and rustlings through the wall.

A lady was at the door. Nia knew from the knock that it couldn't be Mona, who had her own *pom-de-pompom* rap. Ailsa however rushed to the door, stripping off her pinnie, calling out, 'Darling!'

Nia played with her fuzzy felt.

'I did write, Ailsa,' came Topher's mum's hangdog voice. 'I did write to Joe.'

'Oh my goodness. But we didn't realise you meant to come so soon. Are the boys with you?'

'Topher! Topher!' Nia shrieked, and sped out into the hall.

There was no Topher. Just Mrs White in a twinset and pearls, and white leather shoes with a hole through which her stockinged big toe peeped, covered in dirt. She'd put down a large and a small suitcase at the end of the path.

'Ah, it's little Nia! Hallo, little miss!'

'Where's Topher, Missus?' Nia bawled.

'I've left Christopher and Timothy with my mother-in-law, dear. No point in uprooting them until I know what the arrangements are. Is Joe, perhaps, about, Ailsa?'

'No, Irene, he's in the desert.'

'In the *desert*?'

'Exercises. Nothing to worry about. Look, do come in and sit down and have a drink, Irene. Something to eat? Freshen up? Where are you staying?'

In Irene came. She didn't know where she was staying. She had meant to ask Joe's advice. But he was in the desert. How long would he be away? Oh dear. Another two weeks? She looked wan and weak.

'Oh, whatever shall I do, Ailsa?'

'You will be all right. Just sit and get your bearings. That's the way. How did you get here?'

'I flew in a York aircraft. With a lot of public school kiddies vomiting. It was a nightmare.'

'Oh dear. Not pleasant.'

'No, not pleasant at all.' Irene dissolved into tears, hiding her face in both hands, swaying to and fro. Nia backed away from the moist lady who had been spewed on.

Nia could hear reluctance and duty in Ailsa's voice, and then the resolution to do what was required of her as she placed her hand on the back of Irene's neck, where Nia knew it did most good in calming you. 'It's all just been awful, you poor girl. Nia, run and get a glass of water for Mrs White. Run the tap so it's good and cold.'

Nia shuffled in, a brimming glass clasped in both hands. Topher's mother couldn't help smiling.

'Oh you good girl,' she said as she accepted it. 'Aren't you clever, not spilling a drop. You have careful hands like your mummy.'

'You can go off and play if you like, Nia, while we have a chat,' Ailsa said.

Nia slouched out into the garden and swung on the gate, looking down the sandy road, in case Topher was coming, though she knew he wasn't. Then she went into the back garden, sidling her way into position under the open sitting room window.

'Don't be cross with me, Ailsa dear! Don't! Please!' Mrs White wailed.

'Whyever would I be cross with you, Irene? Of course

you can stay here with us, as long as you need. It's no trouble, none in the world.'

Nia went back in and put her hot hand on Mrs White's leg. 'Have you brought your knitting needles with you, Mrs White? Are you thinking of knitting a sock?'

Irene laughed. She said Nia was so droll. She was growing up, wasn't she, a proper young lady. Would she like Auntie Irene to teach her to knit while she was here? Which reminded her, she'd brought a little present for Nia. And Christopher, who'd been such a naughty boy in England, and wet the bed and bit his little brother (such a good child, Timothy, such winning ways) ... Christopher had not forgotten Nia and had staged such a tantrum when he heard Irene was going to see her that his grandma had smacked his legs, you never saw such a spectacle as Christopher in a rage, she told Ailsa, it is volcanic. *He will go to the dogs*, his grandma always said. But Christopher had sent Nia something. Wherever was it? She'd remember as soon as she unpacked her things. Irene raised to Ailsa a spaniel face.

'If it's all right,' she said. 'If you're sure, Ailsa. I'll try not to be a nuisance. It will only be for a limited time.'

*

'Honestly, Mona, what could I do?' her mami said. 'I could hardly turn her away. It's all terribly sad. Still, she's cheered up amazingly. Does all sorts of sweet things with Nia. She brought her out some beads to thread. Now she's gone off to the NAAFI to enquire about a job, and blithely offered to save me the chore of shopping, saying it's quite like old times. Old times! She loathed it here. I don't think

323

she's at all well. She had this funny sort of innocent pash, you know, on Joe. I don't think it meant anything to him. She doesn't bear him the slightest malice, not in the least, for Chalkie – you know. She helps me round the house, till I could scream. I got up yesterday and found her with her head in a turban, down on her knees and scrubbing the kitchen floor – which is perfectly clean, and when I said, *Oh Irene, there is no need for that*, she looked up with this light in her eyes and I could see it was *Joe's floor she was scrubbing.*'

Nia watched Isis in Mona's garden playing with the crickets before she killed them. Cuffing them with her paws, sending them leaping in the grass, then crunching them in her jaws, though she didn't want to eat them.

'And it adds a layer of complication. As if things weren't complicated enough.'

Isis came creeping up to Nia to be stroked; laid back her head and yawned, and you could see the legs of the crickets inside her mouth, in a mouthful of sunshine from the low sun, turning the inside gleaming pink. Nia's tummy tickled with a nasty kind of pleasure to spy that cruel place.

'As well be hung for a sheep as for a lamb,' she heard Ailsa say doubtfully.

Next day the Girl Guides were practising parades beneath the flag in Mrs Wintergreen's back garden. They fell in and they fell out. Whistles were blown and they sang the National Anthem. Mona got fed up with the racket. She leaned out of the bedroom window and barked '*Dis-miss!*'

Irene came back early from the NAAFI. She said she was pleased to meet Mona again. She did indeed remember her: *all too well*, her face said. She seemed inclined to stand to attention while the officer's lady was in the room.

'Do make yourselves at home, everyone,' Ailsa repeated. But Irene wouldn't. The most she could do was to stand at ease, near the door. So Mona felt she oughtn't to sit down and neither could Ailsa. Nia propped her backside against a chair-arm and allowed herself to topple slowly backwards into the seat, lying with her legs in the air. She watched from upside-down.

Irene said she would make the coffee, not Ailsa, who should sit down and entertain her guest.

'I wouldn't dream of it.' Ailsa coloured up. 'The idea. You are my guest, Irene.' She slid past Irene out of the door, returning with a tray.

'How do you like yours, Irene?'

'Oh – however it comes out of the pot. No sugar though. I have to watch my figure, well, we all do, don't we? I was asking dear little Nia when her daddy is expected home. It is so hard for kiddies when the daddies go away. Oh,' she said. 'Oh no!' Her coffee cup wobbled on the saucer. 'Excuse me.' She bolted out of the room.

'Oh *dear*,' said Ailsa. She bolted after Irene.

When they returned, Nia fetched Irene's gift of beadwork. Standing at Irene's knee, she offered it, bestowing herself on the sad lady, because ladies liked it when children did that. Irene's face cleared. Her deft fingers began to thread ruby beads at one end, and she smiled through watery eyes, while Nia threaded emerald ones at the other.

'Do you have children yourself, Mrs Jacobs?' Irene asked.

'Please call me Mona. No. I've no children. But I'm very

325

fond of Nia. You have two little boys?'

'Christopher and Timothy.'

'You must miss them frightfully.'

'Oh, I do. But as soon as I'm settled – they'll be sent for, of course. And Ailsa has been so very patient, though I'm afraid I've rather thrown myself upon her hospitality...'

'Not at all, Irene. We're only too glad to have you.'

'Mona – that's not an English name, I fancy?'

'Well, it can be. Not in this instance.'

'I do so like foreign names. They are so unusual.'

'My mami and Auntie Mona want to go to Palestine,' Nia confided to Irene.

'To Israel?'

'No, the correct name is Palestine. Except to Zionists,' Mona said.

'Oh yes?' Irene seemed to gasp for air. She fetched a deep breath. 'What about the *situation*?'

'The situation?'

'Politically. The tension. It was on the wireless all the time at home, Ailsa. So *dangerous*. Everywhere. Even in Ish. The Egyptians are going to tear up the Treaty, aren't they? What's the word?'

'Abrogate?'

'That's it.'

'We've had very little trouble here,' Ailsa said. 'Mona's family is from Jerusalem, as you know.'

'Oh, really. How interesting. I hadn't realised.' Irene ceased threading the beads but she kept hold of the end so that Nia could carry on threading hers. 'Such an historical place. Well – now I'm here,' she said slowly, 'there's no reason not to go. I'll take care of little Nia. You'd be happy

326

to stay with your Auntie Irene, won't you, darling, and keep her company?'

'No,' said Nia.

Oh no, said Ailsa, they couldn't possibly presume on her. Nia saw her mother looking over her own head to Mona. A nasty tricksiness in her eyes. They were playing piggie in the middle. Nia was piggie. It was only a sort of whimsy, really, Ailsa went on. Just a dream. Anyway Joe wouldn't like it, not one bit.

'How would he know?' asked Irene, an extraordinary expression of guile darting over her face.

20

The side door was unlocked. Joe dumped his kit bag by the kitchen table. Quiet. Putting his head through the hatch between the kitchen and sitting room, he locked eyes with a startled mouse of a woman in Ailsa's chair, her head twisting round, hand clutching the chair-arm, half raising her body. Some terrible thing had happened, then, to his wife and daughter. The thing he had always knew would happen.

'Good Lord alive, Irene. You're back. Whatever's happened? Where's Ailsa?'

The woman was babysitting apparently. But how did she get there? She babbled that Ailsa was *away*, she was taking *a little trip*. He'd been sent home sick, he told her, a week early. The other airmen had envied him his chitty from the MO, but they wouldn't have done if they'd had his gut.

As soon as she twigged that he was ill, Irene calmed right down. Joe swayed where he stood. She guided him to his chair and he leaned his head back, child-feeble. Irene's palm on his forehead was cool. Could he keep water down,

328

she asked? She would help him up to bed and very soon he'd be as right as rain. He hadn't the foggiest where Irene had sprung from. Gave up trying to work it out. Apparently she was staying with them.

'Come on, Joe. Don't worry about anything. It will be all right now,' she soothed. 'Let me get you to bed.'

'In a minute.' Drained and afraid to risk the journey upstairs in case he lost control of his bowels, he rested his head and looked at her. 'Bit of a bad do,' he explained. 'Gyppo cooks. *Eggza-brayed!* Dirty hands. I don't even want a fag,' he lamented. 'The living end.'

'Never mind all that, dear. Don't think about food. As long as you keep drinking. Here you are. Just a teeny sip. *That*'s the way.'

'Irene?'

'Joe.'

'What the hell are you doing here? Where has she *gone*?'

Nia appeared in the doorway and silently stared. She'd been dressed up in a pink satin frock with puff sleeves and a big bow of pink ribbon in her hair. The colour clashed astoundingly with her red hair. Round her neck she wore a long bead necklace, with blue and green beads. She looked as if she were on her way to a party.

'Don't come anywhere near to Daddy,' Joe warned her. 'He might have some nasty germs. Don't want you to get them, do we?'

'Are you home now, Daddy?' Nia asked from the doorway.

'Aye. Home now.'

'Mami's gone to Palestine with Auntie Mona,' Nia said. 'And they wouldn't take me.'

329

'*What?*'

'Never mind that now, Nia,' Irene cut in. 'Daddy needs to rest up. He got a tummy ache in the desert and he's had to come home early. Ailsa will soon be back, Joe, don't you fret.'

'She's where?'

'A trip to Jordan. They call it Palestine but I think they mean Transjordan. Just for a couple of days.'

'In *Jordan*? Ailsa? With the Jacobs woman? And *him*?'

'Who? Oh, no one else, Joe. Just the two of them, of course. No men involved. They went the day before yesterday. Apparently they are going to see for themselves what has happened to the Arabs Israel didn't want. Back on Saturday. I'll explain when you're better.'

She helped Joe upstairs and put him to bed. Then she fended for him.

Caught short. *Duw, duw.* Joe looked down at his unwashed, hairy body. An ape of a man. He should have cleaned himself. Or Ailsa should have done it. Chalkie's widow bundled up the soiled linen and whisked it away. Her fingers fastened the drawstring of his pyjamas and her capable arms laid him down in fresh sheets. Supporting his head, she offered water. When Joe fumbled with words of apology and thanks, she said, 'Oh Joe, I'm a mother of two boys. Nothing here I haven't dealt with before, I can assure you.'

'Disinfect everything, Irene. Taps and so on.'

'I know the drill.'

Joe sank down into a lake of coolness. Later, having slept, he hoisted himself on one elbow and craned to see out of the window. Chalkie's widow was pegging pyjamas and towels on the line.

When he woke again, it was evening; a lamp glowed in the corner. Downstairs the wireless purred and he could hear a friendly chinking of cups and saucers. Everything was normal except that Sergeant *Roberts'* wife was in *Jordan* with Wing Commander *Jacobs'* wife, and who-knew-who-else, leaving his daughter to the late Sergeant *White's* wife, a lady who had apparently come all the way from Birmingham for this exchange. But perhaps it had just been one of those Toc-H excursions, all above board, and perhaps all the wives had gone, and perhaps the darkie woman was there in a supervisory capacity, and her Jewboy husband and that public school queerboy his pal were not there with them, and Irene had got the wrong end of the stick.

Irene was standing at the bedside when he opened his eyes again. Nia and she had gone out when the van came round, and stocked up with Lucozade. She wondered if he could fancy it yet?

'How come you're here and my wife isn't, Irene?' he asked, as she poured a small measure for him.

'I'll explain, if you drink.'

He sipped. The taste was impossibly delicious. Must be on the mend.

Irene had flown out to be near Roy, she told him, to find a position in the NAAFI (which she had done) and to consult him as Roy's most valued friend. This she had undertaken on an impulse and perhaps (if she was frank with herself) it had not been a well-judged action, but she had not been thinking straight at all and who did she have to turn to? And of course Christopher – well, Christopher had been a handful.

'It's his grief for his daddy,' said Joe. 'Bound to feel it, Irene.'

'I know. Don't drink any more now, Joe. Whoa there!' She captured the glass and set it down where he couldn't reach without stretching. 'Take it slowly, I should. But to be so naughty!' she went on. 'Like a little devil. Kicking me. My shins were black and blue.'

'Give him time, eh?'

'Yes. Of course you're right. I can see it now.' She looked shamefaced. 'Why couldn't I see it before, Joe, before you said it? It seems so obvious now.'

'Lovely little chap he is. He'll make you proud of him. Just a little patience.'

'Oh, Joe – *don't*. You'll make me so sad. I seem to get on better if I don't feel anything.'

He made her go on about the flight. She'd taken the last seat in a battered old sardine can stuffed with small schoolchildren with plummy accents – prep school pupils, apparently, coming to visit their lah-de-dah mummies and daddies in Suez. Joe lay still and listened to how paralysingly cold it had been for Irene on the plane, jammed in between these children. She'd sat there, holding a paper bag of inedible food, and thought *What am I doing? What?* At that moment she thought she'd gone off her rocker, truly. The loneliness was worse than at any time since Roy had died. She'd have been glad to jump out of the plane without a parachute.

'Now now,' said Joe, and patted the back of her hand with his fingertips.

'Oh, bless you, I don't feel like that *now*,' Irene said, withdrawing the hand but looking at it with a pleased expression. 'I'm just telling you how it was.'

Ailsa had been terribly kind and taken her in.

'So that's my silly story,' she said brightly. 'Now you can have another sip, if you want one.'

'I'll get up tomorrow morning.'

'We'll see.'

'Tell me about this … thing with Mrs Jacobs.'

'Joe, ask Ailsa yourself when she gets back, I should.'

Her fingers plucked nervously at a small embroidered hanky. Embarrassed she was. For Ailsa, he realised. Defending him from his own wife; or her from him.

'But just to clear off. Clear off just like that,' he complained. 'Don't tell me it wasn't planned. Planned well beforehand. As soon as she knew I was going away.'

'Oh, I don't think so.' Yet he could see that she looked gratified at the thought of the hot water Ailsa had got herself into. Irene was on his side.

'Come *on*,' he said.

'That wasn't my impression. Oh no. They'd just bumped into one another and got talking – and the idea was – mooted. And you know how tremendously intellectual Ailsa is. So interested in historical things. Not like me – a home bird, me, a bit of a feather brain. You know, it's only a four day trip. No more than a jaunt really.'

'*Intellectuals*,' he sneered. Irene had hit upon the word guaranteed to inflame Joe. 'Don't give me intellectuals. Ineffectuals. The rot of civilisation. I won't have any damned intellectuals in my house.'

She can go west, he thought. Ailsa can damn well go west, as far as I'm concerned.

Later he came down to the kitchen, weakly relaxed from

the bath, wet hair flat to his head, spruced up in a clean white shirt. The plain, homely woman at the Primus, Chalkie's widow, turned to greet him, flushed with nervous pleasure.

'One brown egg coming up! One slice of toast cut into soldiers! Cup of tea! You could fancy a cup of tea, Joe?'

'Oh aye. If it's no trouble, Irene.'

Marmalade and Marmite stood on the table cloth and letters were stacked in the last compartment of the toast rack, as he had seen them on Chalkie's breakfast table in that other world, when he'd pop his head round the door first thing: *Wotcher, both!* More often than not, poor old Chalkie was in the dog house and could only reply with a rueful half-grin. Joe perched himself awkwardly at his own table, not sure how to behave. Irene's back was turned to him and she was humming. Glancing at the way the tiny pleats of her tartan skirt rippled over her hips as she moved, a qualm went through him as if some intimacy had taken place between them last night, which of course was not the case. She had been present as a nurse, that was all.

Now Irene bustled round, chatting to Nia, as Joe nibbled and read. Although he didn't want to eat much, he knew he was on the mend. They sat over a second cup of tea, while a subdued Nia went out to play.

'My Roy is here,' Irene said. 'That is why I must be here. It's so silly, I know – when he was alive, I couldn't wait to get out. I was afraid of everything, every fly, every Arab, even the chai wallah and the sweet little one-eyed bottle-collector. Now the fear is all gone, Joe. When I went back to Blighty, I saw there was no Blighty for me there any more. No place for me.'

334

'Your Roy wouldn't like to hear you talk like that.'

'No, he would scold me.'

Joe couldn't help but smile. Nobody could have imagined the mild Chalkie scolding Irene. Chalkie might stand up to the nagging a bit more, he'd occasionally suggested to his pal, thinking, she wouldn't nag *me* if I were in his shoes, *oh* no. He lit up two fags and handed one to Irene. Moving from table to armchair, Joe's eye was caught by the sun staining a corner of the Gyppo carpet he'd got himself into debt for, before he'd left for manoeuvres. Only been able to pay half the sum they'd agreed and he'd given the wog a chitty for the rest.

The autumn colours were hypnotic. In his mind's eye, Ailsa lay naked on the carpet, legs splayed wide open. Good God. And then, hunched into herself, grunting and rasping with an animal noise while his fingers slipped on the slick flesh, tick-tick-ticking *down there*, where it seemed to spasm in what must be – her climax.

He blushed beetroot red. What kind of woman behaved like that? With her innocent daughter in the house?

In his depleted state, Joe recoiled from the woman's shamelessness. She should have resisted him. It was all very well to say, *But we are married, what's wrong with that?* It could not be right. Some things were not natural. He could not imagine Mam and Dad behaving like that on the parlour floor. Who had taught Ailsa these tricks, and when? Virgin when they married, he had been. She'd not actually said that she was. He would never have dreamed of asking.

How could you know? The blood on the sheets? Could have been the other woman's thing. Joe had only glimpsed the bloodstain. It seemed to him now that, when she'd stripped the bed in the morning, she cleverly covered the bottom sheet with the top sheet and whipped them both up together. He'd helped by looking away. All he'd cared about that morning was that he should not have hurt her by his roughness.

The whole thing had seemed so coarse and crude, looked at from her angle. How could women possibly like or want that dark thick *thing* to be poked into their soft tissue?

'Did I do very wrong to come out?' Irene asked him. Her plaintive tone pleaded with Joe to take responsibility for her. It denied on his behalf the fact that, if it had not been for Joe, her husband would still be with her.

'It was, well, a biggish sort of step. I'm not sure where you go from here.'

'That's what I need to find out.'

'Aye. What about the boys?'

'I shall find some path, I believe I shall. Whatever people think. The boys will come to me when the time is right. I want you to do something for me, my dear, when you are up to it, not before. Will you take me to visit Roy? Will you do that for me?'

Late afternoon. They walked together over immaculate turf, as green as England, an oasis of growth and order in the midst of the wilderness. Rows of white stone lozenges and wooden crosses quivered in Joe's shaky gaze. He remembered bearing the body to the hole that had been dug for Chalkie. The light burden of his friend had weighed a ton in the lead coffin. Now he stood back, as Irene ran forward a few steps, with girlish eagerness, and crouched. She placed her hand flat to the turf and stroked

336

it. She had put on lipstick and washed and set her hair. Joe had caught glimpses of her through the half-shut bedroom door in her hair net and slip, applying varnish to her nails.

She was not weeping. She turned and looked up to him: 'Would you sing, Joe?'

'Sing?'

'Sing something for Roy.'

'Well, oh, I don't know about that, Irene *fach*. What should I sing?'

Reddening, he looked over his shoulder. There was only Nia practising cartwheels over by the stand of trees and a wog workman with a rake and a barrow, busy at the officers' end of the cemetery.

'Oh, never mind, sorry. You're not up to singing. Just a whim.' She got up and came to him. 'We used to listen to you singing. It was quite a joke between us. I think you must have been in your bath. Whoever heard you first would call the other: *loofah concert!* We'd stand by the open window and listen. It choked Roy up.'

Joe stood to his full height, took a deep breath and plunged into *Bryn Calfaria*. He followed it with *Iesu Mawr*. She asked if he would sing *Myfanwy*. Of course he would but it was not a sacred song, he said. Wasn't it a love-song? Yes, he said. Then it was a sacred song, Irene replied; she thought so anyway. Love between man and wife was sacred. It was a sacrament.

By the time he was singing *Myfanwy*, Nia had crept over and taken Joe's hand. Pitying tenderness for Irene welled up in him. He put his arm around her shoulder and did not take it away. They all three stood in the ringing

337

silence that followed the music, their bodies casting a slant, single shadow.

*

He would not reproach her. She was his wife. She was Ailsa. Decent through and through. Of course she was. That would never alter. He had begun to feel and know this after he'd sung to Chalkie in Fayid Cemetery.

Myfanwy was a sacred song. If it wasn't, what was?

Who had laid Ailsa down on that carpet to love her? Her husband. Who had she shown herself to? Joe. Who had sworn to be faithful to her, to have faith in her? Joe. He remembered how shy they'd been when first together. She had hardly seemed to enjoy the sexual act at all. He'd felt her body cringe when he entered it. They had learned together.

She had needs. Yes, Joe thought, a decent woman can have needs. When they got home to England, he'd buy a piano. Mam would store it for them when they were posted abroad. And the girlie could learn to play. She'd have a teacher. Nia would grow up with advantages. It was Egypt that had put things out of joint between himself and Ailsa. Once they were home, there would be balance and harmony. He would send Ailsa and Nia home as soon as possible. The Jacobs pair had done the damage. Them and Egypt. Not safe to keep his family here where mounting tensions made it clear that there would be an armed uprising.

Because after all, he thought, sitting forward with his forearms on his knees, pinching the stub of a cigarette between finger and thumb, Ailsa was not Irene. This

338

seemed to explain everything. Ailsa had her passions and they were a bit less commonplace than recipes for toad in the hole, which Irene had animatedly proclaimed she'd be cooking for supper, if he felt he could fancy it. Ailsa would have turned up her nose at such a vulgar dish. In that respect Ailsa was not unlike Mam, who took his wife's part, because she saw and valued that hint of the remarkable in Ailsa. *Diamond in a coal tip*, she'd called her. But Ailsa, unlike Mam, he thought, stubbing out the fag, was a quiet one. Still waters. She kept her thoughts and feelings to herself. She said, *I wish I were more spontaneous, darling, but believe me, it is all in there*, covering her left breast with her hand.

Upstairs, he knelt by their bed and pulled out the box where she kept the Jacobs woman's gifts. Here it was, cradled in tissue paper like a pair of new shoes, though it smelt of age and decay. Sitting on the bed, he opened the book at the frontispiece where a librarian had stamped, 'Property of HM Navy. SS *Empire Glory*'. Light-fingered Mrs Jacobs had lifted it from the troopship. He whistled through his teeth. It wasn't something he did or condoned. Officers did what the hell they felt like, riding roughshod over the decencies. Even a pencil or roll of tape from the office Joe would scrupulously return. That was how he had been brought up.

The book was in Gothic script and looked to his eye vaguely Nazi. Joe sat for a while turning the pages.

On the dressing table lay another book, open with a scribbled sheet of paper and a pencil lying on top of it. Dante, he read, *The Inferno*. Italian or Latin, with a facing translation. He read a few lines in English. Beautiful they

339

were. The scribbles on the sheet of paper were lists of words with ticks or question marks beside them. You sat in a person's private space and you read the clues to her life.

And what did all this say about Ailsa? *Her hunger. To know more.*

He felt now as if he were defending his wife against a voice that spoke with his dad's snarling suspicion of educated folk. Of those who wished to make something of themselves. He understood why Dad sneered in that way. But this was not Joe's way. He replaced the Nazi book in its box and slid it under the bed.

He rummaged in the drawer with Ailsa's nighties. Her green diary seemed to be missing. That proved nothing. Mooching into Nia's room, he woke her from her nap. But he let Irene sleep on. She was quite honestly rather hard work.

Together Nia and Joe cleared away the clutter of toys. Her methodical fingers lined up her bricks in their box. She'd grown, Joe thought, since they'd come out here. Tall and thin she was for her age, like a long-legged foal. Chattering away to her golliwog and teddy. Not too long till she'd be off to school, and presumably some day there'd be a brother or sister for her to play with, making her less of an odd little bod. Perhaps that was what Ailsa really needed, to stabilise and fulfil her.

He began to sort a wicker basket full of screwed up papers, blue papers that had once contained the salt in a bag of crisps, hair slides and whatnot, which magpie Nia insisted were important treasures. A thimble of Ailsa's, a teaspoon smuggled from the cutlery drawer.

A rubber johnny in an unopened packet.

'What the hell's this, Nia?'

'I don't know. What is it?'

'Where did you get it?'

'I don't know.'

'Well bloody well think about it!' he barked. Had she picked it up in the street? It could not be his because it was not the sort he used.

'No need to shout, you Welshman,' she reproved him, clapping her hands over her ears.

'I *will* shout, unless I get an answer. Great Scott, you can't go playing with things like this.'

'Why, what is it? Is it electric?'

'No, it's not elecric. Where did you get it though, girlie? I do need to know.'

'I got it off of Mona,' she told him, darting him a guilty look, which said she knew something naughty, which she ought to keep to herself.

'*From*, not *off of*, Nia. Only common people say *off of*.'

'Yes, but I didn't steal it or nothing.'

'You found it?'

She nodded.

'Where? I'm not cross, don't worry.'

'On *Habibi*'s side of the bed.'

His heart was hammering. It all came out. His wife and daughter had stayed the night – how many nights? – in the Jacobs' house at Masurah.

'Which bed was that then?'

'The big bed. I had a little baby bed through the wall.'

'Did anyone tell you not to tell me?'

'No, they didn't.'

'Who didn't?'

341

'Not anyone didn't.'

There were lots of bedrooms, Nia confided, in Mona's house. Not *poky* like here.

I will kill him, Joe thought.

Nia yawned. She squirmed and said she had to do a wee-wee. Then she began to grizzle and babyishly to repeat over and over that she wanted a strawberry and vanilla ice cream.

Joe put the foreign johnny in his pocket, where his fingers could take avid note of it.

How big was the bastard's cock? She liked kissing cock. Oh aye, he knew. He had been amazed to discover the things she liked doing. He knew her thoroughly. He knew what grossness she was capable of. She had shown him.

A fire of fear consumed him. The smooth, hairless body of his lean, slim, public school rival knelt above Ailsa, fitting the johnny to his cock with one practised hand. And Ailsa waiting in silence, lying in her beauty for the taking. Ailsa who pretended to love Joe's squat, hairy body that had laboured in the steel mill, which was all he was fit for.

'I'm off down the mess,' he called to Irene.

'Right-oh, dear. When will you be back?'

'Late. Don't wait up.'

'What about – ? Never mind.'

'What about what?'

'I was going to say, the toad in the hole.'

They were out in the front. Joe had the tarpaulin off the Tiger and was revving it up.

'Sorry about that,' he said. 'I'll have to miss out on the toad in the hole.'

'Joe. Dear. Please take care on the motor bike. Please.'

'Don't worry, Irene.'

She came and placed both hands on the handlebars.

'I'm bound to worry. I can see how upset you are.'

He denied it. He was not upset. As the Tiger took off, Joe let rip but his heart was ice. The roaring speed, the wind whipping past his temples and the belly of the beast throbbing between his legs killed the hurt stone dead.

But he could hardly go to the mess, he realised, slowing. If anyone in authority saw how well he'd recovered, it would be straight back to the fucking desert with a black mark against his name. Into Ish, then. Get plastered in the Hollywood Bar. As Joe reached the outskirts of Wogtown, he came upon a football match in the middle of the road, and swerved to one side, where he paused. The blokes were playing football with melons, the produce of an elderly Gyppo in a *gallabiyya*, who stood by his handcart, wringing his hands and pleading in gibberish. The fellaheen's whole crop had been dumped in the road. The blokes were rowdy and pretty squiffy by the looks of things. One lumbering squaddie had a whistle and was pretending to referee. Another was commentating.

When the melon in play had burst, a winger would grab another from the pile, the old Gyppo meanwhile weeping, tears in full flow.

'*And* it's McConnachie now, passes to Smith who dribbles the ball – but *oh*! he's lost it to Jack Black, who – *oh*! yes! he *scores*! – Jack Black scores up a date palm!'

The poor old Gyppo had had it coming. But Joe could not look into his face; he looked at his robe, at halfmast, for he was six foot tall if he was an inch, and his white skirt rode up his skinny legs like a surplice without a cassock.

343

They'd calm down in a minute.

But now the footballers were playing with four or five melons all at once. They were getting bored, he saw, but were unwilling to give up until the game had finished according to the rules. Joe had seen troops kicking over market stalls and shooting holes in a rowing boat as it crossed the canal. Fledgling officers liked to play a game of whipping the tarbushes off natives' heads as they sped by in their cars. Kickabouts happened only when the peasant resisted the legitimate desire of thirsty lads for a fruit or two from a stall or when the bastards had cocked a snook at the Empire.

Now the squaddies were applauding their goals. The game was all but over. Several melons were left intact on the road and the old man, aided by a half-naked small boy, crept forward to pick these up. One had rolled near to the Tiger, perfectly positioned for Joe's tyre. He could hear it now: *splat*! Tempted, he revved the engine. His blood was up; it seemed to storm through his heart. This fucking hellhole. The bastards that widowed Irene. You looked into their melting eyes and saw betrayal.

The boy ran directly into the path of the bike. The look he gave Joe was ghastly with desolation. Too late, Joe switched off the ignition and started to dismount, meaning to pick up the melon himself and pass it to the child. But the boy already embraced the damaged globe in his arms and was off on his bare feet, to put it in the nearly empty barrow.

The noise of the larking blokes drew off. Joe rested the Tiger on its prop and went to help pick up the last fruits, damaged but perhaps still worth something to the Gyppo they'd beggared. The old man looked at him and nodded.

His face registered no expression.

Joe took off for Ish, a sour taste in his mouth. Into the Hollywood Bar. Ordered his first Stella, which came on a silver platter, accompanied by three little bowls containing peanuts, olives and onions. The olives and onions he could not look at, but the salted peanuts went down nicely. He sat with the frosted Stella between his wrists. The windmill on the ceiling turned its blades slowly, creating a gentle draught. The cheerful hubbub of off-duty airmen and soldiers comparing tattoos at the next two tables would have been soothing, had his heart not been spasming.

Several Stellas on and Joe had forgotten the sources of his trouble. Or rather the trouble had retreated behind him and leapt on his back like a monkey, clinging while he sang along with the blokes, with Geordie Abel at the keyboard, to the tune of *Abide With Me*:

There's a street in Cairo,
Full of sin and shame,
Rue Ali Baba is its awful name...

The singsong swallowed him up; he raised his glass with the rest. The men swayed as they sang, filling their glasses with frosted Stella betweenwhiles.

They discussed the one-legged purveyor of pleasure at the Moascar Garrison. Joe had never seen her and suspected she was a legend. Peg-Leg was reputed to operate in a pitch against a wall at the edge of Moascar, supporting herself with a crutch on one side and the shoulder of her next customer on the other. On payday the queue was said to go all round the block, one bloke beavering away, while

345

she haggled over prices with the next in line.

'How'd she lose the leg?'

'Run over by a bleeding British truck.'

'Get away.'

'True. She gets a fucking British Army pension.'

'Place of a thousand claps.'

'They'll stone her to death one day, the Gyppos.'

'You had a go, mate?'

'Nah. Gyppo-Bints have razors in their privates. True.'

'Give her a medal. Good service to the Crown.'

'Come on, Taf.'

'Not me, boy,' said Joe.

'Come on.'

'I said, *no*!' he bellowed, getting to his feet, red with rage, his chair toppling back behind him.

'Keep your hair on.'

Off they went to look for Peg-Leg. When Joe tried to get up to make tracks, his beery head was swinging about and he threw up on the street.

*

His wife and the Jacobs woman arrived home a few minutes after Joe. Ailsa burst in through the back door, calling out Nia's name excitedly, though it was dark and their daughter was in bed. Joe, busy taking off his socks, looked up from a job that had turned out to be quite an ordeal, since bending over increased his nausea. He stared at Ailsa, fuddled. Then he handed her the sweaty sock. As his lawful wife, she ought to have it. She took it from him. What the hell was she wearing? A skirt red as a slick of blood, some kind of wrap-around affair that showed her knees as she

346

walked. A dark head in a white beret loomed in the doorway behind her. Mrs Jacobs' cowlike eyes seemed somehow to precede their owner into the room – radiating intensity and busybody curiosity. How dare she make herself at home in his quarters? She hadn't seen him.

'Budge over, Ailsa darling. I've brought all the bags. How is my little Nia? … Oh, Joe. How nice to see you.'

Joe leapt to his feet, one sock on, one sock off, and saluted.

'Thank you, Ma'am,' he said.

'Joe – oh don't,' Ailsa faltered.

'Do you want me to go?' asked the Wing Commander's woman.

'He's had a few,' Ailsa said, under her breath.

Joe continued standing stiffly to attention, holding the salute like a fucking *Heil Hitler*.

'Stand easy, men,' said Nia, in her nightgown. Her fingers gripped the place between her legs, as if to stop herself peeing. He had told her not to do that in company – they had both told her, more times than Joe cared to remember. She'd have to be smacked if she carried on like that. Like mother, like daughter.

Joe brought his hand down but when the darkie woman began to speak, he saluted again, barking, 'Sah!'

'Joe, dear,' said Irene. 'Do come through and sit down. I'll make a nice cup of coffee. Mrs Jacobs is going home now, she's just run Ailsa home from their interesting trip, hasn't she? Nia's been as good as gold. But poor Joe came back umpty. Nia, say hallo to your Mummy and then it's up the stairs to beddy-lands.'

Joe allowed himself to be led as far as the kitchen door;

then turned to watch his wife, face like a Belisha beacon, crouch to hug and kiss their daughter. But Nia pursed her lips in a pet, thrust her head back. Then she dodged past her mother and shot headlong at the Jacobs woman. Nia shoved at her, punching her head into her belly, beating at her with her fists, propelling her out of the back door. Ha! thought Joe, that's wiped the smile off your ugly mug, Missus. Not a word had been spoken. Nia shut the door and stamped up the stairs. From the sitting room window Joe saw the intruder falter down the path. The headlights of her sports car went on. She started up the engine and sat for a moment before driving off.

Ailsa said, 'Joe darling, let me explain.'

'Is this individual speaking to me?' he asked Irene.

'I'm so sorry,' said Ailsa. 'The opportunity came up. You weren't here to ask. There was no harm in it.'

'Oh, *the opportunity*! Take off my sock,' he said.

'What?'

'Take it off. My other sock.' He jabbed his foot in her direction and wriggled the toes. 'Now. Sock. Take it off. Jump to it, woman.'

'Don't be soft,' she said. 'I'm not taking off your sock. You've been drinking. You ought to go to bed.'

'Me go to bed?'

'Yes,' she said. 'You. Sleep it off, then we can talk.'

Irene brought coffee, which he accepted. 'Order her to remove my sock, Irene,' he said.

'Oh come here, I'll take it off,' said Irene, and did.

'Now give it to her.'

Irene dithered. Ailsa snatched the sock out of her hand and took it into the kitchen. When she returned, he caught a shushing look on Irene's face as she informed Ailsa, 'He came home badly sick the day before yesterday. He's really been though it. Not himself at all.'

'Oh no,' said Ailsa. 'I'm terribly sorry. Joe, how rotten for you. How awful that I wasn't here to take care of you.'

'Never mind. I had *her*. And toad in the hole. Whassamatter?' he demanded as his wife flushed and flinched. 'I'm not talking dirty, boy. Not toad in *her* hole, I said toad in *the* hole, batter is that, sausage, great British dish, mind, none fucking better. I leave the toadholing to *you*, Ailsa.'

He heaved himself up and barged past her through the door, churning, haywire, up the stairs, into their bed, out like a blown match.

20

'*Bore da*, Irene. *Bore da*, Ailsa. *Bore da*, Nia *fach*,' he greeted the three of them, where they sat in a row, sewing. See-No-Evil, Hear-No-Evil, Speak-No Evil. A flowery curtain was draped between them over their laps. Three faces looked up warily and he read their expressions: *what mood's he in now?* They all smiled uncertainly. 'What's up with the curtain?' he asked.

'Somebody not a million miles from here swinging on it,' said Ailsa. 'Being a chimp in the jungle, apparently.'

'We can't go swinging on the curtains now, can we, girlie?' he said mildly to his daughter. 'They're not our curtains. Nothing here is ours, see.'

A corporate sigh of relief seemed to be exhaled: the storm was past. They could breathe again. Ailsa stuck her needle in the pincushion. 'It's a clean rip, so we can mend it pretty well.'

'Still have to pay for it when we go,' he said.

Ailsa said, 'Joe, I'm so sorry about everything. I truly

am. What can I get for your breakfast? I don't suppose you're up to fried, are you?'

'A soft boiled egg went down very nicely yesterday,' Irene informed her.

'Oh yes, he likes eggs.'

'Slice of toast will do me. And plenty of tea.'

Over the tea, he apologised to the women for being narky the night before. A bit tight he'd been. Ailsa always over-buttered toast, he thought, as she handed him the plate. Of course he'd never told her this but accepted her offerings as the best, because they came from her. She was making up for years of rationing of course. But now he scraped off the excess of her generosity, leaving it on the side of the plate. He saw that she observed his action and took it silently to heart. But genuinely he meant no rebuff and no odious comparison with Irene's buttering talents. Ailsa had exchanged the sluttish red skirt for the quiet frock with the blue anemones. Joe politely asked after her trip to Jordan.

'Oh,' she said softly. 'Palestine. I do wish you'd been there, Joe.'

'We could have gone any time you wanted. It's only a few hours.'

'I know. I never thought.'

'Never mind. Tell me about it.'

Ailsa gabbled something about the problems of the Middle East. About Zionism, it was so important for us all to understand the injustice ... the crime Israel had committed, the crime that *was* Israel. For they'd all been taken in by Zionist propaganda. Mona needed to visit the frontier, to talk to people, to see for herself the Palestinian

351

refugee camps, to try to contact relatives of hers she had not heard from since *al-Naqba,* the Catastrophe. Ailsa seemed to think she was a delegate on a diplomatic mission.

'So I said I'd go with her, Joe. I'm sorry that upsets you. It was important.'

'How interesting,' said Joe. The film was rolling. Ailsa was lying in her apricot nightie, the Jacobs bastard sliding the straps off one shoulder. *For Jacob*, he thought, *is an hairy man, but I am a smooth man.*

'Yes, it was interesting, very interesting.'

'So what stands out for you, Ailsa?'

'Stands out?'

'Where did you sleep, for instance?'

Irene said she would go upstairs. She'd take her tea up there and leave them in peace to have their discussion. She held out her hand to Nia, who wouldn't leave and denied being a poppet. She carried on pinging a row of glasses on the sideboard with her fingernail.

'And where did Wing Commander Jacobs stay?'

'Oh, *he* didn't come. Of course not. It was just me and Mona. We stayed at a small hotel. I paid my own way. It wasn't expensive.'

Brittle tones, cold stares. Ailsa didn't know him at all, Joe thought. As if he'd resent honouring his wife's bills. Nia piped up: *Zagazig!* she chanted. *Zigazagazig!* On and on, louder and louder, until, moaning *I'm bored*, she hurled herself down and started rolling round the room.

'Don't, Nia,' said Ailsa. 'Don't be naughty now. Don't spoil yourself.'

'Be naughty, Nia, that's fine,' Joe said quietly. 'After all, why not? Your mummy is naughty.'

'You're naughty, Mami! You're naughty!' Nia took up the chant.

He went into the kitchen, shaking, an unlit fag between his lips, and began to fill a watering can in the sink. His plants were looking parched, though he reminded himself that he'd told Ailsa not to bother to heave that heavy can around but leave everything for when he came back. She didn't need to take him at his word, for Christ's sake. *Zagazig.*

As he carried the water out, he realised that the sprinkler at the end was missing.

'Nia,' he said through the window, 'where the hell's the sprinkler?'

Nia paused in the middle of a purple tantrum, relaxing her body long enough to ask, quite rationally, 'What sprinkler?' and to deny that she'd gone off with it.

'Nia, you will have a smacked bottom if you go on like this,' he said. 'Now where's the sprinkler?'

Off she went again, resisting Ailsa's attempt to raise her, drumming sandalled feet against her mother's arms. Joe barged through, wrenched Nia up by one arm and whacked her on the bottom. Hard, once, twice and – one for luck. The blows resounded like thunderclaps. Silence. Then an ear-splitting shriek, accompanied by a stare of disbelieving hurt. The little tyke had had it coming for months. He ought to have been firmer with her from the word go. But because she was a girl, he'd always treated her as fragile; worn kid gloves. Well, no more. She'd better watch her step. He left them to it, shutting the window to muffle the rising siren of Nia's rage. Then it distanced and he could hear Irene distracting her upstairs.

353

Ailsa came out. She touched his arm lightly. 'Could we talk properly, Joe? You didn't need to hit her, by the way. Hit me if you need to take it out on someone. It's my fault if it's anyone's.'

He didn't hit women, he reminded her. But children had to be taught a lesson. Once and for all. He listened expressionlessly to Ailsa's account of what had happened while he was away. Yes, on the whole he did believe her, as she quietly described meeting up with her pal, spending time with her, agreeing to the trip. Ailsa's heart (he could see) was in her mouth. Simultaneously he observed her over his own shoulder, through the eyes of a smooth, distinguished-looking officer of outlandish ways and loose morals. *Zagazig*. He believed her when she said she had seen hardly anything of Jacobs – or of Blondie, except to say hallo – for they'd been away on ops, same thing as him, hadn't they, and if he didn't believe her, he could always check.

In his pocket lay the johnnie. He fingered it. His fingers know she'd been had by this bastard. His nerves tingled with the sheer shock of it.

The fuckers might very well have made home visits.

Ailsa admitted she should not have gone off with Mona like that, leaving Nia. And yet, she said, her forehead furrowing, she should have! she had to! Nia was fine, wasn't she, with Irene. And anyway, Ailsa loved Mona. As a friend. Didn't Joe love his friends?

Love? That was hardly the right word.

Yes it was, she said, it was a word for friendship. *Agape*, she said, *caritas*, as in St Paul, there were so many kinds of love. Love thy neighbour, she quoted.

354

'Chalkie was my friend but family comes first,' Joe told Ailsa, bending to deadhead the blackened chrysanthemums. 'You can't argue with that. Don't try to argue.'

Yes, but it was not a competition, she urged, crouching beside him. Tilting her face up in appeal. Resting her hand on his bare forearm. He had nothing whatever to fear from Mona, she said. Nothing in the world.

'So what's this?' he asked straightening and diving his hand into his pocket, where the change jingled as he fished for the packet. Pressed it into her hand.

'It's a contraceptive,' she faltered.

'Ask me where I got it.'

'Where?'

'In Nia's toy box, that's where. In Nia's toy box – a fucking rubber johnnie. So: is it yours?'

'Is it *mine*?' She tried to hand it back but he wouldn't take it and allowed it to fall on to the earth between them. Ailsa bent and picked it up.

'You idiot! Of course it isn't mine. How could it be? I cannot believe we are having this conversation.'

They stared at one another. Then she said, 'Is it perhaps *ours*, Joe, and she's taken it from your cabinet?

'No.'

'How can you tell?'

'The wrong sort.'

'Then I have no idea.'

'She said you slept in the Jacobs bungalow.'

Ailsa flushed. Joe saw he'd nailed her. 'Yes,' she said. 'We did. But not with Mona's husband, for goodness' sake! With Nia in the house? With Mona there? I know you're jealous, Joe,' she attacked. 'I've always known *that*. That's how you are. We took each other warts and all. But that's not my wart, pal, that's *yours*.'

He grabbed a wrist as Ailsa turned away, holding it hard. The violent action lessened his violent feeling, which turned into a soft throbbing of exquisite hurt along his veins.

'So who did you sleep with?'

'I shared a bed with Mona, if you must know. As I expect Nia told you. And it was no secret.'

'Weren't there enough beds in the house? Was there a bed shortage? Don't they run to a camp bed?'

'You are making an ass of yourself. We are *friends*.'

'Friends?'

'It was for comfort.'

'What did you need comforting for, for fuck's sake?'

'Let go my wrist. Let go. Now.'

'Sorry.'

The skin on the inside of her arm was red where he'd gripped it. She rubbed it with her other hand but without making a big thing of it.

'You just can't keep up this thing with Mrs Jacobs, Ailsa. I thought you knew that.'

'Perhaps *that* is what I need comforting for, Joe.'

For a moment he could see it. Ailsa's good mind finding its equal. The Jacobs woman was in no way attractive to him: the heavy face and build, the swarthy skin. But he could see a foreign, exotic sort of elegance and seriousness in her. Intellect – a female egghead – and of course the music. That was the secret of it. At the concert in Ish, Joe had seen and felt the pianist's charm. It flattered Ailsa that such a person, from the right side of the tracks, should have singled her out. And Ailsa was worthy of this, more than

356

worthy of any Mona in the world. Mrs Jacobs had once been a refugee, which drew his wife's pity, how could it fail to do so? In his new calm, he saw all this.

But she must know unequivocally that it had to end.

'Darling Ailsa,' he said.

'Is it all right?' She took his hand. 'Will we be all right now? I'd never hurt you, Joe, Never in the world. Not like that.'

She began to speak about what they'd experienced at the border between Jordan and Israel, sharing it with him. Joe saw it all through Ailsa's eyes and felt it through her heart: the two women standing with Arab families in Jordan staring across a mass of coiled barbed wire at another group in Israel, their blood kin and erstwhile nextdoor neighbours. Two Israeli border guards with guns looking on and Mona craning to see if her uncle and aunt were there, still not knowing if they were alive or dead. Asking after them across the wire; the people shaking their heads and the guide reminding her: *Please do not speak, it is forbidden to speak. The people over there will get into trouble, you see, if you get talking to them.* No food or clothing could be passed across. It was forbidden. All people might do was stand and look.

'A line was drawn through Beit Safafa when the fighting stopped,' Ailsa told Joe. 'Half is in no man's land, the other half in Jordan.' He saw her calculate that he was hearing her out; that the more she spoke about political matters, the safer she would be.

When Israel declared itself a state, it expelled a million Arabs. Refugees were living in caves, she told him. Rotting on the hoof. In overcrowded concrete shanties. In mud

357

huts. In camps, waterlogged or at low level in simmering heat by the Dead Sea, in conditions as bad as the German concentration camps.

Joe nodded. He refrained from asking what that had to do with Sergeant and Mrs Joseph Roberts. For an intelligent woman, Ailsa was surprisingly credulous. She swallowed whole whatever one-sided story her pal fed her. Nobody deplored the Yids' terrorism under the British Mandate as much as Joe. The stringing up and booby-trapping of the two English sergeants had been the actions of the lowest of the low. But there was another side to every story. Where were the Jewish concentration camp victims supposed to go if not to Israel? The bloody moon? The Bible told of the Jewish right to the Holy Land. This he had learnt at Libanus Chapel. It was an inalienable right. And in the end the Jews were Europeans and cultured. If they could do what they boasted and make the desert flower, good luck to them. A few Arabs were going to get hurt in the process. Then it would all settle down. But Joe did not propose to argue with Ailsa over this. Ailsa, who had been brainwashed by a stronger personality, would not thank him for pointing out the sentimentality of her position.

He said, 'Do you remember when we arrived and we went through the inventory? There were all sorts of items we didn't ever see back home. "Chamber Pots, Officers, For The Use Of" – do you remember those and the label? And how we laughed? The same backsides. Same piss. Different quality pots. That's just how it is. And the roped off areas at public do's? One enclosure for Air Marshalls and their wives, one for Wing Cos, another for Flight Lieutenants, right down to Aircraftsmen. It's not so much that you can't step over as that you don't. Fraternisation, see.'

Ailsa did not reply. Her lip quivered. But Joe felt sure she had heard. They wandered round the garden, arms lightly round each other's waists, bending in towards one another, inspecting the plants, discussing the problem of Irene. Their hearts still beat up too high. He could feel his, intuit hers. Nia could be heard mindlessly chanting *Zagazig, Zigazag* in the house. Irene, who had been watching the couple from an upstairs window, withdrew smartly when she saw Joe look up, for how could the poor woman be other than disappointed that he had made it up with Ailsa?

'There's just one thing,' he said. 'One thing to clear up before we put this behind us.'

'What?'

'I'm sending you and Nia home to England. That is final, Ailsa.'

'What, and leave you here with Irene?'

Over her dead body, she blazed. Ailsa was not a parcel, to be trussed up and packed off across the world whenever Joe felt like it.

That hit home about Irene. There was nothing between him and Irene, he said, fear in his eyes, keeping his voice down. Nothing whatsoever, as Ailsa well knew. She of course saw her advantage as Joe flushed to the roots of his hair; yet felt impotent to press it. Too cheap. Joe was so obviously not that kind of man.

He was sending them home for their own good, he explained. This hellhole was perhaps the most dangerous place in the world – apart from Israel, where that madwoman had taken her.

'You are the mother of my child,' he said, taking her hand.

She thrust the hand away.

'But you refuse to let yourself be taken care of. You are out of control. That is why you are being sent home.'

'You don't seem to get it, Joe. You can't *send* me anywhere.'

'Oh, I can.'

*

And suddenly he was not the soft, temperamental Joe any more but a sergeant who'd made his mind up, in accordance with regulations. That was how she described him to herself. He'd gone on to notify the Air Force that his wife was returning to Britain; that the quarter would be vacated at the end of the month. He'd booked two seats on the plane and a place in barracks for himself. It would not be long until his tour was finished, he'd said. Till then Ailsa and Nia could stay with his mam in Treforys. He'd apply for a posting to St Athan, somewhere near home, to avoid disrupting Nia's life.

Nia is the important person in all this, he kept saying. Not you. Not me.

In Egypt, Ailsa had lived. Truly lived, with an expanded horizon. She must take her expanded world now and shrink it back into her allotted space. There was no help for it. It's over, she thought, and relief mingled with the gravest disappointment she could remember sustaining since realising that university was closed to her. All her life – except twice – she'd been kept in a box with a few inadequate peepholes, amongst folk who took the inside of that box for the limits of the world.

Joe, who'd been packing, drifted out to tinker with the Tiger. Ailsa sat at the table and lit up. The family trunk lay open on the floor at her feet. She was the cargo that was to be crammed in the luggage, strapped and labelled with Joe's number, Joe's mother's address. Where do I come in? she demanded and in her mind Ailsa childishly hurled the contents out of the case. What would that kind of crazy behaviour do to Nia? She satisfied her rage by refraining from lifting a finger to help. She took a long drag on her cigarette. Ailsa had got out and seen the magnitude of things, the mighty complexities of the political world. The skies over the Holy Land full of thunder. Egypt in its beauty and pain. Even as Ailsa had revelled in her larger view, she'd been afraid. Simply terrified sometimes, she thought, as with this thing of *going to bed with Mona*. No wonder poor Joe was foxed by her action. Ailsa didn't understand it herself. She'd been totally out of her depth.

What had that all been about? A conversation, going on round the clock. Holding Mona in her arms through that last strange night in Jordan, and being held, had seemed a continuation of conversation. Nothing sensual about it. She didn't think so, no.

How could there be? But the memory bred unease. Moonlight had greyed the pillow through the curtainless window. What had they talked about? Chiefly not great issues but the magical years at the Old Brewery, reliving that time in the light of their later reunion. They'd been girls again, with the world before them. And for Mona it had been as if she'd enjoyed in that brief interim a delayed youth: the darkness of losing Jerusalem, losing Julie, had been put behind her by a world war. She'd slipped a leash or noose. *And to think that you were so close all the time! Behind the wall, Ailsa!* The bombs had made life apocalyptic: Mona and Gwen, Bobbie and Billie, Lalage and Anna had acted as if there were no commonplace yesterday and no dull tomorrow. In the great bombsite of London, death burned all around them with a lurid flame that stained their world ruby-red. Ailsa had also sipped at a measure of qualified freedom. But with hindsight, the sobs and giggles of the girls – and their highfalutin' conversation, their bohemianism and free love – could be made to seem an echo of a mad gaiety of which she'd been a part.

Calm in the shadow of Mona's hair, Ailsa had lain still while her friend slept. She knew she brought comfort in a way no one else ever had, even *Habibi* perhaps. No idea how she'd done it or what it all meant. But it touched Ailsa to the quick that Mona's search for home had concluded in herself. Perhaps in years to come an older and wiser self might carefully take out the memory, when the shiver in her nerves had died, and examine it and understand.

We are like sisters: that is what sisters do, she'd told her husband, acting surprised that he didn't know this.

But she and Mona were not really like sisters and Joe was only obsessed with the difference of rank and with his imagined rival, the Wing Commander.

In Jordan, she and Mona had conspired to suck at the orange of nostalgia. You couldn't help but enter into the illusion that you were made for each other. This was all meant to be. But where could it go? What house was built for them in this world? What certificate was issued? And, like all nostalgia, those memories were finite. The juice

362

would not keep its bright taste forever.

Ailsa was tired with dispute and her own inner conflict, weary of the subject of Mona. Perhaps in the end a simple, clean, orderly life counted as the greatest good. She listened to the clink of tools as, just outside the back door, Joe tightened this, loosened that, tinkering with the Tiger. He sounded almost normal. When she'd come into the kitchen, Joe had grinned at her, wagging his oily hands as if there were nothing wrong between them. He wasn't even drinking excessively; kept everything as near to ordinary as he could, believing – as he had to believe – that they could still retreat to the crossroads and go on together hand in hand. It was as if another Ailsa altogether had carried her away to a cosmopolitan world beyond the bounds of the real Ailsa's imagination and reach.

Yet how stifling it all was. How did one prepare for a lifetime of such dulness? She stubbed out the fag and drifted back to the window. Nia was rocking on the fence and shrieking with laughter of a particularly inauthentic and grating kind. Ailsa would have liked to smack her legs. Each of them had raised a hand against their daughter and punished her for their own shortcomings.

Another baby, Joe had said last night. *A brother or sister for Nia. When we get back to Blighty. A fresh start.*

Till now, he'd never wanted a second child, preferring to concentrate love and attention on their one-and-only. But Nia was becoming odd. She was a weathervane registering the turmoils between her parents. It was not that though, oh no, of course not. If Joe could burden Ailsa with a batch of kids like these poor Forces women old before their time, he would have grounded and controlled her. She'd be unable to fly. Ailsa would be *penned* in a *coop* like a *hen*.

Joe couldn't force another baby on her. She thought of the contraceptive he had found amongst Nia's things, and her face burned. She must be careful. Since he'd been back, she'd insisted she had a bad period and worn her sanitary belt every night. That couldn't go on forever.

Nia hanging over the fence was fascinated by Mrs Wintergreen's recently acquired chickens. She kept them in nesting boxes in a run in her back garden, up against the Roberts' fence. Ailsa could hear Mrs Wintergreen complain that Egyptian chickens were not a bit like English chickens! Oh no! For a start, they stood up to lay their eggs, she said! They had not the sense of an English sparrow! Consequently the eggs often cracked on impact. Arab hens appreciated neither the straw in the boxes, their potato peel mash in a home-made trough, nor the trough itself. They beaked the mash on to the sand and ate it there. They positively liked filth, said Mrs Wintergreen. They were squalid birds.

Still she got nine or ten eggs out of them per week, beautiful quality.

And there was Nia precariously balanced on the fence, exhorting the chick-chick-chickens to lay a little egg for her.

Ailsa felt ashamed. She could take no pleasure in Nia. She went through the motions. But it will come back, she thought, and, jumping up, began to wipe down all the surfaces with Dettol. For I love her. She is my Nia.

I've been drunk, she thought, drunk on Egypt. Joe is asking me to sober up. For quiet Ailsa, it had been a drug, an intoxicant, to be allowed into this bubbling crucible of change.

Peering out at Nia's antics with the chickens, Ailsa thought: Mona has no children. She knows nothing. And sometimes, for all her experience and intellectualism, Mona had seemed to her younger. Ignorant of how we are hobbled, gelded. We are brood mares, Ailsa thought, and always will be. How could it be otherwise? Some of the radical young women exiled from Palestine who were Mona's friends had insisted, in their peerless English: *Once we achieve equality and a share in power – and once education delivers men's minds from their ancient chains – the world will be transformed.* Like Mona, they were Christians and deplored the veiling of their Muslim sisters that contaminated all relations between men and women in the Middle East. *The veil must be abolished! It must and it will!* This had been how they spoke, rhetorically. Ailsa had felt privileged to share their speculations, though she'd rarely spoken up. All that was irrevocably over. She must make a life for herself and for her family in a drab place.

I have stepped over the pale, Ailsa thought, and it won't be easy to go back. Even if I never see Mona again, she'll be in my mind. I shall only have to hear a recording of Oum Koulsoum singing of her passion – *What havoc your eyes have wrought* – and I'll be back there in Mona's and my Egypt, holding hands under the table. And no doubt Joe sees this. He sometimes looked violent. But that time at their lodgings in Bristol Joe hadn't even been able to drown their landlady's kittens in the stream. He'd returned with the mewing box, sick to the stomach and in tears, ashamed. Taking the box from her husband, Ailsa had forced herself to drown them.

For some reason this brought tears to Ailsa's eyes and

her throat swelled: *Me, I killed the kittens*, she thought. He couldn't bring himself to, so I did.

So finish this thing, Ailsa told herself, before you are one hour older. Grovel to him. Cry. Show him the letter. Ask his pardon, you will never do it again, you want to stay with him, you can't bear to be apart. The letter had been written; she shook it loose from the pages of the *Inferno*, the cantos about Francesca da Rimini, with whom she'd so identified. (And you will still have your books, she reminded herself, for the rest of your life. Goethe and Dante will be your comrades. And that inner world of the mind and spirit that burns so bright. You'll have your journal. He can't take that away.)

Joe was her husband. The right and sensible thing would be to share her inner world with Joe.

'Would you post this for me, please, Joe?' she asked as he came through the door in his shirt sleeves. He went to wash his hands. Ailsa had written a subdued, formal statement that she could not meet Mona any more, she was sorry, she wished her and her husband well. 'But read it first.'

'What is it? Irene not here?'

'Gone to work.'

He took the letter, glancing at the address. Startled, he looked up. Then he ran his eyes over the text.

'I'm glad you've done the right thing,' he said. 'But, Ailsa, sorry, so sorry, but it doesn't change anything. I'll miss you like hell but I've got to send you home.'

'You're not! You're bloody not, Joe!'

Snatching it back, she began to rip the letter into confetti.

'You are going home,' he said. 'Whether you like it or not. And you never used to swear. It doesn't suit you.'

'Just listen to me, Joe, and stop parroting. I said, listen.'

'I'm listening.'

'If you *send me home*, that's it.'

She spoke the word *divorce*.

Joe sat at the kitchen table, stirring his tea, an untouched jam tart on his plate, his eyes on a newspaper folded open at some stale news of doings in South Wales a fortnight ago.

'You don't mean that,' he said.

There was an Arab in a stained blue *gallabiyya* at the door, nervously asking for Taffy Effendi.

'*Mafishfaluk*,' Joe said. 'No money. Off you go.'

'*Votre mari … n'a pas payé le tapis, madame. Il n'en a payé que la moitié.*'

Of course, it was the man who'd sold them the carpet. 'He says you owe him for the carpet, Joe. You've only paid half. Is that right?'

'Go in,' Joe ordered his wife and daughter. 'I said, go in.'

Through the upstairs window, Ailsa watched them confer. The carpet-vendor handed Joe some notes, rather than the other way round. Then her husband ushered him in through the side door. When Ailsa came downstairs the carpet was gone. Neither of them mentioned it.

'Where will you go, Irene?' she asked their guest when she returned from work.

'I've found a dear little flat in Ish. Just the ticket. Two bedrooms. Overlooking the NAAFI. I can move in at the end of the month.'

*

367

At the eleventh hour Joe changed his mind. A colossal qualm came over him. He was physically sick. He sobbed; tried to get the whole thing reversed.

But the RAF was having none of it. The quarter had been reallocated. The quartermaster would be round to check the inventory. Every trace of the Roberts presence at the house in El-Marah must be wiped away.

They sat down together at the table. The relief made Ailsa feel weak; her limbs were jelly. They'd get through this after all and perhaps they'd both be wiser for it and work out a better balance between them. Through it all they'd continued to love one another, hadn't they? That was paramount now. She reached for his hand and threaded her fingers with Joe's in the old familiar way. Now was the time to let him know she had a fall-back plan.

She'd never been going anyway, Ailsa told him.

Joe stared, stunned.

'What do you mean, not going anyway?'

'I couldn't accept, Joe – I can't accept –'

'Can't accept *what*? You mean, you let me book the seats on the plane and you never intended to go at all?'

'I didn't *let* you, did I? You did it against my will. You can't do that to a grown up person. You haven't the right to send me anywhere. I told you that, Joe. I'm not *impedimenta*.'

'What might that be when it's at home?'

'Baggage. In the Roman Army. And the womenfolk were baggage too, just so much of an impediment.'

'Ta for letting me in on that, Ailsa. Thank you so much for enlightening me about the Ancient Romans. So where did you think you were going?'

'Well, to friends, for the time being.'

He saw it all now, his face said. And he wasn't seeing the spirit of compromise in which she meant to offer a way through the maze, a second chance for them both. Joe was rapidly checking back through their days together to ascertain the extent of her calculated betrayal.

'Do as you bloody well like,' he said. 'Go west. I don't care. I wash my hands of you. But my daughter – *my daughter*, Ailsa – she is not going anywhere.'

His lips were white. She saw how he was inside. A layer of skin was ripped away. His hands shook.

'*Our* daughter. And don't speak to me like that.'

'I'll speak to you any way I want to speak, woman. You got that? Any way I fucking like.' He was on his feet and looming over her. 'Just fucking do as you're told.'

'Sit down.'

He did sit down, to her surprise, with a look of confusion. He was flying above himself like a kite in a gale. She was too. If she could find the right words, Ailsa could earth them both. But the words that came out of her mouth were harsh and bitter.

'Nia will be coming with me, Joe. That's the end of it.'

'Oh and you think your precious Jacobs pals will tolerate having a brat bawling in the middle of the night and getting under their feet all day?'

'I'm only going to them *pro tem*. Obviously I can't presume on them. After that another friend has found me a room in the house of a widow.'

'A *widow*?'

'A lady who lives in the Greek quarter.'

'A Greek "lady"?'

'An Egyptian – and, yes, a *lady*, Joe. She lives downstairs from Nobby. She's his sister-in-law. She has a lovely little girl, about Nia's age.'

'Nobby Bowen?'

'Yes.'

'Don't make me laugh! You and that pathetic twit of a slob of a dreamer!'

Ailsa said nothing but she knew her face told him how disgusting, coarse, moronic he was. What a Taffy, what an illiterate! Love him? Love that ugly monkey of a man? She didn't even like him, her face said.

He could read her like a book, Joe told her. Ailsa was so transparent, it was laughable. She thought he was too much of a dimwit to see what she was up to. Her and her *secret diary*. In code! Did she think he couldn't work it out?

How dared he read her diary? Flaring up, Ailsa got to her feet and shrieked at him like a fishwife. How dared he? A diary was private.

Had she ever heard the word *degenerate*? he asked her. Did she know the meaning? Joe could tell her one thing. She was not taking his daughter to live with the wogs. Never. Nia would be dead of typhoid in the year. She'd be in Fayid Cemetery with Chalkie.

'Oh, so you're going to take care of her, Joe, are you? How are you going to manage that then?'

Joe was going to hit her now, wasn't he? The knowledge flashed through Ailsa. She saw the fist, the punch landing with a crack, herself staggering and crashing against the table edge, the blood-gush from her temple. The premonition was so vivid that she leapt to her feet, hand at her temple.

'That's it now! That's *it*, Joe!' she shouted. 'You've had it now. You've had your chips. And to think I'd hoped this would give us another chance.'

'What do you mean?'

'That I'd be nearby. We could have cooled down a bit, and seen each other, and you'd have come to see Nia – well, of course you would, Joe! I never thought of parting her from you. But if you're going to hit me, forget it. You'll never see either of us again.'

'Just hang on a minute, Ailsa. Steady down. I haven't hit you.'

'No, but you were going to.'

'No. No, I wasn't.'

He hadn't; that was true. There was still time. They looked at each other abashed, embarrassed, trying to remember what it was they'd said. How to disown the squalor of what they'd said.

'Well,' Joe said, and patted his pockets for cigarettes. 'Well now.' He flashed her a blue glance, hurt and yet sharp; offered the box. 'Got a point you have, Ailsa. How would I take care of her on my own?'

'And don't forget you were wanting us to go away to Wales where you'd never see us. This is the better way surely?'

But in the event he'd played dirty.

21

They were lying at anchor with thirty-three other ships at Port Tewfik, waiting for the convoy to enter the Suez Canal. The pilot would come aboard and they'd sail at 7 a.m., announced the Captain.

At 8 the pilot had not yet arrived, but, *insha'allah* he would do so at any moment. When a couple of hours later the pilot did come aboard, the immense convoy could move. Behind the *Terra Incognita* lay a luxury yacht, a floating gin palace, the Tannoy informed them, owned by some famous billionaire. Ahead sailed a rusty container ship belonging to the United Arab Shipping Company. They would reach the Bitter Lakes by around two in the afternoon. Nia went up to the forward deck and felt the familiar give in her stomach and a fizz of excitement as the cruiser crept forward over the green-blue water. The deck vibrated in the soles of her feet and the rail in the palms of her hands. A pleasant breeze rippled the flag, tossing her hair around.

Hardly expecting to sleep at all, Nia had slept instantly

and deeply, her head a theatre of dreams, all colourful and adventurous. She'd awoken in the night with a sense of boundless relief, and in the ship's soft throbbing she'd felt as if she were being carried by some force that meant no harm. She'd caught the tail of the dream. But all she could remember was a cornfield or desert, it might have been either, a great wash of ochre light over the whole field of vision. A place of boundless forgiveness. And yet the dead were there.

Nia's dead slept here in Egypt with the Pharaohs, not just her father but in some real way, for all that her ashes had been scattered on the Long Mynd, Nia's mother too. Something in Ailsa must have died and been left behind when Mrs Joseph Roberts had been flown home. Nia sensed, in some obscure way, the presence of her parents in the timeless landscape. And Topher's parents too – and whatever wove the Whites and Roberts together. Topher had rung late the previous night, in an odd, hectic mood. What's she like, what's this Mona Serafin-Jacobs like? he'd wanted to know. Why haven't you phoned, what has she told you? Since Nia had left for the Middle East, Topher complained, he'd been seeing his dead mum everywhere. Accusing him. What if I fly to Alex, he said, and meet you there? OK, Nia? I've got this feeling that we ought to go to El Alamein and see where our dads were war heroes together, what do you think?

The ship slipped forward. This is it, Nia thought, and excitement fizzed again. She'd be seeing the world inhabited by the spirits of her young parents. And the body of her father – where was he?

She hadn't yet asked Mona where Joe was buried but

she would ask her now. Perhaps his remains had never been found.

The *Terra Incognita* slid beyond the wharf's derricks and cranes, oil containers and concrete buildings, into the canal's narrow strait, between the green, palm-shaded agricultural land of the west bank and the yellow dunes of the east, the Sinai Desert. Nothing lived in that wilderness. It was arid and always had been. She could imagine the desolation of the Chosen People wandering there for forty years. In the endless wars of modern times, the blood-soaked Sinai had been over-run by the Israelis, retaken by the Egyptians, a map of fluid boundaries from generation to generation. The *Terra Incognita* sailed between lush Africa and dry Asia, a contrast like a dream. Sinai was beautiful, its dunes like an Alpine *piste* before the skiers come out, glowing rose at sunrise.

The Suez veterans, white-haired men in shirtsleeves, flocked to the forward deck for this high point of their pilgrimage. They stood looking out through binoculars or focusing video cameras, as the ship made its stately way through the strait. They drew alongside their young conscript selves.

It's always the poor foot slogger who has to get the politicians out of their mess...

Their animals live in the same house with them...

Dear old Ish...

Didn't the Jewboys bomb it?

And another of the Gyppos' stunts was to lay trip wires over the road to decapitate our motor cyclists...

Nia's heart clamoured to visit the unknown Joe. But how could it be urgent? After all these years: he would never change. He's fast asleep, she thought, and always will be and doesn't know I've come. He knows nothing whatever about me. Yet the steady sense of presence remained.

She hung on to the railing to get a grip on the haunted feeling. Mona in denims, looking half her age, came to stand alongside Nia, resting her elbows on the rail. The hairs on Nia's arm rose as if the two of them had touched.

'What are you thinking, Nia?' asked Mona, not looking into her eyes.

'We're together, after all. I'm truly glad to be here with you.'

For the first time Nia reached out of her own accord to take Mona's hand. The two were of nearly equal height, Nia an inch or so the taller. And Ailsa formed a ghostly third, joining them, joined by them. For a moment Nia's face rested against Mona's dark hair, as her mother's must have done. This was the woman Ailsa had loved. Had loved beyond reason perhaps and without understanding the nature of that love. It had cost them both everything.

'I wish I'd known the Ailsa you knew,' Nia said. 'If only I could tell her I've seen you – that I understand... I feel I'm much more like her, more in tune with her, than I ever realised.'

'Oh, you are, make no mistake. You are very like her. But you're also like the little girl I got to know on the *Empire Glory*. And I feel ... haunted.'

It was as if Mona softly collapsed, like the last of the sand pouring through the waist of an hourglass. Her face was grey.

'Do you want to go down to your own cabin? Are you all right?'

'No, I'll just sit here with you.'

375

The canal widened as they slid into the Little Bitter Lake, on whose west bank Egyptian military depots had taken over British bases, with hangars and barracks. Water towers and watch-towers commanded the horizon. Cars tiny as Dinky Toys bounced along the paths. Nia heard herself ask, 'What exactly happened to my father, Mona?'

'Ah. What did she tell you?'

'Nothing directly. She'd clam up if I asked about him. I've always had the impression that he'd been killed by terrorists in the guerrilla war in the run-up to Suez – but I can't remember anyone ever saying so. He was some kind of hero, I know. I've never had much time for heroes.'

Mona's face told her at once that whatever had happened to her father was indeed the worst thing one could imagine. Nia had always thought of him as a heroic *murdered man* like Topher's dad. In her mind's eye she'd seen him lying in a gutter in his own blood. Her mother would waken from nightmares clutching her throat, unable to breathe. Screaming in the early hours of the morning, so that the boys and Nia had also awoken shrieking, and the only sane person in the house of hysterics had been Archie, making Mam Horlicks, bringing her inhaler, padding across the kitchen in his bare feet, with tousled hair, saying in his calm way, *It's only one of her dreams, go back to sleep.*

Wer reitet so spät durch Nacht und Wind? ... Who rides so late through night and wind?...

'He was murdered, wasn't he?'

*

The stately and imperturbable voice of the newsreader announced that the Egyptian government had fulfilled its threat to abrogate the Treaty. British forces would henceforth constitute an enemy army on Egypt's sovereign territory. All cooperation had been withdrawn from the British: fresh water and food, means of transport, communication and electricity. Local workers were ordered to cease employment with their foreign occupiers and find alternative work. Violent rioting, arson and looting in Cairo and Port Said had escalated. The announcer reassured listeners that, although destabilisation would give comfort to the USSR, and the situation was undeniably both tense and dangerous, British forces in the Canal Zone stood more than equal to the challenge. Within easy flying distance, the Sixteenth British Airborne Brigade awaited orders in Cyprus, troops who could reinforce the Canal Zone garrison at short notice.

So there was to be revolution. Egypt was about to explode. The group sitting round the Jacobs wireless set wore sombre but calm and unsurprised expressions.

More murders, thought Ailsa. Chalkie, though nobody had guessed this, was just one of the first. This was the beginning of some holocaust. The Middle East was sliding into war.

She could hardly bring herself to care. When Joe had taken Nia, the Jacobs held out their arms to her: *This is your home, Ailsa. For as long as you need it. Isn't it, Habibi?* But they were strangers. Only Nia mattered. Ailsa's breasts ached, as they'd done when she was ready to feed Nia. Not so very long ago. It had been as if the sleeping baby had intuited that the milk for her had come in, opening her clear green smiling eyes as Ailsa lifted her from the crib. Easing me, thought Ailsa, by taking what I was placed on this earth to give her – and only I could give.

Where was Nia now? Egypt was about to explode – and mother and child were apart.

A charming Palestinian professor of politics, displaced and working in a tobacconist's shop in Ish, was holding forth. His education at Eton and Cambridge had made him more pukka than the English.

'What's the real issue? The corrupt Pashas of the Wafd government are hiding behind the British occupation. When you lot have been sent packing, the Wafd will be the next to go. They will all fight one another – the Commies, the fascist Young Egypt, the Free Officers, the Wafd, the bloated king. But, mark my words, the Muslim Brotherhood will be the beneficiaries of this bloodbath.'

Ailsa listened in a dream, not quite sober. Her mind was full of crackly chatter like sweeping waves of interference in an ill-tuned radio. Her glass was perpetually charged with wine but she didn't notice the taste; her stomach was a sink. What the hell am I doing here amongst these people? None of it seemed real. For all the sincerity and sympathy of her welcome, Ailsa felt unhinged and all the fight had gone out of her since Nia had been removed. If only, when Joe had ordered her to go home, she'd gone quietly, taken Nia and boarded the aircraft for Brize Norton. They would be together. There'd have been some sort of a chance for herself and Joe. She missed her husband, home and child. Missed them till she burned with longing. Not Joe as he was now. The Joe he'd been before she defied him. It was so strange to know he'd finally handed over the quarter at El-Marah; that some other couple was sleeping and waking in their bed, eating at the well-scrubbed table and looking out through the windows that had framed the view for her family. Yet she had seen it as a chicken coop and likened herself to one of the birds penned by Mrs Wintergreen.

Awakening in the night, Ailsa had for a moment imagined herself there in El-Marah, only to find herself in these fine cotton sheets, soft as silk, single in a narrow bed, the pillow damp with tears. Her face lay up against a wall. She'd switched on the lamp, feeling her husband's absence. Missing the close intimate embrace that went on all night in your sleep, so that your soul did not need to patrol its perimeter.

She would go to Joe and ask his pardon.

But then surely the rage would well up again in herself. It wasn't Joe's anger she feared but her own. Only mourning was strong enough to suppress it – mourning for Nia as if her daughter had died.

Nobby Bowen took his leave. His wife and two of his sisters in law would be round later on that evening, one of them being Ailsa's landlady-to-be with her little girl. The thought of lodging with a mother and child was a dagger in Ailsa's heart. Struggling to appear involved in the conversation, she automatically accepted but did not drink a glass of brandy and water. Mona, why do you carpet your walls? she wondered. Ailsa had neither walls nor carpets, and how odd that lack seemed when you had never expected to feel the want of either. I possessed everything I needed, she thought, and I went and chucked it away. Oh well done, Ailsa. You've really surpassed yourself. She'd stranded herself in a strange country where at the best of times there were few obvious safety nets.

Mona was a displaced person. That was her constant

theme, on which she harped day and night. But look at me, Ailsa silently told her. Are you worse off than I am?

He'd played dirty.

Ailsa could never have imagined or predicted that of Joe. Of *her* – Irene – of course one could believe anything. Irene was a besotted creature of loss. She could hardly be considered responsible for herself.

Joe had appeased Ailsa with emollient words; seemed reluctantly to concede to her plan to stay in Ish. He'd run the bath for her and even crumbled last Christmas's bath salts in for a treat. *Now you have a nice long soak, cariad. Take your time.* Ailsa had steeped herself languorously in soft water and fragrance. She'd hummed to herself. She'd heard the house go silent, so perhaps father and child had taken a nap. When she'd finally emerged, swathed in a towel, a turban round her head, Ailsa knew at once there was no one in the house. So perhaps they'd gone out for a walk?

'And not just mobs on the street either,' the professor was still lecturing them. Egypt now had *jihad* battalions, trained in the Arab–Israeli War and determined not to repeat the fiasco of their easy defeat in the Sinai Desert. There'd be guerrilla freedom fighters in the Canal Zone, backed no doubt by the Soviets and armed with Kalashnikovs. It wasn't just the British who'd have to look out. He predicted a reckoning day for all Europeans and outsiders: Greeks, Albanians, Levantines and of course the Jews who'd been not only tolerated but accepted as brothers through all these centuries. And even the Coptic Christians.

Ailsa thought again of Chalkie's murder. That death had

been the harbinger. And look what it had done to Irene. It had turned her into a parasite on another woman's husband. It had caused her to abandon two little boys in the Midlands and replace them with a girl she didn't even particularly like, as far as Ailsa could see. What was there between Joe and Irene? Ailsa was unsure now.

Habibi said it was a pity Clem Attlee hadn't had his way. We'd have been long gone if Clem's view had prevailed. Attlee had seen quite clearly that Britain couldn't afford an empire *and* a welfare system.

'Are you all right, sweetheart?' Mona asked Ailsa.

'Oh, fine, thank you. A bit tired.'

Whatever do I look like? Ailsa wondered. Do I look as mad and empty as I feel? She throbbed with longing for Nia. Incommunicably. Mona loved Nia too, of course she did. But it was not the same. You brought a sword, Mona, she thought. You were the agent of separation. Your need is predatory. Look at you sitting there in your Sloppy Joe pullover with your hair soaking from the shower, your feet tucked up and your soles all dirty, your dirt on display. And *that* look on your face: *who can I gobble next?* How in God's name did I not see through you? And *Habibi*, lovable idealist as he is, has dislodged the barriers we need for safety; he does it every minute of every day, he can't help it. He's a loose cannon. Ah yes but he was also and undeniably a healer: *Habibi* had healed Hedwig, talking to her in her depression not as psychiatrist to patient, not even as man to woman, but person to person. This human equality was what the gods could not countenance, it seemed. It threatened their stranglehold on mortals. Norman's raving about *Habibi* to Joe, praising him to the skies, had tipped the balance in the end and soured him irretrievably, at the moment he might perhaps have been reconciled to his wife.

'Ailsa,' Mona pleaded. 'We can go round to Irene's flat. Just say the word. We can confront the woman – and Joe, if he's with her. Take Nia home. I'll run you there – any time. Shall we go now?'

'How would that be right though, Mona?' Ailsa asked. 'We can't just snatch her.'

It was the judgement of Solomon all over again. Cut the child in two! The real mother automatically renounces the child. How can she do otherwise? Then the wise king intervenes to return the child. The true mother has powerful allies on the throne and in the Heavens. What allies did Ailsa have? The RAF? *Habibi* had pressed her to report Joe to the Commanding Officer. But he would surely have rather larger issues on his mind than a domestic tiff between a sergeant and his renegade wife. And the deeper Joe got into trouble, the deeper his rancour.

'Well, perhaps tomorrow,' Ailsa said uneasily. 'Thank you, both. I think, if you don't mind, I'll just go and lie down.'

But she didn't move. Her limbs and eyelids were heavy with booze. Not used to it. She looked at Mona without the least feeling and Mona flinched. She withdrew to the grand piano, beneath the portrait of Julie Brandt-Simon, and began to play a bright, flamboyant piece by Hummel or Dittersdorf. She played with glittering clarity, and with the emotional reserve appropriate to the music. The sonata had been composed in a more elegant age, when elite culture and a dream of reason had gone hand in hand. The figure of Julie Brandt-Simon in a brilliant red gown towered over the luxurious room, her expression severe, like a judge in scarlet. Once Nia had played with the cat under that piano, bursting out in terror when a *fortissimo* storm thundered down into her lair. As they'd moved towards this bitter climax, Nia had caught all the bad notes. She'd detected her enemy and taken measures to expel her, beating Mona with her fists and butting her with her head when they'd swanned back from Palestine. Too late. Ailsa ought to have listened to Nia. The child was a divining rod.

What was Mona thinking and feeling? Lonely probably. But why should the queen of such a castle and courtiers be lonely? Ailsa shrank back into herself, buried in her own anguish and the cynicism it brought with it.

Habibi's military uniform was a disguise. He'd kept it on after the War because Mona wished to go east. It didn't suit him, he didn't suit it and he was wrong to wear it. Cadging a lift to the Orient, the Jacobs had said on the *Empire Glory*. Now he bent over Mona at the piano, reading her disturbance; stroked her hair. Mona turned her head, looked up. The two exchanged a look so private and nakedly intimate that Ailsa had to turn her head away. A door closed softly in her face. Good, let it close. That's that then, she thought, standing as far outside their home as if she'd been in the desert.

It struck Ailsa that the Jacobs always seemed to have a third party in tow, whether Alex or herself. What was it all about? For a long while, mesmerised by Mona's spell, Ailsa had been content that nothing be labelled. She'd never made much of Alex, so quiet and (was this the word?) insipid. An echo or shadow to *Habibi*. Arms draped round one another's shoulders; private jokes; a conspiracy of rueful smiles and intent looks. Had it all been some sordid game between them, stemming from the romantic goings on at the Old Brewery, a game which she, in her naïveté, had not understood – but which her husband, in his coarser way, had smelt out? Had she, Ailsa, been brought in for the purposes of symmetry?

She's led you wrong, that woman. You don't want to live like that, Ailsa. You're too good for the likes of her.

Ailsa could go to her husband and confess that she'd seen through Mona. She had never intended to blow their family apart. It was not too late. She pulled herself together and began to gather up handbag and cardigan. Joe would take her back. Or at least patch up some practical solution. As she got to her feet, the doorbell sounded. Alex went off to answer it. Ailsa heard his heels clicking over the floor; the front door opening; an exclamation, then a wild cry of pain or of joy. A whirlwind of a child was entering the house.

Ailsa raced barefoot out of the living room. Through the hall, Nia in her green bonnet and velvet suit, cheeks fiery red, came hurtling towards her mother. Ailsa snatched her up. Nia clamped both legs round Ailsa's thighs. The child's cheek and forehead burned against her mother's face.

'It was wrong,' Irene said. 'Nia knew it was wrong. Even *he* knew it was wrong.'

'But is she all right, Irene? Is she ill?'

'No. No, don't worry,' Irene stroked the back of the limpet child who was silently glued to Ailsa so that they formed one creature. 'Bless her, she couldn't eat much – or drink, that was the thing that worried me. Perhaps if you have some fruit juice, Mrs Jacobs?'

Somehow Ailsa managed to prise the limpet off to the degree that Nia could drink. She sat on her mother's lap and fished out the ice cubes with her fingers.

'You're not thinking of taking her away again, are you, Irene? Because she is going nowhere,' Ailsa said. '*Nowhere* without me. Do you understand? How *dare* you take her away? Does Joe know you've brought her round?'

Irene shook her head. Never for one moment had she intended to keep Ailsa's daughter from her mother, or so she said. But Joe had been beside himself. He'd arrived at her flat with Nia, wanting Irene to babysit her in her own flat. She'd agreed to take the child for a night.

'I don't regard that as an excuse, Irene. You should be ashamed,' Ailsa hissed.

In stalked the cat, Isis. With a cry of joy, Nia greeted her, cuddling the heavy body in both arms, nuzzling Isis's head and looking into the green lamps of her eyes. The two of them curled up together on the sofa and fell asleep. Irene explained in whispers that Joe had forced Nia on her. It had been no picnic. Irene had taken her into her own bed but Nia had just sat bolt upright, sucking at her sheet, and all she'd say was, *What are you wearing a hair net for in bed, Missus? Did you knit it? Where's Topher? Where's Uncle Archie?*

'Eventually she dropped off,' said Irene. 'Oh, thanks, Mrs Jacobs, I'd love a cup of tea. Do you mind – English tea, real tea? I think we need to speak to Joe. And, Ailsa, I know I've been impossible. I came back here and plonked myself on you... But when I saw Joe like that...'

'Like what?'

'Off his rocker really, Ailsa. When he arrived at my flat

with Nia, he was crying his eyes out. Quite incoherent. He seemed to be saying that there was something wrong with you, you couldn't look after Nia, would I babysit in my own flat? At first I took it that you must be ill. But then I thought: *he's drunk*. It seemed best to take her for a night. No idea where you were, to telephone. Actually, Nia was terribly well-behaved, bless her. She sat and played with my jewel box and we went through my photo album of Roy and the boys. It was very unsettling. Nia was so polite. Not like her at all. Then yesterday Joe arrived again and I'm afraid he'd had more than a few, Ailsa, he was tight.'

'What did he say?'

'Oh – he wasn't all that nice.'

Whatever had gone on, Irene was not saying, except that she'd had to order him off. She blushed and patted the back of her hair, fingering rapidly round the edges of it to make sure that every strand was tucked in. She didn't meet Ailsa's eyes.

'The fact is, I'm in a false position out here. The scales have just fallen from my eyes. As it says in the Bible. Sounds jolly melodramatic, I know, but that was how it was. I came back here to be close to Roy.'

She frowned; her fingers twisted a handkerchief in her lap.

'But I had *left* everything I had of Roy in Britain. Timothy and Christopher. What was I thinking of? There is *nothing* of Roy here. Nothing. But Joe, you know, is a lovely warm man. He is, really. At heart. I'm afraid I rather – fell for him, Ailsa. Very wrong of me.'

'Irene,' Ailsa reached across to take Irene's hand, thinking, *You are not the enemy, you never have been.* 'I knew that.'

'You did?' Irene cringed into herself, blushing profusely. 'Joe reminds you of Roy, that's all.'

'Do you forgive me then, Ailsa?'

There was nothing to forgive, Ailsa said. They understood one another. Irene would work out notice at the NAAFI and then go home to England and try to make a life for the boys. Years it would take, she said, decades, finally to believe that there was no Roy on this earth. But she had begun to believe it. She would never see him again. But so it was. There was no replacement. And she might as well get used to it.

'You will marry again perhaps,' Ailsa said. 'I think you will. When the time is right.'

'Who would want to marry me?'

'Plenty of men. They'll be queuing up.'

'Well, he would have to be a very special man.'

'Of course.'

Irene smiled. 'Will you come back with me, Ailsa? Oh, thank you, Mrs Jacobs. What lovely looking biscuits, so unusual. Are they foreign?'

This was the answer: to move in with Irene until something could be sorted out. Ailsa put her belongings together; lifted the sleeping Nia on to her shoulder. She allowed herself to meet Mona's eyes only at the last minute. They were red and swollen with crying. How did you say goodbye to someone for whom you felt opposite extremes of emotion? Did you promise to keep in touch? Or not acknowledge the moment? They would not see one another again, not if Ailsa had any say in the matter.

'Toodle-oo,' said Irene as they climbed into the taxi. Mona and *Habibi* turned together on the dark drive and went back into the yellow light of the bungalow. No parting kiss; Ailsa was glad Mona had made no motion to kiss her.

*

Dusty, propping up the bar in the Mess at Fayid, had reached the maudlin stage. He was off on his hobbyhorse about how the A-rabs maltreated their animals because they were subhuman. The A-rabs, not the animals. Animals were superior to humans any day. *Sacred bleeding trust*, he kept saying, his language slurred, *that's what it is, mate*. He'd beat up any A-rab he saw hitting or kicking his donkey. He repeated the story Chalkie had told Joe about how, on guard duty with Roy White, Dusty had fired to kill a marauding wog, only to find when the sun came up that he'd assassinated a poor old Eeyore.

'Oh aye?' said Joe. He wished Chalkie had not been mentioned. It was like a hellish toothache you'd temporarily forgotten about. Then someone mentions teeth and the evil that sleeps in your mouth wakes up, screaming blue murder.

Dusty said that the Ancient Egyptians were a far cry from the modern Gyppos. They were a different race, see. Superior. The Pharaohs worshipped animals. Their gods were hawks and cows and jackals, even dung beetles.

'Oh aye? Another?' Joe was pissed and his head muzzy, except for the memory of his pal, clear as day, which he tried to deaden by drowning it in another beer. But Chalkie would not be chased away. Joe saw his friend's light, wiry frame. His ready grin. Five foot four in his socks but like the miners in the pits at home, Chalkie had as much strength in him as many broad-chested six footers. No side.

Boy of few words. The genuine article.

What about going on the town? someone suggested. A couple of other boys joined them. Merry they were. Looking for a bit of fun, a bint or a spot of trouble. *Target practice!* someone yelled. The bastard wogs had torn up the Treaty. That made them fair game.

They spilled out on to the forecourt, ready for anything. Somehow or other the four airmen fetched up at the ammo dump. Fancy that, look where we are! Well, now that we're here... They helped themselves to Service revolvers and ammunition. In civvies rather than uniform they were but the sergeant, seeming a bit skew-whiff himself or perhaps just a simpleton, didn't turn a hair. He signed out the firearms just like that. Then they borrowed a Land Rover for transportation. Singing at the tops of their voices.

And sang all the way to Ish, Joe yodelling a descant. He'd been drinking steadily all day. Now he bellowed: 'We'll keep a welcome in the hillside!'

Far, far gone he was. Not a care in the world.

They staggered out of the Vic. The fucking Jeep had been stolen by a fucking arse of a wog. Which was the kind of underhand thing fucking wogs did. No scruples, see? That meant the boys had the fucking obligation to steal a fucking wog's car in reprisal. Smashing the window of a battered old Austin, they broke in and shot off racing round Wogtown, tyres squealing, hands on hooter, driving at anything that stepped into the road.

Dusty in the driving seat was fired up and blasting on all cylinders. *Get the golliwogs, get them, get them*, he repeated.

Joe saw where they were. He remembered, with a black,

sick qualm, the wrong that had been done to him. His wife had been seduced. His child had had to be farmed out to another woman, and that woman not the brightest button in the box. The pervert Wing Co who'd blown a bloody great hole in Joe's life lived just down here in Masurah. He knew the house; had reconnoitred.

'Turn right, boy,' he told Dusty. 'By there, go on. Now right again. Straight ahead. Left! – I said left! Now stop.'

All the windows of the bungalow were lit up, none of the blinds or shutters being closed. Its whiteness was as milky as the three-quarters moon that hung above the roof. They piled out of the car into the chilly air; mounted the steps to the veranda. Stealing to the window, they peered through. Some kind of concert. All the faces were turned to the source of the singing, just out of Joe's vision. If you could call it music – a tuneless dirge that took Joe back to the caterwauling of the Great Oom at the De Lesseps House, to which he'd been treated. The mooing of a passionate cow. He scanned the profiles of the audience, standing round with drinks in their hands. White, brown and black faces. He was sure he could see Black Sambo, the Ethiopian golliwog saffragi who'd been at the bus stop with Nobby Bowen and claimed to be a prince in his own country. And Bowen was here too, with his tart of a Gyppo wife. Bowen who'd recognised Joe's wife that Saturday morning as they got off the Liberty bus, causing Ailsa to skip off sharpish before she was caught in her deceit. So: not just Jacobs but Bowen. They'd all had her. They'd educated her. To kneel on hands and knees like a bitch on the carpet, to be taken from behind. Joe retched. He felt sick to his stomach. His view tilted, righted itself and swooped sideways: he propped himself against Dusty's back, chin hooked over his pal's shoulder.

'Fucking A-rabs,' whispered Dusty. 'And niggers. In with bleeding RAF officers. Would you believe it, Taf?'

'Oh aye. I'd believe anything. Roomful of fucking degenerates.'

There was a cat in the window. A huge creature like a lynx. It sat back on its fat haunches; bared its teeth and snarled.

'Puss! Puss!' cried Dusty, making a chirruping sound between his lips. 'Come on now, nice pussy!'

The cat poured itself away from the window sill. The song seemed to be over in there. They could hear clapping. Some geezer laughed, a peal of laughter. Want to share the joke? Come out here and share the joke. A record was put on the turntable: some wailing nonsensical female wog-noise without a fucking tune. Joe was paralytic. He swayed where he stood. Passing out. Dots in front of his eyes. Everything he saw was a seething mass of dots. It made him livid. Shoving his mate out of the way, Joe craned at the window to try and spot his wife among the crowd. He saw the hind quarters of some lanky bastard in a cream polo neck sweater with lah-de-fucking-dah swept-back hair, holding forth on some subject with camp hand gestures. No way to see if he was talking to Joe's lawful wedded wife. But the lady of the house was there, wearing a low-cut blue gown, bending to light a fag from a lighter offered by a bald bloke in a grey suit. Even in full evening dress, she was untidily put together, strands of hair escaping from a pearly slide. Straightening up, Mrs Jacobs caught sight of him; locked on to his gaze.

Yoo hoo! He waved. *Décolletage* was the word they used, wasn't it? That was the word. *Yoo hoo, slut!*

This was the woman who had prostituted Joe's wife to her own husband. Ailsa must be in there with her. Under her wing. Not really her fault. Sleeping beauty.

Joe was round at the side of the bungalow before he knew what he was about to do. He laid his shoulder to the door but it was on the latch and he tumbled in, striking his forehead a ringing blow on the wall opposite. Stunned, he stood still a moment. Where was she? He was taking Ailsa home. She'd come with him if he had to drag her. It was not anger that he felt for her, he had no wish to punish her, although she must be taken, by force if necessary.

Joe lurched into a room where the bastard party was going on. The room froze and all at once unreality set in as if Joe had stumbled on to a theatre stage. Faces gazed at Joe's hands in horror. Or at his genitals. Flies undone? He glanced down: no. In looking down, he realised the revolver was pointed straight at them.

He at once lowered it to his side. His stomach gave a violent heave and he was aware that he might throw up any minute. Serve the wankers right if he puked up all over them.

Dusty was not far behind him. He came cannoning into Joe. Joe stumbled forward. Stopping dead, he gaped round at the wogs in the officers' quarters.

'Fucking bastard niggerloving traitors!' he yelled. 'What have you done with her?'

It all happened at once. The fair-haired nancy who followed Psycho Jacobs around like a bitch on heat stepped forward with a smile on his face, offering a hand to Joe.

'Come on, Mr Roberts, have a drink, you don't need that, do you?'

'Sergeant to you!'

Joe brought the gun up and motioned the pansy back. He looked round for his wife. She was not apparent.

The room suddenly seemed to explode. Joe's head exploded with it, and the main light went out.

Dusty had fired his revolver into the chandelier and splinters of glass were raining down on their heads. Screams.

The queerboy was coming forward again, very slowly.

'Let me have it, Joe, come on.'

Let him have it, thought Joe.

The queerboy yelped the moment before the gun went off. The shot went wide, as it had been intended to do. But some other man at his shoulder gave a gargling, rasping shout and a body slumped. Frothing blood leapt out of the skull of that man who was falling, falling, behind the queer boy.

Something launched itself slithering at Joe's legs. Something nightmarishly soft and fleshy. That cunt of a cat, of course. He wheeled and shot down towards it.

The pandemonium of screaming and the woman singing her dirge on the gramophone went on and on.

Joe reeled round and shot the gramophone to pieces with an ear-splitting report. The cat appeared on the window sill, outside the pane.

Dusty looked down, shrieked like a woman and ran, whimpering.

Joe did not run. He looked down where Dusty had been looking.

It was a child. He hadn't known there was a child in the room. Mother and daughter had been sitting behind the door. Joe looked down and saw the child's scarlet hand, held out in bewilderment. Blood leapt from the hand to saturate the woman's turquoise head scarf.

23

A vast crowd in the square roared and surged. The noise was deafening.

It woke Ailsa up, half dreaming she was at a rugby match at St Helen's and all the Welsh boys roaring in ecstasy over the genius of Haydn Tanner or Bleddyn Williams. For a moment she was foxed: but oh yes, of course, they were at Irene's flat in Ish. Dainty and dinky, Irene had said it was, just the job. They needed to be nearer to Joe, Ailsa had brusquely told Mona, unable to look her in the face. Punishing her friend. But for what? Mona would cry; she'd cried already. How beastly Ailsa had been. But it couldn't be helped, it had to be done. Ailsa marvelled at her own ruthlessness and at the way her tender feeling had turned round into animosity. She remembered Nia thrusting Mona out of the door when they'd returned from Palestine, butting her in the stomach, her head a weapon. Children registered everything. Babes and sucklings. Nia knew Mona was death.

Whether this was fair or not, Ailsa neither knew nor cared. It was probably an injustice. But this was a matter of survival.

Oddly enough she'd slept deeply, Nia in her arms, hopeful now of reconciliation with her husband. A stronger character than Joe, she had the power – if she used it tactfully, bit her tongue, acted weak, as she'd signally failed to do – to build peace between them. After a good night's sleep, she'd awakened to the sound of this pandemonium of anger in the square.

Irene, padding round in her white quilted dressing gown, said, in a no-nonsense voice, not to worry, she'd barricade the door to the flat: they'd be safe as houses, no one could get in – and up here on the fourth floor they were well out of range of the mob. Ailsa, peeping through a chink in the shutters, wondered at Irene's composure. She'd always been such a mouse. Chalkie's temperate spirit seemed to live again in her.

The two women peered down on a choppy sea of countless heads. Demonstrators still poured out of the station, presumably from Cairo and Port Said, to swell the tide in the square. Their arrival had been timed to the hour after the mass departure of the husbands from the flats and Army Mansions for Moascar Garrison. Astounding numbers kept on arriving, greeting one another in an ecstasy of brotherhood. Young, excited faces raised from the crowd, looked up, straight into Ailsa's eyes, or so it seemed, with glittering smiles. Many were in *gallabiyyas*; others were students in shirtsleeves. It fascinated Ailsa to be up here, out of harm's way, at a point of vantage and able to study a crowd from above. A bird's eye view. The mob was one organism; it flowed here and there, with no head and no tail, an elated creature of the moment.

Ailsa thought of the boy protester who'd run slap bang into her in Ish last year. They'd punched out his front teeth. The military police had carted him off to who knew what humiliation. British violence had been the hammer to his anvil. He'd been waiting for, praying for, planning for this day. He'd be one of these youngsters in the crowd beneath her. He'd have known beyond all doubt that this day would dawn, for *Allahu Akbar! God is great!* The crowd cried as one voice, raising fists to the infidel women in the flats. The individual was nothing; even the mob was nothing; their lives were nothing. God was great.

The crowd nearest to the flats began to direct its protest against the women and children inside and on the flat roof. Would they come flooding up the stairwell, assault and loot? Would they rape the women, exposed without their menfolk, torch the flats? Rage swelled from a hubbub to a baying chant in English. *Filthy British Infidels Go Home! Unity of the Nile Delta! Aggressors Out of Misr!* Women in the block who'd gone up to the flat roof with their Kodaks to get a view retreated as the hail of stones and bottles began.

'Hallo there! Coo-ee! Don't worry, it's only Mrs Grey!' a voice chirruped outside the barricaded flat door. How this petty official was enjoying herself. What a platform for the battle-axe's officiousness. Learned, Ailsa guessed, in the war and always seeking a heroic outlet. 'Come up to the fifth floor, please, ladies. We've set up an emergency committee. This may take a while and it will be nice for the kiddies to play together – and we'll all keep one another's spirits up.'

Community singsong, Ailsa mouthed, shaking her head with a grimace. Irene raised her eyebrows. No, they wouldn't come – but thanks anyway.

There was a pause. Then Mrs Grey said, 'Well, on your own head be it, Mrs Roberts. If you wish to come, Mrs White, do not let yourself be swayed.'

Doubtless the woman had recognised Ailsa's voice, remembering her transgressions on the *Empire Glory* and keeping up with the gossip ever since. Odious to think one had been the centre of tattle amongst such women as *that*.

Nia, who had been making cats' cradles, held up a string shape on spread fingers and thumbs, asking in a casual sort of voice, 'What are those nasty men doing, Mami? Are they coming in here to kill us?'

Ailsa and Irene swooped on her with comfort and endearments. Perhaps they ought to have gone up with the others? They agreed to go at any sign of immediate danger.

'I expect Daddy will be here soon,' Nia said, glancing across at the door which Irene had barricaded with a table.

As Nia looked up, anticipating her father's arrival, the expression in her green eyes, somewhere between trust and bewilderment, so reminded Ailsa of Joe that she ached to hold him close and be held by him. Joe and she were mutually present in their daughter, almost as a haunting. They were married in the bone structure of Nia's face, her build, the shapes of hands and feet. The inheritance of Joe and herself intricately braided, intimately dissolved together in the chemistry of Nia. She sat Nia on her lap and prompted her to a new cat's cradle.

She picked the web off Nia's fingers; Nia plucked it off hers. Soon, Ailsa and Nia and Joe would be back together.

All they needed for the road was a bit of decency and tact. And this Ailsa must supply, she saw, because at those times when he saw red, Joe probably couldn't.

'Oh yes, the daddies will be here in two ticks,' Irene promised. And it was surprising how she rose to the occasion. 'You won't see those nasty men for dust then!'

'We shall see Daddy very soon, sweetheart,' Ailsa said. 'And we shall all be lovely and together again.' She would eat a fair-sized portion of humble pie if that was what it took – and the rest they would talk through like sensible folk.

The mob hurled itself against the NAAFI. Setting the perimeter fence on fire with torches, it stampeded the entrance, breaking through by sheer pressure of numbers, aided by several Egyptian policeman. Out the men staggered with loot. Crates of food. Carrier bags of cigarettes. Taking back a token share of what was due to them. Flames burst from the store and smoke billowed high in the air. Two cars had been overturned and torched.

Gunfire. The sound of lorries and Jeeps from Moascar. A cry went up from the top floor: 'The Lancashire Fusiliers!' Cheers and applause upstairs, Rule Britannia, wild whooping and stamping as the women swarmed up to the roof.

Now the darkie devils were for it! a lady shrieked. *By God those stinking savages had it coming!*

Bren guns were set up. Lorries with a platoon of troops from Moascar made for the store, shooting presumably over the mob's heads or down at its feet, till the crowd wavered and fell back, spilling into the surrounding streets. A blanket of near-silence lay over the square, like a fog that mutes all sound. The two women tremblingly smiled, thumbs-upped at one another. They clasped hands briefly. Tying on her pinafore and bustling out into the kitchen, Irene put the kettle on and promised bacon and eggs.

'That's enough excitement for one day,' she said.

The deafening report and echo of Sten-guns from the nearby streets came with such sudden violence that it seemed to erupt just outside their rattling window-pane. Irene rushed back in. They peered out into the square: soldiers with fixed bayonets were haring along. The shattering echo of the guns in Ailsa's skull triggered a storm. The shots went on and on. She reeled away from the excessive light. Ergot, she must have ergot.

Order had resumed, with the installation of barbed wire; the carting off of corpses. The firing that had sounded so near was actually coming from side-roads. 'For they are jolly good fellows!' sang the British women on the roof. Men in *gallabiyyas* were herded across the *Place de la Gare*, hands bound behind their backs, Irene reported. Now they were being loaded into trucks. 'Off with the velvet gloves!' cried a woman on the roof. The disorder in Ailsa's head gathered force. Fragments of light whirled in her right eye; her stomach turned over.

She slumped down in a chair, shading her eyes. There was an impression of being back at the Old Brewery. The girls next door had flown. Ailsa was alone in the eerie silence between doodlebug explosions. Joe was in the Western Desert, far beyond summoning, there was no Nia at all, and Ailsa was left cowering, imminent death suspended above her head. She was going to die. She'd had it. Now. The bomb fell – elsewhere. The partition between the flats, with its flaking, bile-green skin of paint, shook convulsively. Windows rattled; crockery jangled on the shelf; a naked light bulb swung around on its lead.

'Mrs White! Mrs Roberts!' Rapping on the door. 'Open up, please!'

The door was opened. A whispering took place.

'She's not very well.'

Ailsa looked up between one bolt of lightning and the next. What was the word for what she'd got? She pointed to her temple to try to alert Irene. Meanings were there but not the words for them. But when she'd searched around and the words reappeared, they'd been deserted by their meanings and fell away into limbo. She saw Irene usher the two RAF policemen into the flat. Hats in hands, they looked at her with anxious, compassionate eyes, holding back from whatever message they had come to deliver.

24

'Does Mam know, *cariad*?'

'I spoke to her last night.'

Joe flinched and turned his head aside. The calm, even tenor of their conversation faltered only a fraction before their tearless eyes met and held one another again. Husband and wife held steady. They stilled the moment by pure willpower, not looking back, not looking forward.

'What did she say?'

'She's coming. She'll be flown out, darling. Don't worry, it will be in time.'

'Ah. And what about Dad?'

'He's not so well. She'll maybe come on her own. She's a strong woman, remember, your mam.'

The Military Policeman in the corner of the room peered straight ahead, quite detached, as if he'd caught sight of something fascinating on the wall opposite him. Everyone had been kind, gentle, tactful with the two of them. Ailsa felt ringed round with human decency. No moments in her life could ever be more precious or important than these, in which she and her husband shared quiet meetings, seated across the table from one another, keeping their balance. Three hours they had left after today, one hour on each of three consecutive days. They were not supposed to touch but in practice nobody objected to their holding hands. They were allowed to embrace and kiss at arrival and departure and they both looked forward to these moments, like teenagers at the cinema.

Human decency, yes, but not from the British Government. Dusty, who was to be hanged with Joe, had no one capable of fending for him. His wife had completely gone to pieces, leaving Dusty in the pitiful condition of having to notify his own parents, for it was War Office practice not to inform relatives of any trouble or problems regarding their kin. It was up to the airman to let his parents know, 'if he wished to do so'. Ailsa and Irene had visited Dusty and rung his mother in Widnes. But Mrs Miller already knew. She had read the news in the paper two hours previously. Dusty was the third of fourteen children. But Mrs Miller would fly to Cairo to say goodbye. Neighbours would take care of the little ones. There was a neighbourhood collection towards her flight.

For the War Office had refused to fly the condemned men's parents out. Ailsa had kept this information from Joe. She was glad now that she had beside her the refunded money from the carpet, a sum which would amply cover Joe's mother's ticket. It had been difficult to arrange the telephone conversations with Mam, none of the Treforys family being on the phone. In the end Ailsa was able to arrange calls for Mam every couple of days at the minister's house; the expense of these calls also came out of the carpet. After her first whimpering cries and rush of tears for her beloved boy, Gwenllian had taken the news of her son's crime and sentence with extraordinary resolution, her voice sounding so close that it had startled Ailsa.

Had Ailsa initiated an appeal? had been Mam's first thought. But incredibly there existed no right of appeal from a court martial sentence. And the court had made no recommendation of mercy for either man.

'What's wrong with Dad then?' Joe asked carefully. Every subject they broached had to be considered and phrased with care, in case the spirit level of their balance should shift.

'Oh, his chest. You know, Joe, the usual. But he'll come if he possibly can. Of course he will.'

Joe's father was in a bad way. Ailsa had not burdened Joe with this knowledge. But he knew anyway. She saw it in his eyes. They were going to their graves together.

She'd copied out a poem for him, Donne's 'Valediction Forbidding Mourning':

So let us melt and make no noise –

'I'd actually rather Dad didn't come, Ailsa, if he's not so good.'

'Of course. Don't worry about that.'

No tear floods nor sigh tempests move –

Ailsa had launched a petition to the War Minister. She had written to King George with all the eloquence at her command, begging him to intervene. Joe's mother's MP had also written to the King, pleading extenuating circumstances. It was no good. The murder of a British officer at any moment counted as treason, the most heinous

404

crime. The arbitrary wounding of an Egyptian child at such a sensitive moment was political dynamite.

Joe had aimed his revolver not at an individual but at the edifice of Empire. At deference. At rank. How utterly ironic this was, Ailsa thought. For Joe believed in and lived by duty and hierarchy. At Port Said he'd saluted *Habibi* and Alex, cleaving the Roberts and the Jacobs families asunder. His salute had reminded them: *this is not a suitable or proper relationship.*

Ailsa's deviance had brought him to this. But he would not hear of it.

Now everyone seemed to want Joe and Dusty gone – shrouded, buried, covered over – as rapidly as possible. Joe himself did not for a moment question the justice of his punishment.

The firmness makes my circle just –

'Do you get any sleep at all, *cariad*?' he asked.

'I don't want all that much sleep. Waste of time.'

And makes me end where I begun –

Ailsa had fitfully drowsed last night, awakening at the point in her recurrent dream where she stood outside a door. She seemed able to wake up in the nick of time before the door opened. What lay beyond it Ailsa did not ask. She and Nia had been moved to a Nissen hut in Fanara, away from the terrorist dangers of Ismailia, for no white person was safe now beyond the barbed wire, the watch towers and the tanks. Each day brought fresh murders, strikes, gun battles, ambushes and bombing. British atrocities multiplied: bulldozers and Centurion tanks had demolished fifty Egyptian mud houses that had been built in the way of a source of water to which the British must have access.

405

We seemed to be a nation that could not learn. Its brain was primitive. It could only repeat the misdeeds of yesterday. Yet this customary thought came to Ailsa dispassionately; her sympathies had shrunk to the horizons of one plight. The war, for it was a war, though no one said so, between Egypt and its occupiers, held no intimate reality for her. Six thousand troops had been flown in to the Canal Zone and a thousand families, including the Websters and the Breans, evacuated. The Roberts family could have been amongst them, disembarking at Southampton from the *Empire Sunderland*. Home.

Hedwig and her son had been amongst the evacuees. That Joe had shot her beloved *Habibi* – who had seen her through a bad time – Hedwig could hardly credit. *Habibi* had led her back to the country of sanity and given Eric a mother. She'd jounced the bundled baby in her arms, smiling into his face as she spoke to Ailsa, while he crowed, flailing at her face as if to snatch the smile. Then he'd crammed his fingers in his mouth as if to taste and drink the delicious smile. *Ailsa, I pity you from the bottom of my heart that you have such a husband.* Ailsa had flared up: *Joe is still my Joe. Whatever he's done.* She'd wanted to say that Joe hadn't gone to Masurah with the intention of killing *Habibi* or hurting a child; it had been a mistake. But how could you apologise for such heinous offences? The words went to ash on Ailsa's tongue. Hedwig had understood that one has to remain loyal to one's husband, right or wrong; a wife's binding duty. But in that case, should one not have chosen more wisely? She hadn't put these formulae – these Prussian platitudes – into words. But Ailsa had heard the message. And all the while, the weather in Hedwig's face had altered with every breath, melting for her boy, clouding for Ailsa. Eric had battened lips on his mother's cheek and blown a raspberry. Involuntarily, both women had laughed aloud. *Habibi was the best kind of Jew*, *exceptional*, Hedwig had said. *He had the warmest heart. Mind you, it's always the best that are taken.* Ailsa had not replied. She'd thought, yes, six million of the best. Hedwig was nothing to her. She lived in a different world. The two would not meet again.

This morning Ailsa had awoken sensing snow on the ground: muted sound and an eerie quality to the light. Her mind's eye had hallucinated snow mounds on dustbin lids; thick coils on washing lines; the purification of dark spaces by a freezing grace of whiteness. She'd slipped out of bed and opened the curtains to find no such thing, but an apricot dawn, of a colour so tender that she'd gone outside into the winter air to bless her eyes with it.

Holding at bay the obscene thing.

January here could be as sharp as Shropshire. Time and the seasons had taken leave of their senses. Ailsa had hardly noticed the year's turning. Three months had gone by since the crime: it was 1952 already. The authorities had rushed through the court martial and the executions. Archie had written to her every day. He would be on the next plane if she wanted him. *Do not under any circumstances come*, she'd telegraphed. *On no account.* For she was all Joe's now. The two of them were all in all to one another. Grafted into the one stock. Ailsa could not be doing with well-meaning outsiders, even a cousin, weakening her with kindness, diluting the passionate outpouring of her heart's best blood to her husband. Looking back through the window, she'd seen Nia lying asleep on her camp bed, bathed in a flush of rosy light, up to the neck in a grey military blanket. One of Nia's arms was flung above her head, her body skewed, as if she'd been casually dropped like a rag doll. The blankets were rough and scratchy, their hairs piercing sheets and nightie. Nia's skin was a tormented mass of eczema, where the insidious fibres rubbed it; there were open sores and scars, for Nia couldn't help but scratch in the night. She never asked after her father. Not a word.

There was no more strolling round Ish on shopping trips: so Irene told Ailsa. Ish was out of bounds. They hate us, Irene said. Well, of course they've always hated us, but they couldn't afford to show it openly, could they? The servants have all downed tools and stopped working for us. Poor souls, they and their families will starve. I knew of course, Irene said, all along. I foresaw it. Even before Roy was taken. Standing at the sink, Irene had paused, her sudsy hands suspended as she washed a vest of Nia's. Then she'd said: *we shouldn't be here at all, we should never have come in the first place, you were right. It isn't their fault. It's ours. We should stay at home and mind our own blooming business.*

Ailsa could not express her gratitude to Irene for remaining with her. So she said nothing about it. She reserved all emotion to herself, permitting it to collect behind a huge dam forever in the building. Irene could easily have gone home with the evacuees but had chosen to stand beside and behind Ailsa and Joe, who had crossed into another world, another time zone altogether. A place of greater stillness.

*

'I sleep OK,' Joe told her. 'Odd, really.'

'Oh do you, darling? I'm so glad. Mind, you've always been a good sleeper.'

'Aye. I try not to drop off and then I do.'

Everything was simple now. Ailsa lit cigarettes for both of them; slipped her husband's from her mouth between her fingers; passed the lipstick-stained end between his lips and smiled with her eyes into his eyes in an ordinary way that heartened him.

She had removed her watch and hidden it in the deep pocket of her skirt. In the windowless room there was no sun to shift the angle of shadow and tell tales about time passing.

'Time, I'm afraid, Mrs Roberts.'

They rose to their feet as one, with a scraping of chairs. The policeman turned away. A bear hug. The softness of Joe's clean-shaven jaw on her throat and the scent of soap; his chest against her breast; his arms powerful around her. She clasped his head between her palms as they kissed and, as they drew apart, brought them down to cup Joe's face in a gesture reminiscent of Nia's. A gesture Nia had caught from Joe.

*

He was suspected
And then arrested
For making whoopee

So Dusty sang, tunelessly on and on, in his cell. The poor bloke had cracked. A shambles of a man, he'd been cracked for a long, long time. He was sand-happy and should have been repatriated some time back. Dusty had not killed anyone at the Jacobs house: all he'd done was to shoot a chandelier to pieces. Did he deserve to die? But the request of Dusty's counsel that he be tried separately from Joe had been denied. The prosecutor had told the court that although Roberts had killed the British officer and wounded the Egyptian child, Miller was equally guilty of murder because he had brought and fired a stolen service revolver in the house.

Pour encourager les autres Dusty was to die. That was what it came down to. Joe surprised himself by minding about this very much. When they were first brought to the condemned cells, Joe had heard his pal weeping, shrieking, banging his head against the cell door. The medics must have given him something to knock him out as he'd quietened down since and only, occasionally, sang. Joe wished Dusty would change the record.

Day and night, eyes peered at Joe through the judas hole. The light was never switched off.

He kept his mind fixed on Ailsa. The compass point quivered but held true. Quiet and still, she held him in the palm of her hand.

A good smell of egg and bacon wafted into the cell. His mouth watered. When his breakfast arrived, Joe was pleased to see fried bread, mushroom and tomato heaped on the tin plate in addition to the egg and bacon. An enamel mug of strong, scalding tea washed the meal down a treat. His body surprised him by its stubborn power to eat heartily and sleep deeply. Joe put the greasy plate down on the floor, with the empty mug on it.

There was a small creature, an insect whose name he did not know, striving to climb upwards towards the small, high

410

window. Joe had at first taken it for a fleck on the wall, whose random mottlings and blemishes his eyes had got to know in the past months, as they absent-mindedly roved the walls. He watched in fascination as the living speck journeyed over the blank surface past other specks that were not alive. Sitting on his bed, resting his forearms on spread knees, hands hanging loosely, he continued to track the creature's odyssey. When he lit up a cigarette, he lost sight of it. No, there it was, having made half an inch of progress.

It was a spider. He would tell Nia about the spider.

When they came to collect his plate, Joe asked for pen and paper. He began to write to his daughter, doodling a cartoon of Incy Wincy Spider climbing up the spout, going on to tell Nia he loved her and her Mami more than anything in the world.

Ti'n werth y byd, cariad, he wrote: you're the world to me. But somehow in his rage and jealousy he'd lost sight of this simple fact. That Nia was a pearl beyond price, entrusted to him and Ailsa who was also *werth y byd*.

When Nia had cried in the night as a baby, Joe was always the first to leap out of bed, to run to her crib, lift her, lullaby her, give milk. It was quite comical, his brothers had said, how he adored that child. They'd roared with laughter to see him kneel and roll up his shirtsleeve to test the temperature of Nia's bath water with his elbow. If Nia was sick, Joe cleared the mess. If she fell down, he'd clean and kiss and bind the wound. He'd sit her on his shoulders and take her round Hendrefoilan Park. They'd laughed because they thought they'd found their brother's weak spot and because as yet they had no children of their own to wring their hearts. But Nia was not his weak spot. She

411

was his strength. He'd always understood that and ought to have set his course by that knowledge. Every hair of her head was numbered. Simple as that. He owed Nia boundless love and protection. What would her life be like, her father and protector a hanged criminal? He was unstrung to think this thought, he wanted to howl: the *terrible thing* that stalked him and which he and Ailsa together held off in their common vigil, advanced.

He was no good with words. But Ailsa would certainly tell Nia the right thing. He could trust her to find appropriate words. Or to judge if it would be better for Nia to forget him altogether. To say nothing. How would she be at ten years old, at twenty? If she found out?

The breakfast all came up, into the bucket. He blew the vileness from his nose, wiped his mouth. Joe crushed the unfinished letter into the envelope, writing Nia's name on it.

All done in a mist, he thought. *Making whoopee.* Widowed the woman Ailsa loved. Shot a cat but the cat was a child; and he'd thought upon bursting out of his drunken stupor that it was Nia he'd shot.

Mona Jacobs had spoken up for Joe at the court martial. He'd hardly been able to believe his ears.

She'd testified that Sergeant Roberts had been upset, understandably upset, and he'd clearly been drinking hard. It had been obvious to her that Sergeant Roberts had come to her house with a view to frightening herself and her guests, throwing his weight about, no more than that. When he'd threatened Flight Lieutenant Ince, he'd made a conspicuous point of firing wide, aiming at a gramophone. And her husband had most unfortunately moved – almost dived – sideways straight into the path of the bullet. Why he had made that move she had no idea: he'd always tended to be clumsy. Perhaps, as Ince also testified, Wing Commander Jacobs was trying to get between Sergeant Roberts and his friend.

And when his gun had gone off at the little Egyptian girl, Sergeant Roberts had thought he was shooting a cat.

A cat? Sergeant Roberts has something against cats?

He deflected his anger from myself and my guests to the house cat.

A man in His Majesty's Royal Air Force breaks into a senior officer's home armed with a loaded service revolver and 'accidentally' kills one person, your husband, and wounds a child of five?

He wanted to teach me a lesson. He disapproved of my friendship with his wife.

Mrs Jacobs had failed to make a good impression, showing none of the natural emotion to be expected of the newly widowed. She had taken the trouble to dress up in a square-shouldered navy jacket and skirt – smart enough but, with her hair cropped so close to her head, the outfit had given her a mannish look. Mrs Jacobs hadn't blamed her husband's murderer. Had shed no tears. Instead she'd opened the door on an unsavoury corner of the world of the British officer class – parties, loose morals, Commie sympathies, perverse friendships with foreigners and lower ranks, indiscretions and breaches of taste. Swanning round in Arab robes. And she was herself a foreigner. A constant procession of coloured persons had been coming and going, according to the neighbours, who'd been sure that the Jacobs were spies. Mrs Jacobs had admitted to taking Sergeant Robert's wife to the Israeli border during his

413

absence. Joe's defence painted Mrs Jacobs pitch-black, presenting her husband's death as a crime of passion. But what good was that, when a child had also been attacked? Joe was visited by flashing pictures of the little girl's blood on his hands, on his clothes as he'd bent to her. He had to die for this. He couldn't bear to live with it.

The court had stared with avid eyes at the Wing Commander's widow and they'd sized up the sergeant's wife. *Lesbians?* The word had never once occurred to him: how odd. In the war, he and the boys had passed through Siwa, a byword for Arab moral decline, where the women they passed in scarlet robes, hair matted with chicken grease, were said to practise inversion. In Siwa they'd turned to it because their men were all homos. Joe didn't see how lesbianism was anatomically possible in any case.

Ailsa had hardly looked at her one-time friend. Her blue-green eyes had rested on her husband throughout the three days of the trial. She'd sat unflinchingly upright in her seat, wearing a dark costume and a blouse fastened at the neck with a cameo brooch. Her face pale, she'd looked sombrely beautiful, entirely collected. Superior. Hearing of his jealousy and his wife's equivocal carryings-on, the court's sympathies had swung from Ailsa towards himself. But their sympathy could do him no good. Joe was going to swing, that had been a foregone conclusion. And he had nothing to urge against this, except that he was the father of Nia. When his own turn had come to speak, Joe told the squalid truth precisely as he remembered it, pleading guilty and acknowledging full responsibility for his actions.

According to the Commanding Officer, who visited Joe daily, the public executioner, Albert Pierrepoint, was not available for the task of executing the two airmen, for he was needed in Ulster. One of his assistants would be flown over in the garb of a Squadron Leader to despatch them. Naturally this official was highly trained and competent or he would not be employed to do the job.

Perhaps the man was here already?

Joe glanced over to the judas hole, through which the executioner might already have studied his physique and stature, assessing his neck muscles to ascertain the length of the drop. This assessment and calculation were essential to ensure instantaneous death rather than slow strangulation. The procedure had been explained in detail to Joe and he had listened attentively.

White cap on face; noose round neck; pin whipped out of catch; lever pushed; drop. Eight seconds flat. And off you went on your final posting into eternity. Easy as winking.

Joe, seasoned by the Western Desert, was stalwart about death. And somehow it helped that he happened to know exactly where he and Dusty would lose their lives – in a disused railway repair warehouse close to Fayid village. In the late summer of the year before last the shed had been converted for three army blokes who'd gone on a drunken spree in Cairo and shot a native watchman. Driving past on the Tiger, Joe had seen the shed with the gallows and hanging pit.

His thoughts roved back to Chalkie, not as he had been in the last months of his life at El-Marah, but seven years previously in the Western Desert. They'd entered Cyrenaica, an Italian colony on the Mediterranean. And this must have been early in the war when the boys were grass-green lads, a cocky swagger in their gait, contemptuous of an effeminate enemy. The Italians, in full flight, had left behind in their dugouts quaint little sewing kits with threads, thimbles and needles; cases of red wine and tins of tunny fish and tomatoes.

Chalkie, laughing his head off, had come rolling a whole Parmesan cheese, big as a cartwheel. Cutlery and cruets littered the desert. The bodies of dead Italians lay about like trippers taken poorly on holiday, amongst chocolate wrappings and fag packets, their letters and postcards – of Naples, Milan, Rome – scattered around them for five miles over the wind-blown sands. *Mama carissima, dearest Mummy, I love you more than life*, the Flight Lieutenant who knew Italian translated aloud. *May the Blessed Virgin preserve you until the glorious Fascist army returns in triumph*. The officer had dropped the page into the general litter of letters. Spoke supercilious words about the enemy's flamboyant emotionalism: *The Italian egg has been cracked and found to be rotten inside*.

They are just men like us, sir, said Chalkie, in his broad northern accent. *That's the long and the short of it*.

The Flight Lieutenant, hardly more than a boy, had had the grace to wince and bow his head. He'd blushed scarlet and said nothing.

The unsent letters of the dead had glowed for miles pink and peach under the falling sun. Homewarding bombers glided distantly across the bloody sunset and the next morning everything was buried in blown sand, as if it had never been: men, mules, stores, swords, letters.

Dusty was off again, *making whoopee*. Foghorn of a voice, no excuse for it. Joe stood up and challenged Dusty with '*Cwm Rhondda*, Bread of Heaven'. His chapel tenor soared up to *want no more … want no more*. Dusty, defeated, was silent. Then, as Joe began to tread the verge of Jordan, Dusty joined in: *Bid my anxious fears subside*.

*

There was a young WAAF at the door, a package in her arms. Ailsa received her husband's personal effects, tied up in a brown paper parcel. Oh, thank you. Sign for it? Right. Here? Sorry, said the girl, so sorry for your loss. Thank you. The door closed. Ailsa unpicked the knot. Three brown envelopes, one each for herself, Gwenllian and Nia. Joe's watch. His reading glasses. His Bible and a copy of *The Reader's Digest*. A half-finished bag of coconut mushrooms. His carpet slippers.

Your husband died dauntlessly, that is the word, the Welsh Congregationalist pastor had said. And with good humour.

She would be with him till the world ended, she'd told Joe on their last day. Every step, every breath of the way.

But don't you be grieving. Marry again.

Every single breath. I'll be with you.

His dad was near the end of the road; he could not last more than a few days: should she come or not? Joe's mother had asked. Just say the word.

Stay with Dad. He'd want you to. I'll be here for both of us. He knows that.

All that concerns me, Joe had said, is that you and Nia are safe and well. And if you marry again, *cariad* –

I shan't. Don't talk about that.

Aye, but bear with me.

Go on then – but I shan't.

417

If you do remarry, and I hope you will, let it be someone who'll be a good father to Nia.

Aye, he had such a voice, said the pastor, such a spirit. Any music in a condemned cell, you know, is extraordinary. Not the expected thing. Joking with his pal he was. Shook everyone's hand. Thanked us all for our trouble.

Went off, I can truly say, as if catching a train.

Nobby would be here soon, to escort Ailsa and Irene to the cemetery. Their request that Joe be buried next to Roy White had been refused. As an executed man, Joe had to be buried at the perimeter of the cemetery and at an angle to the other graves. Not so Dusty. For Dusty had not directly killed anyone. In this way the Air Force had expressed its private view of where blame lay. Nobby had gone to the Commanding Officer and protested vehemently at the insult to Joe's family, in laying him at an angle. Precedent, he'd been informed. Not a matter for debate.

Never mind, said Ailsa. You tried. What does it matter? They are beneath contempt.

Mona, appearing out of nowhere, took Ailsa's hand. Joe's widow stood in the middle, between Irene and Mona. There was a stiff wind, dashing the palm leaves back and forth.

A kestrel banked on the wind. Sand streamed across the turf. Nobody wept. The three widows' faces under the rippling of shadowy veils were stone.

*

The plane banked steeply and then throttled back, releasing the pressure on the passengers' chests. Nia craned up to the window to see the yellow of the desert, the flashing

418

blue-green of the Great Bitter Lake. Her mother did not want to look out: she clamped her eyes shut and seemed to be in a tense, grumpy mood. Was she going to be sick? Nia hoped she would use the sick bag if so. Nia pouted and glared, bringing her face as near to her mother's as it would go. Crosspatch-Mami didn't even blink though she was not asleep, only pretending. Then she opened her eyes, passed her hand over her forehead and let out a sighing breath. At the aerodrome, waiting outside the hangar, Mami had lost her temper; she'd slapped Nia's calf hard, for nothing! For nothing at all! Nia hadn't been dawdling, she hadn't been rude. It wasn't fair. The place on her leg still smarted, not very much but it felt red.

Nia decided to pick her nose. She made a little drama out of it, waggling an imaginary bogey on her finger tip, causing the lady over the gangway to turn her face away in disgust. Even this had no effect on her mother. And anyway there was nothing in Nia's nose worth picking. They'd be staying with *Mam-gu* in Treforys. Nia didn't remember her. Auntie Mona was another person she didn't remember. She remembered Auntie Mona's cat, Isis. The plane had levelled out; a voice told them it was safe to unfasten their seat belts. Refreshments would be brought round by the staff. Nia entered into a tussle with the seat belts, thrashing her body to and fro. In the end Mami reached across and released it; although she said nothing, she smiled with her mouth. Awaiting Coca-Cola, Nia looked down at the world below, where sand met sea in a curving tongue of brilliant green.

Nia had soared far, far beyond the earth. Or rather, the world had fallen, was still falling. The sea spread beneath them, turquoise and formless. When Nia looked again, the plane was sailing through a gauze of white clouds that broke to reveal a dazzle of snow-capped mountains. Must be flying over Italy, her mother said: those were the Alps. Mami brought her face nearer to share the view. Mami's face was white with powder, her lips were dry and flaky, she should put Nivea on them, Nia reflected, and there was a nasty purple crust at the corner of her mouth. Nia reached out to touch it.

Her mother winced away. 'Don't, Nia, don't touch. That's a cold sore. You might catch it.'

A nasty, life-like doll Nia didn't like came into her mind. Its eyes opened and shut when you put it down and picked it up and it cried if you pressed its chest. It had long curly lashes and peroxide hair. Hester, who could do a wee wee if you liked, which you didn't, reminded Nia of Mrs Webster's smelly baby who had dirtied a nappy with yellow-brown poop. That doll was supposed to be the pride of Nia's life. *Your own little baby, darling!* She'd buried the doll in the sand and built a castle over it. And had forgotten it.

25

'Any passengers at present on deck may be interested in seeing a flight of flamingos on the starboard side!' the Captain announced over the tannoy. Nia raised her eyes to the birds, luminous pink against the sky. Their necks and heads with the great dredger-like yellow and black bills were stretched out in front; their orange legs trailed behind. The flock wheeled and turned in the blue air, a sight full of wonder. As one mind, it veered towards the canal's west bank. Presently the Captain announced that the flamingos could now be seen on the port side, flying back the way they had come: everyone galloped across to view them.

But he must warn passengers, added the Captain, that not all the wildlife they would meet in the area would be as acceptable to them. The Timsah area is abundant in flies, he said. I have warned you.

As soon as he had said this, a man in Nia's head came down from a great height and crouched beside her. His eyes were smily and pale blue; his grin lop-sided. The man was holding a lemon-yellow canister of spray decorated with a huge picture of a fly with multiple eyes; a pump was on one end and a puffer on the other. He said the flies must all be killed with DDT. *Germs on their feet, see. No, it's not nice, my beauty, but we must keep you safe.* Fly paper hung from the top of the window. Coughing and sneezing, eyes streaming, Nia fled from room to room but all rooms alike were full of stinky chemicals and she was running over a carpet of twitching flies.

The *Terra Incognita* would shortly be entering the narrow canal leading to Lake Timsah. Soon be there: Nia's heart beat up.

It was too early to form a judgement on the murdered man, for murdered he had been, by the British State. It all came out in a rush: Nia could hear the tremor in Mona's voice as she delivered this news. And yet Nia had always known, hadn't she, in some unconscious way? Mona pointed across the turquoise waters to the western shore, marked by a hazy line of trees, saying 'Joe's grave is in the Fayid Military Cemetery, over there. And my husband is there also.'

Joe Roberts had killed Ben Jacobs. And shot a little girl, an Arab child, who'd lost three fingers through the attack. He'd been court-martialled, found guilty and executed. One of the last executions by the British on Egyptian soil. The bastard, the bastard, Nia thought. Why was Mona excusing him? Heba had been in the corner with her mother, directly behind him, Mona insisted; Joe simply didn't see her there. He said he'd felt something butting at the back of his legs and he thought he was shooting a cat. And he was completely drunk.

'But what is hard to put across, Nia, is that he loved you dearly. You were the apple of his eye.'

How Mona could talk about his loving her in the same breath as apologising for his injuring a child turned Nia's stomach; her scalp crawled. You couldn't call that an accident, like a car collision. Why would anyone shoot a cat anyway? Her father sounded a vile man. A racist. A drunk. A thug. No wonder Ailsa had never spoken of him. What had brought her to marry such a bastard? No wonder she had found it hard to love the bastard's daughter.

Not much of a war hero, were you, she inwardly sneered. The shame that had tainted the Copsey household issued from this deed like a revolting smell that had followed mother and daughter wherever they went. It slimed their hearth with invisible pollution and they had both lived as if they were guilty of having caused it, randomly accusing one another of unrelated offences. They weren't guilty. *He* was. She thought of Ailsa coming in from endlessly polishing those vintage motor bikes she kept in the old barn and never rode; she'd scour specks of oil from her hands and forearms with a scrubbing brush, as if about to perform an operation. Slender hands with immaculate nails like ellipses. Clean as they were, she'd lather and rinse all over again, turning her hands this way and that in the light until she was satisfied. Having dried and creamed them, she'd gather up her rings from the window sill in that careful way she had: her wedding ring, the diamond engagement ring and one ring that was not Archie's. Nia had known of course that it had belonged to her father, the war hero.

Nia recalled a characteristic action of her mother's, long-forgotten. Ailsa would kiss the rings, with the mouth that was silent as the grave about the past, as she replaced them on her fingers. It had been a little ritual. Had she forgiven Nia's father then, in her heart? *Oh poor Mami, what did you go through without any help?*

Not strictly true. For Archie had been there: it always seemed to Nia that Archie had been there from the beginning. Certainly he knew it all. He was the kind of man made happy almost exclusively by having power to create happiness in the other. Well, he had not been able to do that for Ailsa but he'd known himself necessary to his wife. How quietly he'd kept watch, patrolling her borders. When she got home, Nia could talk it all through with him. Archie would break the silence now. The thought of this conversation rolled the stone from the tomb. She could have wept now but, from long practice, held back the tears.

'What are you thinking?' Mona asked.

'I don't know what to think. If only she'd told me. I deserved to know. I could have helped her. She must have destroyed the goodbye letters Joe wrote in prison. Tell me everything you can remember, Mona. Please.'

Nia learned that there'd been a debate about whether such a criminal could or should be buried in consecrated ground. In those days the laws against witchcraft had still been on the statute books. There had been all sorts of links back to the remote and superstitious Middle Ages: codes of shame and deference were more medieval than democratic. So Mona said and Nia believed her. In the end the Air Force had agreed to bury Joe Roberts in consecrated ground but lying at an angle to the other bodies. It was this detail that lacerated Nia and opened her to Joe, turning her

424

emotion in its tracks.

Well then, you paid your debt. The more they abandoned you, the more I turn to you, she told her father in her heart.

The bank slipped past as they moved through the Great Bitter Lake, leaving Joe's resting place at Fayid far behind; they passed the Big Flea, a far-off ochre mound shining in golden air, the only feature you could call a hill on this level landscape.

Strange scenes floated before Nia's eyes. Herself and that wretched golliwog standing on a bed at a wire netting window looking through a mesh grid at an Arab walking deeper and deeper into the desert. The Arab was a grave and dignified figure. He moved without hurry. And whether it had just been just the once that she watched him, or repeatedly, or whether there had been just the one man, or she had made him up, Nia could not tell. She saw him now as if in a film, moving with a certain slow and impressive dignity, until he vanished into the horizon. But where was he going? What was out there for him that he could see and she could not? Nia leaned forward till she was looking straight down into the canal, to where it heaved and slid back against the side of the ship.

For a moment, Nia had drawn level with the dead on this ship, whose forward motion was imperceptible and mimed stasis. We do come abreast of our dead, she thought, and then we overtake you. I am older than you ever were, Joe.

Ahead the container ship led them forward at a snail's pace. Morning was turning into afternoon. Nia fetched sandwiches and tea from the Lido, where Poppy had been sunbathing. As they ate, Nia tried to turn the conversation.

She'd heard enough for the moment: it had to sink in. But Mona would not let the topic drop. For decades she'd been waiting to get this off her chest and would not be gainsaid.

'Joe was not a vile man. Get that out of your head at once, do. Joe was a lovely man. Your mother loved him dearly. He deeply loved her.'

'You say that in spite of everything?'

'I do. You need to understand the times, to judge him.'

'You'll have to convince me of that.'

Mona had gone to visit Joe in prison – the first and last real talk she ever had with him. Mona had put out her hands to Nia's father and it had felt strange to touch the hands of Ailsa's husband – whom she'd injured, she'd wronged. She'd told him: *It was an accident, Joe, when it came to it. You did not mean to shoot Ben. I saw that.*

'So why the hell did he bring a gun then? If he wasn't thinking of shooting anyone?'

'To threaten us. He was drunk. Your father was not a killer.'

'But what made you visit him? My father had killed your husband.'

'Because I saw it all. I saw exactly what happened. The truth is no less the truth because one is personally involved. I testified for your father at the court martial. I believed well of Joe, Nia. And perhaps less well of myself. You know,' she said arrogantly, 'I have always had charisma. I eclipsed him.'

Presumably Mona had borne witness for Ailsa's sake. All very well to act high-minded and talk about abstract Truth. But was Mona, with her vaunted *charisma* and presumably a life-time of making people fall in love with her, really so

426

very high-minded? Perhaps she had not loved her own husband. Clearly she was reluctant to talk about him. What had been the nature of the bond between Ailsa and Mona? What was the power Mona had exercised over Nia's mother? A form of coercion it must have been, the coercion exercised by a powerful intellect and will, allied to a quality of attraction one still felt radiating from the woman. Displaced in every possible world, Mona was insecure and insecuring. Impossible to imagine the diligently correct Ailsa ever stepping out of line. For, yes, she believed in class, didn't she? Slavishly, as Nia had taunted her. But presumably Ailsa had fallen back on this belief after her challenge had not only failed but led to carnage.

Time was awry. The *Terra Incognita* was sailing far too slowly. Suspicions of grey mist settled on both banks and the sun began to dip and redden. As the light seeped away, it was unclear whether the convoy would complete its transit by daylight after all. Nia kept on hoping, willing the ship forward. Hints of twilight darkened the water and shrouded the banks in smoky purple and pink. Only the Sinai on the east bank still shone, a bleached primrose yellow fading to silver-white as the cruiser inched forward.

Lake Timsah, when they reached it, was bruise-blue; the light just about held, illuminating Ismailia on the northern bank. The delicate structures of mosques, tall towers of apartment blocks, advertisement hoardings and the green beauty of the garden city slid nearer.

The *Terra Incognita* glided across the lake, and in the gloaming the war memorial on the east bank appeared, a giant scimitar commemorating the heroic Egyptian dead of the October War of 1973. On a concrete plinth stood a host of Egyptian visitors, eking out the dying light to look out across the Sinai – *their* Sinai, for which so much blood had been shed. A giant scimitar rose into the air, encircled by palm trees and a captured Israeli tank. The scimitar marked the moment when Egypt, humiliated by Israel's occupation of the Sinai, struck back at its enemy. The October War. Egypt had crossed the supposedly uncrossable canal with assault craft, commandos and bombardments, and demolished the hated Bar-Lev Line, fortified observation posts on sand ramparts along the canal. How calm the city looked as they neared it, the fishermen standing up in their boats to wave and call out to the Europeans. Family groups wandering beneath palm and eucalyptus trees or seated at round tables waved to the liner from the green shores of Ish. Off-duty soldiers idled along the bank in couples, rifles slung casually over their shoulders. Many-coloured washing hung like bunting from a thousand tower block windows. The passengers on the *Terra Incognita* were out photographing the welcoming Egyptians, who in turn were photographing them.

Two men, one white, one Arab, jumped up and down on a jetty, waving and obviously yelling. The large, paunchy white guy in a forget-me-not blue shirt and a red baseball cap was positively bouncing. The passengers laughed and pointed. Poppy put her binoculars to her eyes.

'Oh my God,' she said.

It could not be, but was, Topher.

They waved back. The whole ship waved back. As they drew away, Nia's mobile rang.

'Ha! Gave you a surprise there. This is Bahgat, my driver. He's from Istanbul but he's lived here for yonks.

Wave, Bahgat. The lanky lady with ginger hair is my old pal, Nia. The dark beauty is her daughter.' Bahgat waved exuberantly. They waved back. 'But is *she* with you, Nia? I can't see an old lady.'

'Shush, Topher ... Mona is standing beside me here. What on earth are you doing? I thought you said you were coming aboard in Alex?'

'I am. Aren't you pleased to see me? I'm touring. Seeing for myself. Listen, Bahgat is going to take me to Alex and then he's at our disposal. I thought we might nip over to El Alamein – and then, what do you think about staying on for a week in the land of our fathers, Nia?'

'What – *Wales*?'

'No, you clown. Ish. I'll spirit you away to the *real* Egypt,' he said rather grandly. 'You're not going to see anything from that imperialist colonialist hedonist heap of junk. Are you? Bahgat will bring us back here and pay our respects to our dads. About time, eh? I'm going to do this for mum. My driver – my good *friend* rather, aren't you Bahgat?' and he whispered, *'comes very cheap.'*

The ship eased its way past the harbour and into the canal. Past the president's holiday villa they sailed towards El Ferdan and the famous swing bridge. Dark swooped down. They could not see the bridge. It was cold and pitch black. Disappointed, the veterans went below for supper and when they reappeared, the ship was far out on the moonlit Mediterranean, past Port Said.

*

Bahgat drove like a man possessed through the streets of Alex, his palm thumping the horn, cheerful and theatrical.

429

He dodged and wove through vehicles laden with humans, livestock and baggage, all jostling bumper to bumper. Pedestrians wandered blindly and at their leisure into this blaring chaos. Riding up on the pavement, Bahgat engineered a moment's cunning advantage, just missing a donkey cart as he dismounted and headed with squealing tyres for an invisible break in the traffic. Presumably he knew what he was doing, Nia thought, looking out of the window at the squalid, rubbish-strewn streets that were alive with shoppers and sellers and old men seated outside shops in the midst of the throng.

'Don't you worry, *habibi*,' he said. 'Bahgat takes care of his family. *Habibi* means darling or sweetheart, you should know that. You are Bahgat's darlings and he takes care of his own.'

The crumbling sepia stucco of great colonial houses rose high above the road's pandemonium. Down dark, festering alleyways criss-crossed with washing lines, Nia could see old tyres, cinders and heaped garbage. The endless poverty of the Middle East.

She thought of Mona on the plane for Berlin. They'd parted calmly, with every sign of affection. Everything that needed to be said had been said. But Mona, it seemed, was not yet satisfied, not quite. At the last minute she had clung on, holding up the queue.

When can we meet again, Nia?

Oh, well, I'm not sure.

Soon?

Once, staying with *Mam-gu* in her teens, Nia had been caught in a riptide at Langland Bay: she'd swum and swum against the peremptory current. She did not intend to repeat her mistake.

Mona, this has been amazing – and thank you.

If I am spared, insha'allah, *I shall see you again.*

Beyond the city centre, they hurtled on a straight highway past an oil refinery and lakes whose waters were blood-red with minerals and mint-green with salt. The coast road led along the Mediterranean, seen by glimpses through half-built sites for holiday homes. Lush gardens were bursting with figs and date palms, and vast conical hives Bahgat said were for pigeons, kept for food – *as all you English keep chickens in your back gardens, habibi.* Topher sat back in his seat, uncharacteristically withdrawn, suffering from an upset tummy, he said, but that was not it. The banter had been temporarily knocked out of him. Nia understood without being told. It had all come too late. He'd waited till Irene's death to enter the portal that led to his mother's and father's love. Nia had done the same. And perhaps that was natural. She placed her hand over Topher's and kept it there. He smiled without turning his head and she saw quite clearly the boy in the man: a boy who'd built grand castles with her, shown her his willy behind the shed and accepted as a gift her loathed hair ribbon, expressing his devotion by tying it into his own mop of white-blond hair. She wondered what Irene had thought of *that*.

At El Alamein there was little to see but an immense plain of sand, white-beige, with scrub and outcrops of grey rocks as if someone had strewn cinders in every direction. Hot wind rushed across the plain and tossed dust in their faces as they wandered round three war memorials: British, Italian, German. A plane left a disintegrating trail of smoke.

431

It seemed only yesterday that their fathers had endured in this desert and retired to their rest.

'Mona told me everything, Topher,' Nia said. 'My first father was executed. He wasn't a so-called hero at all.'

He was silent.

'What is it?'

'Sorry, Nia, but I know.'

'What?'

'Mum told me.'

Topher had known for over twenty years. His mother had blurted it out one Christmas after a sherry too many. *In strictest confidence, Christopher*, Irene had added, shocked at herself, making Topher promise on his honour not to breathe a word to Nia. She'd cast about for something sacred enough to make him keep his oath. The Bible? No, Topher was a heathen. On his father's picture then. Ailsa would never speak to her again if he didn't keep this to himself, his mother impressed upon Topher; it would be a betrayal. And Topher had kept the secret. But he'd written a poem about it for Nia, which she could see when they got home. And in any case, who was he to tell her this bad thing? They both began to cry, in one another's arms, rocking to and fro.

'My father wasn't a hero either,' Topher said, as Bahgat set off for Ish and the cemetery at Fayid. 'My dad was a dad.'

*

She'd visit him one last time where he slept at Fayid – yes, and *Habibi* too, and Chalkie. They all slept there, where Africa met Asia, far from home and within thirty yards of

432

one another. The time was ripe, for her mastectomy had not worked. Mortal illness was also a beginning of sorts and opened a road – though she'd infinitely rather (who in his right mind would not?) have been struck by a nice clean heart attack in her sleep and gone out like a light.

Ailsa was as excited as a child to board the plane for Cairo at Birmingham. Archie had encouraged her, bless him, and here she was, flying over the Marches and the Welsh hills, feeling fit as a flea, as if a plane could lift you clean out of your skin. They levelled out and Ailsa looked down at the Severn floodplain, the rain-saturated patchwork of fields, the russet and ochre of autumn trees, and felt she was *herself* again, breasts or no breasts. An adventurer quitting her native soil for unknown territory.

Only Archie knew. All these years he'd lived with Joe's ghost. Ailsa settled back in her seat, her mind on Poppy. She'd lived to see Joe's grandchild and now it was as if she carried to her young husband gospel news.

Forsan Island proved a good choice of hotel, basic but clean and air-conditioned. It had its own sandy beach, palm leaf sunshades, a picturesque view of Ish and Timsah. What more could Ailsa have asked? The November weather was warm rather than hot, relaxing every fibre. Having rested on her bed for several hours, she arranged a flannel in the bra of her swimming costume, to pad it out decently, and went to sunbathe and swim. She tried out her Arabic on a young woman bathing in full hijab and veil. Ailsa watched and admired a young man, whose legs had been amputated in the October War, as he swam off like a fish on his own into deep waters.

She slept like a log, waking to the muezzin's call to

prayer, a haunting shimmer of sound through the clarity of the dawn light. Later she roamed Ish. It had changed: how could she have imagined otherwise? Bombed by Israel in '67, the city had been rebuilt; all the street names had been altered after the Revolution. Ailsa savoured the scents of spice and petrol and coffee. In a pavement café, she ate fresh lute that had certainly been swimming in the lake hours previously: unbelievably tasty.

She wouldn't risk El-Marah. No sense in that. There were corners of her mind she never visited: wisely, Ailsa was sure. But her feet found their way to the Jacobs bungalow. *Oh you were, in times gone by, my sister or my wife.* A strange delusion for which to forfeit everything. Ailsa had donated the volume of Goethe Mona had filched from the *Empire Glory* to some church bring-and-buy sale at Church Stretton, twenty years earlier. But you couldn't censor words known by heart. Nor did she wish to. As Ailsa stood shielding her eyes from the dazzle that bounced off the white bungalow, it seemed impossible that her friend could fail to appear on the balcony in her sunglasses and sit down at the rickety trestle table with her book and a tall glass of lemonade. And *Habibi* would be somewhere inside listening to a record, the cat on his knee. His chair was next to the grand piano, in the shadow of its black wing, beneath the portrait of Julie Brandt-Simon.

She'd *hated* Mona when Joe died. That had gone on for years. But waiting here outside the bungalow, sun warm on her back and hair, Ailsa felt both Mona and *Habibi* all about her. *Habibi* in calm and clemency, the *andante* passages; Mona in the storm that powered the music. Ailsa had fled them both and she'd been right to run. But aren't our ghosts, Ailsa thought, born of our love?

Faces peered from the window at the white woman. The door opened. Out came a child holding a brimming glass of water and offered it to Ailsa. Ice cubes and a slice of lime. From his mummy. *Shokrun*. Ailsa drank the deliciously cold water and smiled over the glass at the shy lad.

Later she bathed again with Leila. Her uncle had been killed in the siege of the police station in Ish in 1952. That had happened just after Ailsa's and Nia's repatriation. They'd been staying in Treforys. She'd seen in the paper that we'd murdered fifty or sixty Egyptian auxiliary policemen when they refused to disarm. Of course, the way it was presented, there'd been no option: regrettably the British had been forced to shoot them, they were terrorists, criminal elements. That massacre had been the touch paper for the arson and killings in Cairo. And then the Revolution.

It had been snowing outside in Treforys; the kiddies were sledging on tea trays. Bent over the newspaper, shivering by an inadequate British coal fire, she'd heard Nia outside squealing with blissful but rather high-pitched excitement. Ailsa had closed the paper with a mental shrug. A few more Egyptians dead in Ish: oh well. What's that to me? Shrugging on her coat, she'd stepped outside and, catching a gleam of Nia's joy, had smiled a brief, wintry smile. But nothing had mattered, she didn't care about anything. Cynical and black through and through, Ailsa could only fall back on civilised manners. Nia had been a torment: Ailsa had looked at her and seen his face.

Her heart beat high, riding in a taxi along the coast-road to Fayid, in her cream skirt and jacket, clasping in her lap a foaming bouquet of white and purple flowers. I'm coming to you now, *cariad*. The silent driver's mournful brown eyes met hers in the mirror. He said nothing and that suited her well enough. A bridal day, Ailsa thought, the white wedding we never had. The road forked to the left; they drove down the bumpy track, more slowly now. The immaculately tended cemetery was an oasis of green, pearled with water-drops from the sprinklers; behind it the Bitter Lake. Eucalyptus trees towered, casting pools of shadow.

Here at the perimeter she found him: Joseph Elwyn Roberts. First his name and dates; then 'Husband of Ailsa, father of Nia'. He had been buried at an angle to all the others, to signal his shame. Ailsa dropped to her knees and laid the flowers across the breast of the grave. She sat back and gazed at the stone.

But she felt nothing. She tried to speak to Joe. But where was Joe? Not here, surely. Ailsa had no sense of his presence. It had all been over a very long time ago. Nothing left. Or nothing significant. She could not cry.

Unease deepened. The hum in Ailsa's ears grew. Am I ill? Am I going to die out here, so far from home?

Six months at the most, the consultant had said. She had made him tell her the truth. The ashes had fallen, cold in the grate.

Her entire thought now was to get back to the driver before she collapsed. She made herself walk. But which way? The world spun slowly on its axis and the stand of eucalyptus by which she had set her course seemed mirrored by another in the wrong direction. Righting herself, she walked until she was within calling-distance of the driver, dozing at his wheel.

Do what you came to do. Turning, Ailsa retraced her

steps to Joe and sank down, the full skirt belling, settling softly around her, around them both. Nobody was looking. And if they were, who cared? She obeyed her heart and threw herself on her front over the earth that covered him, face in the flowers. Tears came as they would, and words too, about their daughter and their granddaughter.

Ailsa's skirt was stained with green; her hair wild. Never mind.

The driver started the engine and they made their way along the sandy track to the main road. A convoy of army lorries passed the taxi and then the road was clear until a motorbike tore hell-for-leather into view behind. A heap of old junk if ever Ailsa had seen one, a pre-war German model, by the looks of it, held together with spit and elastic bands. Two teenagers were joy-riding, in jeans and t-shirts. They buzzed the taxi, fell back; swept out to ride alongside and, grinning, waved in to her. Ailsa laughed and waved back. Her driver spoke for the first time, in his lugubrious way: he would show those jokers; young people were the living end; they had no respect. He put his foot down to throw them off.

With a mock-salute from the boy riding pillion, the bikers overtook and vanished in a gale of exhaust up the road to Ismailia.

Acknowledgements

I owe my thanks to the generous friends and correspondents who allowed me access to their memories, thoughts and knowledge of Egypt in the period running up to the Suez Crisis, 1948–56. Successive governments denied that the violence of those years amounted to a war: Suez veterans campaigning for this recognition achieved in 2003 the award of the General Service Medal 1918–62 with 'Canal Zone' Clasp, for those who had served in the zone during the terrible years, 1951–54.

I owe a vast debt to Suez veterans who helped me to research this book. Foremost amongst these is Geoffrey Richards, whose *Queen Farida's Gone Away: Canal Zone Memories* is an unpublished autobiography of his Egypt service. Geoff was a remarkable volunteer to an army that included so many cultured, serious and thoughtful young men, whose mentalities stood in striking contrast to the casual racism endemic in the British military. Deeply interested in Arabic culture and haunted by Lawrence of Arabia, Geoff made Egyptian friends, learned Arabic and entered into Arab culture and religion. In recent years he has edited a newsletter, *Suez Canal News*, culled from news articles of the period, documenting the imperialist adventure that exploded in the 'Suez Crisis' of 1956, when Britain (in conspiracy with France and Israel) invented a pretext to invade Egypt and retreated ignominiously in response to American pressure. In 2003 Geoff entered into a generous correspondence with me, answering my questions about everything from Arabic music to motorcycles. He supplied me with maps, scanned documents and little-known photographs of the aftermath of violent actions by the British in Egypt and read the manuscript, pointing out errors.

I thank my friend, William Travers, who served in Egypt as a national serviceman from 1950 to 1952. A young postman in civilian life, Bill was conscripted as a sapper into the Army Postal Service. As a member of the Army Emergency Reserve, he was called up again in 1956, as he has detailed in his unpublished memoir, *A Soldier's Story: Recalled to the Colours, 1956*. Here Bill records his verdict on the British Suez intervention: 'I hope to prove that ... Dulles and Eisenhower were, throughout the Crisis, the only Western voices of reason.... They responded logically to a legitimate claim by a legitimate power, and Britain and France must shoulder responsibility for the debacle known as the Suez Crisis of 1956.' Bill's narrative is a detailed account of the experiences of the soldier on the ground in Port Said in the mayhem of an unequal battle and of his sympathetic concern for Egyptian citizens, deprived of water supplies and suffering the horrors of bombing. In a generous and moving correspondence over nearly a decade, Bill has shared with me his memories and thoughts about his experiences.

Other Suez veteran correspondents were Ken Brock, Peter Evans and John Grant: I thank them with all my heart.

I should also like to thank John Carey, Merton Professor of English at Oxford (retired), for sharing with me his memories of National Service in Egypt in a memorable and illuminating conversation. Gordon Campbell, Professor of

Renaissance Studies at the University of Leicester and expert on the Islamic world, has in a generous correspondence shared the wisdom gleaned from his travels in the cause of education and women's equality in the Middle East.

Since I have been the recipient of so much personal information and help from these sources, I must emphasise that any mistakes and bendings of historical fact are my own. The novel's political perspectives and its iconoclastic spirit are attributable solely to the author.

The Suez Crisis, with its lies and pretexts, may be read as a palimpsest for the ruinous and self-destructive neo-colonialist Middle Eastern policies of modern governments, evoking the question phrased by Doris Lessing: *What if we are a people who cannot learn?* It is no accident that the roots of this novel lie in 2003. The words of Aneurin Bevan at a peace rally in Trafalgar Square in November 1956 echo eerily with government claims made in 2003 that the Allied intervention in Iraq was necessary police work: 'Sir Anthony Eden has been pretending that he is now invading Egypt in order to strengthen the United Nations. Every burglar of course could say the same thing, he could argue that he was entering the house in order to train the police.'

I thank Helen Williams, Menna Elfyn, Barbara Prys-Williams and Nigel Jenkins, for comradeship in protesting against the Iraq War.

In my programme of reading, I came upon choice spirits with whom I have felt a human meeting, taking place on the page between us. One such book is the Palestinian Raja Shehadeh's *Palestinian Walks: Notes on a Vanishing Landscape* (2007); another is *Who Knows Better Must Say*

So (1955) by the American anti-Zionist Jew, Elmer Berger. Ghada Karmi's *In Search of Fatima: A Palestinian Story* (2002) is the memoir of a refugee driven out of Qatamon as a child. Ali Salem, humorist and humanist, is an Egyptian writer, a sharp observer of the modern world whose refusal of prejudice would render him a one-off job in any society. His *A Drive to Israel: An Egyptian Meets His Neighbors* (2001) recounts a journey of recognition for which he took a lot of stick in his own country. His wisdom is a salutary but caustic eye-salve: 'There is no end to the pain felt by most people when you suddenly raise their curtain of illusions and lies.'

My daughter, Emily Brooks-Davies, acted as my secretary in the early stages of research, meticulously filing documents and compiling chronologies. Grace, her sister, was my travelling companion on two research trips to Jordan and Egypt. I owe them and Robin so much. My greatest debt in the writing of this book is to my dear partner, Frank Regan, who died before it could be published. Frank, who had spent some years serving in Egypt as a conscript, shared with me his memories, wisdom and experience. He was my rock and remains my guiding star.

Stevie Davies

PARTHIAN

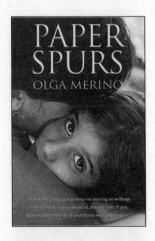

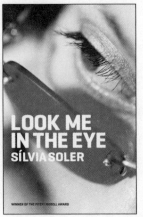

www.parthianbooks.com